D. B. John has lived in South Korea and is one of the few Westerners to have visited North Korea. He co-authored *The Girl With Seven Names*, Hyeonseo Lee's *New York Times* bestselling memoir about her escape from North Korea.

Also by D. B. John

Fiction

Flight from Berlin

Non-fiction

The Girl With Seven Names, co-written with Hyeonseo Lee

STAR OF THE NORTH

D. B. John

Harvill *Secker*
LONDON

1 3 5 7 9 10 8 6 4 2

Harvill Secker, an imprint of Vintage
20 Vauxhall Bridge Road,
London SW1V 2SA

Harvill Secker is part of the Penguin Random House group of companies
whose addresses can be found at global.penguinrandomhouse.com

Penguin
Random House
UK

First published by Harvill Secker in 2018

A CIP catalogue record for this book is available from the British Library

penguin.co.uk/vintage

Hardback: 9781787300477
Trade paperback: 9781787300484

Typeset in India by Integra Software Services Pvt. Ltd, Pondicherry

Printed and bound in Great Britain by Clays Ltd, St Ives plc

Penguin Random House is committed to a sustainable future
for our business, our readers and our planet. This book is
made from Forest Stewardship Council® certified paper.

In memory of Nick Walker
1970–2016

So much about North Korea is stranger than fiction. It is a hereditary Marxist monarchy whose people are sealed shut from the outside world. They are told that they live in a land of plenty and freedom, yet children are sent to the gulag for the thought-crimes of their parents, and the regime has used starvation as a means of political control. Such a state has, over the years, behaved in a way that outsiders might find very difficult to believe, let alone understand, so readers may be interested to know which elements of the novel draw from fact.

To this end, there is an author's note at the rear of this book that should be read only after reading the novel, as it contains plot spoilers.

Prologue

Baengnyeong Island
South Korea
June 1998

The sea was calm the day Soo-min disappeared.

She was watching the boy make a fire out of driftwood. The tide was rumbling in, bringing towering clouds that were turning an ashy pink. She hadn't seen a single boat all day and the beach was deserted. They had the world to themselves.

She pointed her camera and waited for him to turn his head. "Jae-hoon . . . ?" Later, the photograph she took would show a strong-limbed youth of nineteen with a shy smile. He was dark for a Korean and had a dusting of salt on his shoulders, like a pearl fisher. She handed him the camera and he took one of her. "I wasn't ready," she said, laughing. In this photograph she would be in the act of sweeping her long hair from her face. Her eyes were closed, her expression one of pure contentment.

The fire was catching now, wood groaning and splitting. Jae-hoon placed a battered pan onto the heat, balancing it on three stones, and poured in oil. Then he lay beside her where the sand was soft and warm, just above the high tide mark, resting on his elbow and looking at her. Her necklace, later the object of such sorrow and remembrance, caught his eye. It was a thin silver chain with a tiny silver pendant in the shape of a tiger, representing the Korean tiger. He touched it with the tip of his finger. Soo-min pressed his hand to her breast and they began to kiss, foreheads pressed together, lip and tongue caressing. He smelled of the ocean, and spearmint, and cuttlefish, and Marlboros. His wispy beard scratched her chin. All these details, everything, she was already telling her sister in the airmail letter she was unconsciously composing in her head.

The oil began to spit in the pan. Jae-hoon fried a cuttlefish and they ate it with chili paste and rice balls, watching the sun sink to the horizon. The clouds had turned to flame and smoke, and the sea was an expanse of purple glass. When they finished eating he took out his guitar and began singing "Rocky Island" in his quiet, clear voice, looking at her with the firelight in his eyes. The song found the rhythm of the surf, and she felt a blissful certainty that she would remember this all her life.

His singing stopped midnote.

He was staring in the direction of the sea, his body as sprung as a cat's. Then he threw aside the guitar and leapt to his feet.

Soo-min followed the line of his gaze. The sand was cratered and lunar in the firelight. She could see nothing. Just the breakers thundering in a dim white spume that fanned out flat on the sand.

And then she saw it.

In a small area beyond the breaking surf, about a hundred yards from the shoreline, the sea was beginning to churn and boil, stirring the water to pale foam. A fountain was rising, just visible in the dying light. Then a great jet of spray shot upward with a hiss, like breath from a whale's blowhole.

She stood up and reached for his hand.

Before their eyes the roiling waters were beginning to part, as if the sea were splitting open, revealing a black, glistening object.

Soo-min felt her insides coiling. She was not superstitious, but she had a visceral feeling that something malefic was making itself evident. Every instinct, every fiber in her body was telling her to run.

Suddenly a light blinded them. A beam surrounded by an orange halo was coming from the sea and was focused on them, dazzling them.

Soo-min turned and pulled Jae-hoon with her. They stumbled in soft, deep sand, abandoning their possessions. But they had taken no more than a few steps when another sight stopped them dead in their tracks.

Figures in black masks were emerging from the shadows of the dunes and running toward them, holding ropes.

Date: June 22, 1998, Case ref: 734988/220598

BY FACSIMILE TRANSMISSION

REPORT by the Incheon Metropolitan Police at the request of the National Police Agency, Seodaemun-gu, Seoul

Orders were to determine whether the two missing persons last sighted at 14:30 on June 17 had departed Baengnyeong Island prior to their disappearance. Respectfully submitted by Inspector Ko Eun-tek:

1. Security video images procured from the Baengnyeong Island Ferry Terminal establish to a high degree of certainty that no one resembling the missing persons boarded the ferry during any of its departures within the relevant time. Conclusion: the missing persons did not leave the island via the ferry.
2. The coast guard reported no other shipping in the area at the time of the missing persons' last sighting. Due to the island's proximity to North Korea, marine traffic is highly restricted. Conclusion: the missing persons did not depart the island by any other boat.
3. A local resident discovered yesterday, next to the remains of a campfire on Condol Beach, a guitar, footwear, items of

clothing, a camera, and wallets containing cash, return ferry tickets, IDs, and library cards belonging to the missing persons. IDs for both persons match the personal details supplied by Sangmyung University. They belonged to:

Park Jae-hoon, male, 19, permanent resident of the Doksan District of Seoul whose mother lives on Baengnyeong Island.

Williams Soo-min, female, 18, United States citizen who arrived in the country in March to enroll as an undergraduate.

4. At 07:00 today the coast guard commenced an air-sea helicopter search operation over a range of 5 nautical miles. No trace of the missing persons was found. Conclusion: both persons drowned by misadventure while swimming. The sea was calm but currents have been unusually strong, according to the coast guard. The bodies may by now have been carried some considerable distance.

With your agreement, we will now suspend the helicopter search, and humbly recommend that the missing persons' families be informed.

PART ONE

The seed of factionalists or enemies of class,
whoever they are, must be eliminated through
three generations.

—Kim Il-sung, 1970
Year 58 of the Juche Era

1

Jenna was jolted awake by her breath forcing up a shout.

She was breathing hard, eyes wide, her vision distorted in the lens of the nightmare. In the confused seconds between dream and waking she could never move her body. Slowly the dim dimensions of the room took shape. Steam hissed softly in the radiators, and the distant chimes of the clock tower counted the hour. She sighed and closed her eyes again. Her hand was at her neck. It was there, the thin silver necklace with the tiny silver tiger. It was always there. She threw off the duvet, feeling the chill air settle on her perspiring body like a linen veil.

An indent formed silently next to her on the bed. Amber-green eyes made mirrors in the faint light. Cat had materialized from nowhere, another dimension, as if summoned by the chimes. "Hey," she said, stroking his head.

The clock radio switched a digit.

"-retary of state has condemned the launch as 'a highly provocative act that threatens the region's security ...'"

The kitchen tiles were icy beneath her bare feet. She poured milk for Cat, microwaved the cold coffee she found in the pot, and sipped it, steeling herself for the backlog of voice mails on her phone. Dr. Levy had called to confirm her appointment for 9:00 a.m. The editor of *East Asia Quarterly* wanted to discuss the publication of her paper and asked, ominously, if she'd heard this morning's news. The older messages were in Korean and all from her mother. She skipped through them to the original one—an invitation to lunch in Annandale on Sunday—in which her mother sounded dignified and hurt, and Jenna felt guilt rise inside her like an acid reflux.

Cradling her coffee, she stared out at the gloom of her yard but saw only the bright interior of her kitchen reflected in the window. She had to force herself to accept that the hollow-eyed, underweight thirty-year-old staring back at her was herself.

She found her sneakers and running pants in a heap beneath the piano stool, tied her hair back, and headed out into the cold on O Street, meeting the mailman's unsmiling stare. *That's right, buddy, I'm black and I live in this neighborhood.* She started to run through the halftones beneath the trees, down to the towpath. Georgetown had a Sleepy Hollow feel this morning. A chill Nor'easter carried leaves across a brushed-steel sky. Pumpkins leered from windows and doorsteps. She was sprinting before she'd even warmed up, the breeze from the canal blowing the bad dream from her hair.

The man gave a weary smile. "We won't get anywhere if you won't talk to me." Beneath the coaxing Jenna sensed the bedrock of his boredom. On the notebook rested on his knee, he'd succumbed to a doodle. She was focusing on a pastry crumb lodged in his beard, just to the right of his mouth. "You say it's the same nightmare?"

She exhaled slowly. "There are always variations, but it's basically the same. We've been over it many times." Without thinking, she touched the necklace at her throat.

"If we don't get to the heart of it, you'll keep having it."

Her head slumped back on the couch. She searched the ceiling for words, but found none.

He rubbed the bridge of his nose beneath his glasses and looked at her with a kind of exasperation and relief, as if he'd reached the edge of the map and could abandon the journey with a clear conscience. He closed his notebook.

"I'm wondering if you'd be better off seeing a bereavement counselor. Maybe that's what's wrong here? You're still feeling your loss. It's been twelve years, I know, but with some of us time heals more slowly."

"No, thank you."

"Then what are we doing here today?"

"I'm out of prazosin."

"We've talked about this," he said with an exaggerated patience. "Prazosin won't address the original trauma that's causing your—"

She got up and reached for her jacket. She had on her white shirt and slim-fit black pants, her work clothes. Her shiny black hair was tied back in a loose knot. "I'm sorry, Dr. Levy, I have a class in a few minutes."

He sighed and reached for the pad on his desk. "All my patients call me Don, Jenna," he said, scribbling. "I've told you that."

The image appeared as if through a window in space. China was a million points of light, its new cities brash clusters of halogen and neon. Towns and villages without number glittered like diamonds in anthracite. In the lower right of the projector screen, the shipyards and container ports of Nagasaki and Yokohama blazed sodium amber into the night. Between the Sea of Japan and the Yellow Sea, South Korea was fringed with glowing coastal arteries, its vast capital, Seoul, a brilliant chrysanthemum. The center of the image, however, was a swath of darkness. It was not ocean; it was a country, a mountainous land of unlight and shadow, where only the capital city emitted a faint incandescence, an ember in the ash.

The class, seated in semicircular tiers around the lectern, gazed at the satellite picture in silence.

"As you all heard this morning," Jenna said, "the North Koreans launched another Unha-3 rocket yesterday. If, as they claim, the technology is peaceful, and the *kwangmyongsong* satellite is in orbit to monitor crops, then this is the view they'll have of their country by night . . ."

"*Kwangmyongsong* as in, like, 'bright star'?"

Jenna switched on the lectern lamp. A Korean American girl had asked the question. The name did sound ironic. In the galaxy of lights on the screen, North Korea was a black hole.

"Yes, or brilliant star or guiding star," Jenna said. "The name is rich with symbolism in North Korea. Anyone know why?"

"The cult of the Kims," said a boy in a Red Sox cap—another Korean, a defector Jenna had recommended for a scholarship.

She turned to the screen and flicked forward through shots of Pyongyang's traffic-free boulevards, of triumphal arches and mass games, and found the image she was looking for. A quiver of mirth rippled across the room, but the faces of the students were rapt. The photograph showed rows of drab citizens bowing before a full-length portrait of a portly smiling man wearing a tight-fitting beige casual jacket and matching pants. It was surrounded by a display of red begonias, and beneath it a slogan in red-painted Korean script read: KIM JONG-IL IS THE GUIDING STAR OF THE 21ST CENTURY!

"In the official state mythology," Jenna said, "the Dear Leader was born in 1942 in a secret guerilla base inside Japanese-occupied Korea. His birth was foretold by the appearance of a bright new star in the skies above Mount Paektu. He himself is sometimes called Guiding Star—*kwangmyongsong.*"

From the back of the theater someone said, "Was his mother a virgin?" The class snickered.

At that moment the overhead lights blinked on and the dean entered. Professor Runyon, Jenna's boss, was in his fifties, but his stooped shoulders, bow tie, and corduroy jacket made him seem about seventy, and his parched, thin-air voice closer to eighty.

"Have I missed a joke?" he said, peering at the class over his reading glasses. Leaning into Jenna's ear he said, "I'm loath to interrupt, Dr. Williams. Would you come with me, please?"

"Now?"

In the corridor outside he said, "The provost just called me. We have a visitor from ... some *opaque* government body." He gave her a bemused smile. "He wants to meet *you*. Know anything about this?"

"No, sir."

The Riggs Library was a vaulted Gothic chamber that housed the antiquarian books. It was deserted except for a man in a dark-gray suit standing with his profile toward them. He was holding a coffee cup and watching an impromptu soccer game being played on the lawn.

Professor Runyon cleared his throat and the man turned. Without waiting for an introduction he stepped forward and shook Jenna's hand warmly. "Charles Fisk," he said, "from the Institute of Strategic Studies." He was tall, strongly built, and in his early sixties. His nose was slightly bulbous and cleft at the tip, his hair silver and crinkled, like carpet cord.

"Dr. Williams is an *assistant* professor in our School of Foreign Service," Runyon said, still with a trace of bemusement. "We do have more senior staff available, who might be more—"

"Thank you, sir, that's all," the man said, and handed him the cup.

Runyon stared at it for a moment before inclining his head as if he'd been paid a compliment and creeping backward toward the door like a mandarin courtier.

When the door had closed and they were alone, Jenna's only thought was that she was in some kind of trouble. The man was observing her with an odd intensity. Everything about him, the cavalry bearing, the bone-crusher handshake, the formal friendliness, said "military."

He said, "I apologize for dragging you out of class." The voice was deep and well modulated. "May I call you Jenna?"

"May I ask what this is about?"

He was smiling and frowning at the same time. "My name is not familiar to you? Your father never mentioned me?"

She kept her gaze neutral, composed, but she felt mildly alarmed, as she did whenever anyone revealed even the most trivial knowledge of her family.

"No. I don't remember my father ever mentioning a Charles Fisk."

"Served with him in signals intelligence. US Eighth Army in Seoul. That was, oh, many years ago now, before you were born. He was the highest-ranking African American in the garrison. Did you know that?"

She said nothing, continuing to meet his gaze. A memory was stirring at the back of her mind. Of her Uncle Cedric, her father's brother, throwing earth onto the casket as it was lowered into the ground, and her arms tightly holding her wailing mother, and the air filled with the smell of damp leaves, and, standing in the background at a respectful distance, next to the cortège, a row of men in long military coats, baring their heads to the rain as a bugle was played, then replacing their caps with visors pulled low. With the certainty of intuition she knew that this man had been among them.

A bell chimed in the clock tower. She glanced at her watch.

"You have no further classes until three," he said. "I asked the provost to reschedule your teaching."

"You what?"

"I told him I needed your advice on a matter of national security."

Jenna was too surprised to stop herself. "Bullshit."

He looked at her benignly, a wise great-uncle with a wayward niece. "I'll explain over lunch."

Jenna followed Fisk's broad back as the maître d' guided them to a table. The restaurant, on 36th Street, was in a Federal Period town-house decorated with equestrian antiques and Limoges china plates. Portraits of the Founding Fathers gazed over a paneled dining room filled with the murmur of male conversation. She was feeling bang out of place, and annoyed. This man who claimed to have known her father, this total stranger who had hijacked her day, had brushed aside her protests with the ease of one who invariably got his way.

"The Maine lobster is very good," he said, flicking open his napkin and smiling at her as if this were her birthday treat.

"I'm really not hungry—"

"Let's have a dozen oysters to start."

The waiter was quizzed on the merits of particular sauces, a bottle of Saint-Émilion was ordered and tasted, and glasses poured (again, her objections were waved away with a smile). It was an ostentatious display of good breeding, and she wondered how much of it was a show for her benefit. Slowly, after she'd taken a cautious sip of the wine, and conceded the futility of resisting such overwhelming bonhomie, Jenna felt her annoyance give way to curiosity.

She said, "My father never talked about his friends or colleagues in the army. I'd always assumed—"

"He was a private man, as you know."

The thought crossed her mind that this was some elaborate confidence trick.

"How well did you know him?

"Well enough to be best man at his wedding."

This was a surprise. Her mind instantly pictured that miserable red-brick Lutheran church in Seoul where her parents had married. She had always imagined it was just the two of them and a pastor. Her mother's family had stayed away and had refused to give her a second, Korean wedding, as was the custom, going so far as to shun her for years afterward.

"When he brought your mother to Virginia I kept in touch with him. Later, I served with him again at Fort Belvoir ..."

He began to reminisce, recalling legends and anecdotes about her father from a time before she was born, or had been very young. Some she knew; others she'd never heard, but it was becoming increasingly evident that this man knew a great deal. He was even familiar with the more recent history, the decline in her family's fortunes—her father's drinking and his discharge from the army, her mother starting a modest business as a wedding planner to make ends meet—all of which he related in a kindly tone, an old friend remembering the family saga, occasionally glancing at her as he doused an oyster in wine vinegar and lemon juice before tipping it into his throat. And suddenly she began to see, with a rising panic, where this was leading. He was getting closer, skating in slow, decreasing circles around the subject she would not speak of, the abyss into which she would not look.

He noticed her discomposure, and stopped, his fork poised in the air. Sighing, he leaned back in his seat and gave her a defeated smile, as if to show her he was dropping all pretenses. In a gentle voice he said, "You're afraid I'm going to mention your sister."

The words dropped from his mouth like rocks. Jenna went very still. The hum of conversation and chinking of silver on china faded to the background. She could hear her own breathing.

The next course was placed in front of them, but Jenna continued to stare at him.

"You know," he said softly, "I sometimes think the things that are really worth talking about are the things people absolutely refuse to discuss."

Trying to keep her voice level she said, "Who are you?"

His expression changed slightly, becoming colder, more serious. "I'm a spook, and I really did know your father. I've been keeping a professional eye on you for a long time. You needn't look so surprised." He broke off some bread and buttered it, watching her. His eyes were a pumice gray and had acquired an unnerving directness. "You're a valedictorian with academic grades that are off the chart. You're a National Merit Scholar with the highest IQ recorded in Virginia. Your doctoral thesis was so exceptional it guaranteed you a fast-track academic career. 'The Evolution of the Workers' Party as the Kim Dynasty's Instrument of Power, 1948 to the Present.' Yes, I've read it. You grew up in dual cultures, with dual languages. You spent three months last year in Jilin Province, China, perfecting your grasp of North Korean dialect. You're fit and athletic. You were a finalist in junior league taekwondo. You run. You keep to yourself; you keep secrets. You're highly independent. A set of skills and qualities like that wasn't going to pass us by unnoticed."

"Who is us?"

"We're the Agency, Jenna. The CIA."

Jenna let out a soft groan. She had the sensation of having been set up, and felt foolish for not seeing it coming. This was followed by a flash of anger at the realization that her father's memory had been used as a lure.

"Sir ..." She put her cutlery down next to the barely touched main course. "You're wasting your own time and mine." She touched the phone in her pocket, wondering whether it was too late to unpick the changes this man had caused to her teaching schedule. "I should get back to work."

"Relax," he said genially. "We're just talking."

She looped her handbag onto her shoulder and moved to get up. "Thank you for lunch."

The bass register of his voice cut easily through the sounds of the restaurant, even though he spoke quietly. "At 06:00 Korea

Standard Time yesterday the Kwangmyongsong rocket blasted off from the Tonghae Satellite Launch site in North Korea's northeast, in violation of multiple UN Security Council resolutions. It carried no satellite. Its technology was entirely hostile." Jenna froze. "We tracked the launch. The rocket's third stage fell into the Philippine Sea, where it was picked up by the US Seventh Fleet before the North Koreans could recover it. They were testing the heat shield for a long-range thermonuclear missile, which they'll soon be aiming at our west coast. Your food's getting cold." He had begun eating. "Grilled sea bass in a champagne sauce ..." He closed his eyes. "Perfection."

Her mind was whirring through scenarios. She was barely aware that she had sat back down. "My God," she mumbled. She had a sudden image of a shooting star high over the Pacific. *Kwangmyongsong*. "This means—"

"I want you to work for me." He'd spoken with his mouth full of steaming food. "In the clandestine service."

She did a double blink. "I'm ... not CIA material. You may think you know everything about me but you don't know that I see a shrink once a week. I take medication for nightmares."

He gave her a pleasant grin, and she realized that he knew that, too.

"I've been recruiting agents for decades. It's given me a gift for psychology, you could say. You, Dr. Williams, may be one of the most promising candidates I've ever met." He leaned toward her confidentially. "You're not just smart. You have a powerfully personal motive for serving your country."

She looked at him warily.

"You know what I'm talking about." Again, his voice was full of sympathy. "I have no answers for you. You may never learn the truth of what happened to your sister on that beach. But I offer secrets. I offer the possibility that one day a door may open and you may know. Her disappearance haunts you. I'm right, aren't I? It's made you cold and lonely. It's made you trust no one and nothing, only yourself."

"Soo-min drowned," she said weakly. "That's all there is to it."

His voice fell to a murmur. He was treading with care now. "No body was found. She may have drowned ..." He studied Jenna, reading her. "But you can't rule out the other possibility ..."

Jenna closed her eyes. This was her most private article of faith and it was being contradicted. "She drowned. I know she did." She sighed unhappily. "If you knew how many years it's taken just for me to say those words ..."

She stopped and gulped. Suddenly she was fighting back tears and had to look away.

She left the restaurant before he could stop her. She was out of the door and onto the street, breathing in great mouthfuls of sky, walking back to the college as fast as she could, the wind catching at her hair and coat and sending leaves eddying around her.

2

Baekam County
Ryanggang Province, North Korea
Same Week

Mrs. Moon was foraging for pine mushrooms when the balloon came down. She watched it glide between the trees and land on a fox trail without a sound. Its body shimmered and the light shone straight through it, but she knew it wasn't a spirit. When she got closer she saw that it was a deflating polyethylene cylinder about two meters in length, carrying a small plastic sack attached by strings. *Strange*, she thought, kneeling down with difficulty. And yet she had been half expecting something. For the past three nights there had been a comet in the sky to the west, though what it signified, good or ill, she could not decide.

She listened to make sure she was alone. Nothing. Just the creaking of the forest and a turtle dove flapping suddenly upward. She slit open the plastic sack with her foraging knife and felt inside. To her astonishment she pulled out two pairs of new warm woolen socks, then a small electric flashlight with a wind-up handle, then a packet of plastic lighters. And something else: a red carton with a picture of a chocolate cookie on the lid. Inside it were twelve cookies, sealed in garish red-and-white wrappers. She held one to the light and squinted. *Choco Pie*, she read, moving her lips. *Made in South Korea.* Mrs. Moon turned to peer in the direction the balloon had come from. The wind had carried this thing all the way from the South? A few *ri* farther and it would have landed in China!

The sky to the east was bleeding red light through the treetops, but she could see no more balloons, just a formation of geese arriving for the winter. Now that was a good omen. The forest whispered and sighed, telling her it was time to leave. She looked at the Choco Pie in her hand. Unable to resist, she opened the wrapper and took a bite. Flavors of chocolate and marshmallow melted on her tongue.

Oh, my dear ancestors.

She clutched it to her chest. This was something valuable.

Feeling flutters of excitement, she quickly put the items back into the sack and hid the sack in her basket beneath the firewood and bracken fern. Then she hobbled down the forest track, licking her lips. She'd reached the lane that ran along edge of the fields when she heard men shouting.

Three figures were running across the fields in the direction of the forest—the farm director himself, followed by one of the ox drivers and a soldier with a rifle on his back.

Goatshit.

They had seen the balloon go down.

All day she worked the field in silence, uprooting corn stalks with the women of her work unit, moving along the furrows marked by red banners. Enemy balloons were seen in the sky at dawn, one of the women said. The army's been shooting them down and the radio's warning everyone not to touch them.

A biting wind swept down from the mountains. The banners flapped. Mrs. Moon's back ached and her knees were killing her. She kept her basket close and said nothing. At the far edge of the field, she could see only one guard today, bored, smoking. She wondered if the others were searching for balloons.

When the watchtower sounded the siren at six she hurried home. The distant summit of Mount Paektu was turning crimson, its crags etched sharply against the evening sky, but the houses of the village, nestled on a slope of the valley, were in deep shadow. The Party's face was everywhere—in letters carved on stone plaques; in a mural of colored glass depicting the Dear Leader standing in a field of golden wheat; in the tall obelisk that proclaimed the eternal life of his father, the Great Leader. Coal smoke drifted from the chimneys of the huts, which were neat and white with tiled roofs and small vegetable patches at the rear. It was so quiet she could hear the oxen lowing on the farm. The temperature was dropping fast. Her knees had swollen up painfully.

She pushed open her door and found Tae-hyon sitting cross-legged on the floor, smoking a roll-up of black tobacco. Under the exposed bulb his face was as lined and rutted as an exhausted field.

He'd done nothing all day, she could tell. But it was important to her that a husband shouldn't lose face, so she smiled and said, "I'm so happy I married you."

Tae-hyon looked away. "I'm glad one of us is cheerful."

She lowered her basket to the floor and slipped off her rubber boots. The electricity would go off at any minute, so she lit a kerosene lantern and placed it on the low table. Her concrete floor was spick and span, the sleeping mats rolled up; her glazed kimchi pots stood in a row next to the iron stove; and the air-brushed faces on the wall, the portraits of the Leaders, Father and Son, were clean and dusted with the special cloth.

Tae-hyon was eyeing the basket. She had not found a single mushroom in the forest and had nothing but bracken fern and corn stalks to add to the soup, but tonight, at least, he would not be disappointed. She took the plastic sack from her basket and showed it to him. "On a balloon," she said, dropping her voice. "From the *village below.*"

Tae-hyon's eyes bulged on hearing the euphemism for the South, and followed her hand as she took out each item and placed it on the floor in front of him. Then she opened the carton of cookies and gave him the uneaten half of her Choco Pie. His mouth moved slowly as he ate, savoring the heavenly flavors, and in a gesture that broke her heart he reached out and held her hand.

Tomorrow she would scatter an offering of salt to the mountain spirits, she said, and travel into Hyesan to sell the cookies. With the money she would make, she could—

Three hard knocks sounded at the door.

A cold terror passed between them. She swept the items underneath the low table and opened the door. A woman of about fifty was on the doorstep, holding up a battery-operated lamp. Her head was wrapped in a grimy headscarf and she wore a red armband on the sleeve of her overalls. Her face was as plain as a blister.

"An enemy balloon was found in the forest with the package removed," she said. "The Bowibu are warning us not to touch them. They're carrying poison chemicals."

Mrs. Moon bowed. "If we see one, Comrade Pak, we'll report it."

The woman's hard eyes moved from Mrs. Moon to the room behind her, then narrowed in contempt as she regarded Tae-hyon sitting on the floor. "Everyone in the hall by eight," she said, turning away. The light of her lamp danced along the path. "Correct revolutionary attitudes in the workplace is tonight's theme ..."

Mrs. Moon closed the door. "Poison chemicals, my foot," she muttered.

She lit the stove to prepare dinner, while Tae-hyon studied each of the items from the balloon, holding them close to the lantern.

He felt the socks and pressed the wool to his cheek; he wound the small handle of the electric flashlight and shone it at the ceiling; he ran his finger over the labels and trademarks of that mysterious parallel universe, the South. Then the plastic sack caught his eye.

"Something else in here," he said, opening it up.

In her haste to leave the forest that morning Mrs. Moon had not noticed the bundle of loose paper flyers at the bottom of the sack. He held one to the light.

"'To our brothers and sisters in the North, from your brethren in the South! You are in our prayers always. We miss you and care about your suffering. We await with joy the day when North and South are reunited through the love of Our Lord Jesus Christ ...'"

Tae-hyon squinted at the flyer. An extreme wariness entered his voice.

"'Hasten the coming of that day. Rise against the deceiver who tells you that you are prosperous and free, when in truth you are impoverished and in chains. Brothers and sisters, Kim Jong-il is a tyrant! His cruelty and lust for power are without limit. While you starve and freeze he lives in palaces like an emp—'"

The flyer was picked out of his hand before he could say another word. Mrs. Moon heard her breathing sound ragged. Suddenly she swept the rest of the flyers from his lap and in one movement crossed the room, opened the stove, and thrust them onto the coals.

Tae-hyon was staring up at the portraits on the wall, his mouth open, and it was at that moment that the electricity went off. In the flicker of the lantern the eyes of the Leaders seemed to glitter, and a condemned look came into Tae-hyon's face. "The Bowibu ..." he whispered. He began running his fingers through his hair, a habit he had when he wished something wasn't happening. "They'll know ..." His voice was hoarse. "They'll know we've read those words. They'll see it in our faces. They'll make us confess ..." He looked at his wife with an animal fear. "Take these things back where you found them ..."

But Mrs. Moon was staring into the flames behind the small glass grille of the stove, watching the flyers blacken and curl.

Something in those words had sent her back through time. A lifetime had passed since she'd heard that name, fifty years at least.

Our Lord Jesus Christ ... A name erased from history. Suddenly the memory opened like a secret drawer: her mother and a group of grown-ups in a room with the door and window closed, and a verse being read from a big, heavy book, and a candle lit, and words chanted in unison. And singing. Quiet, soft singing.

A lamb goes uncomplaining forth, the guilt of all men bearing ...

From long habit she pushed the memory back into the dark, and locked it away with all the others. She turned to her husband, who had covered his face with his hands.

"No one will know," she said.

She opened the front door and stepped out into the cold. The sky blazed with stars, and there, low in the west above the mountains, was the comet, bright with two tails.

3

Annandale, Virginia

Jenna's mother still lived in the house where Jenna and her sister had grown up. The row of faded clapboard bungalows was set back from a road lined with mature horse chestnuts. The front lawn was neglected and strewn with leaves, but the flag hung from its pole, the pride of a first-generation American.

Han's plumpish figure was at the front door as Jenna's car pulled into the drive. She was wearing her Jeju Island souvenir apron and had on a new fuchsia-pink lipstick, which, with her bubble perm, made her resemble a potted flower. Jenna stooped to kiss her and caught a waft of frangipani.

"You're as thin as a chopstick," Han said, cupping Jenna's face with both hands. She examined her daughter for a moment, as if looking for clues—a new outfit, a greater care taken in the styling of her hair, the application of some makeup—that might signify whether she was happy, or, more to the point, was dating someone.

The house was filled with the complex aromas of grilled beef and something caramelized and gingery.

"Omma, smells wonderful," Jenna said. She went through to the small dining room. "You shouldn't have gone to such ..."

Suddenly her suspicions were on high alert.

The table was laid for three. The best china and tablecloth were out, and a dozen colorful *banchan* dishes of bean sprouts, kimchi, spinach, toasted seaweed, and tiny fried fish were arranged in a neat array. When she saw the chilled bottle of soju on the sideboard—alcohol was seldom allowed in the house—she knew she'd walked into a trap.

"Sweetheart ... ?" Han had taken off the apron, revealing a stylish blouse and a too-tight skirt. She had hoicked her face into her hostess smile and was looking over her daughter's shoulder into the living room. Jenna turned.

A man of about forty was standing at the far end of the room next to the cherrywood table with the family photographs. He bowed to her, revealing a bald patch.

"It's my pleasure to meet you, Jee-min-*yang*," he said.

Jenna flinched.

"This is Sung Chung-hee," Han said in a high, affected voice. "He has a real estate brokerage in Fairfax." She took Jenna's hand and led her toward him. "He's kindly agreed to value the house today."

"On a Sunday?"

"I've told Dr. Sung he's welcome to stay for lunch." Han addressed people as "doctor" if she thought they needed buttering up. In a stage whisper she said, "I knew Sung-*nim*'s aunt in Seoul; his younger brother is an account executive for Samsung Electronics."

"I'd be delighted," the man said, "if it is agreeable to Jee-min-*yang*." He spoke the Korean of the homeland, not the sloppy second-generation language Jenna habitually spoke at home, peppered with English and slang. No one but her mother called her Jee-min.

A hiss of hot fat came from the direction of the kitchen.

"Do excuse me," Han said, turning the hostess smile to a higher watt. "I must check on lunch. Jee-min, why don't you show Dr. Sung the house?"

She's timed this perfectly, Jenna thought.

In a silence Jenna made no effort to fill, the man's fingers fidgeted, as if needing to smoke. He occupied them by removing his glasses and wiping them in a handkerchief.

"Your mother tells me you have an English basement apartment in Georgetown. Must be a small place for a high rent."

"I earn a living, Mr. Sung, and my cat takes up no space."

She hadn't used the honorific form required, but he seemed not to notice. Instead he smiled, as if given a cue.

"Soon, maybe, you'll need a home with plenty of space. Children need more room than cats."

Jenna felt a real depression settle on her. "Right now I'm kind of focused on my teaching."

The man's eyes hardened very slightly and another silence opened between them.

If anyone asked her what her type was, she could never picture or describe the man, but she knew he wasn't one of the Mr. Sungs of the world—an émigré with all the patriarchal family baggage. She was drawn to very few men, but by some dismal law of inverse proportion, too many men were drawn to her, suitors who evaluated her for damage and desirability, the frigid mixed-race girl who was already thirty years old.

From the table of framed photographs her sister's gaze met hers, as if flashing her a warning. Around the girl's neck the silver chain shone against her skin, which was a beautiful ginger-brown cast, the color of waffles and syrup, much darker than the porcelain face of her mother, Han, who stood next to her in the picture.

Mr. Sung followed her gaze. "Your school graduation," he said, bending to examine the photograph.

She thought of correcting him, but her mouth got ahead of her. "Look, Mr. Sung, my mother means well. She worries about me, and feels it's her duty to make introductions ... The thing is ... I don't want to waste your time."

A moment of surprise showed on his face, but she could almost see him reminding himself that he was not in Korea now. Instead he nodded, ready to negotiate.

"You speak plainly with me. I value that. I have no patience for ladies who hide their smiles behind their hands and tolerate anything men say. But Jee-min-*yang*, if I may be plain with you ..."

Her phone buzzed in the pocket of her jeans. She knew that to answer it in front of him would be to show grave disrespect. She answered it.

She recognized Charles Fisk's voice straight away. "Turn on Channel NewsAsia—now!" He hung up.

"I do not wish to be indelicate," Mr. Sung said, "but in terms of your making a desirable match with a family of good standing, you'll forgive my saying that there are factors that need to be overlooked ..."

She picked up the TV remote and flicked through the channels until she found it.

"You are not a pure-blood Korean ..."

On screen an ash-haired Asian lady in a pale-blue suit was giving a press conference. Rows of microphones, camera flashes, no smiles.

An anchorman was saying, *"Mrs. Ishido will give evidence tomorrow to the United Nations Humans Rights Council here in Geneva. She is expected to tell investigators that the victims include hundreds of foreign nationals from at least twelve countries, and will urge the Council to increase pressure on the Kim regime to release information to the victims' families ..."*

The lady held up a photograph of a boy in school uniform and began giving a statement in Japanese. Now an interpreter was speaking across her in French-accented English.

"My son was fourteen when he vanished from a beach near our hometown ... We now know that he was abducted ... and taken to North Korea ..."

Mrs. Ishido looked up from her statement and faced the cameras.

"... *in a submarine.*"

The air around Jenna went thin. Suddenly nothing else existed but her and the woman on the screen, whose effort to hold back her tears were setting off another barrage of camera flashes.

Sounds filtered through, but they seemed far away. A tinkling noise as her mother carried in a tray with three small glasses. The front door slamming; a car engine starting.

"Omma ..." Jenna whispered, without taking her eyes off the screen. The interpreter continued, in a strangely disconnected voice.

"*I believe my son ... is alive ... in North Korea ...*"

"What's happened?" Han said. "Why's the TV on?"

Han turned to the window to see Mr. Sung's car driving away.

Jenna heard her mother put the tray down and slump to the sofa. When she spoke her voice was faded, used up. "I'm only trying to help. You're at an age when most Korean girls are married. I just want you to meet a premium man ... I want to give you the kind of wedding I never had ..."

Jenna was still staring at the screen, too shocked to move. The news item was finishing. Then the woman, Mrs. Ishido, was gone.

"... A reception at the Shilla Hotel, a banquet in the imperial style, limousine, silk *hanbok* dress, dry-ice machine, the whole works."

"Omma." She turned to her mother. All the strength gone out of her voice. "When Soo-min vanished ..."

Han looked up and for the first time Jenna saw how aged she was beneath the makeup.

"Soo-min is hidden by God. Why do you upset me more?"

Later, at home, Jenna removed the old cookie tin from under her bed. She had not opened it in years. She took out the items and laid them on the bed: Soo-min's purse, containing her library card, loose change in Korean coins, return ferry ticket, and a passport picture of the two of them together, aged sixteen, making faces in a photo booth; Soo-min's camera case, which had grains of white sand inside; and her camera, from which the two photographs had been recovered by the police.

The one of Soo-min was slightly blurred. Her eyes were closed and she was laughing. Just visible above the neckline of her T-shirt was the silver chain, the one Jenna now wore. In the background the dunes glowed a reddish gold, and in the top right the moon was rising. The second photograph showed the boy, whose name, Jenna had later learned, was Jae-hoon. He was kneeling in the sand, wearing only swimming trunks, glancing up from cutting a fish. His face was half shade, half gilded by the slanting rays of the sun. To the left of the picture the tip of a guitar case was visible, lying on the sand, and behind him was the ocean, calm and dark.

Just a short time after these pictures were taken ... how long? An hour? Half an hour? A few minutes? ... her sister and this boy had vanished from the face of the earth.

Jenna buried her face in the bedspread. *Oh my God.* Had she been wrong all these years?

She could not have explained why, but she felt a strong certainty that the choice she made next could be decisive and final, and that there would be no turning back.

Fisk's voice was raised against the noise of a cocktail reception. She heard the notes of a piano and the hubbub of voices and laughter. She waited a moment while he moved to a quieter spot.

"You watched it?" he said.

"That woman in Geneva, Mrs. Ishido ... What made you ... ?"

"Out of the hundreds of reported North Korean abductions, only her story mentions a submarine. It would explain why ... I thought you should know about it."

Jenna felt the phone burning next to her ear.

He said cautiously, "After she's given her testimony to the UN tomorrow, I could show you the case file."

"No," Jenna said, absently. Her mind was far away on Baengnyeong Island, on that remote beach facing westward across the thundering surf. In twelve years this was the first whisper of evidence connecting to Soo-min, like a sea breeze blowing through the keyhole of a long-locked door. She was damned if she was going to have it filtered and redacted for her by a spy agency. "I have to meet her in person, Mrs. Ishido ..." she said firmly. "I have to hear it with my own ears."

4

Kim Il-sung Square
Pyongyang, North Korea
Sixty-fifth Anniversary of the Founding of the Workers' Party
Sunday, October 10, 2010

A fug of Chinese pollution lay over the city, making the light so diffuse that the Tower of the Juche Idea on the far bank of the river, normally the imposing focus of the vista from the square, could be seen only in a beige outline.

Cho Sang-ho surveyed the scene from the seats reserved for his family on the south side. His rank in the Ministry of Foreign Affairs equaled that of a lieutenant colonel, and his stiff dress uniform, seldom worn, was making him itch and sweat uncomfortably. To his left he had a good view of the Grand People's Study House and the terrace where the leadership took the salute. He could see all the way down Sungri Street, the direction from which the parade would come, now densely hedged with silent crowds. Across the great square itself thousands of troops from the ground forces, navy, air defense, and Red Guards waited in rigid formations, like companies on a battle map. Behind the troops, in fields of red and pink that stretched all the way to the bank of the Taedong River, fifty thousand citizens, standing in perfect straight lines, held up sprigs of paper flowers representing kimilsungia, the flower of the

Great Leader, whose spirit endured eternally, and kimjongilia, the flower of his beloved son.

He felt a tap on his shoulder and turned to see the broad face of General Kang, creased into an enormous gold-filling smile. He was seated with his two teenage daughters. In heavily accented English he whispered, "Good morning, Lieutenant Colonel Cho. How are you this day?"

The daughters dissolved into peals of giggling behind their hands. Kang, one of the Ministry's veteran diplomats, had been practicing his English with Cho in preparation for a high-level mission to the West.

"I am in good health, Comrade General. Thank you for asking."

Cho's arm rested around the small shoulders of his nine-year-old son, who was known to everyone, after some joke Cho couldn't recall, as Books. The boy wore the red neckerchief of the Young Pioneers. He was moving his lips as he counted the formations in the square, until he gave a loud hiccup that caused Cho and his wife to share a silent chuckle. Of all the women present, each in their colorful *chima jeogori* national dress, Cho thought his wife the most beautiful. Her powdered face was a perfect oval; she'd applied a dark-red lipstick, which took some of the wryness from her smile, and in her hair wore the mother-of-pearl barrette he'd bought for her in Beijing.

"Twenty-four detachments," Books whispered, turning his face up to him, "but I didn't count the band. Where's Uncle Yong-ho?"

Cho glanced at the empty seat to his right. Where indeed was Yong-ho? He'd picked a fine occasion to be late.

The silence was becoming oppressive. A flock of pigeons took sudden flight, clapping wings echoing across the space. Overhead, six great balloons bearing the star of the national flag, tethered at points around the square, swayed gently. On the roof of the Party headquarters, directly above the Great Leader's portrait, plain-clothes Bowibu agents watched the crowds through binoculars.

A commotion sounded to Cho's right, and there was Yong-ho, apologizing to a uniformed grandmother festooned with medals, the matriarch of a large family that occupied most of the row, each of whose members were standing to let him pass. He crept along toward Cho like a guest late for a wedding, beaming his smile at every individual in the row.

"Forgive me, younger brother," he said, sitting down. "You're not going to believe my news ..." Cho's brother was pale and his hands were trembling, which might have alarmed Cho had it not been for the irrepressible good mood on his lips. He leaned in closely and Cho caught a sweet hint of soju on his breath. "They're giving me the top job."

"Seriously? First Deputy Director?"

Yong-ho gave a chuckle. "Better than that." He leaned into Cho's ear and lowered his voice to a whisper. "You're looking at the new chief—"

An instant tension ran through the crowds. In the center of the square the bandleader had raised his baton. Two giant LED screens on the river side lit up; the left proclaiming LONG LIVE THE WORKERS' PARTY OF KOREA! and the right KIM JONG-IL IS THE GUIDING STAR OF THE 21ST CENTURY! Bugles were raised; the band played the opening chords of "The General of Korea," relayed from every building through loudspeakers, and the spectators in the rows stood up. A gradual welling-up of applause that had begun below the eaves of the Grand People's Study House was now rolling into the square in a crescendoing ovation as men, women, and children began acclaiming with their hands above their heads and yelling with all the strength in their lungs. *"MAN-SAE!—MAN-SAE!—MAN-SAE!"* The noise was tremendous.

"I can see him!" Books shouted, grabbing Cho's sleeve. "I can see him!"

The fifty thousand citizens waved their paper flowers rhythmically, creating a shimmering mirage of red and pink. Hundreds of white doves were released and circled above.

The distant figure of the Kim Jong-il was emerging onto the terrace, followed by an entourage of politburo members, senior Party cadres, and generals in sand-colored tunics with gold trim. The noise rose to an electrifying roar. The great man acknowledged the crowds with a gentle wave of his hand, as if blessing them, and Cho felt his power like an arrow from the sun. *Dear Leader, Dear General.* How humble this man was in his simple worker's clothes! How frail from the hardships he'd endured for the people's happiness.

Tears pricked Cho's eyes, and almost at the same moment everyone around him began to weep. The cheering mixed with wailing. General Kang's big face was contorted with sobs as he clapped, and his daughters cried hysterically.

Cho crouched down and Books climbed up onto his shoulders. To lift him high above the heads was no effort at all, he was so light. In a choking voice Cho cried, "Who do you thank for your happy childhood?"

"The Great Leader Kim Il-sung and his blessed son Kim Jong-il, the General of Korea!" he shouted.

Cho's wife clapped her hands, mascara tears tracking down her cheeks. "*Man-sae!*" she cried.

The sun, filtering through the haze, glittered on the distant generals' tunics, drawing Cho's eye to the dark figure standing slightly apart from them on the terrace, a stout young man in a black Mao tunic, the Dear Leader's youngest son. The crowds had noticed him, too, because now there were streams of whispers running in every direction, causing the applause to subside. People were remarking on the young man, whose face was as plump and serene as the Buddha's, as if a new god had been revealed to them.

"Appa, who is it?" Cho's son said.

"A great person born of heaven," Cho said. "One day, when you are older, he will be your teacher and guide."

Yong-ho leaned again into Cho's ear. "They're making me chief of staff to the new boy's private secretariat," he said, nodding toward the stout young man on the terrace, the Dear Leader's son, "with the honorary rank of colonel ..."

Cho turned to him in astonishment. He put Books down.

"The appointment will be announced in a few weeks," Yong-ho said.

The band played "Hold High the Red Flag," and the first formation of helmeted troops bearing regimental banners—an artillery unit from the Front—was marching toward the Grand People's Study House in a high parade step. The stamp of boots shook the ground. Drums beat time. The applause rose to a frenzy.

"You're not joking, are you?" Cho said over the noise. He gave a loud laugh and shook his brother's hand violently. "You bring honor upon us all. Have you told Appa? I think he might die of pride." But before Cho could lean over to his wife and pass on the news, Yong-ho grabbed his arm.

"There's just one thing, younger brother, and I'm telling you now because I don't want you to worry ..." His smile wavered. "An appointment at this level is conditional on me having a spotless class background ... The Bowibu will make a full investigation."

"Naturally." Cho was confused for a moment. "They must speak to Omma and Appa—"

And then it struck him.

It wasn't their beloved adoptive parents the Ministry of State Security, the Bowibu, would investigate. The parents with exemplary class backgrounds who'd taken in two wretched infant boys and raised them as their own. It was his real parentage that would be uncovered. The parents he and Yong-ho had never known. A pool of cold fear gathered in the pit of his stomach.

He turned his face back to the parade. A detachment of the People's Navy was passing in white tunics and caps, presenting AK-74s with bayonets fixed and barking "KIM–JONG–IL! KIM–JONG–IL!" The crowds joined in.

"Relax," Yong-ho said. "The risk is small."

"We know nothing about our real parents and grandparents. We don't know whose blood we have." Cho couldn't believe he was saying this. "Elder brother, this investigation must not happen. You must withdraw from the appointment."

"Come on. Look at us. Do you honestly think we're the seed of capitalists, or collaborators, or traitors who fought for the South?"

"We don't know."

"Our Dear Leader himself said last year at Mangyongdae that the Revolution is carried out by our thoughts and deeds, not by family background. Times are changing. Besides, the Party is damned grateful for what I've done and knows I've earned this . . ."

Yong-ho's voice trailed away, his face suddenly clouded. He was a tall man with faintly cratered skin; hard, intelligent eyes; and nails bitten to the quick. The tailoring of his Chinese suit concealed the wire-thin physique of a high metabolism. His fingers trembled, needing a cigarette. In the complex political landscape of Pyongyang Cho knew that his brother was a significant player, though he never talked about his work. If anyone asked, he described himself as a fund-raiser.

"If you're wrong about this," Cho said coolly, "do I need to tell you what could happen?"

Yong-ho's good mood seemed to have evaporated and Cho detected anxiety in his voice. "One simply does not turn down a job offer from the Leader, younger brother. I've told you not to worry. I am protected."

Cho thought about this. It was true that Yong-ho was one of the Admitted, an elite group of protected cadres. But an onset of

36

cynicism told him that no one, even at that level, was protected from the crime of having bad blood.

The band was playing "Ten Million Citizens Will Become Bullets and Bombs." A unit of the Women's Brigade was passing the saluting terrace, nylon-stockinged legs moving as if they were a single automaton. An odd fact, Cho thought, that women's bodies were better suited to the goose step than men's. Behind them on Sungri Street, assorted military hardware—the tanks, missile launchers, and APCs—was in formation, ready to roll into the parade.

Cho's wife caught his change of mood and stopped cheering.

"Here." Yong-ho reached into his jacket and handed Cho a small gift box made of fine-quality white card stock. "Something you can impress the white devils with. On your foreign trips."

But Cho was sunk in preoccupation. He forgot his manners and pocketed the box without thanking his brother.

When the event was over, Cho's driver was caught in a long line of waiting government cars, so Cho, his wife, and Books made the twenty-minute walk back to their residential compound in Joong-gu. The main boulevards were crowded with departing citizens and troops, the city still reverberating with the tumult of the parade. Ahead of them, marching along the center of Somun Street, hundreds of students in white shirts were heading back toward Kim Il-sung University carrying tall, streaming banners and singing.

"Glory to Korea! Your star shines ever bright.
We follow our Dear General, who leads us to the fight!"

In the hazy autumn light every building seemed bathed in triumph. Books was chatting to his mother about child heroes who had fought the Japanese, but Cho remained silent, his mind filled with thoughts of Bowibu officers opening a case file, unearthing old birth records, exposing to the light the names and faces he'd never known, his real family. How long would it take them? He had no idea. A spasm of terror ran through him.

At home he closed the door of his study, steadied his breathing, and told himself to calm down. Yong-ho was one of the Admitted! None of the organs of state, not the secret agents of the Bowibu, not the regular police, nor the army could touch him without the express permission of the Leader himself. And what could be so worrying in his real family's past? His grandparents would have been dirt-poor peasants scratching about in pig shit like everyone else two generations ago. He poured himself a cognac from the decanter on his bureau and put a cassette tape in the stereo player. Swirling his glass in his hand, he sat back in his armchair, humming the refrain to "Hey Jude." There was a short list of Western pop songs categorized as harmless. He'd bribed the music curator at the Grand People's Study House to tape them for him. He felt himself begin to relax. Yong-ho's appointment would bestow honor and a great prestige upon the family. He was worrying about nothing.

Suddenly he remembered Yong-ho's gift. He retrieved it from his tunic pocket and opened it. Inside the box, wrapped in tissue paper, was a wallet of soft, grained leather, with a label in English. HAND-STITCHED IN ITALY. It was a beautiful thing. Where had his brother obtained such a luxury? He ran his finger over the redundant card-holder pockets—no North Korean owned a credit card—and opened the bill compartment. Inside he found three American hundred-dollar bills, so crisp they might have rolled off the printing press that morning. *Like new*, he thought, and when he held one up to the light, he caught a faint whiff of fresh ink.

5

Hôtel du Lac
Left Bank
Geneva, Switzerland
Mid-October, 2010

The morning rush hour was starting when Jenna got to her hotel. It was on the Left Bank, a few blocks back from the Promenade du Lac and the glittering expanse of Lake Geneva, a sliver of which she could glimpse through a gap in the solid, wealthy apartment buildings. Her room had a tiny balcony overlooking a street of shops and a streetcar stop. If she craned her neck out she could see the Alps, brilliant white in the morning sun. She lay down on the bed exhausted, listening to the whir of the streetcars, thinking it was too noisy to get any rest. She fell into a deep sleep almost at once.

All week Soo-min had been present with her, a genie released from a lamp. In the bathroom mirror she'd seen Soo-min behind her, watching her through the steam. At the piano she imagined she'd seen, for one hair-raising instant, a second pair of hands to her right, accompanying her. She'd awakened with a start in the dead of night, convinced she'd heard Soo-min whisper her name. Her sleep had been thick with dreams of her sister, which played in a rich, saturated color, making the dream seem more real than the faded world she woke up to. Inevitably the dreams slipped their way down, through a fissure in the crust of sleep, into a darker level, the underwater hell of the nightmare, but she had long gotten used to that.

Jee-min was the first to be born. Soo-min had followed her out of the womb thirty-two minutes later, and for that reason always addressed her, when they spoke in Korean, as "elder sister." Jee-min's best friend was her mirror replica: Soo-min had the same laugh, thought the same thoughts, was cast in the same DNA. Their tics and foibles were indistinguishable. Each was an extension of the other. They shared a habit of not finishing sentences. They both inclined their heads and twirled their hair when spoken to. They loved lists and would wear colored hair bands on their wrists as reminders. They had no sense of direction and would easily get lost, even at the mall. Neither would eat boiled vegetables and made a puking face if anyone mentioned them. They were grouchy if they didn't get nine hours' sleep.

The twins' upbringing in Annandale was nothing out of the ordinary. The family's income was enough to get by; their father indulged them; their mother was strict. They studied harder than the neighbors' kids, though not as hard as the Chinese kids, and excelled at sport and music, taking their piano lessons together. On Sundays they joined their mother in the Korean congregation of the United Methodist Church. They followed the same fashions and fads as all the other girls they knew.

And yet Jee-min and Soo-min Williams stood out in every way. It wasn't just their startling intelligence. Some quality of contentedness they carried, some nature that was both shy and outgoing made people instantly warm to them. At school the identical two, Jenna and Susie, as they called themselves, were famous. Half Korean, half African American, with hair tied back in a large bunch, they had bold, freckled faces, and an easy, athletic poise—at thirteen they were the stars of the hockey field and the tallest girls in the school. At sixteen they were finalists in the Virginia Schools Taekwondo Championships. In training they sparred with each other. Boys were reluctant to take them on. They did not lack friends, yet they both knew that they each had only one true friend, and when you had a friend like that, there could be no other. Theirs was an exclusive club of two, and mischief was their relief from the regimen Han enforced.

Report cards were pinned to their bedroom door so that they began each day with a reminder to strive. Coming second at any-thing was a fail in Han's book, but the twins rarely came second at anything.

In their midteens, as they thrilled in shared revelations of devel-oping bodies, they applied makeup to each other's faces and styled each other's hair, each the mirror for the other. During dinner they'd quietly spit out kimchi into handkerchiefs when their mother's back was turned—garlicky breath was a kiss deterrent. Meeting boys for dates was absolutely forbidden by Han, but with ready excuses to be out of the house—at taekwondo, at friends' houses, at the library—their mother's law was easy to circumvent. After lights-out Jee-min would climb into Soo-min's bed for whis-pered discussions about boys, twining their legs and linking fingers, their heads on the pillow, facing each other very close, breathing each other's breath.

Their parents had always told them that separation would hap-pen, though why this was inevitable or necessary was never really clear to the twins. Not long after their eighteenth birthday they embarked on separate gap years before beginning college. Soo-min was enrolled on a music foundation course at Sangmyung Univer-sity in Seoul. Jee-min took an internship in a senator's office on Capitol Hill.

At Washington Dulles International Airport they hugged and cried. Jee-min gave her a sister a good-luck charm, a silver chain with a tiny silver tiger as a symbol of Korea. It was the only thing she had ever bought without her sister being present. Soo-min fastened it around her neck straight away. Her flight was called, and the moment of parting was agony. The twins would not let go of each other's hands, and their parents, too, became distressed. Han's face was heavy with guilt, as if she were seeing the effects of some needless and cruel experiment. Jee-min began missing her sister the instant she'd passed up the elevator and out of sight.

She was at home reading in the backyard when she felt it—a tremor in the genetic skein that connected her to Soo-min, no matter where they were. First came a visceral contraction in her stomach. The next moment she experienced an overwhelming horror welling up inside her and then dying down, leaving saliva pooling in her mouth. She telephoned Soo-min's hall of residence in Seoul but she was not there, even at breakfast time. For all of the next day, and the day after that, the silence from Soo-min confirmed what Jee-min already knew. She became acutely agitated, pacing the house and pulling at her hair, and lost all appetite for food. Her parents asked her what was wrong, but all she could say was that Soo-min was in danger. As the days went by she watched her parents' puzzlement ripen to worry and finally to panic as their calls were not returned.

The news, when it came, was by telephone. Jee-min knew it was the call because her father, Douglas, was silent for a long time listening to the voice on the other end, and reached for Han's hand. An Inspector Ko of South Korea's Incheon Metropolitan Police was asking if he had heard from his daughter. She had not returned to her college dorm in three days.

Inspector Ko said that a woman who lived on Baengnyeong Island had reported the disappearance of her nineteen-year-old son, who had failed to return from the beach with a Korean American girl. The woman was convinced that her son had run away with Soo-min. The inspector conceded that this was a possibility.

Teenage lovers occasionally escaped the pressure of their families, he said, but in almost all cases they made contact within a day or two.

A Seoul tabloid newspaper obtained the pair's college ID photos, Soo-min's and Jae-hoon's, and ran a story under the heading HAVE YOU SEEN ROMEO AND JULIET? with a hotline to call. The police displayed an official missing-persons notice in all bus and train stations. Soo-min's photo showed her wearing the necklace, and Jee-min provided a description of it. It was the one item she knew for certain that Soo-min would always wear. Within a week there had been sightings of the pair in Busan, Incheon, Sokcho, Daegu, and as far away as Jeju Island. Inspector Ko cautioned Douglas and Han not to get their hopes up. None of the sightings turned up a single lead.

Han went to pieces. She veered between tearful hysteria, insisting that Soo-min would call at any moment, and a strange, vacant-eyed listlessness that Jee-min had never seen in her before. It was Douglas who took charge. He confined Jee-min to the house, afraid that she'd try to harm herself, or attempt to make her way to Seoul. For days he implored her. Was there some secret of Soo-min's he should know? Was she troubled by something she'd kept hidden from her parents? What was so terrible in her life that she'd want to run away with a boy she barely knew? Her parents were clinging to this hope, that Soo-min had been a romantic fool and would soon return.

Jee-min knew that her sister had not run away. It was inconceivable that she would have made a decision like that without telling her. She also figured, rightly as it turned out, that Soo-min had only just met this boy, Jae-hoon, and had not yet written to tell her about him, which she would have done in a long, intimate letter.

Douglas was granted leave from Fort Belvoir, and made the grim journey to South Korea. For a month he enquired and searched. He combed the beaches of Baengnyeong Island, showing his

43

daughter's photograph to anyone who'd look, attracting stares, the tall black man in search of a lost daughter. He met the mother of Jae-hoon, who was as clueless and as distraught as he was. They held hands and cried and prayed together. "My son was a strong boy," she said. She refused to accept that he had drowned. In the Itaewon District of Seoul she and Douglas handed out flyers printed with the pair's photographs and searched the internet cafes and *noraebang* bars, where runaways went to find jobs. They met Inspector Ko, who gently told them that the simplest explanation was usually the right one. The abandoned possessions on the beach strongly suggested that the pair had got into difficulties while swimming. When Douglas returned home he was not the same.

A profound emptiness descended on Jee-min's parents. If a body had been discovered they could have mourned Soo-min and buried her. And maybe, in time, their grief would have eased a little. But their child vanished without trace, and this began to eat away at their hearts. Han changed from being a woman who knew every-thing to a woman who knew nothing. She had always had so much energy she could not sit still. Now she took sedatives and slept through the afternoons. One morning she walked out of the house and did not return until breakfast time the next day, by which time the police had been called. Her face was puffy and smirched and her clothes were dirty. When Jee-min asked her where she'd been she simply stared glassily. Douglas began to drink. Six months after Soo-min's disappearance, he was discharged from the army.

Jee-min missed her sister so acutely it was actually a physical pain. She and Soo-min had always moved in each other's slip-streams, lived in each other's warmth and light. Now she was alone in a cold headwind with no shelter. Emptiness did not begin to describe what she felt. And yet ... Jee-min could not truly mourn her sister. Something inside her, a pilot light that wouldn't go out, told her that Soo-min was alive. There had been so many times when the two of them had shared wordless understandings, moments of despair or joy communicated from a distance—not by a phone or letter but by some kind of genetic magnetism—and she *felt* her twin's presence. As everyone around her began giving Soo-min up for dead she took comfort in the living power of this link, though she knew that facts and logic were against it. If Soo-min wasn't dead, where had she gone? Why had she gone?

Jee-min chased these questions around in her head, constructing and discarding endless scenarios for what had happened on that beach, hardly sleeping, until the morning came when she realized she would go insane if she didn't act on her hunch. She herself would go to South Korea. She mentioned nothing of her motive to her parents, not wanting them to go through the agony all over again if she was wrong, but she did not think she was wrong. Soo-min was alive. She *knew* it. Instead, she told them it would give her comfort to see that beach with her own eyes, and Han agreed to take her. The visit to Inspector Ko, however, Jee-min contrived to make alone.

Inspector Ko's wife had opened the door. The house was in a leafy residential street on a hill overlooking the port at Incheon, not far from where the ferries to Baengnyeong Island departed. Jee-min was shown through to a veranda fragrant with jasmine and tomato vines. A hibiscus looked extravagantly purple against the azure sky. Inspector Ko was sitting in a cane chair. Jee-min bowed to him.

He expressed his sympathies and condolences. It had been his final case before retirement, he said. "Your poor sister, and that boy, with their futures ahead of them ..." He poured her a cup of jujube tea. He had a tough, melancholic face. His hair was fine and white, and cropped very short, like a lawn after an early frost. "To drown like that, although ..." He paused, stirring his cup. "I admit that even I had my doubts at the time. The sea was calm. They were both strong and fit."

"They didn't drown," Jee-min said firmly. I believe they're alive. I feel my sister's presence. I'm not imagining it. I want the case reopened."

Inspector Ko studied her over the rim of his cup.

"You ... think they might have been abducted?"

A shadow crossed Jee-min's face. This was a possibility she had tried not to think about.

He fell silent for a while, watching his tea cool, weighing what he was about to say. "Sadly I can't even offer you that hope, small comfort though it would be. Your sister and that boy never boarded the ferry back to Incheon. Nor did they leave in another boat. Baeng-nyeong Island lies in a sensitive area—just twenty kilometers from the coast of North Korea. Very little shipping is allowed near it and the coast guard reported no boats in the area on the evening your sister disappeared." He sipped his tea and squinted into the horizon. The port of Incheon, sparkling under the noon sun, was dotted with container ships. "If someone abducted your sister and the boy, they'd have to have done it right under the noses of the coast guard." He looked at Jee-min with pity. "And I think that's unlikely. I am deeply sorry to say it, but my conclusion hasn't changed. They drowned."

Before Jee-min could speak, the veranda door slid open. Inspector Ko's wife was handing him an envelope.

"Ah. Yes." He passed the envelope to Jee-min. It was sealed and marked with a case number. "The island's local pastor found this on Condol Beach last week. Spotted it in the mounds of seaweed that wash up there. He handed it in to the police station. It matched the description you gave."

Inside the envelope was a clear plastic evidence bag and inside that was a fine silver chain. The tiny tiger was corroded to green by seawater. The clasp was broken.

When Jee-min came to, Inspector Ko was fanning her face with a newspaper. She felt the wooden floor of the veranda hard against her ear, and had a sideways view of a glazed plant pot. She turned slowly over onto her back and stared at him, feeling a noise rising inside her chest, which emerged through her mouth as a howl. Her body began to tremble and refused to stop. She felt a crippling, agonizing wound, as if her heart had been torn and one half wrenched from her. Nothing had prepared her for the pain of the world she was now in.

Her twin was dead.

Jee-min returned home hollowed out, utterly changed. Seeing that necklace without its owner shattered her belief in the most shocking way. She was forced to confront the fact that she had deluded herself into believing the impossible.

She had no true identity separate from her twin. Soo-min had been the completed half of Jee-min's being. The "we" that formed her self was destroyed. There was no real concept of "I." She was now a half person with no idea how to navigate the world. Soo-min was dead, but she remained imprinted in Jee-min's body, in her heart, in her soul. She would forever be living with a ghost.

In September the following year she enrolled in her first semester at Johns Hopkins University in Baltimore, but she was now disembodied from her own life and from those around her. She was overtaken with tiredness and unable to engage with anyone, or to care. She stayed in her dorm and skipped lectures and meals. She was never seen in the hall cafeteria or the common rooms. People who tried speaking to her saw a young woman whose mind was far away, sweeping the rippling surfaces of something dark and fathomless. She had no grounding. She was weightless, floating in black empty space. Gone was the open personality that made people instantly smile when they saw her. She had lost her curiosity, her friendly manner, her positive attitude. She withdrew deep into herself. Her friends drifted away. She had given up hockey. She had closed the lid of the piano and wouldn't open it again for years. Even her name, Jee-min, seemed to fade like a memory, until she no longer thought of herself by that name. To the outside world, and to herself, she was Jenna.

By Christmas of her first semester, her tutor had referred her for psychiatric counseling.

Jenna spent two months at an institution secluded among the hills and oak woodlands of West Virginia. The psychiatrist diagnosed a form of post-traumatic stress disorder. The numbness and disbelief and survivor's guilt she was feeling, the man told her, were a vital part of the grieving process and needed to be experienced, stage by stage. "Going over and over an event beyond your control is a normal reaction. It shows that your mind is trying to come to terms with a massive change."

Every night she was present with Soo-min on that beach. She held her hand and walked through every moment with her in exhaustive detail. Every heartbeat, every blink of the eyes, every footstep in the sand down to the water's edge. She changed the dialogue, the timing, the angles, but no matter how many times she hit Replay and went through it all over again, the end was always the same. Soo-min drowned.

"It may take many years, but time will heal," the psychiatrist told her. And when he said this Jenna regarded him coldly. She knew it was a lie. Time was simply a sentence she would serve until she died.

Her supervising professor was surprised to see her again before the end of the spring semester, but Jenna had already decided that work would be her coping strategy. The prospect of a long leave of absence—free time for her mind to implode—filled her with dread. Work was her refuge and her salvation. She began insulating herself from her pain through study, ignoring the world unless it concerned her studies. She studied from the moment she sat down for breakfast until the books and papers slipped from her hand as she fell asleep in bed. She straightened her hair, and with her weight loss looked quite different from her former self, Jee-min. When it was pointed out to her that she was neglecting her fitness she took up endurance running, which required no team or

48

company, and bought a new loose-fitting white *dobok* for taekwondo. She trained alone in the early morning when the gym was deserted, practicing her palm strikes on the standing bag and working up a sweat with her side kicks and spinning kicks, stretching and focusing between each form. She liked what she thought of as the "tao" of taekwondo, where power came from speed and strategy, not strength and aggression.

By the time she had graduated summa cum laude she had already been accepted for postgraduate doctoral research. Her thesis was so organized that by the time she had completed it early she had already published several well-received papers on East Asian geopolitics in academic journals. Her peers were taking note of her talent. When she applied for a teaching position at Georgetown, the college indicated to her, without actually saying so, that she had no real competition for the post: it was hers.

That year Douglas died of liver cancer. He had ignored calls to stop drinking; his health had declined sharply and he hadn't seemed to care.

"Just you and me now," Han said to her in the strange girlish voice she had adopted. She and Jenna had swapped roles. Her mother had become infantilized by the losses. It was Jenna who had to keep an eye on her and check on her every week. Han developed an obsession with finding Jenna a match, as if this were a final maternal service she had to fulfill before she, too, faded away.

That day on Inspector Ko's veranda marked a boundary that divided Jenna's life as distinctly as geological time in layers of rock. Before it, events had sequence and clarity; after it, everything blurred together. Slowly she carved out an existence. She saw Dr. Levy once a week. She visited her mother once a week. Seasons changed; semesters, students came and went. She took prazosin to alleviate the nightmares, but mostly they continued, the same dream, over and over on an endless loop. The boy plays his guitar for her sister. The two of them are bathed in a golden light.

Darkness falls and they walk hand in hand toward the sea. The waves rise, black and viscous, and then one enormous wave, monstrous, crushing. Soo-min opens her mouth to scream, but the sound that comes out is a ringing bell. It sounds again and Jenna awakes to realize the hotel telephone is ringing next to her bed.

For a moment she has no idea where she is. Dazed, she answers it.

"Dr. Williams? I've called at a bad time?"

"No."

"This is Mrs. Akiko Ishido." The voice is Japanese and as clear and thin as porcelain. "Could I trouble you to meet me at the Hôtel Beau-Rivage in twenty minutes? I don't have much time, and I know you've traveled far to talk to me."

6

Hyesan
Ryanggang Province, North Korea

It was still dark when Mrs. Moon left the village. The open truck was crowded with women muffled against the cold, and was stuck in first gear. The thing was Soviet made and older than she was. She clenched her teeth as they descended agonizingly along hairpin bends, squeezed her eyes shut when they swung out over pine-clad precipices. Soon the road wound through foothills pimpled with graves that made long shadows in the dawn's light.

They turned another bend and she had a sudden, steep-angle view of Hyesan, spread out along the valley basin like some vast cemetery. Hundreds of squat houses were separated by dirt alleys and dark streets. Smoke from thin flues mingled with a white mist coming off the Yalu River. Mrs. Moon shuddered. To the north she could make out the bronze colossus of the Great Leader standing with his back toward China. She squinted at him through the morning sun. *From here you're only as big as my thumb.* Her cataracts were getting worse.

Hyesan was the only city she'd visited in years, and it looked like the ass-end of nowhere, even to her. Cratered roads, an ox pulling a cart. A few shabby apartment towers with cracked walls rising above the houses. Men sitting peasant style on the edge of the road doing nothing, waiting for nothing. A silent, once-famous factory.

She walked the last block to the city center, stopping to wash the dust from her face in a ditch at the side of the road. She was drying herself with her apron when she saw sudden movement in the corner of her eye. Two children, one in a filthy army coat many sizes too large, were right behind her. "Off with you!" she yelled, and grabbed her basket before they could swipe it. She would have to keep her wits about her. There were *kotchebi* on every corner, the vagrant children who flocked like swallows at planting time, picking pockets and snatching bags. For protection she joined the end of the line of factory workers marching to work.

The city center was a broad square on which were located the main train station, the state bank, a beauty parlor, a pharmacy, a hard-currency store where illegal money-changers hung about like flies, and one imposing colonnaded edifice, the city bureau of the Party, decked with a slogan in massive red letters that dominated the square. KIM JONG-IL IS ALL-EMBRACING OF THE PEOPLE, LIKE THE HEAVENS!

She entered the gates of the train station, and immediately found herself in another world. The goods yard buzzed with activity. Merchants shouting in Mandarin heaved huge sacks of goods. Weather-beaten ajummas stood about gesticulating over prices. Two teenage soldiers patrolled with rifles on their backs. About fifty stalls, some with awnings made from blue Yankee rice sacks, were arranged in aisles, with the cries of swooping birds joining those of hundreds of women traders.

"*Sassayo!*" Come and buy.

Mrs. Moon covered her nose and mouth. Her boots felt tacky on the concrete. She passed tarpaulin mats glistening with dog meat, pork cuts, poultry. Mounds of potatoes reached as high as her waist. Anything that wasn't food was covered in Chinese script. Detergents, crockery, electrical appliances she couldn't name. Money was changing hands everywhere she looked. Faces were lit by money. There was an edginess, too, an urgency, as if all this enterprise could be banned at any moment on a whim from Pyongyang.

A couple of street informers loitered, watching, eavesdropping. She could spot them a mile off.

At the end of an aisle she found a noisy open-air canteen where customers sat hunched over bowls of hot rice soup. Yellow steam rose from pans simmering on portable gas burners, and she suddenly realized she was hungry. She would eat something first, then find a buyer for the Choco Pies.

A voice behind her said, "Ajumma, something for those wrinkles?"

She turned to see a grandmother gesturing with a paper fan to a display of putty-colored Koryo remedies. Bottles of dried fungi, deer's placenta paste, every kind of useless goatshit. *Wrinkles indeed.*

"How much to rent a stall?" Mrs. Moon said.

"Five thousand won, dear," the woman said, fanning the canteen's steam away.

"A month?"

"A week." She smirked at the shock on Mrs. Moon's face. "There are cheaper spots nearer the loudspeaker."

As she waited for her bean-paste stew Mrs. Moon's mind was working. *Five thousand won!* Who had that kind of money? Tae-hyon earned more than she did, but his wage was two thousand won a month, and that was when he was actually paid. He hadn't worked since the coal mine flooded, and the ration coupons they gave him weren't worth a bird's fart.

A steaming bowl was slapped down on the table in front of her. She sniffed it. It smelled tangy and fresh. She took a mouthful. It was good. Across the crowded area she noticed two other makeshift canteens like this one, run by traders competing for customers. *Good food in a place like this ...* A small girl in filthy rags darted under the table, snatched up a string of gristle, and ran off.

"One hundred and fifty won, ajumma," said a young woman with a money belt, taking Mrs. Moon's empty bowl. Mrs. Moon felt in the pocket of her apron and froze.

Her money was gone.

Frantically she checked another pocket. Empty.

"*Kotchebi*," the young woman said with feeling. "Those kids are everywhere …"

Mrs. Moon delved into her basket, pulling the cloth away with her heart in her mouth, but then breathed easily. Her treasure was still there.

"I can pay with this," she said, holding up a Choco Pie.

The young woman's eyes widened at the sight of the red wrapper. She pushed Mrs. Moon's hand down, out of sight.

"Are you sure?" she said, furtively accepting the Choco Pie and slipping it into her money belt. She lowered her voice. "If you've got any more of those, ajumma, I'll give you twenty yuan each for them."

Hard currency? Without blinking Mrs. Moon said, "I was thinking thirty yuan each."

In truth she had very little idea how much a Chinese yuan was worth. But the young woman had an honest face and Mrs. Moon had a talent for reading faces.

"How many've you got?"

"Ten."

The young woman put down the empty bowls, ignored a man shouting an order for food, and did a quick sum on a scrap of newspaper. She was small and slender, with large, attractive eyes marred by a slight cast in one of them. Her hair was permed in curls and tucked into a sunflower-yellow headscarf. Her feet were so small she wore girls' shoes.

"It'll take me a few minutes to get the cash. Here …" She went over to the kitchen area and returned with a portion of *soondae* dipped in chili flakes. She smiled sweetly at Mrs. Moon and gave a small bow. "Have this while you wait, ajumma. My name's Ong, but everyone calls me Curly."

Mrs. Moon vacated her place on the bench and sat in the sun against the iron column of the bridge. She could see this was the low-rent end of the market—the traders had no stalls. They arranged their goods on straw mats on the ground. She ate the *soondae* slowly, savoring the burn of the chili, the way it made the blood sausage edible. Above her head a quavering voice issued from the loudspeaker, to a background of stirring music. "... *Fighting against thousands of enemies, braving snowfall and starvation, the red flag fluttering before the rank* ..." To her right, she watched crowds gather on the platform to meet a train from Kanggye, which was clanking in, couplings bumping, trailing sparks from the overhead cables and bringing a reek of latrines and scorched copper.

Curly returned, out of breath, and put three red notes into her hand. The Choco Pies were sold. "If you have anything else from the *village below*," she whispered, "you know where to find me." She winked and left. Mrs. Moon stared at the notes in her hand.

She crossed the square toward the hard-currency store where the money changers hung about. She had no intention of changing the money. She wanted to know what she had. One of them led her to a corner to conduct business, and it was then that she received her biggest surprise of all. In exchange for her 300 yuan he was offering her more than four thousand won in tattered, rotting notes. She gasped incredulously. Two months of her husband's labor equaled ten chocolate cookies from South Korea? She wanted to cry miserably and laugh at the same time. With a pang of shame she realized she would conceal this from Tae-hyon. She could not bear to see him lose face.

She walked away from the money changer, clutching the yuan in her fist.

"Hey, ajumma! All right, a special rate for you ..."

She returned to the market and walked with her head held high past the grandmother selling Koryo remedies.

Life deals you three chances, she thought. *This is one of them.*

Within an hour she had made her purchases. A five-kilo sack of rice and one of dried noodles, a liter of good-quality cooking oil, a bag of rice flour, jars of syrup, mustard sauce, fish stock, and soybean paste, and her biggest investment: a new steel pan.

There are those who starve, those who beg, and those who trade.

She was in business.

7

Hôtel Beau-Rivage
Quai de Mont-Blanc
Geneva, Switzerland

"He vanished from the end of our street, near the beach. He'd just said good-bye to a friend after soccer practice and was on his way home to finish his homework before dinner. The streetlights had only just come on. He was fourteen. We were devastated."

Mrs. Ishido stirred her cup and took a sip. She and Jenna were the only guests in the modestly named tearoom, a high-ceilinged belle époque salon with gilt chairs and brocaded drapes. French windows gave a postcard view of the lake and the Jet d'Eau rising like a geyser. The alpine sky bathed the room in a crystalline light that refracted in the chandeliers. At the far end of the room a shaven-headed man, too big for his suit, sat watching the door. The Swiss authorities had insisted on providing a bodyguard, Mrs. Ishido said, to protect her from North Korean assassins while she gave evidence at the United Nations. "They'd have killed me long before now if they'd wanted to silence me. They don't care what the world thinks of them."

She was about sixty, Jenna guessed, and dressed in an elegant navy suit with beautiful Japanese pearl jewelry. Her hair was an ashy white, and her face lined by sorrow, but there was something striking about her, the tatters of a remarkable beauty. She sat bolt upright like a queen, a posture in which Jenna saw the determined dignity of a mother who had endured the worst that could happen to her: having her child stolen. She could speak a little Korean, she explained, from her days working for the president of Hyundai Heavy Industries in Tokyo, but filled the gaps with English. On the table between them she had placed the school photograph of her son, Shuzo. Boyish, moon-faced. He was a cute kid.

"My husband reported him missing almost immediately. The prefecture police searched day and night. After a week they put this photo in all the local newspapers. They didn't find a single clue. It was as if the night had swallowed him up. Of course, we'd wondered if he'd run away, the way teenagers sometimes do. We always left the door unlocked and the lights on in case he returned when we were out.

"One year turned into five; five years turned into ten, and without us ever saying so we'd both given him up for dead. Living in that town by the sea became insufferable. When my husband's company offered him a transfer to Osaka it was what we had prayed for.

"And then, eleven years after Shuzo's disappearance, we got the phone call that turned our lives upside down. It was a reporter from the *Tokyo Shimbun*. He told me that a North Korean commando had been captured during a failed secret mission to Seoul. This commando was interrogated by South Korean intelligence officers. He admitted to being a part of a unit that had kidnapped dozens of people over the years and taken them to North Korea. One of them was a fourteen-year-old boy from our town."

She shook her head vaguely.

"Our son in North Korea? We'd never in our dreams considered such a thing. But everything matched. The time and the date. It was Shuzo. This commando had snatched him from the sidewalk ..." Mrs. Ishido paused for a moment and swallowed.

"... bound and gagged him on the beach, zipped him into a body bag, and took him by dinghy ... to a waiting submarine."

Hairs rose on the nape of Jenna's neck.

"He cried and yelled all the way to North Korea. They put him to work straight away. Imagine it, a fourteen-year-old teaching Japanese customs and slang to North Korean spies being trained to infiltrate Japan. Maybe they also thought they could brainwash him and turn him into a spy. The young are malleable.

"We demanded his immediate release. After a lot of pressure from our government, the North Korean regime finally admitted that they had taken Shuzo. Then they informed us that he had become mentally ill and had hanged himself four years ago, aged twenty-one." Her voice broke on the word *one*. The effort to maintain her composure must have been tremendous, and Jenna saw how brittle the woman's veneer was. "I don't believe them," she said, her voice ill controlled. "Why should I believe anything they say? I believe Shuzo is alive ..."

She took a handkerchief from her handbag and dabbed her eyes. Jenna looked away. She wanted to take her hand, but Mrs. Ishido did not invite familiarity. A silence opened between them, filled by the hum of traffic on the Quai de Mont-Blanc and the sound of a horn, the Lausanne ferry approaching the jetty. Jenna was reluctant to press but couldn't help herself. "You said ... a submarine."

Mrs. Ishido cleared her throat and when she spoke her voice was level again, her emotion quickly contained. "A naval spy submarine, Sango class, on a mission from the Mayangdo Naval Base in North Korea. Quite a large vessel, according to the commando." She gave Jenna a sad smile. "No one was expecting a submarine. It was probably the same craft that took your sister. It would explain why she vanished so completely and undetected."

An electric current swept through Jenna, a feeling of exhilaration mixed with a sickening contraction in her stomach.

So there it was. At last someone had said it.

"And I'd always been told abduction was impossible," she murmured.

The bodyguard stood and gestured to his watch.

"Forgive me," Mrs. Ishido said, getting up. "I must catch my flight back to Osaka." She gave a small bow and extended her hand for Jenna to shake. "I hope one day you are reunited with your sister." She began walking toward the door.

"This captured North Korean commando …" Jenna said. "What is his name?"

Even from behind, Jenna could see her tense.

"Sin Gwang-su," she said quietly, and turned. "His name is Sin Gwang-su. He's been detained at Pohang Prison, on the east coast of South Korea." Her face darkened.

"You've *visited* him?"

"No …" She hesitated. "He is a Category A prisoner held in a high-security unit. He is not permitted visitors. But with the permission of the South Korean government I have spoken to him … That's not an experience I would wish upon you. Or even one that might help you to find closure. But sometimes … it's possible to extract some truth from the falsehoods evil tells."

When Mrs. Ishido had gone, Jenna paced alone around in the tea-room. She was feeling such extremes of shock, anger, and euphoria that she did not know what to do with herself. The moments in her life when she felt she needed a drink were so few she could count them on one hand. This was one of them.

Amid the French and German chatter in the lobby bar she heard American voices. Keeping her back toward them she took a stool at the zinc bar near the piano, glanced in bewilderment at the rows of European liqueurs in backlit crystal, and asked for a tall Jack Daniel's and Coke. The pianist seemed to notice her, and the melody he was toying with modulated to a bluer key. Her drink was placed in front of her. She took a generous mouthful. Her hand was trembling.

She was taken in a submarine.

She shook her head as if this were simply incredible, as if some-one had told her, "Your sister became a mermaid and swam away." Not in any of the fateful scenarios she'd imagined over the years had she, or anyone, considered the possibility of a submarine.

From deep inside her came a rage directed at herself. *Did you lose hope so easily? Didn't you listen to your instinct all this time? Aren't you ashamed of yourself?*

The bartender, polishing glasses, was watching her warily. She took another large gulp of her drink, feeling the trembling begin to calm, and exhaled slowly.

She's alive. Oh God, she's alive.

Jenna's skin rose in goose bumps and something dark unfurled its wings inside her. If Mrs. Ishido had obtained permission to contact that North Korean abductor in prison, then so would she. She would speak to the fiend who took Soo-min and Jae-hoon. She would—

"You know, there are cheaper joints for getting drunk in this town," said a deep, familiar voice behind her.

She closed her eyes. *You have got to be kidding me.*

Jenna turned on her barstool. "Please don't tell me this is a coincidence."

Charles Fisk was smiling paternally. He was in a suit but had taken off his tie, as if he'd just come from a long meeting. "Mrs. Ishido's something, isn't she?" He took the stool next to her. "Like a Japanese Meryl Streep."

"What are you doing here?" she said, failing to keep the annoy-ance out of her voice.

"I just dropped by to say hello, that's all. The World Economic Forum's about to start." He lowered his voice. "Between you and me, it's a great chance to squeeze our esteemed allies for intel. Did you know this hotel was called the Beau-Espionage during the war? The bar would have been crawling with Gestapo spies and blonde double-agents hiding cyanide capsules in their garter straps."

Jenna sighed. "Look, sir, I'm grateful to you for connecting me to Mrs. Ishido, really I am, but right now I could use a little private time—"

"There's someone here I want you to meet."

It occurred to her that in another life, perhaps, she might have reveled in being an attractive young woman in the bar of a sublime hotel on Lake Geneva, in the company of a charming and erudite man, but she was simply feeling harassed. She did not want to encourage this evolving relationship with Fisk. He was undoubtedly trying to manipulate her to his own purpose. And yet, he seemed so obviously to like her and enjoy her company that she smiled, in spite of herself. She pondered his large nose and crinkled silver hair, his strong, intelligent, ugly face. His charm was a kind of seduction, she supposed, this bending to his will, and she was not as immune to it as she had believed.

As he led her across the grand Habsburg lobby she realized what had been unsettling her ever since she'd entered this hotel. There were security types everywhere. Men in Oakley sunglasses talking into lapel microphones, standing in corners, observing. On the fifth floor they stepped into a thickly carpeted lobby, where there stood another two men with radio earphones. Fisk directed her along a hallway hung with spotlit nineteenth-century paintings toward a lacquered door with a security entry system. He buzzed, and it was opened by a brisk-looking woman holding a desk calendar. "Go in," she said to him, "but please—five minutes only."

They were in a large, sumptuous suite filled with bouquets of flowers. Second Empire claw-and-ball armchairs and silk divans were arranged in each corner. Flanked by tall table lamps with tasseled shades, an outsized Napoleonic fireplace dominated an entire wall.

From behind a door Jenna could hear a woman talking. She thought she recognized the chest tones of the voice but was too distracted to place it. The door opened and a sleek young black man wearing a three-piece suit beckoned them in.

The woman had her feet up on a sofa, with her back toward them, and was talking on a cell phone. She had a full-throated voice, rather deep, that seemed too loud and abrasive for the room. Jenna glanced at Fisk, who signaled with his finger for her to say nothing. Patterns of light shifted across the ceiling, the sunlight bouncing off the lake. She heard the tick and whir of a fax machine. The woman's blonde hair was stiffly coiffed. A young female hairdresser in a pink uniform was packing away a hairdryer and brushes, and left the room. Finally the woman ended the call, saying "Jesus Christ Almighty," and tossed the cell phone to the young black man in the suit. Jenna smelt her perfume, which was citrusy and strong.

She stood to face them, giving them a bright, embattled smile, and Jenna found herself shaking hands with the United States secretary of state.

8

The Ministry of Foreign Affairs
Kim Il-sung Square
Pyongyang, North Korea

Lieutenant Colonel Cho's day had begun routinely enough. A couple of tedious committees; rice balls and squid for lunch in the office of his superior, General Kang, where Kang had doggedly continued to practice English conversation with Cho. *I did hike of a mountain with my two daughters and afterward we eat some pruits in a lestaulant.* The afternoon was a logistics conference with Section One of the Guard Command to plan the Dear Leader's official visit to China: cortège of three armored trains; a dozen timetables canceled to clear the line; armed detachments of the KPA deployed in every station he passed through; fresh fish and game to be flown out to him and the trash flown back. Small wonder the great man seldom left the country. (The Guard Command had also wanted the Leader's urine and feces collected and returned to Pyongyang to prevent any foreign powers obtaining his DNA. Cho had cautiously suggested they solve that one themselves, as the task was too great a privilege for someone of his rank.)

By six he was sitting in his workplace political study group—this evening's lecture was on the revolutionary principles of Juche poetry—and focusing all his remaining energy into not yawning.

He was shattered with exhaustion. His brain felt as if it were wrapped in wool. His eyes felt scoured and too small for their sockets.

He had not had a good night's sleep since the day of the parade, almost a week ago. His mood veered precariously every time he thought of Yong-ho's imminent promotion, which was several times an hour. One moment he felt such a rush of excitement that he could hardly breathe. The next he was almost hysterical with worry. A background investigation into their real family? Their *real family*. The risk was insane! How could Yong-ho do this?

That morning he'd awakened when it was still dark, soaked in sweat. He was listening for the thump of boots in the stairwell, a hammering at the door. The disappearances happened at night, always at night. He pictured Bowibu agents entering his bedroom, shining bright lights in his eyes, come to arrest him because his family, his *real* family, whose names and faces were unknown to him, had been class traitors, saboteurs, enemies of the Revolution, and that he and Yong-ho, brothers whose genes carried this ancestral criminality, had betrayed the trust of the noblest Leader alive. Then he'd rubbed his face, and breathed in, and breathed out. His real family would have been nothing but rice planters and shit shovelers. There was nothing to worry about.

When his study group finished at seven thirty Cho came home for dinner with his wife and Books, and sat with Books for a while, helping him with his school homework. Then he managed a fitful, half-hour nap in his study before returning to the Ministry around ten, along with his colleagues, for the more important part of the working day—drafting reports and communiqués, analyzing intelligence, and *being present* late into the night. The hours of darkness were the Dear Leader's most productive, and the man himself might telephone his bureaucrats at any time. That was an insight of Kim Jong-il's that was lost on the capitalists: fear was every bit as incentivizing as greed.

When Cho reentered the Ministry's main doors at ten, his department supervisor was waiting for him in a corner of the vast lobby. The man stubbed out his cigarette the moment he saw Cho. "They're asking for you on the top floor."

"What?" Fear breathed down Cho's neck like a draft of icy air. "Why?"

His supervisor's eyes were checking him up and down. "Straighten your tie. I'm to take you up right away." He put his hand in the small of Cho's back and began propelling him across the lobby. "Quick. *Chollima* speed."

Cho felt almost suffocated with panic, as if someone had a rope around his windpipe. *This is it! What have they found out?*

The supervisor followed Cho into the caged elevator; the gate was wrenched shut, and the slow rattle of their ascent was accompanied by the hum of a motor. The supervisor said nothing until they had risen clear of the lobby, then began to whisper.

"Kang's been arrested. At his home this evening." The supervisor's voice was hoarse with panic. "Accused of *spying*. The whole department's in turmoil ..."

"General Kang?" Cho stared at him. "On what evidence?"

The man shook his head. "What's it matter? He's been accused. He's finished."

The wan electric bulb of the elevator flared with the current and dimmed again.

Cho's mind began to race. Spying was a vague and unspecific crime but it was highly contagious. The type of crime that was quickly found to exist in rings and factions, and to have infected whole departments.

Was he about to be accused of spying, as an accomplice of Kang's? *Oh my dear fucking ancestors.* Guilt by association, guilt by heredity. Or had they unearthed something in his real family's past ... and this something was providing corroborating proof ... ?

The elevator juddered to a halt at the top floor. The moment Cho was delivered, the gate shut behind him with a ferrous screech. He turned to see the supervisor descending into the floor, face lit like a Kabuki demon.

Admit nothing, he mouthed.

The silent white corridor led toward an anteroom. He'd seldom visited the leadership area of the Ministry of Foreign Affairs, and then only in the company of General Kang. He began walking slowly past a series of oil paintings on the walls. Large, classic pieces dating from the Three Revolutions. Farmers hailing one another across fields of bumper crops. A blast-furnace worker wiping his brow. His shoes echoed like gunshots on the heated parquet floor, and he felt his panic give way to a strange calm, an acceptance almost, like the profound resignation he'd seen on the faces of the condemned at public executions. The feeling was given depth and poignancy by the love he felt for his wife and son. Who would take care of them now?

A uniformed female secretary stood at her desk as he approached. She smiled at him and he felt pathetically grateful. She raised a finger, indicating for him to wait a moment, gave a tentative knock on the paneled door, and opened it ajar. "Sir, Lieutenant Colonel Cho Sang-ho is here for you."

There was a grunt from inside and she opened both doors onto a large, brightly lit office that smelt of wood polish. A man of about fifty was standing behind a desk, shuffling papers.

"Come in, Comrade Cho, come in," the First Deputy Minister said, without looking up. The red flag of the Workers' Party stood on one side of the desk like a theater curtain, and the Father-Son portraits watched from the wall above him. In a glass cabinet to the left were the sacred revolutionary texts in pristine volumes; to the right, three tall, net-curtained windows looked down onto the sparse lights of Kim Il-sung Square.

Cho entered slowly, conscious of his blind spots to the left and right.

The First Deputy Minister nodded vaguely toward a side table with an old silver samovar and china cups. "Pour yourself some tea."

Two other men were present in the room, seated in heavy armchairs facing the desk. Neither turned to greet him but Cho recognized the tailored Mao suit of the First Party Secretary, sitting with his legs crossed. He was holding a cigarette up near his face at an angle, like a Japanese capitalist in the movies. The other man was the Minister himself, his head a wizened and turtle-like protrusion between the epaulettes on his shoulders. Instinctively Cho made a rapid appraisal. He was fairly sure he could discount the two in the armchairs, even the Minister, who was brought out only for state occasions. The real power in the room was the man behind the desk, the First Deputy Minister. He wore a simple brown tunic without insignia, and carried the absolute authority of Kim Jong-il.

Cho poured some tea and felt the eyes of all of them on his back. An intense concentration pervaded the room. He sensed they had just been discussing him.

"Take a seat."

Once Cho was seated the First Deputy Minister walked around the desk and sat on the edge directly in front of him, drumming his fingers on the wood, and giving him a hard, evaluating stare. He had the face of an apparatchik—thinning hair, thick black eyebrows, and steel-rimmed glasses that magnified his gaze, like a crafty owl.

"Your superior, General Kang, is no longer with us," he said with finality. Cho felt a sweat break out on his back. "We have therefore decided to entrust you with his mission to the West."

Cho's mouth might have slackened dumbly in shock because the First Deputy Minister frowned. "It's not a mission we're assigning lightly, I can tell you that." The voice carried an edge of cynicism. "It pertains to a matter of grave national importance. There is no room for error. The question is: are you up to the task?"

Cho was sitting upright on the edge of the chair and balancing his tea on his knee. He would have preferred to stand. He heard himself say, "It would be my honor and duty to serve to the utmost of my abilities, sir."

The First Deputy Minister swatted away the formulaic remark. He exhaled thoughtfully and folded his arms. "My colleagues here think you're too green and, at thirty-three years old, too young. You've never dealt with Westerners before."

"I speak English to a decent standard, sir."

"Ye-es," he turned and glanced at the papers on the desk and Cho spotted a photo of himself upside down. It was his own file, he realized, retrieved from the Central Party Complex, where secret files on all citizens were kept. Their entire lives were in there: names of childhood friends, weaknesses for alcohol or gambling, infidelity, any remark they'd once made that could be construed as disloyal. "English will give you an edge with those jackals and bastards. I should also tell you that your family connections have been an important factor in considering your candidacy ..."

"My family?" Cho felt his heart become buttery and faint.

The First Deputy Minister walked back to his chair, took a cigarette from a walnut box on the desk, and lit it from an enormous brass table lighter.

"We know your brother's slated to be chief of staff to our Dear Leader's youngest son," he said sucking hard on the cigarette. His dark eyes fixed on Cho. The smoke came out with the words, which he spoke carefully. "In time, though we hope that day is distant, it will be useful for us to have a trusted contact so close to the Successor ..."

A tingle spread across Cho's scalp, as if a mystery had been spoken. He had never heard anyone speak of the succession. Such a notion was dangerous because implicit in it was an acknowledgment that the Dear Leader was mortal, whereas the Party taught that the Leader's life was a continuous series of blessed miracles, unmatched by all his people's mortal lifetimes put together. Even in death, he would not die.

The silence seemed to mark Cho's admittance to a secret circle.

Then the First Deputy Minister said, "We're sending you to New York to open negotiations with the Yankees." A patch of hot pain erupted on Cho's knee, where he splashed scolding tea. "Your objective is to screw them for as much cash and material aid as you can get."

"The leadership needs hard currency," the First Party Secretary said, leaning forward to tip his ash into a thick glass ashtray. "Urgently."

Finally the Minister himself piped up to say how much hard currency was needed. Cho thought he'd misheard the old man. His mind was struggling to keep pace. Astronomical sums of dollars. Make-believe numbers. How on earth would he persuade the Americans to agree to such a thing?

"Any questions?" the old Minister said.

Cho's mind was blank. Finally he said, "What leverage will I have?"

The First Deputy Minister glanced at the other two and something secret passed between them. "You'll have something to bargain with. You don't need to know for now."

The men stubbed out their cigarettes. All four got to their feet. Cho stood to attention. The First Deputy Minister walked back around the desk so that three of them stood in a line facing Cho, and raised a sheet of paper ceremonially.

"Our Dear General's order will now be communicated ..." In a high, sonorous voice, Kim Jong-il's written command to negotiate with the Americans was formally issued to Cho. The Word was spoken, and he felt his life changing.

They shouted, "Long live the General!"

Then they dismissed him.

As he was leaving the room the First Deputy Minister said, "By the way, Cho, you're promoted to full colonel. Congratulations."

Cho watched the unlit streets of the capital slip past the backseat window as he headed home. He was in the grip of so many roiling emotions he could barely hold on to a single thought. He felt a mixture of oppression and elation. To be sent on a mission to the Yankees signaled an exceptional level of political trust in him. So much so that he felt a surge of hope—that he had nothing to fear from the Bowibu's investigation into his family background.

Poor Kang. All those painful English conversations for nothing. Did they take his daughters, too?

The car turned into a street behind the twin towers of the Koryo Hotel. After a few yards it reached the striped barrier at the compound's main gate. Two helmeted policewomen of the Ministry of People's Security shone their flashlights on the license plate and into the car, and saluted smartly when they saw Cho's face. The gate slid sideways and the car purred along a curving road lit by tiny spotlights set into the stone curbs. Late-blooming egret flowers winked in the glare of the headlights. The car stopped in Courtyard 5 and Cho said goodnight to his driver. A nightingale trilled in the branches of the gingko trees. On his Nokia the time was just after midnight.

He leapt up the stairs with the adrenalin singing in his chest. His wife would not mind being awakened when he told her his news. He opened the door of his apartment and his blood froze. A pair of polished boots was on the floor of the vestibule. A murmur of voices was coming from the living room. With panic rising inside him like gas through a liquid, he silently removed his shoes and crept into the darkness of the hall, straining to hear. Then he threw open the door onto the brightly lit living room. Yong-ho was standing there with his military coat hanging from his shoulders. He grinned broadly at Cho and opened his arms to embrace him.

"I thought you'd want to know straight away, younger brother ..."

He was holding a bottle of Hennessy Black cognac and had just given a bouquet of pink azaleas to Cho's wife, whose eyes were puffy with sleep. She was holding them to her nose, trying to look pleased. He took two glasses from the lacquered cabinet.

"The investigating officer called me in person," he said, uncorking the bottle and splashing shots into the glasses. "It's better than we could possibly have imagined."

"What is?"

"Our real family name is Hwang. The records show that our real grandfather was killed in September 1950 in the Battle of Busan. He was posthumously decorated for holding off the Yankees to the last bullet while his comrades escaped ..." Yong-ho punched Cho's chest and gave a loud whoop. "To the last bullet! We're the grandsons of a martyr! That practically makes us demigods, younger brother. And it gets even better. Our real father was a highly respected general in the air force until his death ten years ago." He pushed a glass into Cho's hand and clinked it with his own. Cho saw that his brother was already quite drunk. "Didn't I tell you this wouldn't be a problem?" He downed the drink with a wince.

After the momentary elation he'd felt on hearing this news, Cho felt his smile faltering. This didn't make sense.

"Elder brother ... if we were born into such a family, why were we put in an orphanage?"

Yong-ho shrugged. "Our father must have taken a mistress. Wouldn't have been unusual. And we're the offspring. Who knows? It doesn't matter. Our blood's clean. And it comes from a Class A war hero."

Cho stared unseeingly about the room as he absorbed this second bombshell of the night. He held a vague, imagined image of his real mother, whose face his mind's eye could not see directly, but she was there in the periphery, in the shadows of a bamboo forest at dawn, a mythic figure. Now he pictured her tearfully

71

delivering her baby boys to the state orphanage. What terrible choices had been forced upon her?

Yong-ho settled into an armchair, lifting the neat creases of his trouser legs. "The investigating officer wants to wrap this up. The Party's keen to announce my appointment. And listen to this: they're offering us a little celebration to introduce us to the brothers and sisters we've never met."

"We have brothers and sisters?" Cho said in a daze.

Suddenly he felt relief wash over him like warm spring water. He looked up at the Father-Son portraits on the wall and the faces gazed back at him, full of power and enigmatic calm. The relief he was feeling made him generous. "Are you hungry? We have Swiss cheese in the refrigerator, and there's a jar of Iranian caviar." Without a word, Cho's wife turned and went to the kitchen.

Yong-ho poured them both another cognac. He brought a bottle whenever he visited, and Cho wondered, not for the first time, what his brother was worth. Just one of those bottles fetched a hundred American dollars on the black market.

"And now I have some news for *you*," Cho said, suddenly eager to please his elder brother.

"You're off to light a fire under the American monkey's ass," Yong-ho said, belching as the spirit went down. "You're a braver man than me."

"You know?" Cho put his glass down.

"Heard about it this afternoon. Congratulations. But between you and me, younger brother, your General Kang had been falling out of favor for a long time. He had to go."

Cho was stunned. In some way he couldn't fathom, he felt foolish, and offended on Kang's behalf.

Yong-ho ate the cheese and biscuits ravenously, barely thanking Cho's wife, who made a point of saying she was going back to bed. For a rail-thin man he always had a good appetite. He brushed the crumbs from his mouth. Then, remembering something, he reached for his attaché case and took out a large padded package, sealed with thick masking tape.

"I'm giving you this now for safekeeping. Lock it away somewhere secure until it's time for your trip. When you arrive in New York give it to Ambassador Shin in person."

Cho gave him a quizzical look.

"It's just admin." Yong-ho cleared his throat. "And some funds. He's expecting it."

Cho took the package. It was oddly weighted, like a rice sack. Yong-ho was skillfully avoiding his eye. A worrying thought crossed Cho's mind, but once again the secrecy of Yong-ho's work hung between them. Cho could not pry.

As Yong-ho took his leave and wished his brother goodnight, they embraced tightly, but beneath the affection Cho sensed, in some way he couldn't have explained, that a gap had opened between them.

At the door, almost as an afterthought, Yong-ho said, "That package, younger brother. It goes in the diplomatic pouch, not your luggage. Understand?"

9

Hôtel Beau-Rivage
Quai de Mont-Blanc
Geneva, Switzerland

"Dr. Williams, hi." The secretary of state clasped Jenna's elbow and fixed her with a big blue stare, as if she were being friendly to a large pony. "Fisk speaks highly of your expertise. It's great to have you on board."

Jenna smiled uncertainly. "I don't think I've agreed—"

"Some coffee in here," she yelled over Jenna's shoulder. Her voice was really quite loud. With barely any lowering of the volume she said, "Sit down, both of you."

She had slipped her feet into a pair of white hotel slippers, Jenna saw. Her hair was immaculate but she had not finished her makeup and was wearing a faded Wellesley College Athletics sweatshirt. The famous face was both unsettlingly familiar and utterly strange, as if Jenna had never seen her before. The images of her in the media had conveyed nothing of her personal magnetism, or her lack of height.

The brisk-looking female aide carried in a tray with a silver coffee pot and three cups, which the secretary of state insisted on taking from her and made a fuss of serving the coffee herself. It was a trick of the very powerful, Jenna knew, to make a show of their informality. *I may be a higher being*, it seemed to say, *but see how I am one of you.*

Fisk's glance at Jenna betrayed a droll mischief.

"No one has a damned idea what to do about North Korea," the secretary of state said, handing them the cups, "and that includes the president." She'd given them a strong black coffee without offering milk or sugar. "Sanctions, isolation, threats, rewards, cash bribes—nothing's worked. We're shit out of ideas. That man in Pyongyang is laughing at us. Frankly there's nothing I'd like better than to ignore him, but last week he launched another rocket, and that I cannot ignore." She took a sip of her coffee and flashed her eyes challengingly at Jenna.

Jenna looked to Fisk for help. "I ... didn't know Kim's technology had advanced so fast," she said, hedging.

"I know, right?" The secretary of state shook her head vaguely, marveling at what had become of the world. "A tiny, nuclear-armed communist rogue power, still fighting the goddamned Cold War, now poses a direct threat to Los Angeles."

"I'm no military expert, ma'am."

The secretary of state leaned closer toward Jenna and seemed to hesitate, as if deciding whether to take her into a confidence. Another trick of the powerful, Jenna thought: making you feel you're the most important person in the room.

"I need to know how we deal with a psychopath who spends all his nation's wealth on rockets and lets his people starve. I need ..." She opened her hands in a show of helplessness. "... some *insight* into his thinking. Some psychology. We're not dealing with a rational mind."

"Not true," Jenna said. "In a paranoid, twisted way, Kim Jong-il is highly rational. He's a survivor, playing a poor hand with great skill. His weapons keep him safe from us. Hunger keeps him safe at home. His people think only of where their next meal is coming from, not of rebellion. And he'll kill as many of them as it takes to stay in power."

The secretary of state sighed. "It's coming down to this: very soon we'll have to tighten the screws on him even more, or give him what he wants. But what the hell does he want?"

Jenna had forgotten the resentment she'd felt in the bar. Her mind was sparking with connections. She was thinking of Kim Jong-il. Pudgy, cerebral. Soft spoken with a mild stammer, which was why he never gave a speech in public. Paranoid and capricious. Cold, lacking in empathy. The physical awkwardness of one whose self-loathing had been transmuted into power.

"What does he truly want … ?" She turned to the window. On the distant peaks of Chamonix, resplendent in white, mist lingered in the sun's shadow. "In his heart … I'd say he wants the world to revere his late father Kim Il-sung as a charismatic god-king, and himself as the son messiah. I think he wants to reunify Korea and avenge a pure and innocent race that has been invaded and defiled for centuries, by China, by Japan, by America. A war of reunification would be his most sublime contribution to the Revolution. An achievement in honor of his father. A gift to his son. He knows he'll succeed only with over-whelming power. When he agrees to talk to us it's only to buy himself time to increase his arsenal. It's pointless negotiating with him."

The secretary of state gave an affronted laugh. "He really thinks he could take South Korea by force?"

"With banners flying. And my guess is that he'll act soon. He's ailing now and thinking of his place in history. That missile he's going to point at LA is to make sure we don't interfere. He knows the average American won't risk a nuclear strike for the sake of a faraway peninsula."

"Would he use it?"

It surprised Jenna to realize she had never imagined whether he would actually press the button, but she was in no doubt. "Yes."

The secretary of state fell silent. She seemed to have dropped her public persona and Jenna thought she looked tired and diminished, the weight of the world's cares upon her.

Eventually she said, "Do we have any options?"

"Doing nothing may be your *only* option," Jenna said.

"Impossible. Congress'll have me for breakfast."

Fisk said, "A preemptive strike is out of the question. Seoul is only forty miles south of North Korea's border. The retaliation against our ally would be horrific."

The three of them were on their feet facing the windows, thinking. The mist on the Alps was now shot with shafts of light.

"There is one course of action," Jenna said.

"I am all ears, Dr. Williams." The secretary of state's voice sounded jaded, cynical.

Jenna met her eye. "Kill Kim Jong-il."

The secretary of state gave a guilty chuckle. "We'd never get near him."

Thirty-six hours later, back in Washington and unable to sleep, her body still on Central European Time, Jenna called Fisk. If she waited until morning she feared she might change her mind.

At the end of the meeting in the hotel, when he'd walked her to the elevator, her mind was still thinking so deeply on what they'd discussed that she'd barely acknowledged his handshake when he'd said good-bye.

"I'm hoping you'll reconsider my offer," he'd said. "I could use your help. Urgently."

She'd turned to face him just as the elevator doors were closing.

She had no clear or convincing reasons for her decision, but plenty against—she'd be walking out on her academic career, on her tenure at Georgetown, which she would never get back. But she felt that a door was being opened for her, and some deep and unformulated sense told her that it led to Soo-min.

Fisk's phone went to voice mail.

In the stillness of her apartment her voice sounded small and calm.

"If you want me ... I'm in."

10

Hyesan
Ryanggang Province, North Korea

Years ago, in the days of the Great Leader, Mrs. Moon had been a cook. She'd roll her own noodles from buckwheat and make *naeng-myon*—the tangy ice-cold broth with marinated pork and spicy mustard sauce. Her radish kimchi, fermented all summer in earthenware jars and flavored with ginger and garlic, was so tasty that even her mother-in-law, invalided on a mat and living in the family house, had felt compelled to praise it.

The Great Leader blessed them like the sun ripened the wheat. He was Father to them all, a prophet in whose presence flowers bloomed and snow melted. "Rice means socialism," he told them, and through the years of bumper harvests and fields of flying red flags, his words seemed a self-evident truth.

But the Father died and the world changed. Power passed to the Son, the Dear Leader, and Mrs. Moon learned that hunger meant socialism, too. The ration system that had provided for everyone, twice a month like clockwork, became irregular, then broke down. The farm director called in the army to protect the grain store, and it was robbed by the very soldiers sent to guard it. Tae-hyon's coal mine stopped paying wages. Production dwindled as the power cuts became more frequent, then stopped.

In the worst weeks not a kernel of maize was to be found in the village or in Hyesan, where the steel and lumber mills stopped puffing smoke and the streets fell silent during the day, filled with the dead and the walking dead, their minds hallucinating from hunger. Mrs. Moon trekked daily to the forest, though the skin hung from her arms and her joints were so painful it exhausted her even to lift one foot in front of the other. At these times her mind betrayed her, tormenting her with memories of long-ago dishes she'd cooked. A beef *bulgogi* sizzled to perfection. Steamed cockles served in a spicy *yangnyeomjang* sauce. When she became faint she would lie in the moss between the pines, calling to the spirits of her mother and father, and they would appear to her. Light shone through them, and their words were not in time with the moving of their mouths, but their voices were as clear as bells. They told her not to close her eyes; they told her not to fall asleep.

She learned which roots could be eaten and which made the tongue swell up. She added nettles and raspberry leaves to broth to make it look as if it had vegetables, and tiny snails to make it look as if it had meat. Noodles she boiled for an hour to make them seem larger. She mashed a paste out of acorns, sweetened it with saccharine, and molded it into small, bitter cakes.

The famine deepened, and her foraging was not enough. On the day she saw children in the village picking through ox shit in search of undigested seeds to eat, something inside her changed, permanently. All her life she had been decent and honest, but now she started stealing tools from the farm and selling them for a few cups of corn. She crept into neighbors' yards at night, dug up their urns of fermenting kimchi, and ate it with Tae-hyon. She begged for grains from friends who themselves were starving. She saw hunger drive villagers insane. New graves were dug up and the corpses vanished. Parents took food from their own children. She was glad she had no longer had children to care for. It comforted her to tell herself that. It eased the pain of memory. Not a baby on her back, nor one running alongside her.

You don't know yourself until you know hunger.

The Dear Leader felt his people's agony and wept for them. "I am with you on this arduous march," he told them. "Whosoever may endure these trials shall become a true revolutionary." The television news showed him eating simple meals of potatoes, in solidarity with the people's plight, but to Mrs. Moon's eyes the wealth of his belly looked greater than ever. At the entrance to the village a new slogan appeared on a long red placard.

If you survive a thousand miles of suffering,
you shall receive ten thousand miles of joy!

Mrs. Moon read it and knew it was goatshit. She looked up at the colored-glass mural of the Dear Leader standing in a field of golden wheat and made a vow to herself there and then. *I will never again count on you for anything.* If famine returned, she would be ready.

The villagers began to shirk their work whenever they had something to bribe their workplace director. They grew potatoes and runner beans on the hardscrabble lots behind their houses, and foraged in the forest for mushrooms and berries. Mrs. Moon trailed pumpkin vines over her roof, and hoarded lentils and rice in jars. She grew garlic and onions behind her house. At harvest time she slept under the stars to guard her crop. Her trust in the system was gone. Those kindly souls who'd put others before themselves had been the first to starve to death. The Dear Leader had done nothing to help them. As hundreds of thousands died with grass in their mouths, the food-shortage problem had simply solved itself.

She decided to make rice cakes, something simple to see how things went on her first day. She sweetened them with syrup, rounded them into moist, gelatinous balls, and placed a blueberry and an almond on top of each. Arranged like flowers in her nickel bowl, she covered them with a cloth. She prepared in silence, by the light of the wind-up flashlight from the balloon. She was about to leave the house when a key rattled in her door and it opened. Two officials wearing white gloves were on the doorstep. Comrade Pak was with them, holding a large ring with several dozen keys hanging from it.

From long habit Mrs. Moon assumed an expression of cheerful optimism. "Don't wake my husband," she whispered.

The two officials went to the Father-Son portraits on the wall, took them down, and ran their gloves over the glass and the frames, then held them at an angle to the light, searching for any motes of dust. She cleaned them every day—even in the rainy season, when spots of mold could creep under the glass, they sparkled—but she always watched this inspection with apprehension. The men hung them back on the wall with extreme care, and nodded to her. As they were leaving one of them saw the wind-up flashlight on the table.

Goatshit.

He stared at it for a moment, and went outside. To her horror he was speaking into Comrade Pak's ear. The woman's face hardened, then she entered the house without removing her boots. She picked up the flashlight with two fingers, as if it were something rotten. Now Mrs. Moon remembered that the words MADE IN SOUTH KOREA were printed on it, and felt her heart flip over in her chest.

"Where d'you get this, citizen?" The woman's voice was flat but her eyes held a glint of real malice.

"In Hyesan," she lied. "Please don't drop it. I swapped a half kilo of mushrooms for that."

The woman regarded her with cold suspicion, and left.

Curse that woman and all her ancestors!

Mrs. Moon rushed to catch the truck into Hyesan. The wind off the Paektu Mountains was cold enough to stop hearts, but she felt herself sweating freely. Why hadn't she offered the old bitch a bribe? No, too dangerous. She could tell when people were agreeable to a little encouragement and when they weren't. As the truck lurched and bumped out of the village, she felt fear swelling in her gut like a tumor.

The hands of the station clock stood at 9:00 a.m. The Great Leader's face smiled with fatherly love on the crowds arriving to catch the morning trains. A hail of static announced a departure for Musan.

The sky was a stark blue with a stinging chill in it. At the cheaper end of the market, just beneath the iron bridge, Mrs. Moon saw the same dozen women squatting behind their mats. Two or three were keeping food hot with tiny smoking heaters made from paint tins. Customers were already milling about, picking up a hot snack for breakfast. The loudspeaker was blaring out an army chorus to a background crunch of marching feet.

Mrs. Moon cast her eyes about for the sunflower-yellow headscarf of the young woman who'd bought the Choco Pies—Curly, wasn't that her nickname?—and was surprised when the woman herself spotted her first and greeted her warmly. "A lovely morning, ajumma." Over her coat she wore an apron printed with colorful flowers, and had tucked her curls into her headscarf with a hair clip. She seemed to radiate warmth, some inner contentment that made her stand out from all the other women, who were much older, and muffled grubbily against the cold.

"Who do I pay to rent a spot?" Mrs. Moon said.

Curly laughed. "He'll find you, don't worry."

But as Mrs. Moon put her bowl down and bent painfully to her knees to sit on the concrete platform, she sensed the other women watching her with unwelcoming eyes. When she was as comfortable as she could get sitting on her straw mat she filled her lungs and joined the women's calls.

"*Tteok sassayo!*" Come and buy rice cakes.

Almost at once a soldier in a long green coat was pulling his buddy by the sleeve toward Mrs. Moon's mat. "Two," he said.

"Fifty won each," she said, placing the cakes in a wrap of newspaper. The soldiers seemed very young—rough types with hard brown faces and rifles slung across their backs. They pushed some filthy notes into her hand and walked away.

"Very nice, ajumma," one of them called back with his mouth full.

Mrs. Moon looked at the notes in her palm. They hadn't given her enough. The women were still watching.

"Find another spot tomorrow," a voice said next to her. "We don't want them thinking they can get away with that here." Her neighbor on the sidewalk was a grandmother wrapped in so many layers that only a yellowish nose protruded. Her mat was arranged with bottles of Chinese whiskey and a pyramid of home-rolled cigarettes.

What a grim bunch these women were. They sold dried herbs or bags of tiny fried fish, or batteries and plastic toys, or silver disks that she knew were illegal from the way they were whisked from hiding places beneath mats. But even these tough old birds creased into a smile when Curly spoke to them. That woman was a ray of pure sunshine. When she wasn't helping in the canteen, she had her own mat selling dumplings. Her daughter, a girl of about twelve, sat with her, guarding the takings.

At lunchtime Mrs. Moon experienced her first real test. Customers clustered like bees around the mats, and she was slow in counting out change—"Come on, ajumma, do we look like we're at the seaside?"—but she soon made an interesting discovery. She could sell.

"*Tteok sassayo!*"

Customers seemed to warm to her and stopped to chat. *I must have an honest face,* she thought. But to her dismay this only seemed to deepen her isolation among the women. By midafternoon she'd tried several times to break the ice with offers to guard their wares while they went on errands, or provide change when they'd run out, yet still they kept their voices low around her. A cordon of mistrust had been cast around her, and she could guess why. She didn't blame them. Even the gentlest neighbor could turn out to be a Bowibu informer.

The crowd swelled again with the arrival of a train from Hamhung that was four days late. A reek of oil and soldered steel filled the air. Mrs. Moon watched a line of tiny Pioneers in red neckerchiefs following their teacher. Now and then she spotted women who appeared out of nowhere when the station was crowded, and behaved oddly, weaving through the throng, or loitering in corners and flashing a smile at single men. Mrs. Moon averted her eyes and did not judge. During the famine, even village girls had done that. The figures that frightened her were the older teenage boys. Some were hoodlums, hanging about the market in sullen packs, but others staggered lethargically with gaunt faces, bumping into people, or gazing at things that weren't there. Or they lay propped against walls, muttering, with faces that seemed caught between ecstasy and despair.

It was later afternoon when the police came for her.

There were two of them, wearing the caps of the Ministry of People's Security. When they stopped in front of her mat she bowed her head almost to the ground. Again, the women were watching.

The younger one had a loutish grin and a plain, flat face, like a shovel; the other, whom she later learned was called Sergeant Jang, was the senior and seemed to know all the women by name. He might have been good looking once and still thought he was.

"Are you a Hyesan resident?" he said.

"Baekam County, sir," she said, keeping her voice low.

She sensed everyone around her sit up. The younger one stopped grinning.

"You have a permit to leave Baekam County?" the senior officer said.

"Yes, sir."

She handed him her ID passbook. The travel permit approved by the farm director had cost her a bottle of corn liquor, and the man's scowl had made it clear to her that she'd have to come up a better bribe better next time.

The sergeant examined the ID passbook, turning each page, and Mrs. Moon felt her stomach sink. *Don't ask me in front of these women why I'm a worker on—*

"The October 18th Collective Farm!" he said, raising his eyebrows.

She felt her face burn.

He crouched down so that he was at eye level and looked at her, but with more curiosity than menace. "What was your crime, eh?"

Mrs. Moon stared at her mat.

"All right, ajumma," he said, getting up. He tossed the passbook into her lap. "Two thousand won a week for your spot. Pay me at the end of the day."

After they'd gone, she sensed the women around her relax very slightly. Something in what had just taken place seemed to have resolved some fear they had about her. They began meeting her eye when she looked at them.

By the end of the day the sky was turning a deep orange and a bone-chilling northerly was sweeping down from Manchuria, whirling up eddies of coal dust in the corners of the station. Yet still the crowds stood about in the shadows of the unlit platforms, waiting for trains that ran to no timetable. On the clock tower an electric light came on over the Great Leader's face.

Across the market the blue beams of pencil flashlights danced across goods and money. Mrs. Moon had sold all but three of her rice cakes, and rolled up her mat. Her fingers were numb with cold and her knees swollen and painful. In her apron were takings totaling more than two thousand won. She wanted to feel buoyed by her first day's success, but her failure to make friends troubled her. Curly was the only one who'd spoken to her.

Unable to resist a peek at the money, she opened her pocket a fraction and began counting the notes with the tips of her fingers.

A shadow fell across her.

One of the teenage boys was standing right over her, blocking her light. She recoiled as if he were a wild pig, and pulled her coat together over her apron pocket.

"They said you have the nicest rice cakes," he said softly. The light of a passing lamp illuminated his face only for a second. His eyes weren't focusing, and his mouth was missing teeth. He was insect thin, with pale fingers that looked as if they were made from coral.

He seemed so lost and forlorn that Mrs. Moon's heart softened. "Here," she said, giving him her last rice cakes in newspaper.

He smiled and she saw how young he was. "I can pay with this," he said, revealing a square of folded paper in his palm, the size of a postage stamp.

"What's that supposed to be?"

"*Bingdu*," he said simply.

Mrs. Moon stared at him without understanding. "Go," she said.

The boy took the food and ran away.

A rasping noise erupted next to her. It took her a moment to realize that Grandma Whiskey, on the neighboring mat, was laughing.

"You idiot," she said through a phlegmy cackle. "The kid's lost his mind on that stuff. One wrap of *bingdu* will buy a twenty-kilo bag of rice." The laugh brought on a liquid cough. Mrs. Moon closed her eyes as the woman hacked up a gob of mucus and blew it onto the concrete.

"What is *bingdu*?" she said, without hiding her revulsion.

"You'll find out."

At that moment a whistle blew high and shrill, and the market fell silent. Mrs. Moon thought it heralded the arrival of a train, until she saw the last remaining customers begin to scatter in every direction like rabbits. Suddenly from all around came the hiss of urgent voices as the women cussed and groaned.

"I wouldn't move if I were you," said Grandma Whiskey.

"All traders remain where you are!" The iron voice issued from the loudspeakers. "Stay where we can see you."

About a dozen uniformed men carrying powerful flashlights were spreading out through the market.

Goods and money were being stashed away in a frenzy. Takings were being slipped to accomplices and helpers who darted away into the shadows beneath the bridge and along the tracks.

The police were moving through the market, shining their lights into the traders' faces. The two she'd met earlier—Sergeant Jang and Shovel-face—were among them. They appeared to be escorting an official, a bald man with cheeks so bony they cast half his face in shadow. He wore the brown tunic of the Party. One of the policemen helped him up onto a wooden crate. His eyes swept across the aisles. Every trader was facing him.

"By order of the Central Committee of the Workers' Party, he shouted, "no woman under the age of fifty years is permitted to trade in any marketplace. This rule takes immediate effect."

The women turned to look at each other.

"The rules are changing again?" Grandma Whiskey muttered.

"What's the crackpot reason for this one?" another said.

Mrs. Moon put her hand up to shield her eyes from the beams of the flashlights. She heard Sergeant Jang murmur to the official that no one at this market was affected by the new rule, and then the official noticed Curly. He raised his arm to point at her. The police directed their flashlights at her in a single bright ray. Focused in the glare, she appeared very small and fragile, a doe caught in a hunter's snare.

"Citizen, stand up."

One of the policemen approached her and took her ID passbook.

"Name is Ong Sol-joo," he said. "Age twenty-eight."

"Where is your official workplace, Ong Sol-joo?" the official said.

Curly's lovely smile had fallen. She searched for the official's face, as if hoping to reason with him, but the lights were blinding her.

In a wan voice she said, "The April 15th Vinylon Factory."

"You're a textile worker?"

"Sir."

"And why is a state textile worker selling food for private gain on a train platform?"

Behind her, Curly's daughter was staring at her mother with glassy, horrified eyes. Curly had turned very pale and her head was angled to one side, as if she'd been slapped.

"I asked you a simple question," he said.

The air tensed. No one moved.

Mrs. Moon felt her blood rising. She'd seen this happen on the farm. Some poor wife accused of deserting socialism, when all she was trying to do was put food on the table. Before she knew it she was in a people's trial with a noose round her neck.

"Citizen, if you don't answer ..."

The official became distracted by the sight of an old lady rising slowly to her feet, her knees unbending agonizingly after a day sitting on the concrete. Then all eyes were upon her. Fear and alarm passed across the women's faces.

"I wish to save the respected comrade's valuable time," Mrs. Moon said. "Mrs. Ong is a family friend who has selflessly given her time to help me—an old woman who can't fetch and carry and who does not feel safe on her own. The business she helps out is mine, sir. Mrs. Ong does no trading."

With the bright lights upon her she could only glimpse the official out of the corner of her eye. His head was as bald as a buttock.

Before he could speak Sergeant Jang said, "Comrade Secretary, we must get you to the other markets before they close ..."

For several seconds no one made a sound. But then the official got down from the crate with an exasperated grunt, and the women were in shadow again as the police lowered their flashlights and left. A moment later, everyone exhaled in unison.

The silence was broken by the sound of a slap. Mrs. Moon looked around. The noise sounded again. One of the women at the back was clapping. Slowly at first. Then she was joined by another. Then by Grandma Whiskey. Suddenly every woman was applauding, giving her an ovation. Someone cried, *"Man-sae!"* and the women cheered. Curly came over and clasped her hands, but her face was serious. "Oh, what fine words, ajumma," she said. "How can I thank you?"

Now all of them were gathered about Mrs. Moon, bowing to her repeatedly and introducing themselves. "I am Mrs. Yi, ajumma. If you need sugar or rice flour, you know who to ask ..." "Mrs. Lee, ajumma. I can change that old coat for you whenever you like ..." "Mrs. Kim, ajumma ..." "Mrs. Kwon ..." "Mrs. Park ..." "I'm Mrs. Oh," said Grandma Whiskey. "I've got good Chinese contacts on the other side of the river ..."

It was as if a switch had been thrown and warmth and friendliness were suddenly beaming from their faces. Only Curly was gazing at her oddly, with an expression that seemed to pierce right through her, as if she were searching Mrs. Moon's heart for something. It had the most unsettling effect on her.

One of the women was pouring her a plastic cup of beer from a bottle, but Mrs. Moon smiled and declined, saying that their friendship was all that she valued; another offered her a pair of new gloves. Mrs. Moon began to refuse those, too, but then seized them in her hand. They were Chinese made and of the coarsest nylon. They had given her an idea. "Who sells these?" she said.

*

When she returned exhausted to the village the comet was still in the west, its blue-green glow casting enough light to see the track. Above her the sky was pierced by millions of tiny stars. The stiffness in her joints was flaring very painfully now as she dragged the two voluminous travel bags she'd purchased. The door to her house was in deep shadow as she approached. She was reaching for the doorknob when something uncoiled on the step, making her cry out. The small figure of a boy leapt up and darted away between the houses.

When she saw Tae-hyon's face all her fears came sharply alive. He was waiting up for her, smoking at the table. The lantern next to him cast cadaverous hollows onto his face.

"Comrade Pak was here," he said. The rolled-up cigarette trembled in his fingers. "What's in those bags?"

"One of Pak's informers was on the doorstep," she said.

She dropped the bags to the floor and began to unzip them. She had to explain her plan to Tae-hyon before—

They turned to the window. Footsteps were approaching along the alley between the rows of houses, and through the glass she saw the moving yellow glow of lamplight on the wall opposite.

The hammering was so violent she thought it was going to split the door.

She stood up quickly and opened it.

"Come in, please," she said, as if she'd been expecting guests for tea, and gave a deep, ninety-degree bow. Three uniformed men stepped heavily into the room without removing their boots or caps. Comrade Pak slipped in behind them and hovered at the door. One of the men checked a list in his hand.

"Moon Song-ae, you're coming with us. Husband, too."

"Are we under arrest?" Mrs. Moon said.

The man said nothing, but Comrade Pak, whose mouth was working hard to contain a look of righteous glee, couldn't stop herself. "Of course you're under arrest, you old bitch. You found an enemy balloon and didn't report it. You deserted the farm in violation of your sentence."

Then she noticed the two large bags next to the wall, and her eyes widened.

Mrs. Moon's voice was calm as she addressed the men. "It's true I did not report for work on the farm today. I was trading in Hyesan ..."

"Hoh," Comrade Pak snapped her fingers, disappointed that the confession had come so soon.

"... and the profit I made is in these bags for your commanding officer."

Mrs. Moon gave another deep bow.

The men turned their heads toward the bags, puzzled and annoyed, but their interest was snagged. The smile died on Comrade Pak's face.

Mrs. Moon bent down to complete the unzipping and threw them open. One was filled full with hundreds of pairs of Chinese-made nylon gloves; the other with as many pairs of nylon socks.

"Please present these to your superior, for him to distribute freely to the people of Baekam County, as gifts from our Dear Leader."

Out of the corner of her eye she saw the astonishment on Tae-hyon's face.

11

Camp Peary
CIA Training Facility
Williamsburg, Virginia
Third Week of October 2010

A few days after her return from Geneva, Jenna drove her car up to the security barrier of the CIA's headquarters in Langley. George-town University, Fisk had told her, had agreed to release her from her employment, but not before lodging a small protest about its being the middle of the semester, and expressing wonder that a junior member of staff could have knowledge pertaining to the security of the nation. That was Professor Runyon all over. It bol-stered her feeling that she was doing the right thing.

On her first morning she was wired to a polygraph in a window-less, soundproofed room and gave yes-no answers to inquiries about her past; in the afternoon she took a psychometric evaluation that asked peculiar multichoice questions on themes of personal integrity and honesty, with points allotted according to a secret scoring system. In the following days she was photographed and fingerprinted, her irises were scanned, her DNA swabbed from her saliva, her urine tested for drugs. The background checks, she learned, had already been conducted. Everything happened quickly and without delay, her candidacy fast-tracked. Fisk had bent the rules to exempt her from the deskbound preparatory stints at Head-quarters. Ten days after her first visit to Langley she took the oath to protect and defend the constitution of the United States and was handed a short list of the clothes and toiletries she was permitted to take to Camp Peary, known to insiders as the Farm, the secret CIA training facility in Williamsburg.

Not until she boarded the bus with tinted windows and saw her eleven fellow Clandestine Service trainees—three women and eight men—did she become nervous. All of them seemed to pro-ject a similar image: confidence, watchfulness, a brutal fitness. A few eyes regarded her with suspicion, the newbie being pitched straight into clandestine training, and she felt her anxiety stirred by an undercurrent of dread. Only the guy seated across the aisle from her cast her an interested glance. He was tall and olive skinned with full lips and heavy, muscular arms. Latino or Middle Eastern. She looked away.

A low autumn mist was rolling off the York River when the party alighted in front of an old saltbox farmhouse. Across the vast sur-rounding estate, the silos and barns that concealed an extensive facility were fading to gray as dusk fell. The recruits had passed through two levels of security at the perimeter. Relieved of phones and personal items, there was a sense, as they stood before Fisk, who was waiting for them on the farmhouse steps, that they were entering a closed order, and had left all worldly ties behind. Fisk's large, haggard face was partly in shadow. He raised his hand to them in a greeting, or it might have been a type of benediction.

A sudden whine of propeller engines made them look up. The angled foils of a Reaper drone emerged from the clouds and descended toward a hidden airstrip.

Fisk ushered them inside, away from the noise. The farmhouse, it seemed, was little more than a prop, a sentry box that hid what lay beneath. A large freight elevator took them to a lower level, where a pad scanned Fisk's palm and a laser read his eye. A door opened with a pressurized hiss and they were in a subterranean corridor of humming databanks, purified air, and massive tungsten security doors that opened without a sound.

The recruits followed him in silence. Jenna's eyes were everywhere, taking this in. They reached an area that looked like some type of situation room. Six other recruits wearing headphones were seated in front of screens of what looked like grainy security-camera feed, until Jenna realized it was moving drone footage seen in night vision.

Fisk sat on the edge of a desk and faced them with his arms folded. He was dressed in a black casual jacket and jeans, which had the effect of making him seem older, a grandfather ready to go bowling. He gazed at them for a moment, his face calm, protecting.

"What made you join?" He spoke softly, but his every word was audible, as if he were alone in private with each of them. The sweep of his eyes took in all of them. "You joined because you believe in freedom. You believe in the ideals that founded our nation—ideals which, for a while, seemed to be spreading across the world like the dawn. Today, those ideals are everywhere in retreat. You may think our liberty makes us strong. Do not be naive. It is only our vigilance that makes us strong. In five thousand years of civilization, it is mostly tyranny, not democracy, that has been the lot of humankind. In those brief eras when democracy flourished, it was a rare animal with many predators, short in its life as it was violent in its death. Once again, the forces of intolerance have gathered, and draw their plans against us. They are emboldened, believing that our freedom makes us decadent, full of contradictions, exposed. We happy few, we are freedom's guardians. We are the good guys. It is us who stand in the front line. That's why you joined. You chose light over darkness." His eyes shone as if he were speaking a profound and tragic truth. "But it is in the darkness that this fight is fought, often without scruple or conscience. If our enemies win, their tyranny will be made stronger and more terrible by technology. But if we win, our glory will never be sung, our victory will never be written. We hope only for honor, not fame."

He nodded at them, and stood up.

"Over the next ten months you'll be tested to within an inch of your lives. Some tests you'll know about; others you won't, unless you fail them and find yourself being removed from here. Not all of you will make it to graduation as operations officers. Those who do will be the Agency's elite. Welcome to the Farm. Do your best."

Jenna and the three other women of her class were shown to a cramped barrack dorm lined with bunks. One of them, an American Iranian woman with a GI buzz cut said, "Hey," and jutted her chin out. "I'm Aisha."

Jenna knew it wasn't her real name, because yesterday she had been given her own new identity to memorize, together with a driver's license. She was Marianne Lee, a freelance reporter from the Mission Hill district of Boston. A ten-page typed biography was included, outlining her education, the names and birth dates of her parents, her social security number, and work résumé, complete with links to articles she'd written for the *Boston Globe*.

Jenna smiled and extended her hand. "I'm Marianne."

At dawn the next day the women assembled for a seven-mile endurance run and introduced themselves to the men.

"Menendez," said the tall Latino who'd eyed her up on the bus. He grinned.

Their mornings began at 6:00 a.m. Combat training and field exercises took up most of the days. Evenings were spent in classes learning the basics of tradecraft, starting with encryption. Tradecraft appealed to Jenna's sense of discipline and method, even though its main purpose made her uneasy. An operations officer's most important role was the secret recruitment of assets—targeted individuals who were blackmailed, bribed, or persuaded into betraying their country's secrets to the CIA. She spent much of her first week pondering this, trying to picture herself doing it—in a hotel room, perhaps, watching some hapless foreign diplomat's face turn gray as she confronted him with evidence of his corrupt kickbacks, his gambling debts, his weakness for male hookers, which his embassy knew nothing about. She would wait for the full horror of his situation to sink in, and when the moment was right, she might dangle the lure of money—lots of it—or the offer of asylum in the United States, or expensive treatment for his sick child, paid for by the CIA. She might never see him again, but he was hers. She would be running him, collecting his intelligence with an agreed system of signals and dead drops.

It felt sordid; it went against her nature, but her qualms vanished every time she thought of Soo-min. She was being trained to target a criminal rogue state, a prison that held her sister. To that end she wanted every black art the Farm could teach her. And that meant stepping up to the punishment of the field training, because she was finding that pure hell.

Each time her instructors pushed her to the limit of her endurance, abandoning her in a distant swamp with only a compass, making her drop and do push-ups each time she missed her firing-range target no matter what she was firing, Beretta, Glock, AK-47; then they pushed her even harder, and the old limit became normal. By the afternoons she was bruised, exhausted, humiliated. She reckoned her performance would rank close to the bottom of the class—some of whose members were ex-marines—if not for the one skill in which she outmatched them all. In the classes that taught them gun- and knife-disarming techniques she knew how to direct the energy of the pointing arm away from her, flip the attacker's wrist so that the weapon was pointing back at him, and even throw him over her shoulder. Class H watched in amazement. "Where the hell d'you learn that?" Aisha said. Jenna shrugged. She mentioned nothing of her taekwondo. Her past was her own business.

The instructors had not discouraged socializing—the recruits were free to meet for beers and shoot pool in the Farm's bar—but all of them sensed that they should trust no one and say little. Anything could be a test. One evening she was reading alone in the canteen, a Chekov story she'd enjoyed many times, when Menendez placed his tray in front of her and sat down.

"Where've you been, Marianne Lee?"

Everything about her body language was saying *go away*. "Nineteenth-century Russia."

"Been hoping to see you in the bar."

She closed her book. He seemed faintly amused by the restrictions they were under. Unable to talk openly, their conversation lapsed into a silence in which his physical qualities became impossible for her to ignore. Thick, shiny black hair, a straight nose that ended in a fine point. Enormous hands.

She wished he hadn't sat with her. Later all she could think of was sex.

Slowly, gradually, she numbed herself to the mornings, and channeled her frustration into better control. She stilled her mind and focused. And as the month went by, she began to get it. Her shooting improved until she could hit multiple moving targets and rack the slide of her Beretta with one hand. She won the class's respect as the only trainee commended in the tests for evasive high-speed driving. A loose camaraderie was forming between her and her classmates, and it surprised her to realize how little she was missing Georgetown, or the world outside the Farm. But just as she felt she was fitting in, reality bit her again.

On a surveillance exercise in Williamsburg, Class H formed into two teams. The operation was to tail a quarry wherever he went, replacing the tails at intervals so that the quarry would not be able to detect them or flush them.

When it was Jenna's turn, dusk had fallen. The tail she was relieving was Menendez. He was sitting on a park bench watching the quarry—a man with a prominent Saddam moustache—sipping coffee in a Starbucks about a hundred yards across the street. "The guy's been there for half an hour," he said.

To Jenna's surprise Menendez produced a small bottle of Scotch from his pocket, uncapped it, and took a swig. Then he dropped his face into his hands. "The Farm's driving me crazy," he said. "Feel like I'm turning into a fucking cyborg." He looked at her blearily and smiled. "I just gotta do something human, you know?"

She could not have explained how it happened, but suddenly they were kissing, tongues twining, his hot whisky breath in her face, stubble burning her skin. Her hand was up inside his shirt. She parted from him, catching her breath, and she saw that his eyes were no longer bleary but sharply focused on her.

Some intuition made her turn her head toward the Starbucks. The quarry had gone.

Menendez wasn't smiling. "My orders were to stop you fulfilling yours."

He walked away, signaling with his hand to someone she couldn't see.

Jenna drew her knees up to her chin and sat on the bench for a long time, nursing the familiar loneliness.

Am I really cut out for this?

Three weeks after arriving at the Farm, the trainees of Class H were told they could go home for the weekend. Jenna wanted to visit her mother. A bus was organized to take them to DC. They were only two minutes past the perimeter barrier when a fast-moving white minivan overtook the bus and braked to a halt in front of it, blocking the narrow road. Its door slid open before it had stopped and three masked men in black jumped out, shouting. A screech of tires sounded to the rear and the recruits turned in alarm to see another identical vehicle stopping behind them, trapping the bus. One of the masked men climbed on board, brandishing a Glock. "Hands behind your heads. Everyone out!"

They filed out of the bus like hostages.

Jenna was pulled roughly inside one of the minivans, along with four others. Within seconds their hands were handcuffed behind their backs, hoods were over their heads, and they were being driven away fast on the vehicle's hard slatted floor, guarded by one of the men. "No talking!" he yelled, when one of them ventured a question.

She could guess what was coming. Class H had just taken the course on interrogation and techniques for resisting interrogation. This was going to be the stamina test from hell.

When the hood was removed she was alone in a dim basement with moldy walls and a smell of bad drains. Her hands were still cuffed behind her back; the chair was screwed to the floor. Next to her was a large, bare wooden table.

A door opened and a pale man with thinning blond hair entered. His shirt was undone at the collar. "You are a CIA spy." The accent was Central European or Russian. "This is not a test."

Very good, she thought. "I'm a reporter."

"What is your name?"

"Marianne Lee."

"So it says on your driver's license. You are an American spy. What is your real name?"

Jenna gave him a level look. "I said my name is Marianne Lee. I'm a freelance reporter, from Boston."

He tilted his head slightly and said in a neutral voice, "Your choice."

The door opened again and two men in black T-shirts entered. They uncuffed her hands and lifted her onto the wooden table. Then both got onto the table with her. One of them clamped her head between his knees; the other sat on her legs and held down her arms so that she couldn't move. A towel was thrown over her face. This she had not expected. Suddenly she was unhinged with panic. She heard the sound of water being poured into a metal bucket.

"Let's begin." The blond man said. "What is your real name?"

She struggled and cried out but it was impossible to move. The water started splashing onto her face. Seconds later her gag reflex kicked in, and they stopped. Her lungs were coughing, heaving as she caught her breath. *So, not a proper water boarding, but ... Jesus Christ!* Another moment and she'd have started drowning. When they pulled off the towel she was shaking. The pale man's face was looking over her, waiting.

Jenna stared at him, her lungs working. "Marianne Lee."

The next day she was isolated in a cell with bright lights. The day after that she was locked in a tiny room that was pitch dark and cold, as if by refrigeration, and given only a meal of bread and water. Cameras watched her night and day. Jenna reacted in the only way she knew how. She retreated to the solitary realm deep inside herself, engaging in long, imagined conversations with Soo-min, and in them she found solace. She drew strength. Though she had long been self-sufficient in isolation, she could cherish this living link to her twin. Occasionally she heard a cry and guessed that her classmates were all sequestered in cells in the same building.

Each time she was interrogated the layers of Marianne Lee's false identity were stripped from her one by one, like onion peel, until only the name was left. As time passed, the line between reality and simulation became blurred, to the point where she was no longer certain that this was a test.

On the fourth or fifth day she was seated in the interrogation room with her hands cuffed in front of her when the blond man called her a whore and slapped her across the face. The two goons in black T-shirts were standing behind her watching, for no other reason, she presumed, than to add an air of menace and humiliation. It wasn't a hard slap, but she was at her wits' end and it touched something deep and raw inside her. The effect was instant.

She didn't even think. She leapt out of her seat, pivoted ninety degrees on one foot and extended her right leg in a massive kick to the blond man's upper chest. He went flying backward off his seat, legs in the air, and hit his head on the radiator. In one jump toward the man behind her to the right she gained the momentum to front-kick him under the chin. In a lightning turn she spin-kicked the man to the left, hitting him like a mule in the solar plexus, that delicate strip of the torso that the abdominal muscles didn't quite cover. Three basic taekwondo moves.

One of the goons was clutching his jaw; the other was bent over double, groaning. Jenna stood over the blond man, holding out her hands. "Take the cuffs off."

"Crazy bitch." The man's eyes were clenched shut and he was touching the back of his head. "The point was to see how long you held out, not to put us in the fucking hospital." He'd lost the Russian accent. "We're done here," he shouted at the camera.

Moments later Fisk entered the room. His face was frowning, thoughtful. Jenna's shoulders slumped when she saw him.

"Take me home, please," she said. "I'm through."

"We're going back to the Farm."

"Why?" Her throat thickened and she felt tears coming. "I screwed up again. I'm out of here."

Fisk put his hands in his pockets and looked at her with an odd smile. "Everyone gives their name in the end. But you didn't. In fact . . . you're the first trainee I've ever known to fight your way out of the interrogation."

She stopped crying.

"You just rewrote the manual," he said. Suddenly his face reddened and he was laughing helplessly. "I've got to get hold of that video."

"The hell you are," the blond man said. "I'm wiping it now."

*

That night she lay on her bunk. She was deadened with fatigue but her mind was buzzing, wired. For some reason she was thinking of her father. *The highest-ranking African American in the garrison.* That legend about him had cast the rest of his biography into a shade she'd never fully examined. Her father, Captain Douglas Williams, so private and gentle, had been someone she'd never truly got to know. And yet he, Han, Soo-min, and Jee-min had been a close-knit, loving family for the time they'd had together—the most precious thing she'd had in her life. Nothing would bring that back.

This was about more than Soo-min, she realized. The reason she was here. What was it? Vengeance?

Some valve in her heart opened and she felt an iciness flood her veins to the tips of her fingers and toes, making her skin rise in goose bumps and her breathing slow. Her eyes widened in the dark. Yes, this *was* vengeance. She was ready to deal implacably with those who'd destroyed her family. She was ready to put all scruples aside and make those responsible account for Soo-min.

She was changing; she could feel it. After twelve lost years she was becoming ... grounded, focused. She was being steeled by a clear, cold singularity of purpose. She shivered, pulled the bedspread over her shoulders, and turned onto her side, staring at the wall in the dark.

Fisk had been right. She did have a powerful motivation to serve.

The girl was studying a screen of news footage. Now and then she'd put a checkmark next to a name on a list. Watching over her shoulder, Jenna recognized last month's mass parade in Kim Il-sung Square. The news camera paused on Kim Jong-il's rotund young son, the anointed heir, clapping delightedly at a passing rocket-launcher. The girl's hair was tied in manga schoolgirl braids, making her look about fourteen. "I'm trying to figure out who's in favor, who's out ... ?" she said, glancing up at Jenna. "Depending on how close they're standing to Kim. After a while you kinda get a feel for who's important."

The North Korea analysts at Langley—all of them young Asian Americans out of Ivy League colleges—occupied one pen of a vast cube-farm, a bright, circular open-plan area shared with hundreds of other analysts. Jenna and her group were on a day visit to meet them. Class H had started the course on analytic tradecraft. Across the vast space she could see Aisha introducing herself to the team that handled Iran, and the hulking figure of Menendez talking to the Cuba analysts.

A young guy with spiky hair sat in the next cubicle, leafing through editions of the *Rodong Sinmun*, North Korea's national daily.

"I'm looking for shifts in Party rhetoric," he said, compressing his lips together to stifle a yawn. "Changes of emphasis in the propaganda, that kind of stuff ..."

Jenna was puzzled. *This is intelligence analysis?*

Their manager was the only non-Asian in the team. He was a drab, large-bottomed man called Simms, who gave Jenna a clammy handshake and peered at her myopically through a pair of rimless glasses. His tie matched his eyes, which were the color of canal water.

He showed her into one of Langley's secure, bug-swept conference rooms, and surprised her by speaking in fluent Korean. He dropped his bombshell the moment they sat down.

"The Agency has no assets on the ground inside North Korea."

His voice was a patient monotone.

"Really? I ..." Jenna pushed a strand of hair behind her ear. "... guess I'm surprised that the world's largest intelligence organization has no one—"

"Perhaps you've watched too many thrillers," he said with an unhappy laugh. "We have no sources there. No highly placed officer in the Korean People's Army. No disenchanted scientist leaking nuclear secrets. No honey-trap beauty in Kim Jong-il's pleasure brigade. Nothing." He took the glasses off, wiped them, and held them up to the light. Without them his face was devoid of any interesting topography. "That's not to say we haven't tried to recruit. But I don't need to tell you that the regime's surveillance of its own people is total. Calls and letters are monitored. Radios and televisions are fixed to receive only government channels, travel is tightly controlled, people's thoughts are molded and monitored. One step out of line and a person falls under suspicion. Informer networks infiltrate every level of society, from the politburo to the prison gulag."

Jenna sat back. "Defectors bring intelligence—"

"Sure they do, but their escape routes are often long ones. By the time it reaches us their information is, what, months, years out of date?"

"You've got some of the smartest kids in the country out there doing Cold War guesswork," she said. "Studying line-ups at parades? *Kremlinology?* Isn't that as useless now as when we had the Soviet Union?"

Simms sighed. "North Korea is sealed shut from the world. Signals intelligence yields little. The people make no sound. There is no online traffic; very few cell phone calls; few radio signals, no chatter. The country is silent. And it is dark." He leaned back in his chair and laced his hands behind his head, revealing the damp patches under his arms. "They've given you mission impossible, Marianne Lee. I'd say your chances of successfully running your own asset inside the North are—less—than—zero." He smiled at her unpleasantly. "All you can do is interpret signs ... and watch from above."

"From above? You mean, like, Google Earth?"

"No, Miss Lee. Not like Google Earth."

In a glowing control room deep beneath the New Headquarters Building, streams of satellite images were displaying, one after the other, on enormous computer screens. "We got a lot of hardware up there," Simms said with an upward sweep of his hand. "Terrestrial-facing space telescopes ... Lockheed U-2s flying at seventy thousand feet ... radar imaging spysats—those bad-guys can see through clouds ..."

Seated at the screens were the squints, the spysat analysts, about twenty of them, all men. Over the shoulder of one of them Jenna saw a satellite panorama of some location in Asia—brown mountain ranges dotted with tiny cotton balls of clouds; a patchwork of lime-green rice paddies. Simms said to him, "May I?" and leaned over to put his finger to a touchpad. Slowly the image expanded. With mounting amazement Jenna watched as field and mountain resolved into clumps of individual acacia trees and a long dirt road, and finally to a military jeep with an officer riding in the back. She could see the stars on his epaulettes, the phone in his hand. Simms stood back and folded his arms. "Taken from low earth orbit just now. About two hundred kilometers up. The lens adjusts for distortions caused by heat and air currents." He turned to her with a thin smile. "Classified military technology."

Jenna continued to stare at the screen. North Korea was a walled fortress ... *but its roof was open to the sky.*

That evening at the Farm Jenna submitted a request to spend the analytic tradecraft course focusing on GEOINT, satellite geospatial intelligence, as the field most relevant to her training. The next day she was sent an encrypted link to access the squints' secure server at Langley.

She had never seen detail like it. It was as if she'd been endowed with a superpower, and she played with it a while, learning to wield it. The spectral imaging resolution was formidable. Zooming in, the picture stayed pin sharp to within a square meter. At a missile silo under construction, arrowed and captioned by the squints, she could see the welders on their cigarette break. She could read a red-lettered slogan carved into the slope of Mount Tonghung: WHAT THE

PARTY COMMANDS—WE DO! A fox was running along a trail dotted with pinecones. An old woman served stew from a pan on a train platform. Scrolling southward to the Demilitarized Zone, the weaponized wasteland that formed the border with South Korea, Jenna saw the tented encampments for vast numbers of troops. Eastward toward the coast, she found an ghost-city, rusted and soot deadened, and zoomed in again to find packs of ragged children roaming its streets.

She felt omniscient, all seeing, an avenging angel sweeping over this dark land. In a shot taken on a chill, sunny morning thousands of prisoners stood in lines at a roll call, their emaciated bodies casting long shadows on the ground. This was Camp 15, the Yodok Concentration Camp, where the condemned were sent with three generations of their family to toil in quarries and cornfields. *I'm seeing you*, she thought, studying the ant-like figures pulling carts of rocks. *You are not forgotten.* She looked for Camp 22 near Chongjin, but the imaging was not complete. That camp was so vast that it encompassed farms, coal mines, and factories, all worked by slaves and the children of slaves, born in that place, for whom the camp was the universe entire.

The squints almost never analyzed or captioned this evidence of the regime's crimes, she noticed. "Military targets are their priority," Simms had told her.

This gave her an idea.

She e-mailed a request for spysat analysis of the Mayangdo Naval Base on the northeast coast. Within minutes she received a secure link to hi-res annotated images, with arrows pointing out dry docks, maintenance sheds, and submarine pens concealed beneath bomb-proof concrete. Some of the vessels were even visible in the water as they entered and departed. "Submarine: Romeo class (1,800 tons)," "midget submarine: Yono class (130 tons)," and—the one that sent a chill through her— "Submarine: Sango class (180 tons)."

It looked like some predatory fish returning to its lair. A Sango-class submarine, Mrs. Ishido had said. On a mission from the Mayangdo Naval Base. If it weren't for the water making white breakers around the prow, its blackish-green hull would be almost invisible.

And from Mayangdo, where would they have taken Soo-min? But each time her eyes searched for other regions linked by road and rail to the northeast coast she became distracted by something else altogether.

The images that kept drawing her eye, almost against her will, like tidbits in a scandal magazine, attested to the lifestyle of Kim Jong-il. Children begged for grains in his streets, but the Guiding Star of the Twenty-First Century maintained seventeen palatial homes around the country. Paddocks adjoined private oval race-tracks; she could see basketball courts, and infinity pools nestling among flowered terraces, gated and secluded from the masses. He had homes that were imperial summer palaces with roofs of jade-green tiles, homes surrounded by ornamental gardens with fountains, and hunting parks dense with camphor trees. One was a modern beach villa with a fleet of sports cars and motorbikes. At his main residence north of Pyongyang, protected by four surface-to-air missile launchers (arrowed by the squints), he enjoyed a swimming pool with water slides, a shooting range, and a river jetty where he moored a Princess yacht. Golf carts traversed his country estates. She zoomed in from two hundred kilometers and saw the tracks they made in the dew, the sprinklers on the lawns. A private train station housed his luxurious armored train. And at night, when the country lay beneath a squid-ink blackout from lack of power, each one of Kim's palaces was staffed and lit, forming a constellation in the darkness, so better to fool the scrolling spysats as to his whereabouts.

But it was his villa near the beaches of Wonsan that set her imagination on fire. Enclosed within its grounds were greenhouses, cattle pastures, and wildflower ranges where chickens fed beside mountain streams. Persimmon trees bore flame-orange fruits. She saw the famous orchards, rumored to be fertilized with refined sugar so that the apples grew huge and sweet. She imagined those apples being served on platters at his epicurean feasts, where girls danced and stripped for the entertainment of his cronies, and, ever-vigilant, he watched for signs of thought crime in those faces flushed by drink.

The whole country was in Jenna's sights. All its contours, structures, fields, and networks laid bare for her to see. Mountain and forest; prison and palace.

The emperor—the soldiers—the citizens—the slaves.

Where are you, Soo-min?

12

Three figures were floating toward him. General Kang and his two daughters. "He teach me Engrish," Kang said, pointing at Cho, and his daughters' laughter echoed off the marble walls. Kang's chest was a morass of bullet holes and his body was putrescent. His big cheeks were detaching from his face, like halves of avocados. He sailed over Cho's head. Cho was standing on an airport-style moving walkway that glided along an endless gallery. Books was beside him, holding his hand. In the far distance they saw a blue-white glow, like the light of a star, which was getting brighter as they approached, brighter and brighter until it filled the gallery with its rays. He gripped the boy's small hand tightly with love, but his son was struggling to break free. "Appa," he shouted. "We must leave."

"If we're too far away we'll freeze," Cho said to him.

"If we're too close we'll burn!"

Cho woke a start. A pressurized popping in his ears muffled the sounds. He rubbed his eyes, only half hearing the singsong Mandarin voice announcing the aircraft's final descent to John F. Kennedy International Airport. In the rows in front of his the members of his legation had their faces pressed to the windows. He pushed up the blind and blinked groggily into the pink light. Drifts of cotton candy slipped over the wing, then a hydraulic whining sounded and the aircraft descended into a world of gray. The cabin shuddered as it encountered turbulence, then suddenly the clouds parted and he had a steep-angle view of suburban houses, like matchboxes with tiny cars moving between them. Cho looked at them in astonishment. He had never in his life imagined that he would enter the belly of the Yankee imperialist beast.

At the diplomatic arrivals lounge the legation was met by Ambassador Shin, North Korea's Permanent Representative to the United Nations, and his aide, First Secretary Ma. After they'd bowed and exchanged socialist greetings they were escorted to the exit. Shin was a dour, stocky man with a straight slit for a mouth and gray hair combed straight back. His gruff and insolent manner made it clear at once that he was assuming command of the group. Cho disliked him instantly. First Secretary Ma was a thin, watchful man with curious wen on his left cheek, like a small black leech. Cho met his eyes, and noted warily that there was intelligence in them.

Four others were included in Cho's group: two junior diplomats who were a little younger than Cho, both princeling sons of Central Committee members. They would each share a twin hotel room and be accompanied everywhere by the other two members, officers from the Party's political security bureau—colorless, suspicious men who said little. Neither Cho nor any of them had visited the West before.

Rain fell in orange sparks beneath the sodium floodlights. Their driver, a surly Korean waiting with a black Toyota minivan, slid open the door and Cho saw miniature versions of the Father-Son portraits mounted on the dashboard and angled so they faced the passengers. The driver loaded their luggage into the trunk, and while the others were climbing in, Ambassador Shin said, "You have a package for me, I believe?" The man had lit a cigarette the moment he was out of the terminal building.

"It's inside the diplomatic pouch," Cho said, and watched Shin exhale a mixture of nerves, relief, and smoke.

They fastened seat belts and the journey toward the city commenced. Refreshed after his sleep on the plane, Cho looked eagerly at the ranks of yellow cabs and transit buses, feeling the adrenalin pumping in his chest, his eyes drinking in every detail. So many vehicles of different models and colors.

Just think where you are …

Ambassador Shin turned in his seat and began addressing them about the details of the itinerary, and on how they should comport themselves in front of the Yankees, who would almost certainly try to corral them into some compromising and unpleasant social event, which was to be avoided at all costs. He had the darting eyes of a suspicious, ill-tempered man. The group listened respectfully, but their gaze was repeatedly being drawn to the windows. Within minutes they were on open freeway. The black clouds along the horizon to the west were lifting, and when the great towers of New York City rose into view, their tips shining reddish gold in the dying rays of light, they appeared to Cho as an enchanted city. *This is pure magic*, he thought. It was a world he had never seen, even in his imagination. Some of the spires were stately and ancient, as if they'd stood for a century or more. He'd pictured a city of futuristic mirrored glass, like Shanghai. He thought of how he'd describe this sight for his wife and Books.

The lanes of traffic became a broad, slow-moving river of steel. Soon the minivan had crossed the East River and had joined the ant-like crawl of taillights. *This is Manhattan.* Sidewalks heaved and flowed with office workers pouring en masse down subway station entrances. On the next block a crowd was streaming out of a theater, their chatter and laughter making vapor in the raw air. The show's name coruscated with thousands of tiny white lights. Ambassador Shin continued to talk, as if to distract them from the emotional shock they were experiencing. The minivan was inching forward into the midtown grid behind a white stretch limousine. Steam vented from holes in the road. Shin was talking about the Yankees' media coverage of the rocket launch, but Cho was not even pretending to listen. His window misted up. He pressed the button to lower the glass and saw a man taking cash from a machine in a wall, and workers in Day-Glo vests. A digital display of numbers and fractions of numbers ran across the side of a tower. He breathed in. Food odors mingled in the air—fried pork and onions. A deep bass boomed and throbbed from a car that passed alongside, and three black faces in baseball caps passed with scarcely a glance at Cho. He looked up, and saw a soaring billboard of an underwear model.

After Pyongyang, where streets were dark and deserted at night, the impact of these sights was all the more shocking. In his country, foreign visitors were taken straight from the airport to lay flowers at the Great Leader's feet on Mansu Hill. But here, where were the statues? Where were the monuments? The Yankees were allowing New York City to represent itself.

The minivan became boxed into a mass of traffic at a crosswalk just as the lights turned red. Pedestrians flowed around the vehicle in both directions. Cho's eyes jumped from one face to the next, fascinated. No one wore a military uniform. The blacks and Asians weren't wearing flunkies' livery. He felt an intense desire to talk to one of them. He could speak their language! But almost in the same instant he knew that he wouldn't. He would not be alone with anyone, not for a minute. He would present a face of cold revolutionary virtue at all times. He would never make a friend here.

The lights turned green and the minivan proceeded at a crawl. A man wearing a hat with earflaps sat on the sidewalk holding out a polystyrene cup, and Cho remembered that he'd been expecting to see drug dealers, prostitutes, and lines of workless on every street.

At the Roosevelt Hotel an enormous stars-and-stripes flag fluttered from a pole above the golden portico. The minivan pulled over and the party got out in a trance. Cho saw the same hundred-yard stare in each of the faces in his group. As though drunk, he could not take in the grand surroundings of the lobby. First Secretary Ma was checking them in at the reception desk, and while Ambassador Shin continued talking—the slit of his mouth making a patter of dull, flat sounds—Cho became aware of the well-dressed, well-fed people milling around, of Caucasian faces casting glances at his strange group as though they were envoys from an alien civilization. He looked at his party, seeing them now through outsiders' eyes, and felt suddenly ashamed of them, of the two political officer goons in their shiny Vinylon suits and state-issue rubber shoes, and the lapel pins they all wore of the Great Leader's smiling face.

Ambassador Shin suggested they take an hour to freshen up in their rooms before dinner. The political officers went up first, to remove the TV remotes and the Gideon Bibles from the bedside tables, and Cho and the two junior diplomats followed. In the elevator Cho said to them, "While we're in this hotel . . . you may remove your lapel pins." The two diplomats gave no response and looked down. "We should not have to endure the Yankees' stares," he added, with the sinking feeling that he'd said something irreparable.

His room was spacious and had a comfortable double bed. It was adjoined by a marble-walled bathroom, stocked with thick white towels, which appeared to be for his exclusive use. He walked to the window. The sky was an orange broth that obscured the stars. Far below, on Madison Avenue, a fire truck flashed ruby and sapphire, its wail rising and falling, an echoing curve down a lit canyon.

Two knocks sounded behind him.

He opened the door to see First Secretary Ma standing with a teenage black boy wearing a drum-like cap. The boy was pulling a brass bellman cart loaded to the top with luggage. In his daze Cho had forgotten all about luggage. His heart skipped a gear.

The diplomatic pouch!

He spotted his own suitcase, and the boy retrieved it from the pile, but the pouch was nowhere in sight. Trying to keep the panic out of his voice, he said he was certain there was one more item, and with the help of First Secretary Ma the boy unloaded the entire cart until they saw it, a gray, sealed, duffel-like bag, crushed at the very bottom of the heap. First Secretary Ma scowled at Cho. Cho thanked the boy in English. As he had been told that tipping was a degrading capitalist custom, he presented him with a pocket-sized English edition of *Anecdotes of Kim Il Sung's Life*, of which he'd brought a dozen copies.

He closed the door and slumped his back against it. How could he have been so stupid? He dropped the pouch on the bed and undid the seal. He would take the package to Ambassador Shin immediately. But as he took it out of the pouch his stomach clenched again. A tear down its side exposed the bubble-wrap padding beneath the manila. He ran his finger along the gash. It hadn't been cut. It had split under the crush of that damned luggage. He switched on the bedside lamp and felt gently inside the tear. His finger touched cellophane. He felt ... a bricklike object ... several of them ... wrapped in cellophane ...

The door opened and Cho jumped, knocking the lamp on its side so that its bulb lit Ambassador Shin from below and cast his shadow large upon the wall. Cho must have left the latch off the door.

"The package, please, Colonel." He held out his hand.

For one instant the two regarded each other with naked hostility.

"I'd like to ask you what's inside it," Cho said.

"Admin, funds ..." Shin said vaguely. The voice was calm, but the eyes were warning him. He took the package from Cho's hands.

"We are driving to a traditional Korean restaurant," Ambassador Shin announced, once they had all reassembled in the lobby. "The staff and owner are ... sympathetic," he added confidingly to Cho, as though they were being taken to a safe house in a war zone. "We can talk there."

The minivan made a left off 45th Street and was immediately caught in another snarl-up of traffic. Within minutes the vehicle was at a standstill in a line of red taillights and exhaust fumes, like a solidifying lava flow. A cab driver sounded his horn, which set off a hundred other horns. Ambassador Shin began whispering to First Secretary Ma.

The business with the package had unsettled Cho. He did not trust Shin, and now, trapped by the minivan in a cacophony of car horns, jet lagged and disorientated, he felt a mounting frustration at being in Shin's hands. Eventually he said, "Couldn't we get out and walk?"

Ambassador Shin hesitated. "We must remain in the vehicle until we reach the scheduled destination."

They sat for another half hour in silence, watching a huge sky-scraper topped with a mast that changed color. Red, white, blue. Cho leaned forward. "We can't sit here all night, comrades. I respect-fully suggest we leave the car with the driver and eat there ..."

Over the tops of the vehicles they could see a restaurant with an exterior plated entirely in stainless steel. A sign that said OPEN 24 HOURS flashed in ruby neon. Behind a long window overlooking the street, tables were arranged in individual booths, like the dining car of a train. The interior cast an inviting glow. Waitresses in pressed pink uniforms went to and fro carrying enormous trays of food.

"The Korean restaurant has been prepared for you ..." Ambas-sador Shin said.

"Well, nothing's moving here," Cho said.

The group glanced from one to the other. One of the junior dip-lomats shrugged to the other, who seemed open to the idea, but Shin, First Secretary Ma, and the two political officers remained silent, calculating the consequences.

Cho opened his door.

"Wait!" Shin said, his voice tight with alarm. "You're forgetting where you are, Colonel."

Cho looked at the customers in the booths of the restaurant. Four adolescents, two boys and two girls who looked like high school students, sipped Coca-Colas through straws. A small boy's face was cartoonishly agog when a bowl of multicolored ice-cream scoops was placed in front of him. *Small children everywhere have the same reactions,* he thought. A tired-looking man in a security guard's uniform dined alone with a beer and joked with his waitress. None seemed like the Yankee types so easily identified in the movies—villains thin as beanpoles with hook noses and blond hair.

"We have nothing to fear," Cho said. "Unless you're saying our great Party's ideology can't protect us against gluttonous children and bland food ..."

The interior had a black-and-white checkered floor and a long counter of polished chrome where waitresses shouted the orders. The kitchen was behind a pair of flapping doors with porthole windows. Behind the counter was a display of crystal glasses and bottles and above that an image of a frothing milkshake formed of yellow and pink neon lights. Cakes and sweet pies covered in glazed fruit were displayed on rotating shelves inside a glass case.

A waitress showed them to a booth and handed them laminated menus. "Where you guys from?" she said, wiping the table. The name on her tag was PAM.

"The Democratic People's Republic of Korea," Ambassador Shin said in a monotone.

"Okay!" She gave them a brilliant smile, and walked off.

Once they were seated, another waitress passed by carrying two large trays of hot plates and delivered them to the family sitting in the next booth. Complex aromas of melted cheeses and grilled beef followed her.

Perhaps fearing a weakening of his revolutionary resolve, one of the political officers lodged a tentative protest. Despite being large and dull in appearance, Cho knew he was venomously orthodox.

"Colonel, I'm not sure the food here is appropriate. As our Great—"

"Your objection is noted, Political Officer Yi." Cho was hungry and in no mood for a quotation, but a mischievous thought popped into his head. "Didn't you recognize the meals on that tray? Comrade Kim Jong-il himself invented the 'double-bun-with-meat'—as the solution to feeding our university students. A report in the *Minju Choson* showed him giving on-the-spot guidance to the factory workers who made the patties. The Yankees are capable of the vilest deceit. You must admit, there's a strong possibility they stole the idea from us."

Political Officer Yi crimped his lips, making a mental note.

Cho and Ambassador Shin did their best to approximate the menu into Korean for the others, and in doing so discovered that double-bun-with-meat was offered with a bewildering choice of sauces and cheeses, and with a chicken or spicy bean option instead of beef. The more Cho read aloud the more the party around him nodded their approval, increasingly convinced that the dish had originated in the mind of the Genius of Geniuses himself. In homage to him, they each chose a different variety of it, with fries and salad, and opted for a Budweiser beer, as their own Taedonggang beer, which they'd understood was appreciated in many countries as one of the world's finest beers, was not on the menu.

During the meal Cho found himself discussing the banalities and practicalities of the visit, along with everyone else, each to conceal his enjoyment of the food, which was fresh and came in bountiful portions. By the time their empty plates had been cleared and they had accepted Pam's recommendation of the strawberry cheesecake, followed by coffee, even Ambassador Shin seemed at peace with the world. When the check arrived he picked it up to pay, but Cho took it from him with an assured smile. A sense of pride and occasion came over him. He opened the Italian hand-stitched wallet with the crisp hundred-dollar bills, the gift Yong-ho had given him the day of the parade, and paid. He thought of presenting Pam with *Anecdotes of Kim Il Sung's Life*, but changed his mind and left her a generous tip.

They stepped out onto the sidewalk to a cold, clear night. The city gave no sign of winding down. Streets buzzed with traffic and pedestrians. And lights—lights blazed everywhere, from the display windows of the shops, even though they were closed, and—Cho looked up—in every floor of the office tower opposite, though the workers had gone home. He rubbed his hands together, anticipating the adventure of walking the city block back to the hotel, when a middle-aged man with a thin moustache emerged from the restaurant in a hurry. His name tag said GONZALO. He had Cho's money in his hand, and was holding what looked like a small scanning device with a blue light.

"Uh, sir? I'm the manager. Do you have another method of payment please? We believe these bills are counterfeits."

13

Hyesan Train Station
Ryanggang Province, North Korea

The day was cold enough to freeze rice spirit but Mrs. Moon had never seen the market so busy. A power cut had closed both lines into Hyesan. Two trains were stranded in the station, and stranded trains meant stranded customers.

Her benches were rammed with diners, and a line of people waited to be seated. Steam rose, smoke drifted, chopsticks tap-tapped. Few spoke. Hot soup was slurped straight from the bowl. It was too cold to sit still. The sky was a sheet of platinum, and threatening snow.

Mrs. Moon's money belt was thickening by the minute with grubby, tattered won. Her gas burner was turned up full; the four largest pans were simmering on the cooktop, and she was down to her last sack of charcoal. Curly and her daughter were serving, and Grandma Whiskey, whom she'd hired to help cook, was stirring an aromatic fish stew that was selling for three hundred won a bowl. The missing member of her team was Kyu.

"Serve the police first," she murmured to Curly. She was worried there wouldn't be enough.

A thin cheer went up in the station building, followed by a screech from the loudspeaker that made everyone cover their ears. The electricity was back.

At last she caught sight of Kyu. The boy was weaving his way between the mats and the line of customers, silent and stoic as a cat. He took a final drag of *bingdu* from his pipe, inhaling it to the deepest pockets of his lungs, and blew out a white plume in the direction of China.

"Not in front of my customers," she said.

"We'll need a second table soon," he said, taking up his position on top of the rice sacks.

A horn beeped, causing a small commotion at the far end of the platform. An open-top police jeep was crawling toward the canteen, forcing the market traders to pull their mats out of the way. Mrs. Moon's line of customers parted to let it through. Sergeant Jang got out and walked up to her kitchen area with a proprietorial air, nodding at the customers and rubbing his hands. Shovel-face began unloading the rice from the back of the jeep. It came in pale-blue burlap sacks printed the words UNITED NATIONS WORLD FOOD PROGRAM.

"Ajumma." Sergeant Jang grinned, revealing good yellow teeth. "Your face is more warming than a bowl of hot *mandu-guk*."

"What d'you want?"

"I wonder if you would pay me in yuan today …"

"You can give me five percent off for hard currency. The money changers charge me."

She had not used the honorific terms his rank was due, but she was older than him, and she knew the rice he sold her was stolen Yankee tribute.

"If you say so."

He scowled suddenly when he noticed Kyu, who had lit his pipe again, and beckoned to the boy with a flick of his fingers. Kyu passed him the pipe, which he wiped and put to his mouth, taking a deep drag. When he exhaled, Mrs. Moon noticed an unpleasant gleam come into his eyes.

"And, uh, another thing …" He leaned into her ear and she sensed trouble coming. "The Bowibu arrested four people on a train at

Wiyeon Station this morning ..." His voice fell to a whisper, "for possessing *Bibles. Tiny bloody pocket Bibles, ajumma.*" His breath carried a sweetish hint of alcohol. "I don't want the Bowibu snooping around this station, terrifying everyone, any more than you do." He looked at her meaningfully. "Someone is handing them out to passengers as they board trains. Let's make sure no one's doing that here."

Mrs. Moon sighed. He was making her responsible. "I'll warn the women. If they see anything you'll be the first to know."

"That's all I wanted to hear," he said, straightening up. "This is making the Bowibu ve-ery twitchy." He made a creepy-crawly movement with his fingers. "They see spies and saboteurs everywhere they look ..."

Mrs. Moon watched him go.

"What a cunt," Kyu said.

Barely six weeks had gone by since the day Mrs. Moon had first set her mat on the platform and sold rice cakes, a nobody from the countryside who didn't know the rules.

Her bribe of the hundreds of pairs of gloves and socks had taken care of matters with the county police. Not only was she let off the hook for deserting her work unit at the farm, but she'd made allies of the policemen. They'd done as she'd suggested and distributed the gloves and socks as free gifts to the villagers of Baekam County. Just as she had predicted, the initiative had won them the praise of the local Party, and promotions.

What had happened the day after that, when she had returned to the market, convinced her that her fortunes were flowing in a very good direction.

The women had gathered around her mat in a circle. Curly was among them, hiding the smile on her face with her hand. Whatever was coming, Mrs. Moon sensed that his was her idea.

"We invite you to join our cooperative," said Mrs. Yang, who sold dried fish and batteries.

Mrs. Moon got up off the ground with difficulty and bowed to Mrs. Yang. She knew this was their thanks for saving Curly from the hands of that official during the previous night's raid on the market, but she did not understand what was meant by cooperative, until Mrs. Kwon, who sold plastic toys and candies that had no sell-by date, explained that it was an informal club set up by the women to lend money if any of them needed to make an investment, or pay a bribe. Then they bowed deeply to her, and went back to their mats.

"The offer's there, ajumma," Curly said. "Take it."

"What would I invest in?" Mrs. Moon said. "I'm not much of a trader."

"You said you could cook."

This got Mrs. Moon's mind working. "It's true ... But the ingredients I'd want aren't in Hyesan. I'd be offering the same noodle soup and bean-paste stew everyone serves."

Again, Curly regarded her with that bright concentration. Her eyes were wide and clear, the slight cast in one of then giving her an attractive vulnerability. Her lips were the color of rose quartz and slightly open, forever on the verge of confiding something. Whatever the source of her contentment, she carried it in her heart, like heat inside the earth. The sunflower-yellow headscarf she wore suited her. *Light shines from you*, Mrs. Moon thought.

"What supplies do you need, ajumma? I will get them for you."

Mrs. Moon smiled and pinched the young woman's cheek. "Where would you get fresh beef, and good-quality pork? There's nothing here."

Curly's voice fell to a whisper. "From China."

Mrs. Moon's smile vanished.

This was when she learned that Curly had been to Changbai, on the Chinese side of the Yalu River, more than once. She had crossed at night, bribing border guards she knew at a certain narrow, wooded point of the riverbank near her house, and crept over the ice.

Mrs. Moon's eyes popped wide open. "What were you doing in China?"

But to that question Curly said something vague and evasive about having business with Chinese merchants.

"And if you were caught?"

"I have protection," she said coyly, and looked down.

At dawn the next day, Mrs. Moon scattered an offering of salt to the mountain spirits and gave thanks to her ancestors for blessing her with good fortune. A few stars still shone clear and frostily, but the comet in the west had gone. Whatever course of events it had foretold was now in motion. She felt sure of it. She had asked her parents in dreams what the comet had signified but they had answered in riddles and verses and she hadn't understood.

A lamb goes uncomplaining forth . . .

". . . the guilt of all men bearing," she murmured as she stepped back into the house.

"Mm?" Tae-hyon stirred under the blanket and his leg twitched. "What are your bloody ancestors telling you now?"

Later that day she used a loan from the women's cooperative to buy a new Chinese-made gas burner and two extra-large steel pans, a long, cast-iron tray for the charcoal, and a gridiron. Curly insisted on making the trip to fetch the supplies herself, refusing Mrs. Moon's offer to hire smugglers. That evening she slipped across to Changbai in China, returning the next day with everything on Mrs. Moon's list. White fish and scallops. Good-quality fresh pork and tenderloin beef that could be marinated and cut into thin strips. Ox bone. A dozen different spices. Refined sugar. Root ginger, ginseng, chili sauce, and—impossible to obtain in Hyesan in November—sweet, crisp lettuce. Everything else—the soybean paste, garlic, kimchi, and dried noodles—Mrs. Moon bought in the market. Rice she had to buy from the local racket controlled by the police. Finally she found a carpenter to make her a cheap pine table and two benches out of packing crates.

The day after that, as she'd watched the table being assembled, her nerves were wound so tight she was visiting the lavatory every ten minutes.

The vegetables had been peeled and chopped, the rice washed, and the meat marinated. She had an ample supply of charcoal. Curly and her daughter were on standby; Grandma Whiskey had her cleanest apron on, which wasn't saying much. At 8:00 a.m. she fired up the gas burners and lit the charcoal. An hour later, Moon's Korean Barbecue opened for business.

The day started slowly, with only a modest trade by midmorning, and worryingly few customers by midday. But something strange happened after that. Word of mouth spread from the station to the city square outside, as did the smells of grilling beef and sweet charcoal smoke and steam from two simmering pans, of fish stew and ox-bone soup, and by early afternoon her benches were almost full.

At midday the next day her benches were completely full, with a small line of customers waiting, a line that grew longer throughout the day, even when sparse snowflakes began floating like goose down.

By the end of her first week Moon's Korean Barbeque was the talk of Hyesan. She had a permanent line of waiting customers that included city officials and their families. Customers were paying for their meals with won, yuan, euros, American dollars—the king of the black-market currencies, which Mrs. Moon had not seen before—and, occasionally, with Choco Pies. Soon she had multiple exchange rates at her fingertips. *Bingdu* she refused to accept as payment, although *bingdu*, she realized, was everywhere. The drug had become a currency.

Within two weeks she had paid back all the money borrowed from the cooperative. She had hired additional smugglers to obtain her supplies from Changbai, and she was asking the police to increase the supply of rice. From that point onward, she became the market's unofficial head.

But success brought with it fresh worries. Party officials were breathing down her neck about trading rules that changed as often as the wind. And wherever she looked she saw a peeping grimy face—*kotchebi*, children so hungry they ate raw corn from the ground. She'd fed them once. Now they were a daily menace, swiping food and picking pockets. She needed protection.

That's when she remembered the teenager who'd seemed so lost in the world when he'd tried to pay for rice cakes with a wrap of *bingdu*, all those weeks ago on her first day as a trader. When she described him—the insect-thin boy with a shaman's eyes—the kids knew who she meant. He slept in a boarded-up bottling plant on the city outskirts. His name was Kyu.

In the crumbling factory she found him smoking *bingdu* with a gang of children who stank like rotten berries.

"Not safe here, ajumma," he said, watching her from behind a veil of white mist.

"I'm offering you a job." She covered her mouth and nose with her handkerchief. "And a bath."

Fourteen years of age and short and stunted, Kyu had been abandoned in the market at the age of five by a mother who had gone to China in search of food. A street fighter with a cat's sense for danger, he was a true *kotchebi*. When he wasn't high on *bingdu* Mrs. Moon sensed in him a deep bitterness toward life. If he ever saw his mother again, he said, he would force her to watch him eat white rice. But he had no clear memory of what she looked like. Mrs. Moon understood his grief. She knew how it felt to reach out into the void for the ones she had lost. The memory of them was too painful for her to bear, though they visited her in dreams. Kyu, whom she'd taken under her wing as if she'd known him all her life, would be a grandson's age.

Mrs. Moon fed Kyu all the food he could eat but she suspected he could have survived on love and affection alone. He became her protection, her lookout, her source of news. Nothing happened in the market without Kyu knowing. Over the following weeks his tiny body filled out, until he was strong enough to dominate the *kotchebi*. Any kids wanting to pickpocket or steal at Hyesan Train Station needed Kyu's permission. Without permission, all they could do was beg.

When Sergeant Jang had reversed his jeep back along the platform it occurred to Mrs. Moon that if anyone knew who was handing out illegal Bibles, Kyu would. She was about to ask him when a surge of customers arrived, army cadets drawn by the aroma of sizzling *bulgogi*. The stranded train passengers were eating breakfast, lunch, and dinner at her canteen, despite the cold. This had been her busiest, most profitable day. But by early evening the temperature had dropped further and the market was thinning out. She turned off the gas burner and gave the still-warm charcoal to the *kotchebi*.

The moon hung faint and silken like a spider's egg. Just a few dim lamps had appeared in the windows of Hyesan's houses, but the sky above Changbai on the Chinese side of the river glowed amber from so much streetlight and neon. She'd heard there were cities in China that hadn't existed a year ago. Towers of glass that reached the clouds, they said.

The women were packing up. Mrs. Moon sat in front of the brazier with Kyu, warming herself before the journey home. She watched Kyu's young, old-man face as he tipped white powder from a paper wrap into his pipe.

"Can't you leave that stuff alone?"

The brazier crackled in tongues of flame that reflected in his smoked-glass eyes. He flicked his plastic lighter, held it under the bowl of the pipe, and took a deep drag. "*Bingdu* takes away pain ... It takes away hunger and cold." He offered the pipe to her.

She waved it away.

Just then a train horn sounded, so loud it split the air and echoed off the mountains. An instant tension swept through the station as people grabbed luggage and small children and dashed through the shadows toward the platform, shouting. The Hamhung train that had been sitting in the station all day was departing, and Mrs. Moon suddenly remembered her question.

"Who's handing out Bibles?"

There was a din of banging train doors and a crackling announcement from the loudspeaker. In the sparse lights of the station, she could see families gathering along the platform's edge, waving good-bye.

The spectacle distracted her for a moment from Kyu, and when she turned back to him he was avoiding her eye.

"If you really want to know, ajumma ..."

Passengers with contraband were being helped up onto the roof, where they wouldn't be searched. A whistle rose, shrill and clear in the cold air, followed by the calls of well-wishers, and the train began to move very slowly, creaking its way out of the station. Hands and arms in the crowd on the platform were still passing packages of food and goods up to people in the open windows.

"... The answer's in front of you."

For a split second a blaze of sparks on the train's overhead cables illuminated the whole scene as clearly as a flash photograph.

Mrs. Moon was feeling the cold deep in her bones now, and moved to get up. When she got to her feet she stopped and stood dead still. Without thinking, she looked in the direction of the platform, now in shadow again. She could not have said how, but some sense was making her react to something she'd just seen a moment ago. The scene lit by that flash of sparks persisted on her retina, its impact too vivid to wear off immediately.

One color amid the khakis and grays had stood out.

Sunflower yellow ... In the crowd on the platform she'd seen a bright-yellow headscarf. A young woman passing a small package up to someone on the train ... after it had started moving.

Her heart turned over in her chest.

*

The house lay at the end of a dirt street of low huts with corrugated iron fences. Dogs barked as Mrs. Moon passed each gate. An open drain glistened in the moonlight, flowing toward the river, which she could hear gurgling beneath the ice about a hundred yards away at the end of the street. She knocked on the front gate and listened. To her right was the path that ran along the river, the border itself, where guards patrolled in pairs. Dark trees reached out from the far bank. The river was so narrow here she could throw a pebble and it would land in China.

The house door creaked open and then a key rattled in the gate. It opened ajar, and then wide. "Ajumma," Curly said, surprised. She was holding up an oil lamp that cast a pale light. The yellow headscarf was still tied around her head, covering her curls. Before she could say another word something in the way Mrs. Moon looked at her caused the young woman's expression to change. It was not an expression of bewilderment or guilt, but rather of recognition, an acceptance of a long-expected moment. In that expression all Mrs. Moon's fears were confirmed.

Curly stepped to one side to let her into the house.

Dinner was bubbling on the hob. The room was spotless, with only a few sticks of furniture, and the Father-Son portraits on the wall. Curly's daughter, Sun-i was seated on a mat on the floor unwrapping a package by the light of a candle. The spine of a pocketbook could be seen behind a tear in the brown paper.

"Bibles," Mrs. Moon murmured.

Curly closed the door and leaned against it, her head lowered.

Without raising her voice above a whisper Mrs. Moon said, "What are you mixed up in?"

Curly looked up then and spoke with a quiet defiance.

"We read verses of the book aloud ... in our church."

Mrs. Moon felt a tingling on her scalp. That was a word she hadn't heard spoken in a long time.

Curly's breathing became shallow. "Eight of us. We change the location each time, meeting in different houses, but there are others, ajumma, in Hamhung, Chongjin, even in Pyongyang, worshipping in secret. They read verses copied by hand on tiny pieces of paper. Through God's grace, I know some of the Bibles will reach them."

A chill passed over Mrs. Moon. Even hearing this information could get her executed.

"Where are they coming from … these Bibles?"

Curly continued to look at her. Her eyes glistened slightly, containing the emotions behind them. "From missionaries over the river … I meet them in Changbai … They give me a few each time I visit."

Mrs. Moon felt the ball of fear inside her finally hatch and spread throughout her gut. She said quietly, "Those missionaries are placing you in terrible danger. Do you know what the Bowibu do to anyone who's met Christians in China?"

"God protects Koreans in China. He will protect me here."

A fissure in time opened in Mrs. Moon's mind. The long-ago voices of her parents, reading from a book in a shuttered room, and singing quietly.

She said, more urgently now, "The Bowibu are closing in on you. Sergeant Jang told me this morning they've arrested people found with copies on them. They see everything. They'll find you."

Curly's composure vanished, as if a mask had been thrown off. A look of ecstasy and terror twisted across her face, and for one instant Mrs. Moon thought she was mad.

"If I'm caught, I'll die, and I am willing to die …" Her voice was trembling. "Just thinking of it comforts me and gives me the strength to suffer this place, just as He suffered. He suffered so that we may live …"

Mrs. Moon's mind was a riot of fragmented memory and confusion. "The Great Leader?"

"No, ajumma." Curly bared her teeth in a bitter smile. Her voice became louder and ill controlled. "Not him. He tried to replace God with himself in our hearts. He tried to make us love him instead of Christ—"

Mrs. Moon held a hand up to Curly's face to silence her, conscious of neighbors' ears, alert and listening in the dark, quiet houses. In the silence her own breathing was labored.

"And Sun-i?" Mrs. Moon whispered, pointing at the girl sitting on the floor. "Do you want her to die, too, in a labor camp? Because that's what will happen if you're caught."

The animation drained from Curly's face. Her defiance had burned out and she looked sad and exhausted. She began to weep.

"No," she said through her tears. "Of course I don't want that."

The girl got up from the floor and hugged her mother.

Mrs. Moon said, "Listen to me. You must both cross into China tonight. Get help from your missionaries and never come back."

Mother and daughter turned to look at each other, an odd look of destiny in their eyes.

"You don't have time to think about it," Mrs. Moon urged. She opened the window shutter ajar and peered out, but could see nothing beyond the corrugated iron fence and the dark yard. The street was quiet.

It took no time to pack. They had so little to carry. Curly spent a few minutes in her yard digging at the hard ground to retrieve a buried pot where she'd hidden Chinese yuan, and they were almost ready leave.

"Leave the Bibles," Mrs. Moon said, "I will destroy—" She checked herself. "I will distribute them."

Curly was trembling now and Sun-i kept looking fearfully at her mother. The implications of what they were about to do were starting to sink in.

"Take this," Mrs. Moon said, giving Curly a thick wad of money in mixed currencies from her money belt. "In case you have to bribe a border guard you don't know."

Curly took the money distractedly.

"It's best if we leave separately," Mrs. Moon said. "A group will look suspicious."

Curly extinguished the stove and the oil lamp, and the candle. She opened the front door ajar and listened. The freezing night flowed into the house. The only sound was the rushing of the river beneath the ice. Not a breeze stirred the trees. Above the roofs of the houses the stars shone like ice crystals. The air was so cold it burned their throats, so mother and daughter pulled scarves up around their faces.

Sun-i went first, creeping across the yard to the wooden gate in the corrugated iron fence. There was just enough starlight to see her. She unlocked it slowly, slipped through, and closed the gate behind her.

They waited two minutes and then it was Curly's turn. She bowed to Mrs. Moon and gave her the keys to the house. "When I've reached the missionaries I'll send a message to you with one of the smugglers."

Mrs. Moon heard herself say, "God be with you."

Keeping the house door ajar she watched Curly cross the yard and slowly pull the gate.

The gate flew wide open, a large dog barked, and light blazed into the yard from the street.

A man's voice shouted. A violent, blurred movement, and Curly cried out.

Mrs. Moon leapt back into the house and slammed the door.

She had caught only a glimpse of what was outside in the street, enough to know that the catastrophe was complete. Bowibu, four or five of them, in long dark coats. A police dog. Gloved hands holding Sun-i and smothering her face to stop her making a sound.

14

CIA Headquarters
1000 Colonial Farm Road
Langley, Virginia

The recruits of Class H were in high spirits as they boarded the bus for DC, the start of a full week's leave from the Farm for Thanksgiving, their first break since training began a month ago. Jenna waved them off, saying she had errands to run in Williamsburg. In fact Fisk had ordered her to attend a top-secret briefing at Langley, where a senior South Korean intelligence officer was visiting from Seoul.

He was a dapper forty-year-old in a Dior suit who spoke English with a Californian accent. "Call me Mike," he said, smiling at his hosts like a celebrity. Present in the room were several senior analysts, including Simms, and five uniformed and heavily ribboned military types from the Pentagon. Jenna sat on Fisk's right.

Their attention was being directed to an image on a wall-mounted screen. It depicted the Unha-3 rocket part retrieved by the US Navy from the Philippine Sea.

"We're seeing here the nose cap and third-stage section," a young analyst said, pointing with a cursor, "large enough to carry a two-hundred-kilo payload—the right weight for a tactical nuclear warhead. The altitude it reached indicates a missile range of five thousand kilometers. The heat shield reentered the atmosphere intact. Gentlemen—and lady—this was a highly successful test. The North Koreans don't know that, of course, because we retrieved the evidence from the sea before they did, but the clock is ticking. We know they're building two more, and let us be in no doubt. We are the target."

He sat down and South Korean Special Agent Mike Chang took over.

"They've got the rocket science," he said, beaming his smile and winking at Jenna. "What they haven't figured out is the warhead—and this is the most valuable piece of intelligence we have. The CIA may have no assets on the ground inside the North, but my agency does. My sources are all reporting the same thing: the regime is stuck at second base when it comes to building a nuke small enough to arm a missile. It could be two, five, ten years before they've got that kind of technology."

"I don't get it," said one of the generals, a jowly man with a gravelly voice. "Why are they spending millions of dollars testing rockets if they've got nothing to arm them with?"

"It's bluff," Simms said, folding his arms. "The launch timing was no accident—just a few weeks before that North Korean delegation arrived in New York yesterday? You can bet your ass they'll use this to blackmail us for a ton of aid ..."

Jenna turned her eyes to the windows, thinking. Acres of parking lots, and beyond them, chestnut and beech woods as far as the eye could see, the hills of Virginia turning amber, red, gold.

We're missing something.

She was thinking of all the spysat imagery she'd been browsing for the last few days. Most of it had been discarded by the squints because it showed nothing of military interest. But the North Koreans were masters of subterfuge and concealment ... Some of Kim's homes were rumored to be entirely subterranean, with entrances along tunnels many miles long. If they were able to hide something in a place where no spy on the ground could learn a thing about it, where no squint would look for it, maybe they *did* have something to arm their rockets. But where … ?

She tried to think in the mindset of the regime. *A weapon could only truly be hidden … in an information black hole.*

And that's when it came to her. It felt as if an ice cube had slid down her spine.

"My sources learned one other curious detail," Special Agent Mike Chang said. "Kim Jong-il himself was present at the Tonghae site to attend the launch, in the company of his youngest son and successor. No cameras, no propaganda. A secret visit …" Jenna's eyes opened wide.

When the briefing adjourned for a short break she took Fisk's elbow and guided him toward the windows, away from the others, who were standing about with cups of coffee, talking in groups.

She angled her head away from the room and kept her voice low. "They can weaponize their rockets. I believe Mike Chang's intelligence is wrong."

Fisk turned to look at the horizon, his brow perturbed, as if she'd spoken some fear he'd long held.

Her voice was a frantic whisper. "A sophisticated multimillion-dollar missile test? Kim and his heir both present? They *must* have something … A warhead developed in secret, somewhere opaque to Mike Chang's spies."

"Where?" Fisk turned to her. "We've got every eye in the sky watching the damned place."

"A black site. One of the places the squints never look at … Charles, I need clearance to request spysat sweeps of certain coordinates."

He gave a bemused grimace and turned back to the window. "That's a request way outside a trainee's pay scale …"

She looked across the room. Simms stood talking in his monotone to the jowly general. "I'll need access to the spysat control room in the lower level ..."

"Let me get this straight ..." Simms had rather a small head, Jenna thought, which, with the girth of his midriff, put her in mind of a bowling pin. She couldn't read his expression—the glow from the screens reflected in his glasses, making two blank ovals on his face—but his voice held a faint and unmistakable sarcasm. "You want to tweak the orbit of a spectral imaging spysat to get a better look at ... a prison?"

All the squints had turned to listen.

She said coolly, "Camp 22 is thirty-one miles long by twenty-five miles wide, roughly an area the size of Los Angeles. More than enough room to hide a weapons program."

"There's nothing there. It's a mining camp."

"Which makes it impenetrable, except by satellite. And the imaging is incomplete."

He took off his glasses and rubbed his eyes. "Why that camp, Marianne Lee? Why not all of them?"

Jenna knew it was only a hunch, but it was backed by the strong currency of her knowledge. Defectors, former prisoners, had testified in detail about the internal workings of every one of those hells—except one. Camp 22, in the country's remote northeast, was a place from which no prisoner had ever been freed. No prisoner had ever escaped.

At 06:51 Korea Standard Time, spectral imaging spysat KX-4B, in geosynchronous orbit over the Sea of Japan, adjusted its trajectory. The view from two hundred kilometers up revealed a blue-amber dawn rippling westward, turning the beaches of Wonsan to a peel of gold. For a few moments Jenna was lost to its beauty. Then her programmed coordinates locked on, and the photographs began beaming into her folder. She took a deep breath.

Her first sight of it turned her stomach cold. Enclosed by high, forested mountains and dark side-valleys was a vast area of ash and shadow. In the universe of the gulag, Camp 22 was a black hole, off-limits to all outsiders. The little that was known about it came from the evidence of two former guards who had defected ten years ago. What they had described was almost a country in its own right. Two classes of citizen: guard and slave. Fifty thousand starving prisoners toiling in mines and farms. Guards on a permanent war footing, permitted to beat and kill at will. A total control camp. A zone of no return.

She closed her eyes for a moment and imagined herself as an academic again. *Be methodical, objective. Be rational ... and stay calm.* But as she zoomed in she did not feel very calm.

She started just outside the southernmost gates, seeing the railroad that carried coal out of the camp. A long trench formed a mantrap bristling with metal spikes. Alongside that: an electrified fence and a no-man's-land littered with electrocuted rats. She moved her finger on the touchpad, and her view passed over the fence and into the camp. *Watchtower, machine-gun nest, administration office.* The sun had barely risen. Everything was in a deep shadow cast by the mountains. A few guards patrolling with dogs. No sign of any prisoners. A vast roll call yard, the size of ten soccer fields, empty. Smoke rising everywhere from fissures and holes—coal fires raging deep below ground, perhaps. She kept moving. *Cesspool, train station, coal wagons, crematoria.* A ball of flame like a bright-orange chrysanthemum. *Smelting works, factory, prisoner villages* ... Tiny huts were arranged in neat grids, like city blocks. She zoomed out. They stretched for miles across the black terrain, thousands of them. *Keep moving ... internal prison, garbage pond, execution site, graves, graves, graves ... prisoners.* Vast columns of them, like armies, marching to work under armed guard, some heading toward the black fields, some winding between conical heaps of coal slag toward the pitheads of the mines. One column was half erased by the drifting smoke. It was a vision of inferno, a pit of damnation painted by Bosch. By now she had forgotten the object of her search.

She heard movement behind her. The last squint in the room was zipping up his padded coat. It was the end of the working day.

She said to him, "Can I configure this to live feed?"

He came over to her screen. "Sure, but the picture won't be sharp." He leaned over and tapped in an instruction. "Jesus … what are you looking at?"

Now the columns were moving in real time. More shuffle than march, a legion of the living dead, clothed in filthy gray rags. The guards at their side swung long batons as they walked. The image was much fuzzier. Among the adults were children with large heads, stumbling listlessly; others prisoners were white haired. All of them dragged or limped. A guard lunged into the column, baton raised, and the prisoners flowed around whoever had fallen, like a river around a rock. When the column had finally passed, Jenna saw what looked like a small cloth sack left lying on the cinder road. She reverted to photographic, and got an HD close-up. Half curled on its side, a bundle of rag and bone, was the emaciated body of a young girl. Her china-white face was part obscured, her hair splayed behind her. Jenna felt the thin membrane that separated her objectivity from horror finally break. She put her hand to her mouth.

The squint behind her seemed to be holding his breath, and Jenna understood now why these places were seldom studied by his colleagues. It exposed them to the stress of being a witness. They risked seeing things they could never forget.

Ever since she'd returned from Geneva with the knowledge that Soo-min had not drowned, she'd caught herself many times trying to project her twin into the here-and-now, the present. But when she did so it was always the eighteen-year-old Soo-min that she saw.

She imagined she felt Soo-min's presence again, the genetic link that bound them, but it was thin and faint, like the light from an ancient star. If her mind reached out in search for Soo-min's living, present self, her sister's face appeared blurred, shadowed, as if she were behind frosted glass … or smoke. A terrible fear now gripped Jenna's heart. Had this been Soo-min's fate? A place like this?

It was almost midnight on her watch when she finally found it, in a dark, narrow side valley in the camp's northern extreme. She knew it was what she'd been looking for. It stood out like a space ship, and she guessed they'd not yet had a chance to camouflage it or cover it. A railroad track carried building materials to its entrance, and in front of the entrance was … an orchard? The rows resembled fruit trees, though surely no fruit grew there. By now she was so drained and numbed by the horrors of the camp that her momentous discovery seemed a mere detail.

Simms answered his phone after many rings. She heard a cough and the sound of a toilet flushing. "It's very late, Marianne Lee. This better be good."

"It's inside Camp 22."

"What is?"

"A large, modern complex with state-of-the-art aircon units on the roof, stainless-steel cooling ducts, satellite dish, and an outbuilding that could house an independent generator. All surrounded by electrified double fences."

"I'm sure this can wait until tomorr—"

"North Korea is spending its scarce resources building a high-tech facility in a secluded valley that lies deep inside a gigantic concentration camp. It's located only twenty kilometers from the Tonghae Rocket Launch Site. I'm guessing it's not an indoor heated fucking swimming pool. You better put every squint in the Agency on this tomorrow morning before I tell the CIA director it was right under your nose all along."

*

How could she even think of shopping? The tranquil morning on O Street struck her with the shock of the surreal. Pastel cottages amid brick federal mansions. A college hockey team carrying sticks and equipment. High above, a silver airplane tracing a stream of vapor across the blue. Sleep had proved impossible. Even when she rubbed her eyes, the camp retained its imprint on them, like a photographic negative. It felt good to be home for the first time in a month, and reunited with Cat, who had been cared for by her neighbor, but something in her perception of home had shifted. The dust-covered living room was her previous life frozen in time. Her life before the Farm. The briefcase she'd carried to work every day at Georgetown looked as if it had been abandoned next to the piano by a stranger.

Thanksgiving was this week. She forced herself to focus and figure out what she needed to buy. Apart from her mother she'd invited her dad's brother Cedric and his family.

"You've never cooked for us before," Han had said on the phone. And then, in that complicit tone that made Jenna want to stick pencils into her own eyes, "Have you met someone?" One of Jenna's reasons for hosting was to foil any plot her mother might have to ambush her with another suitor in Annandale.

She pushed her cart along the dairy aisle thinking that she'd never felt so out of place. A weekday morning in the grocery store, surrounded by mothers wheeling carts with toddlers in tow, all bafflingly oblivious to the dangers of the world, the precarious security she worked to maintain. What had been normal and routine now seemed trivial and bizarre.

When she got home Cat was hunger-marching up and down the piano keys.

She was pushing the turkey into the refrigerator when her phone buzzed.

Mother's *number withheld* trick.

"Omma, Thanksgiving is your only American meal of the year. I am *not* serving it Korean style."

"Uh, you're on speakerphone, Miss Lee," Simms said coldly. "The squints are with me in the conference room ..." She felt her face redden. "We're ninety percent sure your object of interest is a laboratory."

"What kind of lab?"

"Probably chemical. It has a water supply from a mountain lake and tanks for storing gases. Could be narcotics. Hard drugs are one of their main exports ..."

"Why build a drugs lab *there?*" she turned to the window. The condensation was making diamonds of the afternoon light. "If they're working on a weapon in secret, locating the lab inside a total control camp makes sense. Nothing about it would leak out."

"We're putting more eyes on it, and we'll inform Mike Chang ..." After a pause in which she thought they were ending the call, one of the squints said, "Good work, Marianne Lee," which was followed by a murmur of agreement from the others.

It was a strange feeling, the morning after a night without sleep. The effect on her wasn't always unpleasant. Sometimes her mind burned more brightly the next day, like a candlewick flaring as it neared its end, and made novel and unusual connections. She tied her hair back and chose music for running. Dvořák. Ninth Symphony, last movement.

She ran along the old iron streetcar rails, toward the university campus, the chill air bringing clarity to her head. She turned up the volume of the symphony and quickened her pace, starting to warm up.

North Korea builds a new, high-tech chemical laboratory inside a concentration camp. She ran a lap around the hockey field, then took a path up the hill toward the playing fields and the observatory.

Laboratories conduct experiments. The camp provides secrecy. Or ...

She slowed to a halt. In the distance the Potomac River was myrtle green and choppy in the low November sun.

The experiments require human prisoners.

15

United Nations Secretariat Building
East 42nd Street and 1st Avenue
New York City
Monday, November 22, 2010

"Ready to face the enemy?"

Ambassador Shin, sitting next to Cho on the back seat, gave his shoulder a small squeeze, to show confidence in him, Cho supposed. Or to warn him not to screw up. Since the embarrassment outside the diner, Shin had assumed an air of amused familiarity with him, which Cho found intensely irritating.

Yong-ho must have known those hundred-dollar bills were counterfeits. The realization that he'd given them as a gift without mentioning this had shocked Cho. It had made him think of Yong-ho differently, as if he had suddenly become someone entirely separate from the brother he loved. But he reminded himself: spreading those counterfeits was one of the very countermeasures against Yankee power that they were all working to bring about. Cho tried to see it as a patriotic act, and not to judge his brother for it.

The Americans had sent a black Lincoln Navigator and two State Department diplomatic security escorts on motorbikes to collect him from the Roosevelt Hotel. He supposed this was a gesture to honor him, but the sight of the motorcade waiting outside the portico in public view, with the motorbikes' rotating blue lights attracting a small crowd of onlookers, had given him a bowel-loosening feeling of dread.

Cho's knee shook. He didn't speak a word to the two junior diplomats in the seats in front of him. More than anything he was worried his English would let him down.

The day was gray and overcast, with a light drizzle falling. The motorcade turned onto 1st Avenue and he saw the outline of the United Nations tower fade upward into low clouds, like an unfinished sketch. Flags lining the concourse hung limp. The limousine was greeted at the main entrance by First Secretary Ma, who escorted them across the vast lobby to the elevators. On the eighteenth floor they turned a corridor and were shown straight into a conference room. Four Americans stood up from their seats along one side of a polished wooden table arranged with glasses, bottled water, notepads, and a display of fresh flowers.

Chris O'Brien, the American UN envoy, was taller than anyone in the room. He ambled toward them with a genial smile, hand outstretched, as if they were new members of an athletic club. "Colonel, great to see you here," he said giving Cho's hand a hearty pump. His head was puce and pink and sand colored, his shoulders too broad for an intellectual.

Just as a jackal cannot become a lamb . . .

"The Dear Leader Kim Jong-il extends his cordial wishes for the success of our talks," Cho said without smiling.

They took their seats. The window framed a blank world of swirling clouds, an empty dimension. O'Brien opened the proceedings with a rambling speech stating the United States's position. He had a poor speaking voice, Cho thought. Strangulated and nasal. None of his words contained any surprises, except that O'Brien spoke as if these were thoughts and opinions he shared with his colleagues, rather than the words of an authorized text. The usual arrogance cloaked in reason and affability. *Last month's rocket launch a cause for deep concern ... Violation of multiple UN Security Council resolutions ... Human rights abuses ...* The same lack of respect for Korea's sovereign desire to live the socialism of its own style. The presumption that it had no right to arm itself against the enemies on its doorstep. Cho observed O'Brien's colleagues as he spoke. The speech was so tedious they barely seemed to be listening, and Cho recognized in their aspects an imperial complacency, a mock seriousness. One of them was dabbing at a coffee stain on his tie. Whatever nerves Cho had felt when he'd entered the room evaporated like the cloud outside the window, now burning off in the morning sun. He thought of the street poster that was all over Pyongyang this week—of an enormous Korean fist smashing down on the US Capitol Building.

He'd had enough of O'Brien's voice. He stood up, and rested his fists on the table. O'Brien looked up from his notes. His speech petered out in his nasal cavity. The Americans stared at him.

"Do you think our country is indifferent to its own dignity?" Cho said calmly.

"No, sir, we are merely—"

"Are you telling us we can't live by our own rules?"

O'Brien opened his hands, that gesture of reasonableness again, an objection forming on his lips. It was not Cho's turn to speak, but he was brushing aside the framework. A revolutionary had no use for protocol. In a clear, controlled voice he stated his position with force. He reminded them of the blood reckoning his country still had with the United States. He wagged his finger to prophesy the sea of fire that would engulf its puppet forces in Seoul if their meddling in his country's affairs did not stop.

O'Brien's brow was furrowed in understanding. At the end of Cho's remarks he gave an uncertain smile and smoothed his sandy hair with the tips of his fingers. "Let's take a short break," he said. As the Americans left the room Cho saw two of them exchange a glance of perplexed amusement, as if he they'd listened to a drunk give a speech at a wedding.

The American with the coffee-stained tie remained seated at the table. He had a long nose and thick, side-parted blond hair. "With the greatest respect, Colonel Cho ..." He was speaking in Korean with a pronounced American rhythm to his speech, which for some atavistic reason Cho found deeply sinister. "We know what's going on here, and we're tired of it. You launch a rocket. You drop menacing hints. You ratchet up tensions to crisis point. You'll wait till you see news headlines like 'North Korea on brink of war!' Then all of a sudden you offer to talk. The world breathes a big sigh of relief, and showers you with aid and concessions. Blackmail's worked for you until now. Not this time. Not any more." He got up, adding in English, "Ain't gonna happen."

At the end of the day, Cho asked directions to the men's restroom. He entered and checked he was alone before splashing water on his face and looking at his reflection in the mirror. He regarded the cold set of his mouth, the blankness in his eyes. Sometimes he did not recognize himself, or feel sure which was the real him. He felt the knots of tension in his back and neck and the familiar ball of dread in his stomach. The Americans had conceded nothing. Now he would have to report his lack of progress to Pyongyang.

When he entered North Korea's UN office on the fourteenth floor, Ambassador Shin, First Secretary Ma, and the two junior diplomats were sitting around the speakerphone on the desk. One of the diplomats was talking excitedly into the speaker, extolling the highlights of Cho's speech and the surprise on the Yankees' faces. The approving grunts of the First Deputy Minister himself could be heard on the other end. Cho stepped forward and snatched up the phone to hear the man's voice in private. He breathed in. There was no glossing this.

"Comrade First Deputy Minister, the Yankees aren't going for it."

"Relax, Cho Sang-ho. From what I've just heard you're doing fine ..." Behind the hiss and crackle on the line, Cho heard him suck in on a cigarette. "There's still one more day to go. Tomorrow could make all the difference ..." Someone muttered a word in the background. Others were listening in. "You'll know what to do."

Cho replaced the handset with a sense of foreboding. The First Deputy Minister hadn't questioned him about the proceedings. Hadn't given orders for the tactics for tomorrow's session. He'd behaved as if these crucial talks, for which the Ministry had spent months preparing, were of no consequence at all. That odd emphasis on *tomorrow*. Suddenly Cho's instinct for subterfuge stirred sharply to life.

He returned to the hotel feeling drained and on edge. He'd been placed in an impossible situation, he knew. He'd come to New York to accept tribute and reparations from an enemy that should have been cowed by the power and range of the rocket, but the Americans seemed unafraid. An incriminating, heretical thought crossed his mind—that a subtler, friendlier approach, with compromises offered, would have been more fruitful, and done much to engender a positive attitude in the Americans toward his country. But with that thought came the perception of a darker truth—that nothing in the Americans' attitude was meant to change. The Dear Leader had written,

The Yankees are the eternal enemies of our masses.
We cannot live under the same sky as them.

He sat on the bed and undid his tie, pulling it upward for a moment, imagining it was a noose. He badly wanted to speak to someone human, to his wife, to Books, who had such a sweet nature that Cho believed him incapable of a mean thought. At school he helped raise rabbits to provide fur for soldiers' hats, and listened with wonder to legends from the boyhood of Kim Il-sung.

He put the chain on the door and felt around the edges of the television for the "on" button. Surely it could be operated without the remote. He found the volume and turned it down low. A fat, brick-colored man with an image of the White House behind him was jabbing a finger at the camera and shouting about "hidden socialism." Cho changed channel. An excited voice introduced the Chevrolet Silverado, available at zero percent finance over forty-eight months, applicants subject to credit checking. He changed again. Multicolored fluffy creatures resembling no animals Cho recognized were singing a song about the importance of brushing your teeth. He turned it off and lay on the bed for a while, still clothed, his hands laced behind his head, listening to the sounds of the city. Soon he was drifting off to sleep on a wing of depression.

Some hours later he awoke in a sweat, disorientated in the unfamiliar room. He had no idea how long he'd been asleep. An alien urban glow filtered through a crack in the curtains and the contours of the room began to materialize around him.

The hammering sounded again.

Cho leapt off the bed and opened the door. One of the junior diplomats was outside in a state of agitation. He rushed past Cho into the room and went straight to the television set, talking excitedly. Confused by sleep, Cho couldn't follow what he was saying. The screen showed footage of houses on fire and a gas station exploding, with BREAKING NEWS at the top. The gas station's signs were in Korean. People were screaming, panicking. A woman was trying to run holding two infants in her arms. Lights pulsed on a military fire engine. His country was attacking Yeonpyeong, a South Korean island in the Yellow Sea, with artillery fire and MiG fighter jets. South Korean marines and civilians were being killed.

Suddenly Cho was wide awake and reaching for the telephone.

16

Hyesan Train Station
Ryanggang Province, North Korea

Mrs. Moon couldn't hear herself think. The loudspeaker was broadcasting at maximum volume. A Party orator's voice crackled with outrage, a massed rally chanted. Every few minutes the broadcast was interrupted by a bulletin from the Front, wherever that was.

In a way the noise was a welcome distraction. If her mind rested for a moment on thoughts of Curly and Sun-i, picturing where they were being held, what was being done to them now, she felt such gut-coiling anxiety it was all she could do to stop herself from fainting. She'd had no sleep, and had been the first to arrive at the market this morning. She'd told each of the women the news one by one. An atmosphere of fear, mixed with something like bereavement, hung over all of them.

She'd slipped out of Curly's house by the kitchen door just as the Bowibu were kicking their way in to search the place. Finding herself in a small vegetable patch she'd squeezed through a gap in the chicken wire and had hidden in a pigsty in a neighbor's backyard. There she stayed for hours, crouched in the frozen filth, listening to the men ransack Curly's house, pulling down the ceiling, tearing up the floor. They were organized, methodical, even though they must have found what they were looking for straight away: the four pocket Bibles were lying on the mat. By the time they'd gone, a bank of clouds was rubbing out the stars one by one. She was in utter darkness and had to feel her way out of the neighbor's yard. She'd long missed her truck ride back to the village. So she crept back into Curly's house, pulled open the back door, and sat among the devastated floorboards until morning. Rest proved impossible.

For the twentieth time she told herself to calm down. She tried to compose her face into its habitual mask of optimism. Panic was suspicious. In fact there was no point panicking at all until she had information, and once she had that, there might be a solution. No, there was always a solution.

Without Curly and Sun-i to serve food, Kyu had stepped in, but the customers did not like being served by one of the *kotchebi*, and scowled down their noses at him without thanking him.

She kept peering along the platform, keeping a lookout for Sergeant Jang. He would be the first one she'd ask for help.

Unable to sit still, she realized her mind was still in shock, which may be why the vision materializing before her eyes didn't especially surprise her.

Walking toward her between the aisle of mats and stalls was the spirit of a young girl. Mrs. Moon did a double blink.

She was about twelve years old, moving slowly and stumbling slightly, as though she were blind. Her face was smirched with dirt and deathly pale, her eyes glassy and half-covered by a curtain of matted hair. The clothes she wore were torn and hung from her in ragged strips—and she was barefoot. That was the detail that unhinged Mrs. Moon.

What ill omen was this? Fear breathed on her like a draft of night air.

Others were noticing the girl, too. They were staring at her and stepping out of her way. Mrs. Moon pinched herself.

She wasn't hallucinating.

Suddenly Mrs. Kwon let out a shriek and ran toward the girl, scooping her up in her arms, and Mrs. Moon snapped out of her trance. The phantom was Sun-i.

The women sent their customers away. They abandoned their mats. They formed a huddle around the girl, as if protecting a wounded fawn, and moved her beneath the bridge, away from the eyes of customers and the bleat of the loudspeaker.

The girl began shaking violently. A blanket was thrown around her and hot tea called for. She was wide eyed but not looking or see-ing. Mrs. Lee was trying to clean her cheeks with a damp cloth, saying "shush," though the girl had not uttered a sound. Mrs. Moon cupped the girl's cheeks in her hands and a flicker of reality came back into the eyes.

"Ajumma..."

She had lovely bow-shaped lips, just like her mother. Her voice was pure air and oddly disconnected, as if she were speaking in her sleep. "Where's my mother?"

Mrs. Moon glanced at the women. Their faces were appalled.

She held the girl's head to her chest, and felt death's shade on both of them.

A small head pushed through the women's aprons and Kyu appeared. Mrs. Moon said, "Find Sergeant Jang and tell him to come here now. Hurry."

It wasn't until later that the women were able to piece together what had happened from the scraps Sun-i could tell them. Outside the house she had struggled free from the Bowibu officer holding her, and had run to the river. They sent the dog after her over the ice. It attacked her and tore at her clothes. Two Chinese men waiting in the darkness on the other side, who may have been smugglers or human traffickers, beat the dog away and helped her up the bank, but she ended up running away from those men, too. She could not explain how she lost her shoes. At first light she crept back across the frozen river in bare feet.

Sergeant Jang found himself penned in by a wall of stony faces.

"Curly ... was distributing the Bibles? Ajumma ... please." His smile had frozen and his eyes darted about, looking for an escape. "That's a political crime. Very serious. You're asking the wrong man." The women's expressions did not change. "You have to understand. The Bowibu share no information about those crimes with us. It's not my business to get involved ...'

Mrs. Lee folded her arms. "I'd say you were a mouse if you weren't such a great big *leech*." She spat a bolus of mucus on the ground. "Always holding out your hand for more, but when it's a favor we need from you—"

"How much to bribe the Bowibu?" Mrs. Moon said. "To release her."

Sergeant Jang grimaced as if she'd screamed in his ear. He glanced about, but there were no customers in earshot. The loudspeaker was broadcasting a victory concert. Massed choirs singing "We Live in a Powerful Nation."

He gave a jittery laugh. "You can't bribe *them*."

"Everyone has their price in this city. How much?"

Sergeant Jang's eyes popped wide and he shook his head. When he spoke he'd acquired a stammer. "They m-might listen to you for, perhaps, ten thousand y-yuan ... But you don't have that kind of m-money ... and what happens if they take offense? No, no, no, no ..."

Mrs. Kwon turned to her in dismay. "Ten thousand yuan ..."

Kyu caught Mrs. Moon's eye and conveyed an idea. His shrug was a question mark.

The brazier cast its amber light onto the iron beams of the bridge. The women sat around it in a circle. Mrs. Moon was on her feet. "If we use the cooperative to raise half the money between all of us, Kyu will obtain the other half in *bingdu*."

Mrs. Yang said, "Is this going to get us into trouble?"

"I'll keep you all out of this," Mrs. Moon said simply. "There's no point putting everyone in danger. I will take responsibility for the offer."

A murmur of protest spread around the group.

"For Curly's sake we must act fast before—" She glanced at Sun-i and checked herself. "—before the authorities reach a decision. Sun-i," Mrs. Moon said softly, "it's not safe for you here. Go with Kyu tonight. He will hide you until this blows over."

"But who'll approach the Bowibu?" Grandma Whiskey said. Her yellow tortoise face was poking out from several layers of headscarf.

"Sergeant Jang will have to find his courage," Mrs. Moon said, "or I'll humiliate him and go myself."

17

United Nations Secretariat Building
East 42nd Street and 1st Avenue
New York City

A Fox News crew filmed the motorcade as it arrived at the UN building. Cho's door opened to a barrage of flashes. Surprised that there
were no Yankee police to stop him from speaking, he reiterated
Pyongyang's line for the cameras—"My country does not tolerate
illegal incursions of its territorial waters and has acted robustly"—
and proceeded into the lobby. He was in high fettle, with his junior
diplomats on either side of him and Ambassador Shin following
behind. First Secretary Ma was absent for some reason, but Cho had
scarcely noticed. The Dear Leader's eyes shone upon him from the
East and had made this happen, just to help him.

There were no amused faces across the table in front of him at
that day's talks. Now his every word carried the weight of a tank
shell. By lunchtime New York time Pyongyang had faxed him the
evening's newspaper headlines—YANKEE JACKALS COWED BY "ATTACK
DIPLOMACY!"—together with the Central News Agency's international press release, describing him, Cho, as a "warrior diplomat"
and reporting that the Yankees had come "crawling back to the
table, terrified that Comrade Kim Jong-il would draw the treasured
sword of the Revolution!" Cho basked in his new authority. He set

out his demands. Within hours, O'Brien's team began alluding to concessions that could be offered to make the crisis disappear. To induce them further, Cho softened his tone. He was generous in victory.

One shadow marred his day. Where was First Secretary Ma?

"He's been detained by important consular business," Ambassador Shin had said, when Cho asked him. *What business was more important than this?* Once again Cho's instinct for plot was roused. Toward the end of the day, when the Americans began firming up their offers and the scale of his triumph was becoming apparent, First Secretary Ma was still nowhere to be seen.

Cho delivered the good news in a long telephone call to Pyongyang in Ambassador Shin's office. The Americans were offering even more than the First Deputy Minister had hoped for—thousands of tons of food aid and hundreds of millions of dollars in cash. When he emerged from the office he checked to make sure he was unobserved, and punched the air. He was buoyed with excitement and relief and grinning like a kid. It was time to go home. He hit the button for the elevator, spun around in little dance, the doors opened, and he was face-to-face with O'Brien.

"Colonel Cho, I was just coming to look for you."

Cho stepped in and O'Brien pushed the button for the lobby. Cho looked down and pretended to adjust his cuffs. He had no small talk to make with this man and was thinking that silence would be entirely appropriate when O'Brien turned to him and clasped his elbow in a most familiar manner.

"We've made a small arrangement for cocktails and dinner at a, uh, Manhattan establishment, which I think you'll like, called the 21 Club ..."

He was smiling warmly—as if nothing of the depth of enmity Cho had conveyed in two days of talks had any effect on a personal rapport.

"Just a relaxed gathering, to offer you some New York hospitality ..."

The grotesque bourgeois sham of his manners! Cho gently disengaged his grip. His orders in Pyongyang could not have been clearer: under no circumstances was the legation to socialize with the enemy.

"The delegation of the DPRK regrets that it must decline your invitation," Cho said with a bow of his head. "Another time, I hope."

O'Brien did a double blink. With a face that grew redder as each floor passed, he said that he was very sorry to hear that, and admitted that he hadn't expected it, because unfortunately it was too late to decline. The two junior diplomats in Cho's legation, who'd been waiting for him in the lobby, were already being shepherded into cars outside the main entrance and driven to the venue as he spoke. They'd been told that he, Colonel Cho, would be joining them presently.

Cho was dumbfounded. "And you didn't think to ask me first?"

Two days of bottled frustration were suddenly on O'Brien's lips. "Jesus Christ, it's a treat, not an insult!"

Cho glared at the elevator's descending digits, which now didn't seem so swift, fearful that he was about to yell something unbecoming of the dignity of his country.

"Sorry," O'Brien muttered, smoothing and resmoothing his sandy hair with his fingers. "I apologize."

The doors had not fully opened at lobby level before Cho was running across the vast marble space, drawing the eyes of the security guards. He reached the main exit in seconds and was through to the floodlit concourse, frantically looking left and right down the avenues of flags, his breath forming white billows on the night air. A snaking line of cars with drivers awaited heads of diplomatic missions, ambassadors, and attachés. But of his own staff there was no sign. They'd left.

His shirt clung icily to the skin of his back. Were the Americans playing a deadly practical joke? He lifted his eyes to the UN tower, blazing with the lights of all nations, and cursed the Yankees in the coarsest language of the army. O'Brien joined him on the curb, panting. His shirt had come untucked from his pants and his tie was askew.

"This car will take you," was all he said, indicating a waiting Lexus. A driver was holding the rear door open. Cho looked at O'Brien as upon a foe who'd outclassed him. He had no choice. He got into the car.

Moments later, as he rested his head against the cold backseat window and gazed at the teeming intersections on Lexington and Park Avenue, he marveled at the twists a life could take. Today he was fêted in Pyongyang. Tomorrow he faced dismissal, or worse. His triumph sabotaged. He felt a rising fury toward O'Brien, who had no understanding of the regime Cho served. It tolerated no slipups. No mistakes.

A sleety rain began to fall as the car turned into West 52nd Street, making the brownstone buildings dark and glistening. Beneath the sidewalk canopy of the 21 Club a top-hatted doorman was opening an umbrella while police officers held back a small crowd. Quickly Cho felt in his pocket for his lapel pin of the Great Leader's face and pinned it in his buttonhole—his talisman against American shamanism. If this display of hospitality was calculated to soften him, he'd show them how unyielding he could be.

The Lexus pulled over, his door was opened. Cameras flashed and voices shouted in the rain.

"DOWN WITH KIM JONG-IL!" Someone jostled violently in the crowd. "DOWN WITH KIM JONG-IL!"

Cho was ushered down the steps and into the club, still seeing orange stars from the camera flashes, through a reception area where there stood four solidly built men in suits with radio earphones whom he knew with absolute certainty were American secret police, along a narrow corridor, and into a private dining room. The door closed silently behind him and he found himself in a world to which he'd never truly been admitted before, not even on his missions to Beijing.

Low, rose-colored lighting reflected in dark paneled walls, on which were hung spotlit paintings of schooners and clippers in sail. A jazz trumpet solo played softly through recessed speakers. Next to a stone fireplace situated at the far end of the room, beyond a long, white-cloth dining table laid with wineglasses and silver, a group of tall, gray-haired men stood talking with booming emphases and wide hand gestures. The offhand ease of power. They stood a little apart from his own Korean staff—the two junior diplomats and two political officers—who looked like a group of refugees, clutching the stems of martini glasses in their fists as though they were trowels. Both groups turned toward him, and their conversation fell to silence. One of the tall American men made a remark that drew chuckles from his group. Cho felt his face burn.

The door opened again behind him and the broad frame of O'Brien entered, brushing the damp sandy hair from his face and sweating profusely. He seemed annoyed and on edge, but quickly softened his face into a more welcoming expression. As he led Cho toward the tall men, and began to introduce each in turn amid much hand shaking and stares of intense curiosity, Cho understood the reason for O'Brien's nerves.

The gathering before him included a world-famous former secretary of state, now slack mouthed and stooped; a senior army general in dark-green dress uniform; a Wall Street CEO; … and one former president of the United States. All assembled here this evening to meet him, Cho Sang-ho, a colonel in the Korean People's Army. He had to compress his lips together to suppress a laugh. *What idiots these Yankees were!* He was living under a charm. For the second time in a day, his shitty predicament was transformed. This was the honey on the cake of his triumph.

Whatever the Americans were intending with this parade of luminaries—a display of power; intimidation; a show of their determination to change his country's course—they had utterly misjudged the significance of a gathering like this to a mass audience of North Koreans back home. Simply by meeting him these men were abasing themselves before the Dear Leader's greatness. They were on their faces paying homage. Pyongyang's propaganda machine would be in overdrive.

"How d'you do, sir," the former president said in a hoarse drawl, and peered at Cho's lapel pin as if it were a second head. A photographer raised a camera to capture the handshake. Cho composed his face coldly. The former president gave a convivial smile; bulbous nose and pinkish-red skin making him seem faintly debauched. His hair was ash white in the camera flash.

"Mr. Cho, tell me what the hell happened today on Yeonpyeong Island."

Cho remembered that the former president had met the Dear Leader and spent time in his presence, and answered the question respectfully.

"You tell Chairman Kim from me that he's destabilizing the whole goddamn region ..."

The conversation was joined by the Wall Street CEO, a sharp-nosed man who reminded Cho of a bald eagle with glasses, who asked why North Korea did not open its economy, as the new China had done with such success.

"The DPRK remains true to the path of socialism," Cho said, accepting a martini from a tray. "The happiness of our people does not depend on the rapacious pursuit of profits."

"Sure, but profits'll put food in their mouths."

Only in the company of the army general, whose eyes regarded him with cool intelligence, was Cho wary. He had been introduced as Charles Fisk.

"Colonel Cho, I'm here to persuade you that nuclear weapons are not the right path for your country."

"General," Cho said, stirring his martini with the olive on its stick, "what, if not nuclear weapons, would get a small country like mine invited to a place like this for a drink with you this evening?"

Fisk threw back his head and laughed. A sincere, earthy laugh. "You have a point."

At that moment Cho was distracted by the boisterous voice of one of the junior diplomats, who was in conversation with O'Brien. He caught the diplomat's eye, flashing him a warning just in time to stop the man accepting a second martini.

"Tell me," Fisk said, moving in closer to Cho. "These long-range missiles you've got dressed up and disguised as satellite rockets ..."

Cho felt the hairs rise on the nape of his neck.

"... What are you hoping to arm them with?"

Was this man was provoking him?

"Forgive my question," Fisk said. "I'm merely curious." He smiled in apology, but his eyes were cold and there was a current of contempt in his voice.

Cho inflated his chest. "We assert our absolute right to a peaceful space program."

"Well." Fisk took a sip of his drink and turned to face the room. "Maybe I'm worrying about nothing. Perhaps it's something entirely innocent you're cooking up in that shiny new laboratory ..."

Cho stared at Fisk. He was being treated with insolence. And he had no idea what this man was talking about.

"Ah!" Fisk's eyes were smiling over Cho's shoulder. "At last."

A slender woman in a dark velvet cocktail dress joined them. Her skin seemed almost African American to Cho, and beautiful, too, but her hair and eyes were Asian. The narrow dress complimented her, though no Korean woman would bare her shoulders so immodestly.

Fisk began to introduce her, but she had already dropped a cool hand into Cho's and explained, in pitch-perfect North Korean dialect, that she worked for General Fisk as a special adviser.

"I am Marianne Lee."

18

The 21 Club
West 52nd Street
New York City

As the guests found their places on either side of the dining table, Jenna saw a momentary discomfiture on Colonel Cho's face. He was not being seated next to the former president or the former secretary of state, but toward the end of the table, opposite Jenna, and away from his staff. She slipped her handbag off her shoulder and gave him a brilliant smile, which he returned with a bemused look, unsure if he was being flattered or snubbed.

A piano arrangement of "'Round Midnight" played in the background. The lights dimmed, casting a luxurious glow onto the tablecloth and silverware. A maître d' wearing a radio earphone ushered in waitresses in black trouser suits who began pouring wine into each glass on the table, leaning in between guests with balletic poise.

Fisk was abiding by the calculation that the more convivial the atmosphere, the greater the chances of the North Koreans relaxing their guard and revealing the mind of the man in Pyongyang who, with a brute and brilliant timing, had triggered the release of hundreds of millions of dollars from the US government in return for calling off a brief, manufactured crisis, and who had demonstrated a shocking will to strike without provocation. The surprise attack on Yeonpyeong Island had set alarms ringing from Tokyo to Washington. Within forty minutes of the news breaking, Fisk, at an excruciating meeting in the White House Situation Room, had been obliged to admit the CIA's intelligence failure to the commander in chief in person, who had come from a black-tie reception, glass in hand, and listened to Fisk with a decided coolness.

This evening's hospitality at the 21 Club, though arranged months previously, was now seized upon. "I don't care if we have to spike their fucking drinks!" Fisk had shouted. "We've got them to ourselves for two hours. That's our window. We work them, pitch them, find out anything we can." The emergency had also caused the other, equally alarming, matter, to move high up Langley's crisis list: Jenna's discovery two nights ago of a secret laboratory inside Camp 22. Her suspicion that this was the lethal part of the rocket program was shared by the squints. She had submitted a report on it to the CIA director himself, and the coordinates were now being monitored daily from orbit.

Fisk had applied all his tact in a bid to dissuade some of the grandees from attending this evening—hardly presences in which the North Koreans were likely to lower their defenses. But looking at the faces around the table, Jenna could see that he'd been wrong. The North Koreans were glowing with pleasure at meeting the former president, and over cocktails even this son-of-a-bitch Cho had become open and approachable. The seating plan had been arranged with care. "We'll have more leverage if a woman talks to him," Fisk had said to her. "He'll be thrown off guard. Do whatever it takes. Charm him, coax him, appeal to his nice side."

"Does shit have a nice side?"

Just after everyone had taken their seats, the stocky, thuggish figure of North Korea's UN ambassador, whom Jenna remembered was called Shin, entered the room. She sensed, from a slight hardening in Cho's eyes, that Cho disliked this man. She continued to watch his face as the wine was poured. Jenna had met many North Korean defectors, but this was the first time she'd faced an unapologetic member of the Kim dictatorship. Like a zoologist sighting a species she'd spent years tracking, she could not take her eyes off him.

Light concentrated in the stem of his glass, illuminating his face. High cheekbones, thick hair sleeked back over a well-proportioned head. *Something of the propaganda poster about him*, she thought. She wasn't sure she found him handsome. The eyes had an arrogance that imbued his face with a very faint brutality. But she couldn't fault his attire. His suit was a tailored fit, and he wore a well-chosen tie and cuff links. To the casual observer he might be an executive from a South Korean conglomerate, Hyundai or Samsung, if it weren't for the refulgent little face on his lapel pin. The bizarre reminder that Korea spanned parallel universes.

She looked up from the pin to see that he, too, was looking at her. He blinked, as if conscious of being rude. It felt like an awkward first date. Something was going to happen, but neither of them knew what.

"I'm sorry," he said in English, taking a sip of his wine. "I've never before met someone of your race who speaks the dialect of the North."

"My race?"

A spoon chimed against a glass.

"Mr. President, honorable guests, ladies and gentlemen ..."

O'Brien was on his feet welcoming the visitors from the Democratic People's Republic of Korea. Jenna smoothed her napkin over her lap to hide a flutter of nerves. Her palms were sweating. O'Brien was speaking in his soft, nasal whine, making light of the two days of talks. He smiled and gestured toward Colonel Cho, whose face remained expressionless.

"Never in my career as a diplomat have I been described as an 'anti-socialist political dwarf who will be crushed by the weapon of single-hearted unity ...'" The audience chuckled into their laps, unsure if O'Brien was hitting the right note, but then, with good timing: "At least, never to my face ..." They laughed, and the tension that had been in the room from the outset was released. Even Cho looked amused. "Whatever our disagreements ..." O'Brien said, speaking through the laughter, "... and they are many, I believe that on both sides there exists a desire for greater trust and understanding in the name of security and, ultimately, peace ..."

A phlegmy mumble of "Hear, hear," from the former secretary of state.

"... which I hope this evening's hospitality will help build." O'Brien raised his glass. "To peace."

"To peace," everyone said, the words overlapping.

Glasses clinked, and a generous humor spread around the table as the weight of that tawdry bargain in the name of peace temporarily lifted from the Americans' shoulders.

The waitresses began placing baskets of bread rolls on the table.

"Food's a language we all understand," the former president said loudly, tucking a napkin into his shirt collar.

Jenna said, "How are you liking New York, Colonel?"

Cho broke off some bread and chewed, frowning in thought. "I have not noticed any of the corruptions I'm told are common in a capitalist city. Drug dealing, prostitution, soup kitchens, and so on and so forth."

Charming.

The first course was placed in front of them. A New England clam chowder.

"Pyongyang is free of vice, I suppose," she said.

"Generally, yes," he nodded, oblivious to her note of irony, "although, of course, like any city, it is not without crime."

The conversation stalled. Her training had not adequately prepared her for this. She probably had only a couple of shots at him before his attention would be drawn by someone else—not enough time to cultivate him, probe for doubts, learn his thoughts. If she was going to get anything out of him it would have to be through flattery or provocation, and something told her he was not easily flattered.

Watching him over the rim of her held glass, she said, "And what are the crimes typical of a North Korean city, I wonder? Espionage, sabotage, antirevolutionary plots, criticism of the Dear Leader … and so on and so forth?"

Cho's eyes narrowed, alert to mockery. "Socialism faces many dangers," he said. "The United States also has enemies who threaten its way of life." He leaned forward, his face an expression of cynical savoir faire. "It treats them in much the same way, I believe."

"We have no Camp 22, if that's the kind of treatment you mean."

Although Jenna had spoken softly it was at a moment when a lull seemed to settle over the table, the wine not yet having loosened conversation. At the periphery of her vision she saw that faces had turned in her direction.

"I know of no such place." An edge came into his voice. "We deal with criminals in our own way. You think their rights are more important than the well-being of a whole society? Imperialists have no right to speak of human rights."

"I haven't mentioned human rights," she said, taking a sip of her wine. "But it's interesting that you have."

He resumed his eating, but she felt too on edge to eat. She had drawn his hostility almost immediately. An armed truce seemed to open up between them. She was conscious of the murmuring currents of conversation around the table, the chime and chink of cutlery on china. She shared a brief glance down the table with Fisk, who looked at her enquiringly. She turned back to Colonel Cho, and changed tack.

A neutral subject. She smiled. "Do you have children?"

He brightened at once. "A son, aged nine, in the Young Pioneers. And you? You are half Korean, I'm guessing. You have family in Korea?"

"A twin sister." Her heart missed a beat. The words had fallen out before she could stop herself.

She blinked, and felt her face redden.

"Really?" He was distracted by the sight of Ambassador Shin engaged in an animated conversation with the former secretary of state. "In Seoul?"

"Not in Seoul ..." Her eyes were fixed on him now. She had a vague awareness that she was losing her focus. Some trip-wired charge deep inside her had released a sudden rush of grievances. Her urge to say them to this bastard shocked her. "I hope to be reunited with her ..." She was veering dangerously off message now, but an emotion too strong to control was overriding all her caution, all her training. She might never get a chance to say this again. "... if your government would permit her to leave."

The spoon stopped halfway to Cho's mouth. He put it down and stared at her.

"Your sister is in my country?"

A siren began wailing in her head, but much too late.

"She was ... taken there. Twelve years ago. From a beach in South Korea. Her name is Soo-min."

He gazed at her for what seemed like a full minute. When he finally spoke he reverted to Korean. "You are mistaken. If you're referring to the unfortunate issue of the abducted people, my government has publicly accounted for all of them, living and dead, and has apologized. The matter is resolved and in the past." He spoke as if correcting her on a point of law. "But apart from that you are wrong for another reason."

"I feel sure you're about to tell me."

166

"The people of my country are racially …" He cast about for a delicate word. "… *homogenous*. A twin of yours would not go unnoticed. I would know about her."

Jenna felt a faintness come over her, as if her knees might buckle if she tried to get up.

"There have been so many Western lies about this," he went on, finishing his soup. "You should understand that most of those so-called abductees voluntarily defected *to* my country—for a fairer life."

"Indeed," she said, trying to iron out the tremble from her voice. "I can't imagine why anyone would think they'd been taken there against their will …"

"What makes you think she's there?"

She pushed back her chair. "Would you excuse me?"

Oh, God. Jenna faced her reflection in the powder-room mirror. *What have I said?* She felt as if her chest were stuffed with hot rice, squeezing her heart and making her breathing labored. *I'm fucking this up.* Fisk had recruited her in the belief that this issue—this very issue—would enhance her capability, not undermine it. She reapplied her lipstick and gave herself a hard, appraising stare.

For Fisk's sake, for Soo-min's—do your job.

When she returned, the main course had been served. Hamburgers, fries, grits, ribs, and Buffalo chicken wings, the soft cultural propaganda of the American common fare, even if the fries, she noticed, had been tossed in rosemary and sea salt, and the buns looked distinctly artisan.

"Mr. Cho," the former president called with his mouth full, "food like this greases the wheels of American diplomacy."

Cho said, "As a matter of fact, it was our Dear Leader Kim Jong-il who invented the 'double-bun-with-meat'—"

The Americans laughed in loud, delighted hoots. The former president dropped his cutlery and gave a sporting clap of his hands.

Jenna was the only one of them who knew Cho wasn't joking.

The discussion became dominated by individuals addressing the table at large and Jenna saw that she would not have another opportunity to engage Cho. All tiresomely *male*, she thought, though each of them gave way respectfully when the aged former secretary of state croaked his Delphic pronouncements from the head of the table.

For dessert and coffee the guests switched seats. The Wall Street CEO was complaining about federal restrictions on asset management to a row of blank Korean faces. Fisk and the former secretary of state were deep in discussion with Cho. Jenna found herself seated with the tall and gangling Chris O'Brien, whom she found far too gentle and amiable a man to be handling a hissing, spitting alley cat like North Korea.

"He's a curious one, isn't he?" O'Brien said, casting a cautious glance toward Cho.

They watched Cho declaiming to his listeners, back straight, fist laid imperiously on the table. From the ill-concealed annoyance on Fisk's face she guessed that he was making about as much progress as she had. She noticed that Cho kept glancing in her direction, and none too subtly, as if he couldn't quite believe how insulted he'd been by being placed opposite her at dinner.

"He's smart, I'll give him that," O'Brien said, speaking from behind his coffee cup. "But the mask doesn't slip. Behaves like he's a true believer. If I were a member of the elite like Colonel Cho Sang-ho . . . with access to hard currency and foreign travel . . . I'd be plotting my exit strategy."

The former president stood to take his leave and conversations around the table petered out. The evening was over.

Guests mingled near the door for a few minutes as farewells were said and hands shaken. Colonel Cho came over to her. To her surprise he said, "Should your duties bring you to Pyongyang, Miss Lee, I would be happy to be your guide."

He looked at her with a strange earnestness. She guessed this was one of the pleasantries said on these occasions, but the remark had a nervy, rehearsed feel to it. He handed her a business card with both hands and bowed.

Jenna accepted it, also with both hands, and mustered a smile. "Maybe I could visit something that's not on an official tour, or talk to people without the Bowibu present."

Cho gave a small, hurt smile that said *let's not spoil the mood.*

She gave him her own card, which simply bore the name Marianne Lee, and telephone number. He bowed again, and left.

"What was that about?" Fisk was next to her, loosening his tie. He looked as defeated as she felt. She checked her watch. It was 9:45 p.m. They'd hardly touched the wine at dinner.

"Stiff drink in the bar?" she said.

He smiled. "That's the nicest thing anyone's said to me this evening."

At that moment one of the Secret Service men approached. "Call for you, sir." He handed Fisk a phone.

Fisk was still smiling as he put the phone to his hear. Then slowly the smile died and his mouth fell open.

"Holy shit … Just keep him there … We're on our way." He ended the call. For a moment he looked stunned. Then there was a trace of amusement on his lips. "Get your coat. We're going to Brooklyn, 71st Precinct Police Station." He turned to her with a glint of excitement in his eyes. "Want a shot at recruiting your first asset?"

The man leapt to his feet the moment Jenna and Fisk entered the room.

"You cannot detain me! I am a United Nations diplomat."

He was about forty, and tall, with a gaunt face and coal-black intelligent eyes. An odd wen on his left cheek looked like a small beetle.

169

"Good evening, First Secretary Ma," Jenna said. "You are free to go, but it's important, for your sake, that we talk first. Please sit. This won't take a moment."

Fisk had briefed her in the car, and the FBI agent had just shown them the evidence bags. She took the chair across the desk from Ma. Fisk hung back, leaning against the wall to show that he was taking no part. Despite the freezing night it was intolerably stuffy in the chief's office. An electric fan ruffled Ma's hair. A fluorescent strip light blinked. Jenna slipped off her coat and watched him glare at her cocktail dress and jewelry, as if this were some offensive joke.

"Who are you? CIA?"

"I serve the federal government in an intelligence capacity."

"This conversation's over." He moved to get up.

Jenna switched to North Korean dialect, without any honorific register. "Sit the fuck down."

Ma froze in surprise, as if he'd been slapped. His eyes moved slowly from Jenna to Fisk and back to her. He sat.

She continued calmly in English. "You'll walk out of here with your money. You can inform Pyongyang that your transaction today went smoothly ..." She thought of the man in the trench coat they'd just seen in the station reception area, quizzing the desk officer. A well-known crime reporter from one of the tabloids. "Not a word of this will get out. As long as one thing's clear ..." She moved her face closer toward him across the desk. "You work for us now."

She was watching intently for his reaction, his succumbing. His shoulders sagged, but she saw no calculation in his eyes, no weighing of the risks, rather a bleak, angry acceptance, a resignation, like a man in his prime given a diagnosis for a terminal illness.

She said carefully, "You will of course be remunerated. We'll set up a secret escrow account ..."

He was shaking his head and she realized that the cough he gave was a dry, joyless laugh.

"You have no idea, do you?" he said, meeting her eyes. "Where I come from, everyone is watched. Everyone. Pyongyang had at least one set of eyes observing me in that parking lot tonight." As if to mock her, he too moved his face closer. "They already know I am here. And they'll know the CIA used the opportunity." The dark eyes sparkled. "Do you know what that means ... you dumb bitch?" His voice rose. "It means I'm finished. Dead."

He grabbed his parka from the back of his seat and left, letting the door slam behind him.

Jenna didn't move. She felt her hands tremble very slightly.

For a few seconds the room was silent except for the whirring of the fan, then Fisk said, "He just called your bluff."

Suddenly she got up and opened the door. The two FBI agents were waiting outside with the duty sergeant.

"The case is all yours," she said.

"What about the other guy?"

"Charge him." She reached for her coat.

"And the media?"

"There's a reporter in the lobby, I believe."

19

The Roosevelt Hotel
45 East 45th Street
New York City

The mood over breakfast was celebratory. Even Political Officer Yi seemed to have abandoned his vigilance, no longer sniffing the air for traces of unorthodoxy. All of them had congratulated Cho the night before, confident now in their association with him, delighted to have the shine of his glory reflected on them. One of the diplomats talked of the decoration that surely awaited him—the Kim Jong-il Medal, or the Order of Heroic Effort, at the very least—to which Cho, holding up his palms and laughing, had dissembled modestly. Ambassador Shin had left a message at reception to say that, unfortunately, neither he nor First Secretary Ma was able to accompany them to the airport today. He hoped they'd forgive this lapse in protocol and wished them a safe journey home.

To hell with them, Cho thought. He was on his way back to a garlanded homecoming.

As they were finishing their coffee they were informed that their driver had arrived and a bellhop was loading their luggage into the Toyota minivan.

At the souvenir shop near the reception desk Cho had bought a small thermometer set into a model of a skyscraper with the words

EMPIRE STATE BUILDING at the base, a box of assorted hard candies, and a junior-size New York Knicks basketball jersey as gifts for Books. He would buy perfume for his wife at the airport, or maybe a bracelet she could show discreetly to her friends. He did not think, in the circumstances, the political officers would object to him taking such items to Pyongyang.

The minivan set off and Cho lowered the window an inch. Cab horns, traffic fumes, coffee, fresh bagels. How easily he'd got used to the sounds and smells of a New York morning. He'd miss this when he got home. It had rained during the night, making the streets seem varnished and glossy. Patches of fast-moving clouds made a theatrical effect, with the vast buildings thrown into relief by moving arcs of light and shadow. Everything and everyone was suffused with a kind of superreality. It was magical—an illusion enhanced by the tiny lights and decorations that had appeared everywhere, in every storefront, restaurant, and lobby, as if by sudden decree. He had never seen a Christmas tree before.

America.

How false his idea had been. In fact it was the opposite of everything he'd thought. He'd considered himself too shrewd to believe the propaganda. Now he saw how deeply it had lodged in his psyche, from the anti-imperialist cartoons he'd watched as a boy to his English grammar course at Kim Il-sung University.

We killed Americans. We are killing Americans. We will kill Americans.

His knowledge of America had been learned from fables written by the Party. None of them matched his experience—the thrilling, vibrant, disorderly reality—of an American city.

He thought of the woman he'd sat opposite at dinner last night, Marianne Lee. Again, he felt an unease about her that he couldn't account for. Her lips on the rim of the wineglass; the way she'd watched him in a way that seemed mocking, curious, and vulnerable all at once. Her bare shoulders. She was undeniably beautiful.

Is that what was bothering him? That he desired her? It was a disloyal thought, and not just to his wife. The Leader took greatest pride in the purity of the race. Foreign blood, mixed blood, was a stain. And yet ... this was not making him feel the guilt he had expected. Had she told him her Korean name? He wasn't sure. Soomin? *No.* That was the *sister.* Cho shook his head absently. Crazy that she thought her sister was living in his country. She really seemed to believe it. Half Korean, half African American ... Extraordinary.

The evening had taken other strange turns, too. His face clouded. He had never heard of Camp 22, though he did not doubt its existence. He simply knew it was better not to know. But what on earth was she getting at? And General Fisk, whispering in his ear about the rocket. *What are you hoping to arm it with?* The capability to place a satellite in orbit must indeed have alarmed them. It was proof that his country had entered the league of technically advanced nations.

He hummed to himself, drumming his fingers on the arm of his seat while the two junior diplomats and the political officers talked among themselves in the seats in front. The lights turned red at a large intersection and the minivan came to a stop alongside a taxicab with the driver's window down. The yellow of the cabs seemed unusually bright today, a rapeseed yellow. The cab driver adjusted his bead-covered seat, scratched the back of his neck, and unfolded the *New York Daily News* on the steering wheel. Cho tilted his head to read the headline.

FEDS ARREST NORTH KOREAN DIPLOMAT IN DRUGS BUST

He remembered nothing more of the journey to JFK. The moment the minivan reached the terminal he ran to a news store, bought the *New York Daily News,* and walked away without waiting for his change, throwing out the pages until he found it.

North Korean UN diplomat was dealing in narcotics, authorities said.

First Secretary Ma Jae-kwon, 41, was arrested by federal agents in Brooklyn after being caught handing over drugs with an estimated street value of $2,000,000 to a known criminal gang. The feds, who had the gang under surveillance, were surprised to discover that the supplier was a diplomat.

Ma has claimed diplomatic immunity and has refused to cooperate, but his contact in the gang, Omar Calixto Fernandez, 32, has admitted to receiving a package containing crystal methamphetamine. The drug, also known as tina and ice, is thought to have been smuggled through JFK in a North Korean diplomatic pouch . . .

Pages slipped from Cho's hands. He gazed around, trying to breathe and steady himself, but his feet were weightless, and the check-in hall's lights had become distant strobes that hurt his eyes. The space around him was a blur that began to spin.

"Colonel?" One of the junior diplomats was at his elbow, regarding him with alarm. "You've turned extremely pale."

20

Regional Bureau of the Ministry of State Security (the Bowibu)
Hyesan
Ryanggang Province, North Korea

The overhead lights hummed to a bright yellow before dimming again. On the neck of the man standing in front of Mrs. Moon, an angry boil winked from between hat and collar. He was called to the desk. She was next in line.

She'd walked past the building three times. It was a squat, gray modern edifice, three stories high, that bore no external signage, no hint of the organization that occupied it, yet she felt sure there was no one in Hyesan who did not know what this place was. The limit of Sergeant Jang's courage had been to find out the name of the arresting officer. She'd been about to walk past a fourth time when she felt the sentries' eyes following her. She breathed in and entered before fear got the better of her.

The two lieutenants behind the main desk ignored her for at least ten minutes. She tried to calm herself by resting her eyes on the only dash of color—a full-length portrait of the Great Leader on the summit of Mount Paektu, coattails flying behind him, arm pointing into the dawn—and by thinking of Tae-hyon, whom she'd left sleeping in bed this morning. He'd have a stroke if he knew where she was now. With a pang of regret she realized what little role he played in her decisions these days. An out-of-work husband was as a useful as a streetlight in daylight. She was wishing she hadn't drunk a second cup of tea with her breakfast when one of the men beckoned her forward with an impatient flick of a finger.

Mrs. Moon approached, feeling her stomach turn to water. "I wish to speak to Inspector Kim."

"There are five inspectors called Kim," he said without looking up. He was cleaning something with a damp cloth—the congealed ink off a rubber stamp.

"The Inspector Kim who made the Bible arrests this week."

The man looked sharply up. "You have an appointment?"

"I have information."

His eyes did not leave her face as he picked up a telephone. Then he dialed a three-digit number and spoke to someone, lowering his head so that she couldn't hear.

"Follow me," he said.

Inspector Kim flicked through Mrs. Moon's ID passbook without interest. Half the space in his narrow office was taken up by a bank of gleaming filing cabinets. On his desk was a telephone with touch buttons instead of a dial, and a television with some sort of keyboard. The room's only other furniture was a metal chair, which she was not being offered, and the Father-Son portraits.

"What do you know about those Bibles, grandmother?" he said, tossing her ID passbook onto the desk. He was a short, brutish man in his forties, with small dark eyes and skin the off-white color of a maggot. The brown uniform was new and fitted well. His revolver belt smelt of fresh leather.

"Nothing, Inspector. Only that you arrested Curly—Mrs. Ong, I mean. She's a trader in our market at the train station. It was a terrible shock for us—me and all the women—when we heard she was mixed up in such a thing. The street kids told us what happened—"

Inspector Kim silenced her with a raised palm. He looked tired. "*Kotchebi* ..." he said, getting up. "Those kids are the eyes and ears. If only they all worked for me."

He pulled open a drawer in one of the cabinets and lifted out a file.

"Ong Sol-joo ..." he said, studying it. Over the top Mrs. Moon glimpsed what looked like a charge sheet with Curly's mug shot taken from the side and face-on. She had on her headscarf. "Also known as *Curly*. Christian. Active member of a subversive criminal element, a house church. Charged with distributing seditious literature. One daughter, Sun-i, aged twelve. Evaded arrest. Still unaccounted for ..." He sat back down and flicked open his notebook.

His pen was poised. He was looking at Mrs. Moon. "Let's have it."

His eyes had a deadness in them that frightened her, as if they were watching her through a tank of stagnant water. They held not a trace of kindness.

"I've come to ..." The room felt warm suddenly. The words she'd prepared turned to stones in her mouth.

Inspector Kim dropped his pen and massaged his eyes with his knuckles. "Look, grandmother, I thought I'd be taking the mountain air today, getting my back rubbed by one of those beauties at the hot springs. As it is I've been on duty all night and now I'm with another old peasant who's wondering who to denounce for a few extra food coupons." His voice rose. "Do you know where this bitch daughter is, or don't you?"

Mrs. Moon glared at him. In some room down the corridor telephones rang and switchboard operators transferred calls.

Oh yes, she could imagine him interrogating Curly in a cell, slapping her about the face. This pitiless cold bastard with his strangler's hands.

Mrs. Moon tilted her head back slightly. Her voice was cool.

"I've come to ask for the release of Ong Sol-joo."

The dead eyes came to life for moment. After a pause he closed his notebook. "What's she to you?"

"A close friend and a good socialist."

"That all?" He leaned back in his chair. His leather belt creaked. "Or have you caught this religion, too?"

"No, sir, I wish to vouch for her excellent character and ask you to let her go."

There was a bored amusement on his lips now. "And you've brought a release order signed by Comrade Kim Jong-il himself, have you? Or you're going to tell me she's innocent and there's been a dreadful misunderstanding. You're a bit late." He laid his hand flat on the file and gave a breathy laugh. "She confessed. We didn't even need to show her the instruments."

"She will make amends for her error."

"Get out, old woman." He snatched up Mrs. Moon's ID passbook and threw it at her so that it struck her on her breast and fell to the floor. "You're lucky I'm keen to go home."

Her joints groaned as she bent to pick it up. She had a sudden image of the portrait in the lobby.

"Did you ever meet the Great Leader, Inspector?" she said straightening back up stiffly. "I was in that presence once. It was like facing the sun." Inspector Kim looked at her uncertainly. Without taking her eyes off him she said, "The morning he visited our farm, workers came from miles to see him. We sat in the field like children, hundreds of us. And when he spoke I felt he was speaking only to me, as if he knew everything about me. He had an aura of great ..." She breathed in as she chose the word. "... dignity. Her voice hardened. "So remember who you represent."

A wariness glinted in his eyes before they went dead again. It was unwise to interrupt a paean to Kim Il-sung.

"You know what my school teachers used to say?" Mrs. Moon smiled and it wrinkled her whole face. "No one in history is greater than Kim Il-sung. Not Buddha in kindness, not Christ in love, not Confucius in virtue ..." As she said this her hands moved slowly to her money belt at the front of her apron. Still her eyes did not move from Inspector Kim. "Inspector, don't you think that a heart as great as his could forgive a young woman her folly?" She began cautiously to unzip the money belt. His eyes seemed hypnotized by the movement of her hand. "You're not saying that her pathetic delusions could harm our Revolution ..."

"What are you doing, grandmother?"

"I am showing you how sorry Curly is for her mistake. We're reminded every day that the Great Leader is always with us. In his mercy ... would he not forgive her?"

She extended her arm toward the desk and opened her fist. His eyes flared as the roll of bills fell from her hand. Red hundred-yuan bills wound tightly by an elastic band. Mao's red eye and chin wart facing up, wobbling as the roll came to a stop. It was as if a light had been shone into Inspector Kim's face—his features were suddenly bright and alert. He stood up, almost knocking over his chair, walked the five paces past Mrs. Moon to the door, and yelled into the corridor. "Get me the duty sergeant!" He turned toward her. "Should've gone when you had the chance, old woman. Now you've—"

The expression on his face made him look oafish; simple even. She was dealing with a human after all.

On the desk was a second, identical roll of red yuan bills, to which she had added a third, and now a fourth. Finally she took out a large clear-plastic sachet of crystalline white powder—hundreds of grams of *bingdu*, worth as much as all the cash—and placed it next to them. His eyes were darting from one to the next. His face went slack, as if he couldn't grasp what was happening, or who she was. Slowly he closed the door and locked it, returned to his chair, and sat down, knitting his thick fingers together on the desk, staring at the bribe. After what seemed like a full minute he looked up and met her gaze.

21

The day before Thanksgiving Jenna got up early to run, despite getting home late from New York the previous night. Warming up along the canal towpath in the predawn gloom, she was determined to cast Colonel Cho Sang-ho from her mind, and First Secretary Ma, and that whole damned evening.

If she'd only trusted her instinct, she told herself, she'd have known that what Mrs. Ishido had told her was true; what Cho had told her was false. Cho was a functionary, a face from a propaganda poster, a minion who followed the regime's script. Such infuriating arrogance, and yet he was probably in no position to know anything about Soo-min. She was so focused on forgetting him, she realized, that she couldn't stop thinking about him. She lengthened her stride to a full sprint, taking satisfaction in her strength, in the sheer physical power her training was giving her. She had never felt so fit. She was striving for full steam, pushing her body toward its top speed, when her phone rang. She slowed down and stalled. Panting hard, she unstrapped it from her arm, frowned at the screen, and had a sudden premonition of fate. The number had the prefix +82. South Korea.

It took her a moment to figure out what the distant voice on the other end was talking about. A man was saying that he was an officer of the South Korean National Intelligence Service in Seoul. He was calling about her application to the Ministry of Justice seeking permission to speak with a special Category A prisoner named Sin Gwang-su, being held at the Pohang Maximum Security Penitentiary.

Jenna went dead still. In the five weeks since she'd begun her training, this had gone right to the back of her mind. She'd sent that application more than a month ago, soon after meeting Mrs. Ishido in Geneva.

He said, "Are you aware of who this prisoner is?"

A captured North Korean commando held in solitary. "Yes, I'm aware."

A long pause at the other end. She tried to think what time it was over there. Late in the evening. "I'm afraid we can't grant this request unless there's a very compelling reason ... May I ask you what your interest is in this prisoner?"

Jenna turned to face the slow black water of the canal, and saw Soo-min's figure reflected back at her.

"I believe he abducted my sister."

The call ended with him promising to refer the matter up the chain. He sounded dubious and noncommittal. She sat down on a bench and dropped her face into her hands. That was a blow she could have done without today.

That evening, when Jenna went to bed, it was a mild, clear night in fall. When she awoke on Thanksgiving Day morning, it was winter. The leaves of her maple tree were furred in frost; the ground diamond hard and sparkling. Through the kitchen window Cat watched her from the top of the yard wall, and yawned a mouth of needles. Voices on the radio chirped and chuckled about the cold front sweeping Virginia. Snow was on the way.

She made her coffee, turned on her laptop, and saw, at the top of her inbox, an e-mail from the South Korean Correctional Service. Her heart began to race.

Her call with the Pohang Maximum Security Penitentiary had been booked for 13:00 tomorrow. It would terminate automatically after fifteen minutes, or immediately if any of the regulations below were violated. There followed a list of topics she was not permitted to discuss with a Category A prisoner, including explosives and anything of a lewd and sexually explicit nature.

13:00 in South Korea tomorrow ... *is midnight in DC tonight.*

Suddenly a horrible fear seized her at the thought of who she would be speaking with. It overcame her with such waves of vertigo that she sat motionless, breathing slowly for several minutes until it had passed.

She had already been dreading Thanksgiving. After weeks inside the closed world of the Farm, she felt unusually exposed to the strain of a family occasion. Now it awaited her like a severe trial. She looked at Cat, still watching her from the yard wall. How was she going to make it through the day?

A smell of roasting turkey blanketed the small apartment. Over the cheer and oompah of the Macy's parade on TV in the next room came the yip of her mother's laugh, followed by the velvet bass of her uncle's, and the chinking of glasses.

A low sizzle emanated from the oven. Jenna dried her hands and reread the instructions for the gravy. The practicalities had in fact calmed her, restored her sense of method, given her a space to think, and she realized that she was actually glad to have the distraction of company. As the morning went on, as she basted and stuffed, chopped and mashed, she succeeded in pushing aside thoughts of the midnight phone call, and the rush of terror she'd felt was now just a trickle of anxiety.

The banter of newly dropped male voices sounded in the yard—her cousins back from their turkey trot. Steam rose from the black frizz of their hair. Cedric and Maya's two adolescent boys entered trailing freezing air and a tang of male sweat. "Yo, Aunty Han." Hot plates were laid. Uncle Cedric uncorked the wine and the boys took their seats, talking across each other over the buzz of the carving knife. "One dude was dressed as Colonel Saunders. He had this rubber chicken under his arm—"

"Are we all here?" Han said in Korean, peering through the window. "I thought I heard a car." She'd been to the hair salon, Jenna saw, and wore a new crimson blouse, with a matching lipstick, and trimmings of gold and pearl jewelry that made her resemble some extravagant Christmas decoration. It was pathetically obvious she'd hoped Jenna was hosting the day in order to surprise them with the introduction of a man.

"We're all here, Omma, and we're speaking English today."

Once Han had led them in saying grace, they wished each other a happy Thanksgiving. Uncle Cedric asked Jenna what was new in her life—camouflage netting, she suspected, for the *man* question. Aunt Maya asked about her new job.

"I'm ... working for the government."

"Sounds hush-hush and exciting."

It is exciting. For a moment Jenna smiled. Her report on the secret laboratory had made it into the president's daily brief—the first thing he'd read with his coffee in the morning. Then her mind turned to her encounter with First Secretary Ma, whose fate she had almost certainly sealed, and the brutality of the Farm, and her smile faded.

The boys ate their pie in front of the game, and Jenna insisted everyone relax while she cleared away. She was stacking the dishwasher when she heard the kitchen door click shut behind her. Han was facing her, leaning against the closed door.

With ominous calm she said, "What's wrong?"

Her jewelry glittered and her face was partly in shadow, which gave an air of melodrama.

"Nothing's wrong." Jenna began wiping surfaces. "It's been a wonderful day."

"You've been gulping wine, which is not like you, and you're far away. It's like talking to someone who's not there."

"Just a little tired," she said, annoyed. Han's sixth sense was becoming honed with age.

Han gave a rough little shake of her head. "This is something to do with Soo-min."

"It's not." Jenna tried not to look away but her face was betraying her, and her mother's expression registered what she saw.

"I'm right." Han remained motionless. Her voice was distant thunder over the ocean. "Why can't you let your sister's soul rest in peace?"

"Omma," Jenna said, knowing she was being cruel. "We all believed that drowning story but now I'm getting nearer the truth."

Han's eyes flared angrily for a moment, then became magnified by tears.

"Oh, here." Jenna plucked at a sheet of paper towel and dried her mother's eyes and held her small plump figure, her mom, whose tears smelt of freesias and ginger lily. "I'm sorry." And she began to cry herself.

Later, when it began to snow in great silent flakes, and the apartment was still and dim and Cat slunk somewhere in the shadows, Jenna sat immobile on the sofa, staring at the phone lying on the coffee table.

The living room clock ticked remorselessly toward midnight. Midnight in DC. 1:00 p.m. tomorrow in South Korea. Just a minute to go. The lights in her apartment were off, but the living room was filled with a diffuse glow of snow reflecting in streetlights. Snow swirled and eddied, building a small drift in her yard that seemed to muffle and deaden her fear, leaving her cold and with a feeling that was something akin to hatred.

The minute hand reached midnight. Almost robotically she picked up the phone to make the call. She had the number written down next to her, and was about to punch it in when a long ringing tone made her jump. It was coming from her laptop behind her. She stood up and stared at it as if something supernatural was materializing on her desk.

A Skype call?

And that's when she remembered that she'd entered her Skype address on the application request to the South Koreans, weeks ago.

It rang twice, three times. She sat at the desk and answered it.

A cacophony of noise and static, from male voices talking, and a face appeared, too close to the screen. The shaven head was brutal in the gray-yellow light. A second later, her own camera connected, and the face locked into hers. The eyes had a ferocious directness. The mouth grimaced, showing canines. Behind him she could see a seated prison guard talking to another who was out of sight.

"Who is this?" the face said, very close, his mouth filling the screen. Violence crackled about him like static. "What do you want with me?" He spoke with the strong accent of the North.

Jenna's throat had gone dry. She opened her mouth but her words had fled.

"No need to hide in the shadows," he said. "Turn a light on over there."

Slowly Jenna reached over, turned on her desk lamp and angled it so that it shone brightly into her face.

She watched him squint at her for a moment and then a look of confusion spread over him, as if there had been some bizarre mistake, and recognition sparked in his eyes.

Jenna nodded, and felt her nails making deep gouges in the seat of the chair.

"Do you see me now?"

22

Hyesan Train Station
Ryanggang Province, North Korea

One of Kyu's *kotchebi* arrived with the anemones Mrs. Moon had ordered. She arranged them in a beer bottle and placed them in the center of a table surrounded by customers, then stood back to admire them. Bright pink with flame-orange stamens, they were a burst of color.

Kyu, watching from his perch on top of the rice sacks, tipped his head back to exhale a leisurely puff of white smoke. In a distant valley a train's horn sounded its funeral-barge note. Midafternoon, and the day was dark already.

Her bribe to the Bowibu had cleaned out the cooperative. The women had little money left, which would make life precarious for a while, and yet a warm humor had spread among them. They told stories that had each other weak with laughter. They made jokes about their husbands that only women could do together. Later, Kyu would fetch Sun-i from her hiding place in the bottling plant. Curly was being returned to them this evening. The flowers were for her.

Curly was being detained at a Bowibu holding camp outside Hyesan. Kyu's face had darkened when Mrs. Moon told him that.

"It's where they throw people caught running away to China," he said. "One week in that place ... no one runs again."

As news of Curly's imminent release spread, people had begun greeting Mrs. Moon with a marked respect. Rumors were everywhere. One had it that a market woman had called in favors from powerful men in Pyongyang; another that she had millionaire relatives in Japan, or connections among the Chinese triads, which even the Bowibu feared. With amazement she realized that these rumors were about her.

The rest of the day at Moon's Korean Barbecue passed in such a frenzy of work that she had no time to think of anything but cooking and serving. Work distracted her from checking the station clock every minute and glancing about for Curly's face. A biting easterly began sweeping down from the Changbai Mountains. The joints in her knees were inflamed and her fingers were stiffening, but as always she waved away Kyu's offer of the *bingdu* pipe.

Grandma Whiskey, whose face was a yellow bud swaddled with scarves, announced that gas for the burner was running low, so Mrs. Moon tied her A-frame to her back and told Kyu she was heading across town to buy a canister.

"When Curly arrives, put her next to the brazier and give her dinner."

As she left the market, Mrs. Moon glanced again at the station clock.

23

O Street
Georgetown
Washington, DC

Jenna watched the confusion on the man's face turn to disbelief. He glanced quickly over his shoulder at the two guards talking behind him, then scrambled to put on a pair of headphones and plugged them in.

He said, "But ... You're calling from America."

"Yes."

"How?"

She focused all her energy into presenting a calm expression. Her pulse was knocking against her throat.

"I can't talk about that. You understand."

He closed his eyes and nodded. "I understand."

His arrogance was in abeyance and Jenna saw that he was older than he'd seemed at first. The aggression of his features had delayed, for a few moments, the realization that he was at least sixty.

The conversation paused. She felt panic again, her mind clutching for something to say without giving herself away. His narrow eyes were watching her, and she remembered a reporter's trick. *Say nothing. Let him fill the silences.*

"Forgive me," he said, forcing a nervous smile, "I am a rough fellow. I thought you'd be another reporter snooping—" The Skype signal cut out for a second or two. "—if I'd known it was you …" He bowed his head, so that she saw the top of his goblin-like skull. Jenna's mind was reeling, but she remained silent. She had no idea where this was going. He put his fist to his chest. "I am loyal unto the death—" The signal cut out again, and the screen froze his face in a grimace of defiance. "—want you to know that. The bastards here offered me a deal," he said loudly and tilting his head up, so that the guards behind him could hear. "I gave them *nothing*."

Jenna shook her head, beginning to warm to her role. She marveled at the power this deception was giving her. "If you've betrayed anything … Do not think you are beyond reach in a prison." His eyes glared with hurt pride. This man, she saw, was unafraid of death. She was improvising wildly now. "I have been curious about you for a long time, Sin Gwang-su."

"Me?"

The signal cut out. Again his face froze, this time in surprise. The delay in reconnecting was longer this time, four or five seconds, and the pounding of Jenna's heart grew faster.

She said, "I owe you a debt of gratitude. For what you did, taking me from that beach. It is because of you that I have purpose, I have pride." She emphasized the words, hoping to imbue them with meaning they didn't have. "You seem surprised."

He shook his head, in admiration. "You … resisted our teachings so fiercely. You wouldn't follow orders. I … Forgive me. Please forgive me. I know we had our differences." He dropped his head again in respect. "I'm just so impressed. It is not always easy to change someone with the Truth."

Jenna felt adrenalin coursing through her. She sensed a path opening. "So … you did not know that I'd left the … facility?"

"I knew that you'd been transferred to Section 915."

The receptors in her brain were sparking. The effort not to show her excitement was tremendous. She managed to shake her head gently, as if reminiscing. "Section 915 …"

He gave a jittery laugh. "… the Seed-Bearing Program was not a project a fellow like me ever got to see, you understand."

"We 915 girls are an exclusive group …"

"You earn your privileges."

The signal cut again, freezing an expression of awe on Sin Gwang-su's face for two, three seconds. The signal returned. "… he has shown you great favor," he murmured solemnly. She felt herself begin to tremble now and knew she could not maintain her composure a second longer. He said, "He made you one of the—"

The signal died and the screen went dark. She waited a minute, feeling herself perspiring as if she'd been for a hard run, but it did not return.

She closed the lid of the laptop. Suddenly she shot out of the chair, clutching her hands to her head.

All her thoughts were shuffled up and scattered, like a deck of cards flung in the air. She threw open the French windows and rushed outside, desperate to cool the blaze in her mind with frigid air. She turned her face upward and breathed in. Snowflakes melted icily on her face. How could it be possible to feel such extremes of emotion at once? She had never felt such horror and excitement, such hope and despair.

What in God's name is the Seed-Bearing Program?

Distantly, in another room, her phone was ringing. She ignored it. But then after a pause it rang again, and she ran to answer it.

Fisk said, "I'm picking you up tomorrow at seven a.m."

"Where am I going?"

"The CIA director wants to see us."

24

Hyesan Airport
Ryanggang Province, North Korea

It was late afternoon when Mrs. Moon got to the depot on the far side of the city. Her contact usually rolled out the gas canister when his boss wasn't looking and she slipped the money into his pocket, but for some reason the place was unattended. Then her eye was caught by the beam of a floodlight sweeping across the clouds from somewhere behind the depot—the airport.

The distant rushing sound she could hear was like the sound of the river after it had rained in the mountains, until she remembered that she was quite far from the river. She turned and peered into the darkness of the road that led back into the city and realized that the sound was the murmuring and whispering of a great mass of people. It ebbed and then grew louder and then she saw it—the shadowy crowd approaching, escorted by soldiers. As they drew nearer she could make out distinct groups: factory workers in indigo overalls, construction corps wearing hard hats, city officials in their Mao suits, uniformed Socialist Youth. Tiny, blackened *kotchebi* were darting ahead and running about. She tightened her money belt and made sure it was zipped and hidden.

What was going on? For minutes the huge throng walked past her. Mothers with children, market vendors, railroad workers. Then she spotted Mrs. Lee in the crowd, and Grandma Whiskey—and Kyu! Who was watching the canteen?

A group of elegant women glided by in their long *chima jeogori* dresses, hostesses from some Party cadre's restaurant, being jostled along the road, their powdered faces stiff as masks.

The next thing she knew a soldier was shining a flashlight at her, and signaled impatiently for her to join the crowd. Then she was being herded with everyone else, moved along in a crush of bodies that was becoming denser by the minute. Everyone was being shepherded toward the airport. Voices muttered, cursed, cussed. It was as if the soldiers had rounded up everyone they'd found in the streets, and emptied the factories and shops and offices of their workers.

A young soldier was gesturing them onward with a sweep of his rifle butt. "What's happening?" she said.

"People's trial."

A few hundred yards ahead, between the heads of the crowd, she saw the single-story airport building with its stubby tower and a smiling portrait of the Great Leader, and the runway, lined with old propeller planes. Parked in the middle of the runway was a dark-green military jeep, on top of which were mounted two enormous floodlights. The movement of the crowd slowed and became an immobile scrimmage as a cordon of police motioned for everyone to spread out along the side of the runway, but still the crowds continued to arrive, several thousand people, so that the mass of spectators along the edge was dozens deep. The whole of Hyesan had been brought here. The smallest children—Young Pioneers in red neckerchiefs and ragged *kotchebi*—squirmed their way through to the front to claim prime positions.

Night was falling like a cloud of ash. The only light came from the floodlights on the jeep and a small electric light above the Great Leader's portrait. A strange, sinister tension was running through crowd. Nerves and fear mixed with the anticipated thrill of horror, as if an act were about to start. Then, in the blackness to the right, at the far end of the runway, two amber headlights came on. The truck must have been waiting there, because now it approached slowly in low gear. As it came nearer to the light, helmeted guards with submachine guns could be seen standing in the back, but it was too dark to glimpse the prisoners through the wooden slats. The wheels bounced across a crack in the concrete and a clink of chains could be heard from inside. The truck came to a halt in the focused beam of the two floodlights.

The rear hatch dropped open and the guards jumped out. They ran behind the airport building and emerged wheeling a long, heavy wooden platform. A collective intake of air was heard from the crowd, like the breath of some powerful beast. The platform had a row of eight, evenly placed stakes, each about the height of a man, protruding from it. The guards maneuvered the platform to a right angle on the runway so that it was on the crowd's left and facing the truck.

The first prisoner was led out, a teenage boy who had soiled himself. His ankles were in chains and a dirty cloth blindfolded his eyes. He was whimpering softly. A few jeers went up, but most of the crowd remained silent and many, Mrs. Moon saw, were looking away. He was followed by a woman of about her own age who might have been a factory worker, and a young man and woman in good-quality clothes whom Mrs. Moon guessed were husband and wife. The husband's cheeks were streamed with tears, but the wife's face, what Mrs. Moon could see of it, was blue with fear. For some reason, she thought it shocking that they were wearing their own clothes, not prison uniforms. After them came a slender young woman in a headscarf, and a young soldier who'd had his insignia and stripes ripped from his uniform.

They were led in a file toward the wooden platform, their chains dragging on the concrete. The final two prisoners were both young men whose clothes had been torn, and she could see that their faces, even with blindfolds, were blackened and puffy from beatings. One of them stumbled and fell and was picked up and carried by two guards. The chains and the tips of his feet dragged along the concrete.

On the platform, each prisoner's head, chest, and waist were being tied to a stake. Then their hands and feet were tied together behind the stake. The whole operation was completed with synchronized swiftness. The guards then stepped in front of each prisoner and forced something into their faces: some sort of metal clasp that sprung apart in the open mouth and expanded it, stopping them uttering a word. Now the floodlights' beams swung fully onto the platform, illuminating in the glare a gruesome sight. Eight condemned, trussed to wooden stakes like carcasses, their mouths grotesque holes in their faces.

In the bright lights the yellow of the young woman's scarf shone as brilliantly as a sunflower, and Mrs. Moon's entrails turned to ice.

Without thinking about what she was doing, she charged into the scrum of bodies, shoving, butting, squeezing her way through to the front. She had a single thought—that a terrible mistake had been made and she had to fix it before it was too late. Soon she was within arm's length of the front of the crowd, but her way was blocked by two soldiers whose backs formed an impenetrable wall of khaki and leather. With a violent lunge she drove her shoulder between them, sending them crashing into people either side of them. Shouts rose around her. "Watch it, you bitch." Someone grabbed her elbow but she struggled free. Finally she was at the edge of the runway where the Pioneers and kotchebi were sitting cross-legged. Their faces drawn by the commotion, one of them rose up from the ground right in front of her and stopped her with his hand. It was Kyu. His shaman's eyes stared fiercely into hers. "There's nothing we can do," he whispered.

Mrs. Moon looked in horror from Kyu to the platform. "Oh, Sun-i ..." she whispered.

Curly's face was expressionless; her skin was cream white, with one livid red mark across her cheek. Guards standing behind each prisoner pulled the blindfolds off in unison, as if they'd rehearsed the act. The prisoners blinked, blinded in the glare. Then—in what Mrs. Moon knew was deliberate theater—the small electric light illuminating the Great Leader's portrait went out, and a gasp arose from the crowd. God's face was veiled; the darkness beyond the floodlights complete.

She had been so distracted by the platform that she had not noticed the row of court officials in black robes that now stood facing the crowd. In front of the judges a microphone was placed, and a Party orator in a plain brown tunic stepped up to it. He stood motionless until the crowd was silent and still. Slowly, he began reading out the names of the condemned, his voice made metallic by a sound system mounted on the jeep.

"... These men and women who stand before you are charged with conspiring to form an antisocialist criminal faction; with distributing seditious literature; and with treason of the first degree. They have made the fullest possible confession of their crimes ..."

He pointed at the platform but his eyes remained on the crowd. He was a small, hard-looking man with a wide, thin slit of a mouth and a grating voice.

"These accused, these criminals, who are corrupt and sick of mind, have plotted to undermine our Revolution by practicing their pernicious religion ..."

One or two exclamations of anger broke out from the crowd.

"They have selfishly conspired to spread untold poison among you, the glorious and pure people of Kim Il-sung ..."

On the platform the teenage boy's eyes began to roll in their sockets. His gaping mouth was drooling, as if he were having a seizure.

"They have turned their backs on his teachings, and on his love ..." The speaker gave a sorrowful shake of his head. "They have reveled in their selfishness, their ingratitude ..."

The crowd seemed to stir and flex as if it were a single organism, reacting to a coarse energy in the voice. As surely as if the sky had clouded over, Mrs. Moon sensed the mood darken.

"So infected are they by the foreign disease of their beliefs ..."
The orator's voice began to rise. "... beliefs wholly alien to our way
of life, that not one of them—not one of them, citizens!—has
renounced the cancer of their faith when offered the benevolent
mercy of Kim Il-sung."

An ominous murmur rippled outward, a sighing and heaving of
anger. Someone in the back yelled, "Shoot them like dogs!"

"These men and women are beyond reeducation. They are
beyond redemption." He opened his arms. "Comrades! Brothers
and sisters! When we find cancer in a body, do we not cut it out?"

The murmuring grew louder, and the children at the front broke
into a frenzy of applause.

"Do we not act resolutely, without hesitation—before it spreads?"

"Yes, yes, yes!" came the chants.

"Do we not act in the only way we can, in the Korean way, with
Korean speed?"

"Shoot them! Shoot them!"

The speaker held up his palms, his face an expression of solemn
duty.

"I hear the justice you, the people, demand. The Party obeys the
will of the masses because the Party and the masses are one."

A gathering swell of applause rose from all around.

"In the name of the Party, the sentence is: death by firing squad!"

The cheer was deafening and Mrs. Moon felt nauseous. The crowd
was in the grip of an ecstasy of vengeance. And afterward, she knew,
no one would recognize the baying beasts they had briefly become.

A firing squad of three soldiers grouped mechanically before the
first prisoner, the teenage boy, and raised their rifles. A gurgling
noise came from the hole in his face. He was scanning the crowds,
his eyes naked with animal terror.

The stutter of shots—*pan-pan-pan*—echoed off the airport
building, to more loud applause. The boy's body twitched and
jerked.

Somewhere a child was crying. Children were hiding in the folds of their parents' clothes. But the faces of the *kotchebi* sitting on the concrete were eager, fascinated, drinking in every detail.

Kyu said, "Come, ajumma, let's get you away."

But Mrs. Moon would not move. She would not look at the next execution, nor the one after. In the periphery of her vision she was aware of the powerful beam moving from one prisoner to the next as the firing squad dispatched each one. But she forced her eyes open for Curly, staring boldly at her, projecting a ray of love toward her. And to her amazement, in the bright focus of light, Curly's eyes were calm, showing no sign of terror, even with that obscene contraption in her mouth. Her breathing, white vapor in the cold air, was steady.

Afterward, Mrs. Moon knew she had imagined it, but if it were possible to read words in someone's eyes, she thought she understood. And though she had not thought of those words in decades, they were still known to her.

Though I walk through the valley of the shadow of death, I shall fear no evil . . .

The firing squad moved in front of Curly and reassembled, and the young woman's eyes settled into a profound peace.

. . . You prepare a table before me in the presence of my enemies: You anoint my head with oil; my cup runs over.

She was gazing back at the soldiers, meeting their eyes.

Surely goodness and mercy will follow me all the days of my life . . .

An order was shouted; the rifles raised.

. . . and I will dwell in the house of the Lord forev—

Shots rang out in the clear night air, and Mrs. Moon's knees would support her no more.

25

The "Forbidden City," Compound of the Workers' Party Elite
Joong-gu District
Pyongyang, North Korea

It was early evening on November 25 when Cho arrived home. He'd been away only five days but it felt much longer. He unlocked the door to find his apartment silent and unlit. *Strange*, he thought, taking off his shoes and carrying his luggage into the hall. His ears still rang with the "Song of General Kim Jong-il" played by the band at the foot of the airplane steps. When invited by the welcome committee to say a few words, he'd praised the inspirational guidance of the Leader of All Socialist Peoples and stood for photographs. Despite the hero's reception, he couldn't shake the old fear he felt whenever he returned home to find his apartment empty. He went through to the living room, noting a fusion of cooking smells. Then he heard a rustling movement in the dark and hit the switch on the wall.

Lights came on to loud applause.

His wife, son, and parents were standing together in a chorus in front of the lacquered cabinet. They'd been joined by some of the courtyard neighbors—two Central Committee men and their wives. All were laughing like children at the joke and clapping their hands. A banner tacked across the cabinet said WELCOME HOME APPA!

in his son's childish hand. Books stepped smartly forward and raised his arm in the Pioneer's salute. Cho knelt down for a hug and for a moment could bury his face in his son's embrace, breathing in the warm dough smell of his skin, and not have to face the room. His wife and mother were either side of him, their faces beaming with pride, trying to embrace him and ask questions at once.

"Appa, what did they look like?" Books said.

"The Yankees?" Cho took off his officer's cap and put it on the boy's head. "Just like they do in the movies."

"Did they smell bad?"

Cho's white-haired father shuffled toward him. "How could you feel safe in such a place? We were worried, I can tell you."

Cho's heart was a swamp of emotions. On the long flight from New York, sleep, even the shortest rest, had been impossible. For thirteen hours one bleak thought had chased another. On the final leg, from Beijing to Pyongyang, in the rusted Tupolev that reeked of latrines and aviation fuel, the junior diplomats and the political officers had begun freshening up and combing their hair in preparation for the welcome reception, while he'd rested his head against the cabin window, staring at the ranges of white mountains, sharp as teeth, and ravines of abyssal shadow. He'd said nothing to them of the report in the *New York Daily News*. First Secretary Ma would be recalled to Pyongyang and to his fate, probably tomorrow. He was already an unperson.

He clasped the frail hands of his parents, smiling at them absently, and bowed to his wife. His father was wearing his veteran's medals. The women's faces were powdered and made up; they'd put on the long colorful *chima jeogori* dresses normally reserved for the Leader's birthday. His wife seemed to read something in his eyes and her smile wavered. "Sang-ho," she said softly, taking him by the arm. "Come and see the gifts." She led him away from the party and into the next room.

Arranged on the dining room table were six or seven bouquets of flowers, a basket of fruit, including a pineapple and bananas, a box of canned meats, a Chinese flat-screen television in its box, and two wooden crates, one of French Bordeaux wines and another of Hennessy Black cognac, his favorite. The most striking bouquet was arranged entirely of blood-red kimjongilia. Cho opened the card.

For Respected Comrade Cho Sang-ho,
who spoke for our country in the true spirit of socialism and revolution.
From his grateful colleagues at the Ministry of Foreign Affairs.

His wife said, "The wines are from the Central Committee of the Party …"

"And the TV is from the politburo," Books shouted, tugging Cho's sleeve. "Can we open it?"

"Wait, the best is to come," said a booming voice from the hall. Yong-ho entered the room in his cap and greatcoat to a cheer from the others. His face broke into an enormous smile for his brother. He stepped forward to embrace Cho, whose arms hung limp, like a manikin's. "Younger brother, you must prepare yourself," he said, squeezing Cho's shoulders.

Cho would not look at him, but he seemed not to notice. He turned Cho toward the window, opened the curtains, and signaled to someone with a wave of his hand.

Lights came on below. In the center of the courtyard, parked between the gingko trees, was a silver Mercedes-Benz sedan. Its upholstery was still in its plastic covering. A uniformed driver pointed the beam of a flashlight at the three-digit license plate, 2★16.

Cho moved his head closer. Cars with that particular date as their license number were few. February 16th, the Day of the Bright Star, the Dear Leader's birthday.

"From …"

"... The great man himself!" Yong-ho shouted, giving Cho's shoulder another violent squeeze. "No checkpoint will dare stop that car! The traffic girls will close streets to let you pass."

The family and neighbors had followed Yong-ho into the dining room and began clapping and laughing again, radiating pure happiness for Cho. Cho smiled inanely and scratched the back of his neck, feeling the weight of new expectations settling on him like a lead yoke.

While the women cleared the gifts from the table and started laying the *banchan* dishes and glasses for dinner, Yong-ho handed out packets of cigarettes to the men—American Marlboros. In addition to his brother and father, there were the two courtyard neighbors, both middle-aged Central Committee men in brown staff uniforms, and one other man Cho had only just noticed, a foreigner standing in the corner apart from the others—a diminutive figure dressed in a linen suit for tropical climates. He had rounder eyes and resin-colored skin. His hair was white and cropped very short, exposing a bumpy, liver-spotted skull. Cho caught his eye and the man bowed with a smile.

Yong-ho put his hand to his forehead. "I'm forgetting my manners. Younger brother, I hope you don't mind my inviting a business associate. Mr. Thein is an industrial adviser from Burma. He'll be our neighbor in the courtyard for a few months."

A foreigner in the Forbidden City?

The man shook Cho's hand and for the briefest moment Cho glimpsed the tattooed serpent coiled around his wrist, with its blue head peeping from beneath a cuff. "Congratulations on your triumph," the man said in accented English.

Yong-ho poured soju into small glasses for each of the men. "My own little brother, a hero of the Revolution," he said, raising his glass. "*Man-sae!*"

"*Man-sae!*" they cried, and toasted him.

Cho downed his shot and held out his glass for another. They were grinning at him now, eager for his experiences. He knocked back the second, trying to summon up a feeling of bravura, but his mind remained pitilessly sober. He forced his face into a smile, and called the women back into the room.

For the next half hour he recounted, for the guests' entertainment, his night out in Manhattan and the Yankee plot to take him to the 21 Club. He exaggerated grotesquely his hosts' immodest clothing and dog-like eating habits, the former president's undignified manner, and Chris O'Brien's cringing, gutless capitulation. He described O'Brien's pinkish sandy coloring and did an impression of him getting flustered and nervously smoothing and resmoothing his hair while protesting in his strangulated voice. The room descended into gales of laughter.

"Sandy hair!" Books cried, laughing.

"But it was all down to our matchless Leader," Cho said to admiring nods from all around him. "He knew how to play these Yankees. I was merely his messenger."

As he spoke he noticed the small Burmese man, Mr. Thein, gazing around the room, his yellow smile beaming on and off like a lighthouse as the guests exclaimed and laughed along to Cho's story.

When he finished they toasted him again, and Cho realized that there was one American he'd left out of his story. The woman whose face kept returning to him in the purple dusk through the airplane window. *How are you liking New York, Colonel?*

At dinner the women served trout soup and steamed *mandu*. The made-up wives of the two Central Committee men smiled demurely, said little, and ate little, like imperial *kisaeng* women, Cho thought, suffering the soju-fueled men's talk and the noxious veils of cigarette smoke hanging over the table. His wife led Books around the table to bow to everyone and say goodnight. The boy went to bow to his grandfather, but the old man was engrossed in a question he was putting to Yong-ho, and Cho sensed straight away that something was wrong.

Beneath the white bristles of his father's eyebrows, Cho saw fear.

Yong-ho's collar was undone and his face rose-flushed and sheened with sweat. He was about two-thirds drunk.

"Nah," he said loudly, reaching to tip his ash into a *banchan* dish that still had pickles in it. "But they'll announce it any day now. More bloody formalities to clear up. The matter's gone up to those creeps in the OGD ..."

Cho stared at him, appalled. The teeming, unformulated resentments he'd been harboring toward his brother suddenly concentrated into a single clutch of fear. Yong-ho's appointment had still not been announced? *The investigation into his real family background was not yet closed?* He'd almost forgotten about it. And why had matters gone up to the Organization and Guidance Department? A bead of cold sweat rolled from his armpit down to his belt. The Bowibu, like every other organ of the state, even the army, reported to the Organization and Guidance Department, the shadowy body through which the Dear Leader exercised power. If things had gone to that level, some issue had arisen that was beyond the Bowibu's power to judge ... He watched Yong-ho give a complicit snicker at some off-color remark one of the Central Committee men was whispering in his ear.

The realization struck Cho like a blow to the neck.

There IS a problem with our family background.

He felt the blood draining from his face. *The matter's gone to the Organization and Guidance Department because Yong-ho is one of the Admitted and can't be touched without permission from the very top.*

Cho looked down at his hands. They had become clammy and feeble, as if tendons had been cut. He couldn't hold his chopsticks. He had the collapsing feeling of a man who'd gone to the doctor with indigestion only to be told he had stomach cancer. The

Admitted were the elite of the elite—only if the Leader had asked to meet a specific person in private and had spent more than twenty minutes talking with them behind closed doors could that person be anointed as one of the Admitted. The Bowibu would never have referred the matter up to the Leader himself unless they had uncovered an extremely serious problem and they were very, very sure of their case ...

A mouth was opening and closing with globs of greasy fish on the tongue. It took him a second to realize that one of the Central Committee men was talking to him. With an intense effort Cho forced himself to appear interested and listen. But his ears soon pricked up. The man was telling him matter-of-factly that the apartment below Cho's had been vacated; the cadre who lived there had been sentenced to six months' reeducation through labor in the mountains, along with his family. Mr. Thein was living there temporarily—Yong-ho's idea. The Committee man wiped his mouth with the back of his hand and gave low belch.

For the remainder of dinner Cho said little, chasing flakes of fish and kimchi around his bowl. He was in a paralysis of nerves and anxiety, all the time having to smile and appear to bask in the glow of his triumph. Only his wife could tell something was amiss. When everyone had finished eating, she announced that her husband was exhausted after the long flight and should rest before his debriefing tomorrow. In ones and twos the guests said their good-byes and left. His parents said goodnight and embraced him and congratulated him again, followed by the Central Committee men and their wives.

But before Yong-ho's peculiar guest could take his leave, Cho said in English, "I'm interested to know what industry you're in, Mr. Thein."

The smile switched on again. He looked as if he'd been set an intriguing puzzler. "I advise your government on synthetic consumer goods, you could say."

"Would one of those consumer goods be crystal methamphetamine by some chance?" He turned to Yong-ho. "*Bingdu* it's called here, isn't it?"

All the warmth went out of Mr. Thein's face. His expression changed to something colder. All pretense gone.

Yong-ho stepped over, his voice low and furious. "What the hell's got into you?"

"Get him out of my home," Cho said calmly. "You and I need to talk."

26

CIA Headquarters
1000 Colonial Farm Road
Langley, Virginia

Dawn had not yet risen when Fisk collected Jenna and drove her along silent streets toward Langley. To a casual observer he might have appeared his usual calm, equable self, but Jenna knew him well enough by now to spot signs of nerves. A slight edginess to his movements. A nick on his cheek from an overhasty shave. The director had summoned Fisk for an 8:00 a.m. meeting the day after Thanksgiving because Fisk was in trouble.

In the underground parking garage of the Original Headquarters Building a member of the director's security detail was waiting for them next to the private elevator. They rode with him in silence to the seventh floor and were escorted through a deserted open-plan area. The sun was just rising above the treetops, sending golden bars of light across the carpet.

In the glass-walled office at the far end the director sat working in his shirtsleeves.

"How am I going to explain it to Congress, Charles?" he called, getting up and walking around to the front of his desk when he saw them approach. He glowered at Fisk from behind beetling eyebrows and a large nose. "Crazy Kim launches an attack against

South Korea, a close US ally, in a transparent ploy to screw us for aid ..." His voice rose to a shout. "... and it *works?*" He threw his arms open and began to pace around the desk, becoming, Jenna thought, more Italian the angrier he got. She liked him. "And this comes just weeks after a rocket test we also knew nothing about." He smacked the paper of a report in his hand. "Was there no chatter out there prior to this attack?"

"No, sir," Fisk said, "nothing."

"Not even a breeze? A whisper?"

Fisk looked down, like a schoolboy.

"Caught napping again, they'll say, yet we have the gall to justify a budget bigger than NASA's."

The director paused for a moment with his back to them, peering at the blue-gold sky through shatterproof glass. "The president is deploying the USS *George Washington* to the Yellow Sea as a show of force, but he wants to combine it with some kind of *peace mission*. Speak softly and carry a big stick. He's also calling for fresh ideas for tackling Kim, and he's not asking the State Department." The director turned and threw the papers onto his desk. "He's asking us."

Fisk began to speak. "Sir, we'll get onto it—"

"Specifically, he's asking you, Dr. Williams."

"Me?"

"Our president is a thoughtful man, and an avid reader. It seems your report on North Korea's secret lab impressed him. Congratulations. I'd like your draft recommendations by the end of the day."

Simms let Jenna use his office, one wall of which was a huge whiteboard covered in photographs and screen grabs, with colored marker lines connecting each.

Her fingers poised over the keyboard. She was feeling alert and clearheaded. And she was feeling a buzz of nerves and excitement.

Fresh ideas, he said . . .

She knew that what she wanted to say was radical. It would over-turn decades of policy. In a sudden burst of inspiration she wrote:

Just as many diets to lose weight can have the opposite effect in the long term, so isolating and punishing a tyrant for his aggression can make his behavior worse. We cannot hope to change a regime by isolating it from change . . .

She explained her reasoning, in bright, plain prose, drawing on her years of thinking about North Korea. She worked through the day, stopping only to eat food out of vending machines. She was so engrossed that she even managed to put to the back of her mind thoughts of last night's Skype call with her sister's abductor, though that, too, was feeding into her excitement.

She concluded with a list of recommendations she knew would raise eyebrows. Using the CIA encryption software that was unique to Top Secret Special Access files, she sent the report to the director, and no one else. He would probably throw it straight into the shredder.

Something else had been at the back of her mind all day, too. As she left the empty building that evening she remembered what it was: the director's mentioning something about a peace mission.

27

The "Forbidden City," Compound of the Workers' Party Elite
Joong-gu District
Pyongyang, North Korea

Cho closed the door on the last guest and turned to face his brother. Yong-ho's face was crimson with rage, his brow dripping, as if he were sweating pure alcohol.

"Mr. Thein was our *guest*," Yong-ho hissed. His voice was ill controlled, struggling to contain a shout. "Have you picked up Yankee manners now? Is that how you speak to—"

"It's over for us. Isn't it?"

Yong-ho stopped. His mouth opened and closed like a landed fish. The dead calm of Cho's voice seemed to derail him completely. Anger evaporated from his face, and was replaced by a dull fatigue. After a long pause he said, "What're you talking about?"

Cho poured them each a shot of soju. He was starting to feel wired and awake, even though it was almost midnight. His body was on New York time. The apartment was silent except for a ticking in the floor as it began to cool, and even though he kept his voice very low, each word was flinchingly clear.

"Whatever crime they've uncovered in our real family's past, our blood carries the guilt. It's just a matter of time before they act. Our rank won't protect us. You know that."

Fear sparked in his brother's eyes and then died down, leaving them empty and dark.

"You're jumping to conclusions."

Cho shook his head slowly and handed him the glass.

"There probably won't be a trial. They'll just make us vanish."

He was breaking a taboo and it was making him feel strangely serene. No one spoke of the reality behind the state's facades. To avoid even thinking about it, it was necessary to maintain two mental sets of accounts, one public, one secret—the ability to know and not know at the same time. Cho had done this all his life. It was the only way to reconcile the daily contradictions between propaganda and the evidence of one's eyes, between orthodoxy and the kinds of thoughts that could land you in the gulag if they were ever spoken aloud. The secret set of accounts was never acknowledged because there was no emotion or idea, no aspect of life, public or private, that fell outside the state's authority. A disloyal remark was all the Bowibu needed for an arrest. Sometimes, simply a look was enough.

He turned to the window and looked down at the silver Mercedes-Benz sedan in the courtyard—his gift from Kim Jong-il—now in a monochrome gloom.

"I don't think they'll arrest my wife. As the daughter of a Heroic Family she's protected. Omma and Appa are safe, because they're not our real parents." He knocked back the soju and winced. "But you and I, elder brother . . ." He felt his chest tightening. ". . . and my son . . . are in real danger."

"You're forgetting something." Yong-ho was mopping his brow with a paper napkin, sweating streams. "Loyalty. The Leader has thanked me in person for my work. He's *embraced me*." He put his hand to his heart. "Do you know what that makes me?" His voice was trembling now, but whether from affronted pride or fear, Cho couldn't tell. "One of his most trusted, one of his most loyal. He values loyalty above everything. He will not forsake us because of some wrong committed—fuck knows—" He made a sweep of his arm. "—*generations* ago."

Yong-ho slumped against the wall.

Cho sat on the low windowsill with his arms folded. Behind him a half-moon trailed a silvery veil across the city. "The closer a cadre is to the top, the more violent his end when it comes. That's how it goes. And as for this work you've done for him ..." Cho shook his head vaguely. It was funny how he'd almost forgotten his grievance against Yong-ho. The counterfeit bills. The drugs in the diplomatic pouch. None of that seemed to matter now. "... that may mean we're in even graver danger than we could even imagine. You know what Appa says about our Dear Leader. Get too far from him and you freeze; get too close and you burn. I think you, elder brother, have been much too close."

A silence opened between them for a moment, until a glass smashed and cascaded as the soju slipped from Yong-ho's hand. His body seemed to crumple from the middle, making him slide down the wall. Folded up on the floor in a zigzag, his sharp knees touching his face, he looked vulnerable, a defeated animal, his tall, cocky stature diminished. Shards of crystal surrounded him on the parquet, and Cho heard a sound like the lowing of a wounded ox. For the first time in his life he was seeing his big brother weeping. He crouched down on the floor next to him and tried to put an arm around him, tried to hush him, but the cry became a keening sob, broken by gasps for air. Some lifelong defense inside Yong-ho was cracking and falling. Cho clasped his brother's head to his own. Soju-scented tears flowed over Yong-ho's cheeks. "I've always been loyal," he said. His shoulders heaved again, his sobbing so loud it threatened to wake the courtyard.

Cho put Yong-ho's arm around his neck and lifted him heavily up onto his feet. "Let's get some air."

*

They sat in the Mercedes beneath the pines of Moran Hill Park. Military police patrols passed them every quarter hour, but the car's 2★16 license plate was a powerful amulet. No one approached them. The air was clear and Manchurian cold. In the light of the half-moon Pyongyang lay sprawled below them like a city of the dead, without electricity except for the red-glass flame of the Juche Tower on the far side of the river, and the floodlit colossus of Kim Il-sung on Mansu Hill, bronze arm pointing into darkness, the nation's destiny. The hemisphere of stars reached to the horizon. Yong-ho opened the sunroof a few inches to smoke and Cho looked up. The Milky Way trailed brightly westward toward the Yellow Sea, and the branches of the pines were black and sharp against it.

"Remember coming up here to look for girls?" Cho said, taking a swig from the soju bottle he was nursing in his lap. He passed it to Yong-ho.

Years ago, in their Socialist Youth days, they'd bring a cassette player up here among the picnicking families in summer.

A smile spread across Yong-ho's face. "You'd dance with the prettiest girl, and I'd have to take turns with her mother and grandmother."

They lit cigarettes, though Cho seldom smoked. He clasped his brother's hand. It was as if they were meeting for the first time since those far-off days.

Cho stared at the glowing tip of his cigarette. The place was so quiet he could hear the paper crackle as it burned.

"Why did you let me travel to New York with a diplomatic bag full of drugs and fake dollars?"

Yong-ho raised his hands to his face. "Younger brother ..." Shame emanated from him in a soft groan. But his confession, once it began, seemed to salve him, and took on a momentum of its own. Faster than Cho could take in what he was hearing, with one revelation eclipsing the next like fireworks in a display, the secrets of Yong-ho's work came tumbling from him.

Cho's first shock was to learn that his brother was the First Deputy Director of Bureau 39 of the Party—in effect, chief of the most secret organization in the country and one of the highest-ranking cadres. He had held the position for four years and reported solely to Kim Jong-il. Yong-ho glanced at Cho, waiting for him to say something, but Cho's mouth was hanging open.

Bureau 39, Yong-ho explained, had been set up back in the seventies to manage Kim Jong-il's personal wealth and to provide a secret powerbase separate from his father. The Great Leader was then in his prime, enjoying the largesse of his patrons, the Soviet Union and Maoist China, and basking in the growing cult of personality his ambitious son was creating for him. Bureau 39 was tasked with raising funds to pay for the cult's extravagance—the statues of bronze and gold, the endless portraits, the words carved in granite and marble. But it was also financing the construction of private palaces for Kim Jong-il, and the luxury cars and watches he gave as gifts to keep his inner circle loyal.

Yong-ho tipped his head back to blow smoke through the sunroof.

"When the Great Leader died in ninety-four the world thought we'd go the way of the old communist bloc, the way of history— liberalize, modernize, Westernize—but the Son had no such intention. He took the title Dear Leader and that's when the madness really started. The deification of his father became more elaborate than the Orthodox Church, and all our country's meager resources went to the military." Yong-ho shook his head and a new bitterness came into his voice. "Our farmers plowed fields with oxen and children starved in the streets, but so what? We had nuclear weapons and a space program." He rubbed his eyes. "The world stopped talking to us. Our country froze in time. We became the most embargoed state on earth. We couldn't raise money through normal trade. But, somehow, we had to pay for a million-strong army, and buy the components of sophisticated weapons.

"So Bureau 39's operations expanded, dramatically. We began inviting crime organizations to Pyongyang—the Tokyo yakuza, mafia from Taiwan, Thai heroin specialists—to share their expertise in narcotics and counterfeits. We let them set up factories and labs here. Imagine it. I hosted banquets for these scumbags in the Great Hall of the People.

"Heroin was a big part of our operation in the early days, but poppy crops kept failing in the rainy season. A synthetic drug like crystal methamphetamine—*bingdu*—proved much more convenient, and lucrative. We supplied the investment and the protection; the gangs produced it to a high purity. They shared their profits with us; we stayed out of their turf wars. Soon, *bingdu* addicts all over Asia were getting high on stuff made here, and Bureau 39 was running the biggest industry in the country, bringing in billions of dollars each year."

Cho was dumbfounded. His country's main industry was crime?

The car's interior suddenly filled with light. The headlights of a patrol jeep were approaching from the lane behind them. Cho was reeling and barely noticed, but Yong-ho was alert, watching in the side mirror. The jeep dipped its lights as if in apology, reversed, and drove away.

Yong-ho stubbed out his cigarette in the car ashtray.

"Of course, we learned from the gangs and started making the products ourselves, and not just drugs. We exported fake-brand cigarettes, fake pharmaceuticals, Viagra, you name it. We diversified into money laundering, using shell trading companies in dozens of countries ..." A note of satisfaction entered his voice. "Our Leader was proud of us. 'Why should a pure race be bound by the dictates of an impure world?' Those were his words. 'Whatever harms our enemies is justified.'

"But shipping these products undetected wasn't easy. So our diplomats became key players. They could smuggle the goods in bags that wouldn't be searched ... and for this our Leader wanted a new breed of diplomat—ruthless, like partisans in the mountains, he said. Our embassies were turned into businesses, ordered to make money by selling narcotics and counterfeit brands to local mafias ... and, of course, by spending the hundred-dollar supernotes. Ah ..." Yong-ho gave a wistful sigh and took another gulp of soju. "I'm actually proud of those. We've used them to pay for everything from hookers to rocket parts."

His laugh was a breathy fume of soju that filled the car, and Cho began laughing too, at the absurdity of it. His embarrassment over the incident outside the diner in Manhattan now struck him as farcical.

"Know how I started in Bureau 39?" Yong-ho was in full flow now. "I ran an operation from a glitzy office in Macao, buying policies from the biggest insurance companies in London, New York, and Tokyo, offering them premiums so high the greedy bastards couldn't say no. Soon I was collecting millions of dollars on claims for nonexistent factory accidents, helicopter crashes, ferry sinkings, mining explosions—all impossible to verify because we wouldn't let their investigators into the country." He smiled ruefully. "They wised up, of course. But when the going was good ... Five years ago I was in that office late one night stuffing twenty-five million US dollars in cash into duffel bags. Next morning it was flown to Pyongyang as a gift to our Leader on his birthday."

Cho remembered. "He sent you a letter of thanks signed in his own hand ..." The whole family had gathered round to read it, glowing with pride and shaking Yong-ho's shoulder. "It was delivered with a box of oranges ..."

"... And a DVD player and a warm blanket."

Cho's face was agog. Then he began laughing silently. "That's what you got for giving him *twenty-five million dollars?*"

Yong-ho nodded.

"*In cash?*"

Yong-ho began to chuckle, too. Suddenly they were both laughing so hard the car shook. They laughed until their cheeks were streaked with tears, and they had aches in their bellies.

After that they retreated into their own thoughts as the city began to stir. The sky was lightening to a deep purple, and drifts of clouds near the horizon were catching fire. A bright, cold day beckoned.

Cho felt dazed with wonder and disgust. He was smiling, he realized—a would-you-fucking-believe-it kind of smile, as if he'd been duped in the most extraordinary scam. Kim Jong-il was running a mafia racket and using the rocket program to hold the world to ransom. He, Cho, was part of a tiny elite bought off with trinkets, while the rest of the population, about whom, now he thought about it, he had only the haziest idea, labored in obscurity ... Who were the masses? Not the rosy-cheeked workers and farmers on state television. Suddenly he had the sensation of a vast cloth of painted scenery splitting and tearing, and behind it millions of souls twisting in agony. He'd seen them—from his car window on the occasions he'd left Pyongyang. Stick figures, breaking rocks in distant fields or doubled over planting rice saplings. Old ajummas at filthy roadside markets. Children with large heads and swollen stomachs.

He felt his mouth fill with saliva.

Yong-ho looked at him then turned his head away, as if he'd read his thoughts. He seemed to be mulling over something, hesitating. "What I'm about to tell you, younger brother, is known to very few ..."

With a sudden premonition, Cho knew. *The abductions.*

Yong-ho flicked his cigarette out of the window and watched it trail orange sparks. "Our Leader said that if we were to know our enemies, we had to get into their minds. He called it 'localization.' Most of the victims, as you know, were snatched from Japan and South Korea.

"Well, the program was a failure. We got some useful information out of them—how our enemies spoke, their slang, their capitalist customs, and all that, but it wasn't worth the effort. And of the hundreds we brought here, only a few were successfully reconditioned."

"Successfully what?"

"Turned into spies and sent back to their home countries. Even the youngest ones had such strong memories of their lives at home that almost all of them resisted our teachings. That left us with the problem of what to do with them. We couldn't just let them go. So the decision was taken to make them disappear—some in accidents, others to the camps."

"But ..." Cho's face buckled, horrified. "The Leader acknowledged the kidnappings. I was there when he apologized to the Japanese prime minister. The victims were repatriated."

"Five of them were." He looked at Cho meaningfully. "Five. The Japanese never found out how many we'd brought here. The families of most of them thought they were dead or missing and have never even guessed they were here."

The saliva in Cho's mouth tasted bilious, his tongue like something bloated and rotten. He wanted to change the subject. "The program ended."

Yong-ho shook his head. "The abductions ended ... but the Localization Program didn't. In fact it got more ambitious." He gave Cho a tentative look that said *Sure you want to know?* "We began sending female spies abroad to entrap men of other non-Korean races."

Cho didn't understand. "Entrap?"

"Become pregnant by them, and give birth to their babies here in Pyongyang. At the same time we enticed non-Korean men here—men with white, black, or brown skin to get certain Korean women pregnant."

"*What?*"

"This was our Leader's solution to the failure of localization, which he renamed the Seed-Bearing Program. We're creating spies and assassins who look foreign—some have blue eyes and blond hair—but who have been brought up learning nothing but the Juche teachings of the Great Leader Kim Il-sung and the Dear Leader Kim Jong-il."

Cho's gasp was a half laugh, as if someone were trying to tell him the sun went round the earth and not vice versa, or that reality was a figment in the dream of a chimpanzee.

"But I've never seen anyone of any other race living here as a Kor—"

Cho stopped. A synapse in his mind was connecting, relating what Yong-ho was telling him with …

The bile was rising in his stomach.

"You won't see them," Yong-ho said simply. "They live in a secret compound, which they never leave, a short drive north of Pyong-yang. Their training and all their needs are provided for by Section 915 of the Organization and Guidance Department. The eldest of them are in their late teens now and almost ready for active service abroad. The Leader has visited them many times. They've been encouraged to look upon him as their father. He brings them treats and gifts—"

The pressure in his stomach spiked. Cho wound the window down and gulped in the freezing air.

"You've gone white, younger brother—"

He threw open the door, staggered, part-run, part-skip, toward the nearest pine, and vomited in wrenching, agonizing heaves.

After a minute he stood upright, leaning his forehead against the rough bark, watching an arc of mucus hang from his mouth, glistening in the moonlight, and wondered if it would freeze before his eyes. The air smelled of pine needles and his mind was now strangely clear. He looked back toward the car. A light flared amber as Yong-ho lit another cigarette, and the synapse in Cho's memory connected.

She was taken. Twelve years ago. From a beach in South Korea.

His brother's voice was muffled. "Get back here before you freeze."

Cho got in and closed the door. "What about women of other races?"

"Mm?"

"You said men of other races were enticed here, for this ... Seed-Bearing Program. What about women of other races?"

Yong-ho shrugged distractedly. "It's possible ..." His humor had drained away with the last of the soju and his face was desolate. "So what're we going to do, little brother?" He exhaled and leaned his head against the window. "I guess it's the soldier's way out for me." He mimed the two fingers of a revolver pointed to the back of his mouth and made a click with his tongue.

Cho let several minutes go by. The first trolley bus was heading down Chilsongmun Street, trailing sparks from the overhead cable. On the river a coal barge cleaved its wake on the slow-moving water, turning mother-of-pearl in the gathering light. On the far side of the city Power Station Number One was puffing a column of pink smoke high into the sky, and beyond it the first row of hills was materializing in the haze, then the row behind, and, very faintly, the farthest row.

"No, elder brother," Cho said, turning the key in the ignition. The powerful engine engaged softly. "We're going to escape."

28

Hyesan Train Station
Ryanggang Province, North Korea

The women were subdued as they laid out their goods. Like Mrs. Moon, they probably hadn't slept. There wasn't a breath of wind. The market was waking to a dead-clear stillness. An air of mourning hung over the station, and the mood throughout the city streets was fear. Mrs. Yang, Mrs. Kwon, and Grandma Whiskey distracted themselves by making a plan for Sun-i: the girl would be smuggled over the river after dark to stay with distant relatives of Mrs. Yang's in Changbai.

Mrs. Moon sat absently on her rice sacks, staring into space. Her mind lingered somewhere between nightmare and the realm of the spirits. Anything her eyes fell upon—a fence post, a headscarf, a uniform—suddenly arranged themselves in a crooked way in her mind and she'd see Curly's body tied to the stake.

Tae-hyon had begged her to stay at home in the village for a few days, and not go near Hyesan. But hiding would change nothing. In trying to save Curly, a condemned criminal, she had made herself known to the Bowibu. She was a marked woman now.

Kyu was assembling the table. She should be starting the cooking but she was unable to perform the simplest task. Sergeant Jang dropped by asking for *bingdu*. She gave him five grams without even trying to extract a favor in return.

She looked down the empty aisle toward the station building. The executions had made everyone lie low.

A group of youths from the Maintenance of Social Order Brigade was clearing the beggars from the station platform. She watched them kick an aged woman who got stiffly to her feet. They kicked again to make her move away. She'd left behind a tin cup and they kicked that, too, sending it clattering across the platform. It was a scene Mrs. Moon had witnessed many times, but this time it fascinated her. She could not take her eyes off the woman, who had difficulty walking and whose hair was matted and dirty, or the stony-faced youths in their red armbands. From deep in her stomach she felt a rage kindle and rise. It blazed brightly for a moment, then died, and her mood darkened even further. She lived in an upside-down world where good was evil and evil was good. It made no sense, but she knew it wasn't right.

A lamb goes uncomplaining forth ...

She barely reacted when one of the policemen came to tell her she was ordered to present herself at the local police station at 5:00 p.m. In the wake of the executions, she learned, a team of Bowibu special investigators had arrived in the city to root out factionalists and subversive elements.

Her name was on a list.

Moon's Korean Barbeque did not open that day. With Kyu's help she sold her gas burner and all her stock. She used the money to buy a new Chinese refrigerator that she would offer to the head of the investigation team to have her name removed from the list. They could accept it or shoot her. It was all the same to her. She had nothing left.

29

The "Forbidden City," Compound of the Workers' Party Elite
Joong-gu District
Pyongyang, North Korea

Cho arrived back at the apartment minutes before his wife and Books woke up. He had not slept in two days and had eaten little, but anger and terror were mixing in his veins like fuel and oxidizer in a rocket thruster.

His mind was sparking with the escape plan he and Yong-ho had begun to hatch in the car. They had agreed to talk again tonight.

He showered and dressed in a clean white shirt, his fingers trembling as he did up the buttons.

How, except with the most affected charade, was he going to make it through his day at work? He was debriefing the First Deputy Minister at ten and would spend the rest of the day reporting on the meetings with the Yankees.

Much of the plan depended on Yong-ho: this morning he would send an urgent commission for two Chinese passports for himself and for Cho, containing forged visas for Taiwan and Macao. Yong-ho could do this without arousing suspicion—Bureau 39 regularly procured false travel documents. For money they would use the hundred-dollar supernotes. If, for any reason, these counterfeits were detected and they were unable to use them once they'd reached

China, then—and this made the hairs on Cho's neck stand on end—Yong-ho would access the Kim family's secret accounts at the Banco Delta Asia in Macao, where he had regularly made deposits and withdrawals on the Leader's behalf.

How much time did they have? It was impossible to know for sure, but as Cho's mind raced he realized that fortune might have thrown them a slender chance. The Leader departed today on an official visit to Beijing by train—Cho himself had organized the logistics with the Guard Command. The great man would return to Pyongyang in forty-eight hours, and Cho's instinct—from years of second-guessing that mind—was that he would defer passing sentence on such a sensitive case until the journey home.

They had less than forty-eight hours to escape the country.

Yong-ho traveled regularly on Bureau 39 business. With luck it was not too late for him to escape Pyongyang tomorrow by air, but Cho could not simply ask for a plane ticket. He would somehow have to make his own way north and slip across the Yalu River into China. Once in China he would use his forged passport to rendezvous with Yong-ho in Taiwan. From there they would seek asylum in the West. Yong-ho had ruled out South Korea. Too many Bowibu spies and assassins had infiltrated the South, he said. Without heavy security, the two of them would be tracked down and killed within weeks.

Making his own way north to the border with China was only the first of Cho's worries. How was he going take his wife and son? Using what documents?

How was he even going to tell them?

There was no possible way of obtaining passports for all of them without giving the game away. And he had never even been to the border. Its mountains were known to him only from legend, the "white hell" where the Great Leader had defeated the Japanese. Even if he could reach there by train, a journey that could last days on the creaking rail network, he had no idea how or where he would get his family over the river. He knew that people crept across in the dead of night, but he had no contacts there, no brokers who could help.

Panic surged through him, making his legs turn to paper. He felt like a man fleeing a monster in a nightmare. Every scenario he envisaged extrapolated to catastrophe. In desperation he realized that the only sure way to save his wife was if she stayed behind. She could claim she had been deceived by a criminal element, and would be believed. Her own status, as the daughter of a Heroic Family, would protect her.

But his son ...

He smoothed the tension from his face, put on the jacket of his uniform, and, smiling broadly, he entered the kitchen.

"Good morning," his wife said, giving him a sideways glance as she laid out the breakfast. "You're as pale as a fish."

Cho couldn't open his mouth. He felt if he opened his mouth he'd fall apart. He picked up his tea and saw the tremor in the liquid's surface. He got up again and excused himself. He locked himself in the bathroom and tried to think, think, but no idea came to him. He leaned his forehead to the cool surface of the mirror and began to mutter softly so that his breath steamed the glass, muttering to whom, he didn't know, but if the spirits of his ancestors could help him, they should help him now.

It was at that moment that he heard Books's voice in the kitchen saying he didn't want his kimchi because it burned his throat. Cho pressed his ear to the bathroom door. His wife was murmuring something about swollen glands and a slight temperature. And then: "I think you'd better stay home from school today."

Cho wiped his face, stilled his breathing, and walked back into the kitchen. As casually as he could, he said, "I'll take him to the doctor, just to be sure."

Five minutes later he had strapped Books into the passenger seat of the new Mercedes and was driving to the University Medical

Hospital in Tonghung-dong, where he figured the staff were less well paid than those at the special hospital for cadres' families. It was still early—plenty of time for him to get to work.

They were directed to a dim waiting room that stank of bleach, and sat on plastic chairs. Books took out a picture puzzle and leaned his head against Cho's shoulder. Eventually a young female nurse with a white headscarf asked them to come to a consulting room. Cho held Books's hand and carried his heavy briefcase in the other. The room was small. There were half a dozen kerosene lamps grouped on the floor for when the power failed. She sat him down, asked the boy his name, put a thermometer in his mouth, felt his throat.

"He'll be fine." She smiled at Cho. "It's a mild viral infection."

Cho's words were deliberate and cold. "I want to see the most senior physician here."

"I don't think that's necessary," she said, surprised. "He'll feel better—

"Do as I say ..." He adopted the manner of a high Party official being provoked. "... or you'll be mopping floors in a dysentery ward."

She flushed scarlet and left.

His son looked at Cho wide eyed. "Am I in trouble?"

"No, no," Cho said, squeezing his hand and trying to keep his voice steady.

Panic again. *Fight it.*

A minute later, a tall, gray-haired man in a clean white coat entered. His face was deeply lined and his eyes had a hardened pragmatism. "I'm Dr. Baek," he said gruffly.

Cho stood. "I'm concerned about the swelling in my son's throat."

The doctor listened to the boy's heartbeat with a stethoscope, looked inside his mouth, and he, too, felt the glands in the throat. Then Cho said to the boy, "Wait next to the car."

Twenty minutes later Cho jumped back into the driver's seat and fastened his seat belt. In his briefcase was a letter typed on the hospital's letterhead stating Dr. Baek's professional opinion that the cause of the throat swelling could not be determined and recommending an urgent examination at the specialist unit of the Women and Children's Hospital in Dandong, where an appointment for tomorrow was at this moment being made. It had cost Cho a thousand euros and two bottles of Hennessy Black cognac.

His mind was speeding on automatic. If he lost focus, even for a second, he feared his nerve would fail and his body shut down. And then he'd be alone, like a prisoner in a cell, with the question he could not answer.

How can I abandon my wife?

He checked the car's speed and slowed down, feeling panic again. Traffic police were on duty at every intersection.

He had accomplished the task in just forty-five minutes.

But if it means saving our son ...

He couldn't look his wife in the eye. Her eyebrows shot up when he told her. "Treatment in *China*?" He showed her the letter, and tried to reassure her—that this was probably a false alarm, but there was no harm in being sure, and the specialist equipment didn't exist in Pyongyang. His sweating was betraying him. He was radiating guilt. He knew she wasn't buying it, but she said nothing and turned to the window. She was afraid.

Later today he would use Dr. Baek's letter to obtain the travel permits he needed for the border region, and if it took another hard-currency bribe to get them filled out right away, so be it.

His wife said, "The Ministry car's arrived. That's not your driver, is it?"

He stepped to the window. A thickset man Cho did not recognize was standing with the Ministry car in the courtyard, looking up at the building, searching for Cho's apartment, and talking into a two-way radio.

Cho felt his stomach turn to stone. But then that strange calm came over him again, a resignation, an acceptance almost. It was as if he wasn't quite there, or this was happening to someone else.

He let out a quiet breath, and almost smiled. The gingko trees had turned a beautiful flame ochre.

It's happening. There's nothing to be done.

His wife may have been puzzled by the lingering hug he gave her, and the kiss he brushed against her neck, and the way he squeezed her hand and was reluctant to let go, but he turned away before she saw the desolation in his face. Books had gone back to bed, and Cho spent a minute watching the innocent repose of his face, his breathing slightly clogged with cold, his sleep untroubled because his loving parents were nearby, keeping him safe.

"No Jung-gil today?" Cho said, getting into the back seat.

"He has been reassigned, sir."

The car glided toward the gates of the Forbidden City and the barrier was raised; it passed the Koryo Hotel, and Cho turned in his seat to see a gleaming black SUV with tinted windows. Its indicator light winked, and then it began trailing his car at a distance of about thirty meters, conspicuous in the boulevard's sparse traffic. It had a white license plate with numbers beginning with 55—an army vehicle.

Cho's driver did not make a right toward Kim Il-sung Square, his usual route to the Ministry, but continued along Sungri Street.

"Where are we going?" he said calmly.

The driver's eyes met his for a second in the mirror, but he said nothing. A streetcar whirred alongside them for a moment, windows packed with weary faces and vacant eyes, like fish in a tank.

Cho looked down at his hands. There was no tremble at all, now that he knew his fate was settled. It wasn't himself he was fearful for. He was thinking of Books, sleeping peacefully. When would they do it, he wondered, the men who would take him away? It was better that he was at home, and they wouldn't do it in front of his class at school. And his wife, how would she react?

Screaming, pleading with them, prostrate on the floor, holding on to their boots as they left, or trying to wrest her son from their arms? Or would she be too shocked and stunned even to move? He thought of Yong-ho, how close he'd felt to him last night in the car on Moran Hill Park, and wondered whether he'd made it as far as the airport.

The car made a sharp left down a narrow concrete ramp and into the bowels of a deep underground parking garage. Cho had been too lost in thought to notice which building. The black SUV was directly behind now. It slowed to a halt as Cho's car stopped, and its headlights came on full beam. Its engine hummed, white exhaust fumes making it look like a demonic tank. Its doors opened at once and four uniformed men stepped out with the visors of their caps pulled low. In the dim tungsten light Cho could not read their faces, or see if any of them were holding handcuffs. He closed his eyes, savoring five private seconds before nothing in his life, what remained of it, would be his any more. He exhaled, opened the car door, and got out, feeling a heaviness in his legs, like a man about to climb a scaffold.

The four officers snapped to attention in a synchronized salute.

Behind them a wedge of light fell across the concrete floor as an underground door opened and two women approached. They were young and pretty, and wearing the starred cap and uniform of the Red Guards, with gleaming black boots.

They saluted sharply and in unison. One said, "Respected Comrade Colonel Cho, it is our honor to escort you."

Cho's mind spun with confusion.

Moments later they had him in a wood-paneled elevator with polished brass buttons. One of the women gave him a shy smile as they ascended, then looked down. He glanced at the ascending lights. He was in one of the big buildings of state. The door opened onto an immense colonnaded lobby colored by light from a high stained-glass ceiling. The Supreme People's Assembly.

More Red Guard ushers were waiting before two enormous rosewood doors inlaid with gold-filigree lotus flowers. They pulled them open, and the roar came out like an ocean crashing on a shore.

He entered the great hall to see the hundreds of deputies of the Supreme People's Assembly standing in their tiered seats, facing Cho and every one of them applauding with abandon. The sound came in thunderous waves. His brain went into meltdown. Cameras flashed in his face. A television crew was suddenly grouped behind him, following him as the Red Guards led him across the floor toward the podium, where he recognized the tall, bald President of the Presidium, holding out a hand in welcome. Behind him a vast stone statue of Kim Il-sung was bathed in a pinkish-blue light and flanked on either side by guards of honor bearing silver-plated Kalashnikovs. Cho was ushered up the steps of the podium to a chair facing the entire assembly.

A bell rang. The applause subsided immediately, and the deputies sat. The chairman began speaking in an incantatory voice, drawing out the vowels with solemnity.

"Deputies, we open today's proceedings by honoring a hero of the Juche ideal, Cho Sang-ho. As many of you will have heard, he engaged with the imperialist jackals as a true warrior-diplomat, embodying the partisan spirit encouraged in us all by our Dear Leader Kim Jong-il …"

Applause broke out again. Cho stole a fugitive glance at the statue to his right. Its belly swelled gently beneath a stone Mao suit. The face was stern.

"The Yankees have more than met their match in Colonel Cho. In fact, I am authorized to inform you that they have today begged us for further peace talks, here, in the Capital of the Revolution, in three weeks' time …"

Exclamations of surprise and triumph arose from the deputies, who applauded again. The President turned and Cho stood.

"Comrade Colonel Cho Sang-ho, for courage against the enemy and for exemplary service, you are awarded the Order of Heroic Effort, First Class."

Cameras flashed again. The President's back was toward the hall as he pinned the medal to Cho's chest. Cho looked into his sharp, waxy features. The man's eyes met his with a flash of pure venom. And Cho understood at once, immediately and with no doubts or second thoughts.

They need me to deal with the Americans.

The medal pinned to his chest, Cho faced the hall as the deputies stood again and the applause broke over him. He tried to muster a look of pride but his mouth felt as if it were cast from iron.

He'd been given a reprieve. Three weeks before the ax fell.

This is power, he thought, as the applause continued in waves. The television crew had moved below the podium to get a clear shot. Their cameras were trained on him and a bright light was being shone on him. *To bestow upon me the highest honor of state, then to disgrace me, kill me, and erase all memory of me.* He looked into the faces of the deputies clapping in the first row, complacent in their epaulettes and badges of rank. *This is how the Leader inoculates you, permanently, against any greed for power. This is how he teaches you the only truth that matters. Purity brings reward. Impurity brings death.*

As he descended the steps to the floor, the wall of applause still thundering before him, he noticed something odd. A few rows back from the front stood a silver-haired man of about fifty who was not applauding, nor was he wearing the deputies' beige uniform, but a plain black tunic buttoned up to his chin. His face was stern and heavily lined but not unfriendly. In the moment Cho's eyes met his, an unmistakable message seemed to pass, like some wise assurance from someone who cared about him and knew him well. It was the most uncanny thing. Cho was ushered from the Assembly Hall by the female Red Guards.

When he turned back to look again, the man was obscured by the standing deputies still clapping.

Cho knew now that his every waking moment would be watched; every call he made would be recorded, every note he sent read. He would have Bowibu shadows and street agents following him wherever he went. They would make his neighbors and colleagues complicit in the surveillance. He could forget about taking Books to China. He could lose all hope of escape. He was already a prisoner. This evening he would ask his wife to divorce him, in the slim hope that their son could escape punishment as the progeny of a criminal element.

When he arrived at his office in the Ministry a man dressed in an electrician's overalls was changing the lightbulb above his desk. A Bowibu agent, as plain as day. He ushered the man out, closed the door, and called Yong-ho's cell phone. A deep, unfamiliar voice answered.

"Who's this?" Cho said. "Where's my brother?"

There was a pause and a change in the background noise, as if the call was being put on speakerphone. "I am a friend of your brother's," said the voice.

Cho hung up.

They'd arrested Yong-ho.

PART TWO

Nothing is impossible for a man with a strong will. There is no word "impossible" in the Korean language.

—Kim Jong-il

30

Airspace over the Sea of Okhotsk
Three Weeks Later
December 17, 2010

Jenna opened her eyes to a cabin shot through with arctic light. The view from the window blinded her. A frozen sea cracked into hexagons, as spotless as icing sugar. Far below, an icebreaker chugged black smoke, clearing a watery trail through virgin snow. Her eyes felt full of grit. It had been an early start from the Elmendorf Air Force Base in Anchorage.

The mood on the plane was subdued; a few laptops were open, but the white head of the governor was slumped forward in sleep.

Her mouth was parched. She looked around for a stewardess and then remembered there was no service on board.

"No calls to make before we enter enemy airspace?"

She turned in her seat to see the jockish blond man who'd winked at her when they'd boarded, and again got the vague feeling she recognized him. She assumed he'd been working on his laptop until she'd heard the cartoon ping of a computer game.

"Chad Stevens," he said, closing the screen and extending his hand. "Asia correspondent, NBC News. I'm guessing you're Marianne Lee."

She shook his hand with reluctance, too sleepy to be social.

He rested his forearms on the tops of the seats. "So ... a peace mission with no official itinerary, no diplomatic protection, no security, and zero communication with the outside world. I guess anything could happen." He had a loud tenor voice that grated on her; it instinctively made her lower her own.

"I guess so."

"You thirsty?" He held up a full bottle of Coca-Cola.

"Oh." Jenna brushed the hair from her eyes and smiled. "Thank you." She opened it, took a swig, and almost sprayed it out across the cabin. The liquid was about fifty percent bourbon.

He gave a hacking, high-pitched laugh and smacked the back of her seat. "Dutch courage!"

On the other side of the aisle, the governor's executive aide, a coiffeured grande dame with pearl jewelry and half-moon glasses, glanced over the top of her *USA Today*. "You fell for it, too?"

Jenna handed the bottle back to him. "It's, uh, a little early for me."

"Drinks are on me tonight. And maybe you could even give me a few words ..."

"Your nightlife options in Pyongyang may be limited, Mr. Stevens. Your chances of a private conversation with me even more so."

"There's always my room."

She laughed unhappily. "That'll be the first place they'll bug." She turned back in her seat.

"Jeez, you're right."

Now she knew who he was. She'd seen his faux-solemn reports to camera and had usually flipped the channel. Nothing about his analysis of North Korea suggested originality or insight.

He was still leaning over her, crowding her space. "You know, one of our spooks told me there's no fifth floor in our hotel. Like, the elevator buttons go from four to six? It's because there's this secret listening station hidden on the fifth floor. There's one in all the hotels for foreigners ..."

Jenna closed her eyes. *Buddy, take the hint.*

She was zoning him out, listening to the hum of the engines, picturing whales gliding under the sea ice, and the ozone swirling in the thin outer blue, but she couldn't get back to sleep. Mention of enemy airspace had drawn her inevitably back to thoughts of Soo-min. Again Jenna's insides knotted with anxiety. What her sister's abductor had unwittingly revealed in that Skype call had electrified her. It was hard evidence that Soo-min had been abducted. But once her euphoria had faded, the hopelessness of the situation set in. It was like being told she'd won the lottery but her prize was on a heavily guarded island from which nothing could be taken. All she could do was sail past. She wondered vaguely what had happened to her "fresh ideas" report to the CIA director.

Outside the window the sky had clouded, turning the ice a pigeon-breast gray.

Colonel Cho would be at today's talks. She had no idea how she would do it, but it was crucial that she engineered a moment alone with him. It would not be easy. Everyone would be watched and accompanied at all times.

And if he wouldn't help her … ?

She would go public. She would bust the whole scandal wide open. Tell the world that her twin had been kidnapped and forced into … *Section 915 … the Seed-Bearing Program …* She had no idea what that could be, though instinct told her it was something fearful and sinister … and had nothing to do with gardening.

But even as she thought this, her resolve ebbed. Going public was highly risky. The regime would deny all knowledge of Soo-min. The shutters would come down and the one small hope Jenna had would be extinguished for good.

Landing gear lowered with straining hydraulics. Brown, bare landscape was rushing past, rising toward her. Not a tree anywhere. The wheels hit the tarmac and wobbled down a runway of filled-in potholes. Banks of earth. Tank trenches? Barbed-wire fences. No lights, no airport traffic. The plane slowed, passing two rusted Tupolev jets with the Air Koryo logo.

The plane turned slowly. A terminal building moved into her field of vision and Jenna felt a flutter of excitement. On top of the building was an outsized smiling portrait of Kim Il-sung, like a billboard for senior-citizen dental care.

Han would have a heart attack if she knew where I was.

Jenna had devoted years to studying North Korea but this was her first visit. Few Americans got to enter the country with which they were still technically at war. She gazed everywhere, hungry for detail.

Outside the terminal a row of men was lining up grimly to greet them. Foreign Ministry and internal-security types by the look of them, military coats flapping in the wind, waxwork faces. Her eyes searched for Colonel Cho but he wasn't among them.

"Here's the hospitality," Chad Stevens said. She noticed that the Coca-Cola bottle had been drained. His eyes were dancing about like a kid's.

The peace mission prepared to disembark with the governor in the lead. As they filed out of the plane, two CIA security officers in flying jackets checked their names off the manifest.

"You're coming with us, right?" Jenna said.

"We stay with the plane, ma'am. Too much sensitive comms gear on board to remain here overnight. We'll be back for you at six a.m."

She walked on, feeling a chill of anxiety.

It was early morning and searing cold. Sunlight slanted theatrically across the concrete, and her breath made patterns of white vapor, yet somehow this was a day like no other she'd known. It wasn't the air, which was fresh and unpolluted, just a faint and melancholy smell of coal fires. Or the rows of soft hills, which seemed to materialize, dreamlike, one after the other. It was the silence. No traffic, no planes overhead, no birdsong.

The white wisps of the governor's hair fanned in the wind as he gave a hearty handshake to someone in the reception party.

Though of pensionable age, and with two years still to serve in the capital of one of the northwestern states, the governor, as a respected former United States ambassador to the UN, with long experience of North Korea, had been the obvious candidate to lead the peace mission. His aim was to defuse tension following the Yeonpyeong Island attack, and to offer more aid in return for genuine concessions. The president had provided a White House military jet. Jenna's official role was to translate. Her real, more sensitive role, had been briefed to her by Fisk, who was still bruised by the intelligence failure over Yeonpyeong. Determined to capture the initiative, he had insisted the mission deal only with a known entity: Colonel Cho.

Daily spysat monitoring had revealed that the lab complex inside Camp 22 appeared almost complete. The speed of construction, using a vast, expendable slave labor force, had been astonishing. Convinced that it had everything to do with the rocket program, Fisk's nervousness was spreading through the defense community. Jenna's secret orders were to link any further offers of aid to a demand that the lab complex be opened to inspectors. Very quickly this had become the primary undisclosed aim of the mission, and it had focused Jenna's mind in the most sobering way. She was certain the regime would refuse, leaving her with no good options.

Behind the governor the members of the mission followed in single file: a *Wall Street Journal* commentator known for her acerbic views on the president's foreign policy; the governor's executive aide, who kept her boss's insulin in her handbag; two State Department East Asia policy experts, both Asian American men in their forties wearing identical Tom Ford sunglasses, and an NBC cameraman assigned to Chad Stevens. So far, only Stevens, whom she wouldn't trust with a child's ice cream, had been friendly.

They were escorted through the deserted terminal building to a cursory customs check, the purpose of which was to relieve them of their cell phones and all communication devices, which would be returned upon departure.

Through the window she looked at the gleaming US Air Force Gulfstream IV. Its cabin door had closed and its turbines were beginning to spin. Without taking her eyes off it she said, "I think we should all stick together ..."

"Good idea." She hadn't noticed Stevens standing next to her. "Me, I hate traveling alone."

"*Geepish.*"

A uniformed customs officer was jabbing his finger at the laptop in Stevens's open Samsonite case.

"*Geepish!*"

"He thinks it's got GPS," Jenna said.

"Tell him it's just a goddamn laptop and I need it for my job."

A cortège of cars waited outside. In the lead was a vintage black Lincoln sedan with the flags of the USA and the DPRK on the hood. The governor was led to the first car. Internal security goons she guessed were Bowibu stood about in black leather jackets. She saw Chad Stevens being ushered into the car behind her, and the others into the cars behind his.

The next thing she knew she was alone in the back seat of a Nissan Maxima with a driver and a security agent sitting in front. The cortège set off at a funeral pace, following the Lincoln sedan.

I'm alone in a hostile country without protection.

Glancing behind, she could make out Chad Stevens's large head in the car following hers. He waved. Incredibly, she was in the mood for that bourbon and Coke.

Jenna asked the two in front if she could listen to the radio.

The pair exchanged a glance. The security agent turned the dial. An exuberant female voice filled the car. "... *announced yesterday at the Kangsong Steel Complex, where the workers themselves kindled the torch of a new revolutionary upsurge that is spreading nationwide ..."*

The road was no wider than a country lane. The cortège passed a village of whitewashed huts with hip-and-gable tiled roofs, which had looked picturesque from a distance, but close-up were wretched, as if the inhabitants shared their homes with livestock. At the village entrance stood an enormous stele displaying the Kims, father and son, in a mosaic of colored stones. The same portrait had hung in the arrivals building. She'd been in the country half an hour. Already she felt there was no psychic space to escape them.

The cortège picked up speed as it entered the city outskirts along a dead-straight, tree-lined boulevard running between endless regimented apartment towers. It looked like one of Kim Jong-il's movie sets, or a vision of the future from the cosmonaut era. Electric trolley buses whirred past; here and there was a Mercedes-Benz with a military chauffeur, tinted windows, and a three-digit license plate.

On both sides of the boulevard, crowds were assembling on the sidewalks outside each tower. Hundreds of citizens in drab clothing were forming into lines five or six abreast and setting off into the low morning sun, marching to work in columns behind leaders holding red flags.

And something strange was happening to the voice on the radio. It was becoming amplified and ambient, an echo that seemed to boom beyond the car and into the chill air between the buildings. It took Jenna a moment to realize that the same voice was being broadcast from loudspeakers on lampposts at intervals of every hundred meters or so.

"... a new high-speed battle for production, comrades! Let us all show socialist solidarity with the heroes of the Kangsong Steel Complex by working the same extra hours ..."

She dropped her head back on her seat.

Welcome to Pyongyang.

31

Hyesan Train Station
Ryanggang Province, North Korea

Something was in the air. Mrs. Moon could not explain what. A power outage had silenced the loudspeaker, which seemed to heighten the tension everywhere. She felt it in her joints, the way rheumatic people feel a storm coming. The morning was overcast. Gauzy clouds obscured the sun, giving a sulfurous tint to the sky. The station was subdued, as if people were walking on tiptoe.

Twenty rice cakes were arranged in her nickel bowl. Her backside was numb from sitting on the ground. She was starting over from scratch, from the very bottom, but she would manage somehow. The team of Bowibu investigators had accepted her bribe of the refrigerator and removed her name from their list, but she knew it was only a temporary reprieve. They'd be back. With luck she'd have her canteen again in a year or two, and could afford to keep paying them off. These thoughts pinged on and off in her mind, like faulty lights, agitating her. Or perhaps it was just this unnatural tension. She wished something would happen to break it.

Kyu was sitting opposite her on a crate, flicking a plastic lighter beneath his pipe. He cocked his head, like a dog hearing a faraway bark.

"You feel it, too?" he said.

32

Ministry of Foreign Affairs
Kim Il-sung Square
Pyongyang, North Korea

Cho sat in an armchair in the First Deputy Minister's office, but-toned up in a new uniform with the medal on his chest. He felt like a phony actor in a war movie, with the Ministry's senior staff grouped behind him as extras, all in their best, with shoes polished and decorations glinting.

The First Deputy Minister was pacing, tea in hand.

"Our main opportunity will come during tonight's banquet, after several toasts of soju." A complicit laughter spread about the room. "That's when we feed our Yankees a side dish of threat, a main course of disinformation, and a dessert of sweet promise. Let's send the old man home thinking he's got peace in his pocket ..."

Their task, as far as Cho could tell, was not to defuse tension at all but to keep it nicely managed. Not that any of this mattered to him now. The Yankees were in the country for twenty-two hours. He doubted the Bowibu would wait that long. He suspected they'd arrest him as he left the banquet later this evening, his role over.

The First Deputy Minister paused to sip his tea and stare owl-ishly through the tall windows into Kim Il-sung Square.

"We must envelop our enemy in a fog to prevent him from guessing our plans ..."

Fog, lies.

Like a compass finding north, Cho's mind returned to his family.

He had told his wife everything, and he was still smarting from the pain. They lived the privileged life of the elite. She had never known disgrace. She had never known Cho as anything other than a dutiful husband and as a doting father to his son. Now, he had to live with her knowing the truth: that his ancestry was stained. That his blood carried a crime so grave that he would be removed from society altogether, though he had no idea what that crime was. Her reaction morphed through disbelief to shock to endless crying in the bedroom. Was he sure? She kept asking him, and although he had no evidence to give her he was absolutely sure. He said over and over how sorry he was, but he had no words to comfort her. He was the problem. The next day, he sensed her shrinking from him, already severing the tie that bound them. The day after that, she turned cold toward him. Feelings of betrayal and regret were showing in her face. She was regarding him anew, as someone else entirely. He couldn't bear to look at her. The stigma had been passed on in the son she had borne! Cho asked her to take Books to her parents' dacha in Wonsan on the east coast while he filed for divorce. And as the acute danger to Books began to dawn upon her, she became desperate to dissolve the marriage, urging Cho angrily, saying her family would pay whatever bribe it took to hasten it. She and Cho were clinging to this hope: that divorce, and her family's connections, would save their son.

Cho had arranged their travel permits himself. That had been the worst moment: seeing Books for the last time, saying good-bye to him on the platform of Pyongyang Station as if Appa would be joining them in a few days' time for a winter vacation. Books had asked him to remember to bring his puzzle book, and Cho had to turn away to hide his emotions.

His own life was over, and he was surprised by how lightly he wore it. He examined this feeling, this lightness in the face of death, wanting to know its source. Perhaps somehow, in his heart, he'd always known it could come to this. Its happening was a relief, and gave him unexpected courage. And with this courage a black smoke rose inside him, a desire to commit an act of vengeance.

He had brooded over this for several days, but when an unexpected opportunity arose, he did not hesitate.

He owed it to truth, to the future. He owed it to Marianne Lee.

Yesterday morning Cho's colleagues had been called to an unscheduled meeting on the top floor. He was not invited. As soon as they'd gone he put his head out of his office door and glanced up and down the corridor. None of the Bowibu agents who had been keeping a watch on him, dressed as cleaners, clerks, and maintenance men, were anywhere to be seen. He had a minute, perhaps. Two at most. The office next door belonged to a colleague named Captain Hyong. Cho slipped inside and closed the door.

With his heart thrumming in his ribs, he tried to steady his breathing.

Section 915, Yong-ho had said. The Seed-Bearing Program.

He picked up Hyong's desk phone to the Ministry's main switchboard and felt his mouth go dry. "Put me through to Section 915 of the Organization and Guidance Department."

The phone was answered immediately with the speaker giving name and rank.

"Lieutenant, this is Captain Hyong of the Ministry of Foreign Affairs," Cho said, trying to sound relaxed and superior. "We require the data you hold on a woman named Lee Soo-min, a Korean American brought here in 1998."

A grudging pause filled the line. "We don't share information about a classified program with another ministry unless—"

"This could give us a crucial advantage in our talks with the Yankees tomorrow. Do I really need to refer this up to the Leader in person?"

Another pause on the other end. "One moment."

Cho heard a muttered discussion in the background.

The lieutenant was back on the line. "A Korean *American*, you say?"

"You heard me. Mixed race. African American and Korean."

Cho heard something being tapped into a computer keyboard.

Hurry.

Holding the phone he glanced again into the corridor and saw two of his Bowibu tails conferring at the far end. Evidently they had just realized he was not in the meeting with the others. One of them turned and began to approach.

Please, come on.

It was at that moment that a document at the top of Captain Hyong's in-tray caught his eye. It listed the names of the American peace mission delegates, with a few intel details about each. His eye went straight to Marianne Lee. He saw the words ... *is almost certainly the former academic at Georgetown University, Washington, DC, named Dr. Jenna Williams* ...

The lieutenant was back on the line. "I've found a *Williams* Soo-min, the only name that matches that racial profile ... Name was changed to Ree Mae-ok. Entered the country by naval submarine at the Mayangdo Naval Base on June 23rd 1998, along with one South Korean male aged nineteen ..."

Cho's head was spinning. *So it's true* ... "Quickly, please, where is she held?"

"The Paekhwawon Compound, just north of the city. That's a strict invitation-only zone ..."

Cho was about to hang up when the lieutenant said, "Should we send over the file?"

Cho left Captain Hyong's office casually, in full view of his Bowibu tail, dangling Hyong's desk stapler from his hand as if he'd just popped in to borrow it.

That evening at home he sat in the dark in his study for a long time, picturing the eighteen-year-old Soo-min, disorientated, terrified as she arrived in his country, staring about at her new surroundings, thinking herself in a waking nightmare. How would he give this information to Marianne Lee, real name Dr. Jenna Williams? *Jenna.* It was a question of timing, opportunity ... And was that all he was going to do? Tell her what he'd learned? He felt himself breaking out in a sweat. *Cho Sang-ho, you are no coward. Surely you can—*

"Any questions?"

Cho was jolted back into the room.

The First Deputy Minister was scanning the faces of his staff through his thick glasses. His eyes settled on Cho.

"Cho, after the talks you will wait for the Yankees at the Yanggakdo Hotel and escort them to the banquet. And remember," he said, addressing the room at large, "if a Yankee asks you about the heightened security presence in the city, you are to reply that it is a 'routine annual drill.'"

What heightened security?

Cho returned to his desk to get his speech. This would be his most shameful part of all: he was to be a ventriloquist's dummy for words written by the Party. He turned into the corridor and passed one of his Bowibu shadows pretending to polish a glass door. For some reason a number of staff were hurrying in the opposite direction. Suddenly his shoulder collided with one of the junior diplomats and the man's papers scattered over the floor.

"Comrade, slow down," Cho said.

"Sorry, sir."

Everyone was on edge. Were they so jumpy about the Yankees' visit? He'd noticed it in the meeting. The way the First Deputy Minister kept peering nervously through the windows into the square.

He sat at his desk and began reading the speech one last time, but was interrupted by shouting in the corridor. An officer of the Pyongyang Police Garrison was approaching, followed by two orderlies holding boxes.

"All laptops, cell phones, and flash drives!"

Colleagues were dropping their phones into the boxes.

They stopped at Cho's door. "All laptops, cell phones, and flash drives!"

Cho tossed his phone in. "What's going on?"

"All communications devices to be registered with the Bowibu. Part of the heightened security measures," the officer said, attaching a sticky label with Cho's name to the phone. "They'll be returned tomorrow."

Puzzled, he went to the floor's reception area near the stairs, where there was a newspaper rack displaying all the dailies and weeklies. He scanned the pages of the *Rodong Sinmun*. It mentioned nothing about heightened security. The only thing that caught his eye was a curiously neutral notice on the first page about "necessary economic measures" that would be announced at midday.

He listened. The building had fallen eerily still. The desk phones were silent. Cho turned to walk back to his office and stopped. Standing at the far end of the corridor was the figure of a man watching him. He had silver hair and was dressed in a plain black tunic. Cho recognized him at once, the man he'd seen among the deputies in the Supreme People's Assembly. Instinctively Cho walked toward him, but the man turned and disappeared to the left. Cho thought of going after him, but at that moment he was distracted by another commotion.

The city's sirens began to wail, dipping and rising in one district, then another. His colleagues' faces were showing fear and alarm. All eyes were turned to the windows. Cho had remained calm until now, but that figure in black had unnerved him. He began to feel a formless, shapeless unease. Then a noise outside caused everyone to move en masse to the windows. Across the vast space of Kim Il-sung Square armed troops and police were running. Then they suddenly divided and scattered outward, like two flocks of swallows, clearing a path, and from the left a long, dark-green gun barrel slowly protruded, followed by the clinking and whirring of caterpillar tracks. Cho watched stupefied as a T-62 tank maneuvered into position in the center of the square.

He picked up the handset of a telephone on the nearest desk. Dead.

Behind him came a sound of hurrying footsteps. He turned to see the First Deputy Minister passing in the corridor, with other diplomats of the negotiation team following behind him. He signaled impatiently to Cho.

"The Yankees are here."

33

Ministry of Foreign Affairs
Kim Il-sung Square
Pyongyang, North Korea

Jet-lagged and disorientated, the members of the American peace
mission were led in single file past state news cameras, which were
waiting for them outside a large colonnaded edifice near the Taedong River. It looked like a side door, rather than the main entrance
on Kim Il-sung Square. A calculated snub, Jenna thought.

Stevens was alongside her. "Feels like a perp walk, doesn't it?"

She could smell the booze.

They were led through two long halls and into a spacious carpeted stateroom, and were invited to sit along one side of a long
mahogany table. On the wall to the left was a vast painted sea scene
of blue-green ocean waves crashing, spraying against rocks. Jenna
craned her head to take it in. The painting took up an entire wall.
She decided it symbolized the regime's steadfastness in tempestu-
ous times.

Neither the governor nor anyone in the party had any idea what
to expect. The North Koreans were maintaining total control over
the visit. The *Wall Street Journal* reporter took out her compact and
made a face as she inspected her lipstick. Chad Stevens's cameraman was excavating something from his nostril with the tip of a

ballpoint. The silence was broken by the governor's fingers drumming the table, and the distant wail of sirens.

Without warning the double doors at the far end of the hall flew open. A large delegation marched in, keeping step as they approached. The governor stood up and shuffled around the table to shake hands, but they marched straight to their seats, lined up, and sat down all at once, with the other members standing behind them. The governor, looking foolish, let his hand drop, and resumed his seat, followed by all the eyes in the room. Seated directly opposite him was Colonel Cho, in a white military tunic and a khaki cap. He'd been given a medal in the shape of star. Jenna tried to catch his eye, but his gaze remained fixed on a middle distance. His high cheekbones were sharper, and there were dark pouches beneath his eyes.

The panorama of hard faces was arrayed before the Americans. No greeting had been offered, no smile. The silence began to fester. The governor's mouth opened in confusion. It was obvious he had expected a word of welcome.

Directly behind her Stevens breathed, "Those Cold War talks with the USSR? Swingers' parties compared with this ..."

Unperturbed, the governor smiled genially, took out his speech, and put on his glasses. He was no stranger to an audience in need of a warm-up. But just as he did so, Colonel Cho laid his own speech on the table. In a ringing voice he began reading. Even weirder, the speech had been printed in a newspaper, in what seemed to be the lead editorial of the *Rodong Sinmun*.

Leaning in close to the governor's ear, Jenna translated the hectoring prose—*Yankee unjust blockade of Korea a barrier to peace! The only path for flunkyist nation-sellers is destruction!* The governor pursed his lips and nodded his head, listening with understanding for the first minutes, taking out his pen and jotting down the odd note, but his expression turned to mounting bewilderment as Colonel Cho turned a page and his voice rose a notch to condemn Yankee venality and moral vacuity until, after some twenty minutes had elapsed and the speech gave no sign of reaching a point or drawing to a close, the governor raised a hand and waved in a high, exasperated movement, signaling for Cho to stop.

Cho looked up.

"Sir, I'm an old man. I fear I don't have time for this, because I might be dead before you get to the end of that piece."

Jenna translated. Another silence followed, as all eyes looked from her back to the governor.

Then the man to Cho's right reacted. He wore thick, steel-rimmed glasses that gave him fish eyes, and a plain brown tunic without insignia. He gave a deep, slow laugh, and Jenna understood what had seemed ambiguous about the whole scene. The dynamic was wrong. Cho was a mouthpiece. This man laughing was the power in the room. The others took his cue and began laughing with gusto, male laughter filling the hall. But Colonel Cho's expression remained somber. For the briefest moment his eyes met hers before settling on his own reflection in the polished wood of the table. As the mirth continued and grew louder she heard its underbrush of cruelty, as if this wispy-haired old man, the governor, was their enemy's strength incarnate.

Later, the governor and his aide were led away to their lodgings at a state guesthouse—"Easier to bug our conversation," he muttered—and the other members of the mission were installed in rooms on the thirty-first floor of the Yanggakdo International Hotel for foreigners, with a view across the Taedong River to the city. The hotel was situated on an island in the river, the only bridge to which was watched. There was no chance of slipping away unobserved and unaccompanied. Minders and guides would be at their side the moment they left the lobby doors, and informers among the hotel staff and drivers would be watching their every move. Their rooms afforded the only privacy, but Jenna felt unsure even about that, and slotted the chain on her door.

She stood at the window for a long time, listening to the chug of a rusted barge dredging shale from the riverbed and the sirens rising and falling, as if the city was readying for an attack. A dark skyline of towers extended to a horizon of ghostly hills. No color or light from commerce; no buzz or bustle, just bare lights glowing in uncurtained apartments, a forest of concrete.

The governor's exasperation at the meeting had resulted in a minor American victory. The man who'd started the laughter, whom they learned was the First Deputy Minister, had signaled for Colonel Cho to put away the speech. For half an hour their exchange across the table was almost a normal discussion, until the governor, opening the brief Jenna had written for him, and holding up a pin-sharp satellite photo, cited the secret laboratory complex as a grave security concern. The First Deputy Minister appeared mystified, then an aide whispered in his ear and the atmosphere in the room changed in an instant. *No one speaks of the camps*, Jenna thought, seeing the faces before her turn cold once again. It was as if some secret line had been crossed. *Too bad.* She would make sure the matter was raised again at the banquet.

The sirens hadn't stopped and were starting to unnerve her. She turned on the ancient Toshiba television set to mask the noise. Pre-school children wearing makeup and pulling exaggerated faces of joy were performing a little dance, putting their hands in the air and singing, *"Let us reap a richer bean harvest ..."*

Cho had sat out the rest of the meeting in silence. Something had happened to him since New York. He'd met her eyes only for a second, and in them she'd perceived not conceit but something altogether unexpected, something vulnerable. She'd seen sorrow and shame and regret. She was sure of it. It seemed borne out by his taking no part in his comrades' laughter. A word alone with him had been impossible. That left only this evening's banquet ...

She hung up her clothes and lay down on the bed. She was exhausted. Within minutes she had fallen asleep to the children's singing, drifting into a restless, shifting dream in which the television set was watching her, the door handle to her room turned, and the chain on the door rattled.

34

Hyesan Train Station
Ryanggang Province, North Korea

It was midday exactly on the station clock. Mrs. Kwon heard it first. Then all the women heard it, and looked up from their mats. It was coming from the far side of the city, a cry like the wind catching the eaves of houses during a storm, or the howls of bad spirits in the mountains. As it drew nearer they discerned the sound of many whistles blowing.

The market stopped to listen.

Suddenly they saw Shovel-face, without Sergeant Jang, running toward them down the aisle, holding on to the visor of his cap. His face was plum red. He signaled for them to gather round.

"If any of you ladies have illegal phones—get rid of them now. And you didn't hear this from me."

The whistles rose again, many together, and were now joined by the wail of the air-raid sirens. The women turned in the direction of the sound, alarm bright in their eyes.

"What's happening?" Mrs. Yang said, but Shovel-face had gone.

"We're at war," Mrs. Kim gasped, covering her mouth with her mittens.

Mrs. Moon sat listening from her mat. This is what had been building all morning. It had made the atmosphere as tense as a drum. The electricity was still out. Without the covering noises of the loudspeaker or the trains, the whistles' notes seemed to gather and fall in ghostly waves of sound.

Then her attention was drawn by a squeaking sound in the square outside the station. She squinted, and through the fence saw a long red object moving into her line of vision. A teenage troop leader was directing a group of Socialist Youth as they pushed an enormous placard supported on wheels, rolling it into position in front of the Party Bureau. In letters a meter high it read LET US DEFEND COMRADE KIM JONG-IL WITH OUR LIVES!

From the opposite side of the square came the growl of an engine—an army truck moving fast. It lurched as its brakes screeched to a stop, and troops jumped out of the back. They began pulling out more placards from the truck. Their officer was shouting, pointing to positions around the square where the placards were to be affixed.

The whistles sounded again, like screams, and closer now. High keening notes behind a violent hammering of nails into walls.

The first placard was up, and a black dread crept over Mrs. Moon. The letters were daubed hastily in white paint.

DEATH BY FIRING SQUAD TO THOSE WHO SPREAD RUMORS!

The air filled with hammering. Customers seated in the market's two canteens stopped eating and stared, as if witnessing someone being clubbed to death. A second placard was up, then a third and a fourth.

DEATH BY FIRING SQUAD TO THOSE WHO SPREAD FOREIGN CULTURE!
DEATH BY FIRING SQUAD TO THOSE WHO ORGANIZE ILLEGAL GATHERINGS!
DEATH BY FIRING SQUAD TO THOSE WHO ABANDON SOCIALISM!

Without a word the women gathered their goods together and started packing up. Mrs. Moon looked about for Kyu. She'd feel safer with him, and he would know what was going on. The hard-currency store opposite the Party building was evicting its patrons; the state beauty parlor had already emptied; the pharmacy had closed.

"*A maximum sum of one hundred thousand won,*" said an iron voice from the loudspeaker.

The volume was explosive, almost rupturing her ears. The current was back. The station lights came on. The city was reeling, not knowing if it was day or night. The drone from the loudspeaker was loud and even. "*I repeat: within two days, up to a maximum of one hundred thousand …*"

The women froze.

They listened through to the end of the announcement.

"*All schools and universities are closed until further notice; all cell phones and memory sticks must be handed without delay to representatives of the Ministry of State Security …*"

On tenterhooks, the women were staring at the floor, waiting for the announcement to repeat from the beginning.

The news swung through the market like a wrecking ball.

"*A new, more valuable currency is being issued. The new won is worth one thousand old won. All citizens have two days to exchange the old banknotes for the new ones, up to a maximum of one hundred thousand won. I repeat …*"

The stillness was like the aftermath of an explosion. As the smoke cleared, devastation stared them in the face.

The state was wiping out what was left of their savings.

Mrs. Kwon sat down on her haunches like a peasant and began wailing with her hands covering her face; others continued to concentrate, listening to the announcement again, stupefied, as if they'd misheard, or its words might change.

All their enterprise, all their long hours, all their hard work.

For minutes they were lost in thought. Then Mrs. Lee gesticulated angrily at the loudspeaker. "All I have left is in won," she

shouted, and dismay turned to anger like damp firewood beginning to catch. The scale of this disaster was sinking in. A moment
later, all of them were talking across each other. How much had
they saved in won? How much in secure, hard currencies—yuan,
dollars, euros?

"Why are they doing this?" Mrs. Yang shrieked.

She'd questioned the unquestionable, but no one appeared
shocked. Her words seemed only to stoke the anger spreading
through the market.

Because to trade is be free, Mrs. Moon thought, and looked down
into her lap.

The whistles rose again in unison, a background noise now to
the hubbub of angry voices.

A young man holding an infant boy in his arms came hurrying
down the aisle. He was approaching the traders who sold clothing;
each of them shook their heads. He reached the women at the end
near the bridge and pleaded. "Please, I've been saving to buy my
son a coat." With his free hand he was holding out a wad of soon-to-
be-worthless won.

His words seemed to trip a switch, and the febrile mood of the
market changed again. Panic followed him down the aisle, like
leaves stirred up by a sudden breeze. Now panic gripped the women
around Mrs. Moon, and panic spread to the customers. Within seconds the market was in uproar. Everyone was trying to spend their
won on anything they could resell.

"A day of ill fortune, ajumma." Kyu had materialized beside her.

Without hesitating she pushed a grubby bundle of won into his
hands—all she had.

"Buy anything that can be resold," she said. "Hurry. Go."

She slumped down onto a pile of rice sacks, dropping her head
into her hand, ignoring the shouting and arguments she could
hear breaking out around her. She felt as if she were sitting on the
shore of a flat dark body of water that stretched on and on, cold, and

forever. For a long time, years perhaps, she had distracted herself from it, ignored it. Now she faced it, and accepted it. It would always be there. It would never change. *There is no future*, she thought. The melody she half recalled played through some door in her memory that opened onto long ago, and her vision became misted and blurred.

A lamb goes uncomplaining forth, the guilt of all men bearing . . .

It brought with it an image of a young woman in a beautiful *hanbok* dress, sitting amid petals in the dappled shade of a cherry blossom tree. Her singing was sweet and lovely and full of hope. Her mother, long dead. Mrs. Moon pulled two of the rice sacks toward her, hugging them to her chest, resting her head on top of them. Her baby sons, only thirteen months between them. How they'd cried and gurgled, how healthy they'd been, how noisy with life. Lost to her, like everything else.

When Kyu returned the sky was fading to gold, with fiery red clouds near the mountaintops. He dropped a weighted cloth bag to the ground. He was dirty, with wipe marks round his eyes, and had a tear in his coat. He sat next to her on her mat without a word, took out a wrap of *bingdu* and his pipe, and performed his ritual with his thin fingers. He didn't need to tell her. The noise of the battlefield had raged all around her. Fighting had broken out as people outbid each other to buy anything they could resell. With one finger she lifted the rim of the bag. He'd managed to buy a stuffed toy bear, a used sweatshirt, and a pig's head. He'd spent two thousand won on goods that would have cost a few hundred this morning. The three bills he had left he gave back to her.

He exhaled the ice-white smoke, and offered her the pipe.

She looked at it. In his small hand it shone like a sacred object. With a sense of ceremony she put it to her lips and inhaled. The drug didn't burn her throat or make her cough. It was smooth and clean, more like mist than smoke. Her brow relaxed, and moments later she cared even less about everything. She turned to Kyu and put her arm around him. His smoked-glass eyes regarded her, full of knowledge, then he rested his head on her shoulder.

"What's your family name?" She had never thought to ask him.

"Don't remember."

"Don't remember? Your name's just 'Kyu'?" That wasn't right. Everyone had a family name. A person was nothing without family. "Take mine," she said.

He smiled shyly as if given a gift of rare and great value. "Moon," he said.

The whistles and sirens were background music now. They'd lost their power to scare her. She took another puff of *bingdu*. Kyu was right. It took away pain. It took away fear, and worry.

She was seeing people drifting into the square outside the station, knotting into groups, talking in front of the Party building, oblivious to the sirens. The voice from the loudspeaker continued its steady martial bleat.

"*By order of the Ministry of State Security, a city-wide curfew will begin at sundown. Any citizens at large in the streets after sundown will face arrest...*"

The last rays of the sun were illuminating the underside of the clouds a deep crimson, but the numbers of people in the square seemed to be doubling and trebling. The *bingdu* was making her see things that weren't there. A growing crowd that was unafraid.

Then she noticed Kyu's face, too, transfixed by the sight, and the women leaving the market and heading into the square as if pulled by an invisible string.

Mrs. Moon stood straight up. She wasn't imagining it. The crowd *was* growing.

Holding Kyu's hand she entered the square. Some faces she recognized—merchants and vendors who knew her—but they were being joined by a multiplying number of other citizens. The whole city seemed to be gathering, drawn out of their factories and apartments, drawn by the gravitational pull of whatever this was. The tension she'd felt all morning had broken. That had felt like a kind of static, but this was something else. She couldn't explain it. It was a force, a magnetism. Someone carried the *yontan* brazier from the market into the square, placing it right in front of the Party building, and people gathered around it, blowing into their hands to keep their circulation moving.

When four, five army trucks with their yellow headlights on full beam arrived in a convoy the crowd watched in silence. Rather than scurry away their numbers were continuing to grow. People were disregarding caution; faces were tense with anticipation. Troops jumped out of the trucks, dozens of them, but faced with an unexpected and very large crowd their whistles fell silent. The standoff lasted a few moments until the cordon of troops parted to allow a captain through. He walked to the *yontan* brazier at the center of the square, looking left and right, shoving people out of the way.

All eyes in the square were on him.

"What's going on here?" he shouted. "Have you no respect for our Party Bureau? A curfew is about to start and you're hanging around like riffraff?" No one in the crowd moved. "This is what happens when the poison of capitalism spreads. Disorder. Disrespect. Selfishness. And since I see so many capitalists here ..." He tipped his hat sardonically toward Grandma Whiskey. "... you may as well hear this now: from tomorrow morning the station market will open for three hours only, from eight to eleven ..."

"*Why?*" said a voice.

The captain stepped away from the fire. His hand went to his gun holster, his face suddenly blank with astonishment.

"Who speaks back to me?"

Mrs. Moon stepped through the throng of people to the firelight and stood squarely opposite him on the other side of the brazier.

"How dare you question me." He was glaring at her, breathing deeply. "You ask me why—I'll tell you why!" He looked about, to address the multitude, and a slight apprehension came into his voice, at the growing audience of faces. "From now on, prices for food, fuel, and clothing will be set by the government ..."

From all over the crowd voices exclaimed in anger.

"The government doesn't know what the hell it's doing." The voice sounded like Mrs. Lee's.

"The ration system will be working again tomorrow, will it?" The sarcasm was Mrs. Kwon's.

"What are we supposed to do with our worthless won?"

Mrs. Yang pushed to the front and showed her face, which was as hard as copper in the firelight. "Burn them for heating?"

"Amounts in excess of one hundred thousand won must be deposited in the state bank," the captain shouted.

A laugh of derision went up. The captain took out his handgun, pointed his arm upward and fired it into the air, making everyone crouch. The shot echoed off the square's buildings, subduing the crowd instantly.

"Markets are breeding grounds for every type of unsocialist practice," he yelled. "The Party is reasserting the people's economy—"

"We are the people."

Mrs. Moon hadn't raised her voice. She spoke in her usual tone, but her words seemed to ignite and flare the moment they were out.

She took another step toward the firelight. "Didn't Comrade Kim Jong-il himself say that the people are the masters of the economy? We are the people." The crowd began to murmur and whisper. The invisible force seemed to swell and grow stronger. She felt her words take power as they left her lips. She felt no fear, just a gathering elation rising inside her. There was something so simple and natural to what she said next, as if she were presenting options to children. "He will have to give us rice, or let us trade."

She tugged her three remaining bills out of her money belt. They looked pathetic, and one fluttered to the ground. She scrunched the other two into a paper ball, held out her arm, and dropped them into the brazier.

The crowd went dead still. Those bills carried the image of the Great Leader, now flaring on the coals. Shock passed across the assembled faces. She had committed an act from which there would be no return, no forgiveness. Night was rolling down from the mountains. Faces flickered amber and gold in the firelight; and eyes were black and sparkling. The captain opened his mouth, but no speech came out.

Mrs. Moon saw movement to her left and right. Mrs. Lee and Mrs. Yang stepped forward to the fire. One after the other they raised their arms out straight and dropped their bundles of worthless banknotes into the brazier. The troops, waiting for an order, did nothing. Everyone seemed too surprised to move, as if some universal law was altering before their eyes. Now Mrs. Kwon did the same. Then Mrs. Kim. Then Grandma Whiskey. Hundreds of thousands of won consigned to the fire. The ink in the notes made delicate flames of blue and lime and fuchsia that reflected in the women's faces. Then the paper combusted brightly, sending orange embers up into the air.

The crowd made an ominous noise, a herd being roused and provoked. "Disperse, everyone!" the captain shouted. "Disperse now or face arrest!"

A woman's shout came from somewhere at the back of the crowd. "Give us rice or let us trade." Another voice, younger and nearer to the front: "Give us rice or let us trade!"

The captain signaled with his hand to the troops and blew his whistle. For two seconds they did nothing. The troops were witnessing their first riot. Suddenly they charged into the mob, ramming people away, kicking them, punching them, knocking them to the ground with rifle butts. The violence, now unleashed, was brutal. The crowd roared, but the chant had caught and spread like a forest fire, with every individual's energy feeding off each other.

"Give us rice or let us trade!"

"Give us rice or let us trade!"

Every citizen in the square was shouting it, venting, fists punching the air. No whistle could drown the chanting. A stone flew through the air, hitting an army truck, then another, smashing an upper window of the Party headquarters. The whole square was chanting in unison.

Mrs. Moon had not seen a sight like it. The world was turning upside down. Iron was melting, stone dissolving. Anything seemed possible.

Suddenly, a gasp rippled through the crowd like the shock wave of a blast. As quickly as it had started, the riot stilled; the chanting stopped. People stared in disbelief. The small brazier cast its weak light onto the shadowy colonnades of the Party Bureau, enough to see that the long red placard erected in front of it that morning had been defaced. The crowd was trying to take in the impossible.

In hurried black letters, two words had been painted above the Dear Leader's name.

DOWN WITH
KIM JONG-IL

The only head not turned toward it, the only figure facing the opposite way, was the captain's. For a moment his face was in shadow, until the firelight revealed his expression. His eyes were wild, unhinged. He was scanning the crowd like a laser for Mrs. Moon.

She began to inch her way backward, slowly, a step at a time, without drawing his attention. Then he saw her. The next thing she knew he was charging toward her, hurling people out of the way. He raised his handgun, holding it by the barrel, with the butt raised to strike.

She raised her arms to protect her face.

Out of nowhere, a small dark shape bowled into the captain's legs, smacking him clear off his feet, sending his cap flying. He landed hard and heavily on his side, his ear to the ground, and howled in pain. Before he could catch sight of his assailant, Kyu was gone. The captain pushed himself up, touched his ear, and saw his fingers sticky with blood.

Mrs. Moon turned and did something she hadn't attempted in years. She ran. The *bingdu* had taken away the stiffness and pain in her knees. Her heart beat calmly; her head was clear. That did not, of course, alter the fact that she was arthritic and sixty years old. She'd made it as far as the rail tracks when the blow came from behind, punching into her back and knocking the wind from her lungs. Loose chippings crashed into her face.

In the background she heard the *tat-tat-tat* of a machine-gun. As her head was pushed into the oily and shit-covered gravel between the sleepers, and the cuffs locked over her wrists behind her, she thought how happy she was to have given Kyu a name.

35

Thirty-first Floor
Yanggakdo International Hotel
Pyongyang, North Korea

When Jenna awoke an orange dusk had settled over the city. The sirens had stopped, leaving an eerie silence. The streets were deserted of people and traffic. She glanced at her watch. She had only minutes to get ready.

The bathroom pipes gave a phantom groan before scalding water sputtered from the shower. She washed and dried her hair quickly, put on her black Givenchy dress, and, after a cool, appraising stare into the mirror, applied some makeup and fastened her sapphire earrings. Taking Soo-min's silver chain from her handbag she hung it carefully around her neck and touched the pendant with the tip of her finger. A Renaissance lady, pointing to a jewel.

It was tempting to let Chad Stevens oversleep, but she'd agreed to pick him up and walked along the corridor in search of his door. The corridor lights hummed and flickered and then went out completely, leaving her in darkness except for the dim emergency exit lighting. This hotel was starting to creep her out. She hoped the elevators were working. The whole building had a deep stillness to it, as if this were the only occupied floor.

She knocked on Stevens's door. No answer. She knocked again, then opened it slowly to see Stevens, back toward her, hunched on the floor over his laptop wearing headphones. Beside it was his open Samsonite case and a half bottle of bourbon. A lead extended from the computer to the square, flat, unfolded satellite aerial perched on the windowsill. On the laptop screen was a BBC World News studio.

"Stevens, what the hell—"

He snapped the laptop shut and shot to his feet as if he'd been caught watching porn.

"Jesus, you scared me."

Jenna stared in amazement. "What're you doing?"

He held his palms up. "Chillax, will you. Keep your voice down. Something big's going on ..."

"D'you think this is a game? We're in North Korea, Chad. Have you any idea what danger you've put us all in by bringing that—"

"I'm sorry, all right? No one'll be any the wiser ..."

She glanced about the room, noting the multiple hiding places a bug could be concealed, listening right now to this jerk confess his crime with his own big mouth.

He gestured to the laptop. "I'm telling you, a massive story's breaking ..."

She sighed and folded her arms, a schoolteacher hearing a lame excuse.

He poured a finger of neat bourbon into a coffee cup and handed it to her. His face had lost its dull frat-boy look. His eyes were alight, his mind working. She accepted the drink. He sat back down on the floor, reopened the screen, and showed her a stop-motion, pixelated image. The ticker running across the base read TUNISIAN STREET VENDOR SPARKS UPRISING. An angry mob was marching through a bazaar, chanting in Arabic. An overturned car blazed, illuminating the crowd. Hundreds of fists punched the air. The signal kept cutting out. He turned off the audio. Then the footage cut to an ID photo of a young man with tight curly hair and large, sad brown eyes.

"This street seller set himself on fire yesterday, in protest against ... everything. It's starting a fucking revolution. There are already crowds on the streets in Cairo. This could spread anywhere ..."

Jenna watched a fuzzy, juddering aerial image shot from a helicopter. Tear gas trailed white smoke as it was fired, creating a sudden round hole in the crowd like an iris dilating. Now pundits were talking soundlessly, from London, Istanbul, Cairo.

"You can bet every Arab dictator will impose curfews tonight. They're on high alert—"

"All the more reason to turn that off, *now*. Jesus, Stevens, remember where you are."

Her words seemed to sober him. He closed the computer and folded away the aerial. "You're right." Then gave her his salesman's smile. "Exciting, though." He knocked back his bourbon.

"You're not even dressed."

"Why don't you go down? I'll meet you in the lobby with the others." She was through the door when he said, "You're looking hot by the way."

He didn't see her roll her eyes.

On the landing for the thirty-first floor the other members of the mission were waiting for an elevator. The two State Department East Asia policy experts were in black tie, which she wasn't sure would strike the right note; the *Wall Street Journal* reporter was power dressed like a presidential candidate with lacquered hair and big shoulders. Stevens's cameraman had on the same bejeaned garb he'd arrived in.

One of the four elevators' doors opened; it was crowded with a group of extremely tall Asiatic men in sweatshirts bearing the words MONGOLIAN FRIENDSHIP BASKETBALL TOUR. There was enough space for a few more.

"You guys go ahead," Jenna said.

The others got in and the doors closed. Again the lights flickered, dimmed, and went out. She wondered if the elevator was affected, but the digital display above the doors showed it descending smoothly to the lobby. In the darkness she noticed a small halo of ruby lights trained on her: a security camera. She moved to the window, out of its range, and gazed at the eastern, residential side of the city. Great swathes were in total blackout. The only pools of light, like icons in a catacomb, were the Father-Son portraits, which made the darkness oddly jeweled. Beautiful, in a sinister kind of way.

Her mind was replaying the scene she'd just witnessed.

A mob rampaging through a bazaar in Tunisia, a dictator's grip on power weakening by the hour under the glare of the world's media.

The fright it must be causing the regime here ...

The realization struck her with the force of revelation.

Kim Jong-il was only as powerful as his ability to control this news. If it leaked into this country, if rumors of revolutions spread, the smallest spark ... the smallest spark ...

The sirens. The empty streets. The troops everywhere. Jenna put her hand to her forehead. *The city was in lockdown.*

A *ping* sounded behind her.

An elevator door opened. It was unoccupied. Where the hell was Stevens?

She stepped in. The doors closed. She watched the descending digits and remembered what Stevens had told her on the plane. Sure enough, the steel panel next to her had an elevator button for every floor from the thirty-fifth down to the lobby, but not for the fifth floor.

She tightened the belt of her coat. The air inside the elevator was freezing. She turned to the mirror to check her hair and makeup. The long descent began to slow. The elevator came to a halt and the doors opened with a *ping*.

In the reflection of the mirror she saw not the lobby behind her but absolute darkness.

In confusion she glanced up at the digit on the display over the door. The floor number displayed was five.

An icy draft blew toward her, carrying with it a wave of pure void. She was staring into a long, dim corridor, as if into the barrel of a gun. The small light inside the elevator buzzed, then went out.

The hands reached in and seized her before she could scream.

36

Fifth Floor
Yanggakdo International Hotel
Pyongyang, North Korea

The hand had slammed over her mouth and nose, muffling her cry. She writhed and twisted, but then a voice hissed in her ear.

"Not a sound, if you want to see your sister."

Jenna went instantly rigid, her eyes wide open. What she experienced was more powerful than surprise.

Cho relaxed his grip slowly, uncertain of her, wary of her reaction. As her eyes adjusted to the dark she saw a corridor lined with doors and smoked-glass walls. A low, white-noise humming filled the space, and with it the hot-wire smell of computer servers.

She held her breath, her heart a tight fist in her chest.

His voice was a tiny exhalation of air, less than a whisper. "We don't have much time. The banquet starts in thirty-five minutes. Do you agree to do exactly as I say?"

"Yes."

"There's a price. Asylum in the United States. I leave with you on your plane at six a.m."

He's defecting? Jenna's mind reeled. She had no power to agree any such thing, and he must have known it. Then she sensed the magnitude of the implications. The North Koreans who defected were poor and hungry. Only once in a decade did someone of this rank—*a regime insider*—defect ...

She said, "You won't get anywhere near the plane—"

"I will, with your help."

Jenna felt frantic. He had released her, but she held on to his hands and turned to him in the dark, very close to his face, conscious of time draining away.

His voice was tight with desperation. "Do we have a deal?"

She would say anything to see her sister, anything at all, and he must have known that, too. "Yes."

He was silent for a moment, evaluating her, wanting to believe her.

Afraid that he might suddenly change his mind, she kissed him suddenly on his cheek.

She sensed his eyes searching hers in the dark.

"Go quickly to the end of the corridor. Do not look left or right. Wait for me on the other side of the door. Be ready to run."

Jenna felt dizzying surges of fear and euphoria. Her legs were wobbling. She began to walk along the corridor. Unable to resist, she glanced to one side. Behind a smoked-glass wall she saw uniformed men sitting with their backs toward her. They were wearing headphones and watching banks of CCTV screens. She glimpsed moving footage of guests lying on hotel beds, guests waiting for elevators, and, on one screen, a woman taking a shower. *Oh, you fool, Chad Stevens. They've seen everything.*

But was she any less stupid? What insane risk was she taking?

After a hundred yards or so she reached the fire door. She looked back and dimly saw Cho reach into the elevator and press a button. The doors closed just as he jumped clear. Then he jabbed his elbow hard against a small panel on the wall, smashing its glass.

Fire alarms rang clamorously, deafeningly, and she put her hands to her ears. Now he was sprinting toward her. One of the doors in the glass wall opened. Then another. Men stepped out.

Jenna slipped through the door before they saw her, hearing Cho yell, "Fire!" Then closer: "Fire! Evacuate the building!"

He caught her elbow. Hurrying down the dim stairwell, lit only by fire-exit signs, they reached the fourth floor, then the third, which was now emptying of people. Maids, security guards, and foreign guests were filing out onto the stairs. Getting clear of the noise was all anyone could focus on. No one took any notice of Jenna and Cho. By the time they'd reached the first floor and joined the snaking line of waitresses, karaoke hostesses, croupiers, bowling-alley attendants, barmen, chefs and more guests, their escape had slowed to a crawl.

They followed the crowd out of a fire door into the freezing night air, keeping their heads down. Directly to their left was the rear of a new silver Mercedes-Benz sedan with the license plate 2★16, parked as close to the fire exit as possible.

"Get in," Cho said, bleeping his key to unlock the doors. They jumped in; Cho slammed his door and turned the ignition, glancing in his mirror.

Less than ten feet behind them, just past the fire door, the headlights of a waiting car came on full beam. But the vehicle was blocked from the Mercedes by the dense lines of evacuating staff and guests, passing in front of its headlights like a barcode. Cho revved the engine, released the hand brake, and slammed his foot down. Wheels screeched and they were speeding away, just as the car behind blared its horn in an urgent staccato. It was trapped behind the crowd, its horn lost in the cacophony of the fire alarm.

Jenna turned to Cho. She was riding a wave of pure adrenalin, and felt her training kick in. *Stay calm and alert.* His face was focused on the unlit road, his hands gripping the steering wheel as if it were a life buoy. *Focus with him.* The car slowed as it reached the checkpoint on the Yanggak Bridge connecting to the city. Guards shone flashlights, and to her surprise, stepped back and saluted. The barrier was raised without Cho even having to stop. Moments later they were across Taedong River, accelerating along vast empty boulevards, past Pyongyang Station, past the Koryo Hotel.

It was a strange, haunting sensation, seeing the grim outlines of towers and state edifices slip past unlit. A city in a nightmare, or a city under siege in wartime, made all the more surreal by a sky lit with stars. Only the Father-Son portraits were illuminated, their lights burning by a current that was never cut. With no traffic and no traffic lights, Cho shot across intersections with barely a look left or right. Again Jenna felt a surge of nervous excitement.

They were heading northwest, as far as she could guess, away from the monuments and the river. They crossed a high overpass, and she saw straight into dim apartments lit by kerosene lamps.

After a few minutes' driving fast, the towers began to thin out, and the city became squalid districts of tiled-roofed shacks, the parts of the capital visitors were never shown. The road deteriorated as they reached the sparse outskirts, and Cho had to brake suddenly to circle a craterous water-filled pothole. When the city limits gave way to hills and farmland, he broke his silence, and spoke in Korean.

"The capital's under curfew. I don't know why. The phone network is down, so at least it means the car following me can't raise the alarm in a hurry."

"What trouble are you in?"

"The minders escorting your group to the banquet will think you're trapped in that elevator. We have ..." He glanced at the car's clock. "... twenty-three minutes before the banquet starts, before suspicions will be raised."

"Are you going to tell me where we're going?"

"I can't promise you'll see her." He stared ahead, preoccupied. "On the way back into the city, I will tell you what you have to do to get me onto the plane."

Suddenly she felt a rushing, hair-raising danger, with strong undercurrents of guilt. She hadn't the first idea how she was going to help him, even if she could, without endangering the others.

There was no possible way of contacting Langley for orders. Unless ... *Stevens's satellite aerial.*

He said, "What time will the plane come?"

"I guess ... only a few minutes before we depart at six a.m. and then it will take off immediately. It's a White House military jet. It won't stay here a minute longer than it needs to."

Cho was sunk in silence again, and she wondered whether he had any plan at all, or if the unexpected lockdown may simply have thrown him a chance.

They had driven so fast that they were now in the countryside and from the top of one hill Jenna thought she glimpsed the ocean. The car slowed again as it followed the high stone wall of a large, gated enclosure.

"Get down in front of the seat." They were approaching a barrier gate. Two squat entry boxes built of reinforced concrete stood to either side of the gate, flanked by rolls of razor wire.

Jenna crouched, and a blanket was thrown over her.

The car stopped. She heard boots approach across the gravel. Again, she heard them step back, and stamp in salute. Perhaps Cho had shown ID, but he had not even opened his window. Something about the car itself—*the license plate?*—was opening every barrier, waiving all formality.

"Don't move," he said. A moment later they slowed for a second barrier. Again, salute, and the car proceeded. "You can get up now."

They were gliding along a road lined with Korean maples, each lit with tiny spotlights set in a landscaped lawn. To the left was a large ornamental lake with a brilliant illuminated fountain in the middle, turning the water to cascading white sparks. The silhouette of a peacock trailed its long feathers, and she glimpsed the floodlit putting green of a golf course. The transformation was shocking, as if they'd crossed a border from Mogadishu to Beverly Hills.

Up ahead on the crest of a low hill was a two-story villa with a red-tiled roof, lit by spotlights set into the surrounding stone paths.

Tall cypress pines gave the place a Tuscan air, and the windows cast strips of golden light down the slopes of the lawns. Driving around a tennis court they passed a covered area of parked luxury Western sports cars and Suzuki motorbikes that looked new and unused. Cho was about to stop when a bright security lamp blinked on, hitting them full beam. He drove on a little farther, finding a spot of deep shadow alongside a thick beech hedge.

"What is this place?" Jenna said.

"A few seconds only," he whispered. "Then we leave—do you understand?"

Jenna's eyes were picking out every detail. She could see some kind of shooting range with targets fashioned in the outlines of soldiers. She wondered if she had seen this place before in the spysat images.

"Did you hear what I said?"

"Yes."

They got out and walked along the edge of the hedge. The air was so cold it burned her nose. Her heels sank into the grass and she stumbled; she reached out and Cho held her hand.

He slowed, gesturing for her to stay in the shadow as they neared the end of the hedge. Music, and laughter, and the sound of many voices conversing—children's voices—were coming from the side of the villa that overlooked the lake. Cho held Jenna's shoulder and together they peered around the edge of the beech leaves.

Inside the villa they saw a children's party. The youngest were eight or nine, but they seemed to range in age up to early adolescents, thirteen or fifteen, perhaps. They were seated on the floor along low tables angled in a square around the room. The music, which sounded like a patriotic Soviet song, was coming from an ensemble of four children playing accordions. All were dressed in Western clothing—jeans, sneakers, sweatshirts—but there was something singularly un-Western about them. They were curiously composed and respectful, but that wasn't it. It took Jenna a moment to see it. Some of the children were blond; others dark skinned and dark haired. Some had blue eyes; others dark brown or chestnut. In fact their unifying trait was in the shape of their eyes. Every child was half Korean. Smiling women in *chima jeogori* dresses were serving them food, and chatting with them affectionately. It took another moment for Jenna to register that the person seated at the head of the table, in a flowing, traditional Korean silk dress, was herself.

In the place reserved for the head of a family sat a woman who was her replica. She was holding a silk fan, and her hair was in the conservative North Korean style of the 1950s, the same as the other women. She was inclining her head and listening to one of the older boys—a youth with East Asian features and striking, corn-gold hair—who was speaking into her ear. She made a polite show of laughter and ruffled his hair.

Soo-min. As plain as day. Just yards away.

Jenna felt her breath become ragged. Could she trust the evidence of her own eyes? It was as if she were seeing a magical animal, a creature of folklore. She took an involuntary step forward, but Cho yanked her back hard by her arm.

The food being served was also unusual—not Korean food but pizza and Coca-Cola and salad. Food no ordinary North Korean would ever see, never mind eat.

A plate was placed in front of Soo-min but she waved it away with an apologetic shake of her head. Then she stood up and the chatter and the music fell quiet. The children got to their feet. She made an animated face and said something that made them laugh. Now the children gave a deep bow, as if she were about to leave.

Jenna lunged toward the window with her arm outstretched, but Cho held tightly to her. She coiled and tried to shove him away.

"We're leaving," he hissed. "Now."

She forgot to whisper. She forgot about everything else in the world.

"I am not leaving without her!"

37

Paekhwawon Compound
13 Kilometers Northwest of Pyongyang
North Korea

His face was entreating, his finger to his lips, trembling, telling her *not a sound.*

We had a deal. He was clenching her arm tighter, aware that he was hurting her.

In the glow from the windows he saw her eyes flare with a tremendous kinetic force, emotions too powerful to subdue, and certainly not by him. He had become an irrelevance to her. She gave a violent movement of her arm that disengaged his grip. Before he could prevent her, she had run across the stone path.

She stopped just in front of the window. Her body seemed to soften and melt before the scene.

Soo-min was still talking, her pink *hanbok* dress shimmering in the golden light. The children had sat down again. She was addressing them as if telling them a story. They listened, rapt.

Jenna reached her hand slowly up in greeting. A young girl was the first to see her, and gave a shriek of surprise. Then all the children's heads turned in unison toward the windows.

And for three long seconds, the sisters' eyes met.

Soo-min's face was blank, then it seemed to open like a flower, from bud to petals of fear and disbelief, astonishment and joy, and Cho imagined he witnessed something of immense power connecting, an arc of pure energy passing between the sisters.

Then Jenna touched the tips of her fingers to the glass, and everything went to hell.

White, saturating lights came on in all directions, and a deafening intruder klaxon pierced the air with long electronic dashes. The children scrambled to their feet and ran from the room, but the sisters' gaze did not waver. Cho watched as an expression of great fear seemed to come across Soo-min's face.

A dog barked, very close.

From around the corner of the house, about twenty meters away, a black shape scuttled into the light.

Jenna turned to see the dog poised, snarling. With shocking speed it leapt for her, teeth bared. Before Cho could even react she had taken a step toward it and shot her right palm smack into the animal's nose. Another step and she had kicked it hard out of the way. The dog howled and ran off.

When she turned back to the window, the room was empty. Soo-min had gone.

Men's voices were shouting from the direction of the lake, and booted feet were running toward them along a stone path. Jenna was pushing hard at the sliding window, trying to force the catch.

Cho yelled, *"Capsida!"*—*Let's go!*

Suddenly she backed away. Two armed guards had entered the room, their eyes scanning along the windows. Cho seized the moment. He lifted her clear off her feet, carrying her at a run around the side of the villa. To his surprise she did not struggle, and against his cheek he felt the soft gasping of her breathing. The Mercedes was bright silver under the glaring lights, the trees bleached a lunar white. The keys were in his hand. He bleeped the doors unlocked and had to lay her into the seat. Her body had gone supine, like someone in shock, or drunk. He threw the gear into reverse and released the hand brake. The car whined backward fast along the gravel to the covered area of cars and new motorbikes. He felt the bumper hit the nearest motorbike with a metallic crunch, toppling it into the next, crashing them like dominoes. He swung the steering wheel and spun the car around, spraying gravel onto the other cars, and accelerated down the tree-lined road along the lake toward the exit.

There was no point in hiding her now. In fact, her face was their best chance of getting out of there.

The first barrier was approaching. Flashlights were shone into the tinted windshield. They weren't going to wave him through.

A young officer signaled for him to pull over. Cho lowered his window. The klaxon was blaring in the guardhouse.

"Sorry, sir, no one leaves the grounds until we have the all clear."

Cho's face went as hard as rock. He held up a passbook with the gold-embossed insignia of the Workers' Party, the ID of an elite Party cadre. If there was one thing he did well it was playing Pyongyang's game of petty hierarchies.

"Do you know who you're talking to, you shit?"

"Sir—"

Cho flicked his head conspiratorially toward the passenger seat and the officer crouched down to peer in at Jenna. Her head was in profile as she gazed ahead, unseeing. She seemed calm, seraphic almost, like someone who'd experienced a vision.

A look of confusion came over the officer's face.

"Open the barrier," Cho said.

The officer reached into his pocket for his cell phone, before remembering that all cell phones had been confiscated and the network was down.

"I have orders to—"

"My passenger must be in the city in a matter of minutes. Don't make me tell you who she's meeting. Believe me, you do not want to be responsible for fucking up his evening."

The officer froze with indecision, and looked at his subordinates manning the barrier. Only now did Cho notice that he wore the crisp uniform of the Guard Command. This was no ordinary unit of troops.

A telephone bell, the old fashioned sort, began ringing urgently in the guardhouse. The compound must have its own internal communications system.

"Your choice, Sergeant," Cho said brusquely, taking out the notebook he carried in his tunic pocket. "Your name?"

Fear streaked across the young man's face. After another agonizing pause in which the telephone continued to ring, he signaled to the two at the gate.

Cho slammed his foot down and shot through before the gate was fully open. He glanced at Jenna but her face was as inscrutable as a stone Buddha. The maples lining the road gave way to silver birches, flashing black and white in the glare of his headlights. The main exit to the compound loomed ahead. He heard the klaxons before he saw the two guardhouses of reinforced concrete, the high wall of the enclosure, and the main gate to the outside. He was certain they would have been warned by internal telephone by now. A spotlight came on, silhouetting a row of four caped and helmeted troops blocking the road, with submachine guns raised.

Cho braked and slowed the car to a crawl. Expecting him to stop, two of the guards parted to either side to grab the doors. He stamped his foot down. The car's wheels spun. One guard did a goalkeeper's dive to avoid him. The side mirror clipped the other, knocking him backward. Voices shouted. The Mercedes roared in low gear, accelerating straight for the exit.

The impact was intense. A ferrous flash of sparks and the gates broke wide open.

The crash seemed to shock Jenna out of her trance. She turned to him. "Stop the car. Let me drive."

"Not stopping now."

The car swerved to the left and picked up speed, hurtling out into almost total darkness. A gauzy veil of cloud had erased the stars, leaving the moon faint and silken, like a moth cocoon. Not enough light to see the landscape. The car's headlights beamed out into black void, with sudden twists and turns in the road revealing themselves only at the last second.

Cho's veins pumped adrenalin. He glanced at the clock. The banquet in honor of the Americans was about to start. The speech written for him by the First Deputy Minister was in his pocket. He pressed his foot to the accelerator pedal and gripped the wheel as hard as he could. The bumping and jolting from the road were tremendous.

"I'm telling them," Jenna yelled, her voice distorted almost unintelligibly by the shaking. "I'm telling them that I've seen her. She's leaving with me tomorrow."

"Do you want to get her killed?" Cho shouted. "If you say anything, she's in danger. They'll deny any knowledge of her, but she'll be in terrible danger. Trust me. You have no idea."

"Trust you?" she shrieked. "Last time we met, you were one of them!"

She was radiating pure wrath. They glanced at each other at the same moment, and it seemed to Cho that a spark of something passed between them, which he hoped was indeed trust. *You are beautiful*, he thought. She was the first Westerner he'd ever been alone with, and they were just inches from each other in the dark.

He said, "Tomorrow, when the plane—"

Something in the rearview mirror caught his eye. Had he just seen a light? Jenna turned in her seat to look. There it was again— two lights, yellow like fireflies, cresting a hill behind him.

Then he heard them—the angry buzz of two motorbikes, closing in on him. Cho dropped a gear for better control and accelerated.

"Watch!" she shouted, raising her forearms to her face. The car hit the enormous hole in the road they'd passed earlier, sending up a plume of deep water. The front wheels bounced, almost jarring the steering wheel from Cho's hands; the car's rear fish-tailed on the wet tarmac.

The road was leveling out and becoming straighter. The clouds parted, revealing a dim view of Pyongyang, black and sprawling like some vast geological formation.

The two motorbikes were coming right at them. Cho saw a flash from one of the bikes. Next thing he knew half of the back windshield became a maze of spider-webbed cracks. The impact of the shot reverberated through the metalwork. He lowered his head and jammed his foot hard to the pedal, as the gun behind him lit up again. Another *pang* as a bullet struck and the rear window blew inward, showering them in a hail of glass. The car bucked and its lights went out, but they were still accelerating.

Over the noise of the wind she shouted, "They're gaining on us."

"We just need to make it as far as ..." He clenched his teeth and the engine roared. They were careening down a straight gradient without headlights. The black outlines of poplar trees shot by in dim moonlight. "... *there*." He nodded ahead in the gloom. Four or five flashlights came on and they saw what looked like sentry boxes on either side of the road. Cho glanced again in the rearview mirror. The motorbikes had cut their speed.

Jenna turned again to look. "They're stopping."

"We're entering Pyongyang. The Guard Command has no jurisdiction here. This is the turf of the Pyongyang Police Garrison." He slowed the car. "Let's just hope communications are still down."

The Mercedes slowed enough for the sentries to see the license plate. Dozens of beams shone into the shattered, lightless Mercedes, sweeping across the faces of its driver and a female, mixed-race Western visitor, traveling without the two guides required by law. The men's impulse to halt this car and arrest its occupants must have been tremendous, but it was protected by powerful magic. To question the driver of a 2★16 car was to question the Dear Leader himself. They stood aside, and the car entered the city.

38

Pyongyang International House of Culture
Central District
Pyongyang, North Korea

In the marbled splendor of the great hall, the diplomatic corps of
the North Korean Ministry of Foreign Affairs were reciprocating
the Americans' goodwill with a banquet on an imperial scale. The
host himself was present only in the form of a vast, sweeping oil
painting, his pudgy figure improbably depicted standing atop a
jeep, leading an army through a snowstorm.

All present turned as Jenna entered, late, but before she could
even mumble a word, two of the Ministry's junior diplomats were
at her side making exaggerated apologies for the "fire drill" at the
Yanggakdo Hotel, which had come at such an incommodious
moment. Cho had returned her to the hotel, where her frantic
minders had been searching every floor for her.

The North Koreans, uniformed and decorated, presented an
immaculate front. The Americans looked like extras from a different movie who had somehow got mixed up in the same studio.
Chad Stevens gave her a lascivious smirk. The governor's executive
aide scowled at her dress. Jenna took her seat, feeling her legs shaking. She brushed a strand of hair behind her ear, and heard a crumb
of windshield glass fall to the floor.

Three powder-faced women entered holding kayagums, zither-like stringed instruments, and began plucking a gentle melody.

The First Deputy Minister nodded to Cho, who stood, smiling, glass in hand, to address them in English, and Jenna marveled at his ability to maintain such composure, betraying no outward sign of the near-death experience they'd just been through, but then, she supposed he'd been conditioned since birth to conceal his thoughts and feelings. From among the voices that must have been screaming inside his head he had selected the tone of a genial and magnanimous pirate who had plundered the Americans' treasure ship, but was happy to treat his victims to a feast and let bygones be bygones. The Americans raised their glasses to the precarious new "understanding," if not in friendship then at least in the spirit of a temporary truce.

Jenna's glass was shaking from her rage.

When the dining got underway, she could not swallow any food. She was supping with her sister's captors! How could she? And behind this sham hospitality these extortionists and kidnappers were laughing at the old governor, laughing at all of them. She was meant to be translating for the old man, who was seated next to her, but even keeping her mind in the room took a superhuman effort—all she could see before her eyes was the scene she had witnessed at the villa.

Soo-min in the flesh, Soo-min alive and real!

She had come so close, to within speaking distance of her prize. She had no intention of letting her slip back into darkness. Surely *now* was her chance to fix this, *now* was her chance to put an end to this outrage.

She put down her glass and felt her hands sweating. She was sweating all over as if she'd been in a steam sauna. Her fury was empowering. Damn it, yes, she was going to make a scene of her own. *Who were they to deny her her own sister!* She took a deep breath, then pushed back her chair to stand up.

In the millisecond that Cho caught her eye he communicated a warning, and her courage was quickly cold-showered by terror.

Do you want to get her killed ... ?

Was she going to risk that? What if he was right? Then thoughts of Fisk crowded her mind, Fisk who was counting on her, and she was overwhelmed by an agony of hesitation and guilt.

At some point while these thoughts were roiling and warring in her head she became aware of the First Deputy Minister peering curiously at her through his steel-framed glasses. She wasn't eating or conversing. She could barely contain the feelings that must be showing in her face, like water boiling behind glass.

She looked again toward Cho. For what? Reassurance?

He was deep in conversation with Mats Foyer, the only non-American Westerner at the table. As the United States had no diplomatic relations with Pyongyang, Foyer, the Swedish ambassador, was the protecting power for the American mission. A tall, angular figure with a choirboy face and a charming grin, he found his glass being liberally replenished by Cho. Was he part of Cho's escape plan? The Swedish ambassador? Cho hadn't told her how he planned to reach the airport when the plane left at dawn, only, if she did not see him, to try and delay takeoff until the last possible moment.

Suddenly all heads turned to the windows. Over the plinking zither music the city's sirens had started rising again, underscored by the crunch of marching feet.

The governor said, "Hell of a lot of activity out there ..."

"An annual city-wide exercise," the First Deputy Minister's interpreter said.

The tall doors opened and a messenger hurried across the hall to hand the First Deputy Minister a note. He glowered at the messenger and then opened it.

The Americans watched the man's face darken. He tried to hide the expression of his mouth by dabbing at it with a napkin,

and somehow Jenna knew. The game was over for Cho. His colleagues seemed to catch the change of humor. The mood around
the table cooled, like a cold sea fog rolling inland. Cho went very
still.

The First Deputy Minister got to his feet and signaled for the
musicians to stop, leaving only the sound of the sirens, which were
amplifying eerily in the cavernous hall.

"We ..."

The man's mouth opened and closed. He seemed unable to find
the words, before urgency compelled him to abandon niceties
altogether.

"Esteemed guests, I regret to inform you of a change to our
schedule. Your plane has been summoned and is now awaiting
your immediate departure. We have taken the liberty of placing
your luggage in the cars that are now outside. They will convey you
directly to the airport."

Something had gone badly wrong. The fear on the North Koreans' faces was contagious. Jenna had a sudden image of the
Tunisian street vendor, from whose body flames were spreading
across a continent.

The Americans looked at each other, stupefied.

"What's going on here?" the governor said.

The First Deputy Minister's face froze into a fake smile. One by
one the Americans got up. The tall doors opened from the
outside.

Stevens said, "We're being thrown out? I'm enjoying the chow."
He grabbed a couple of *mandu* from a dish and put them in his
pocket.

The North Koreans accompanied the party to the top of the landing. The First Deputy Minister, pale with loss of face, attempted a
murmured remark to the governor and proffered his hand. The
governor gave him a curt nod and led the way down the grand stair-
case. The others hurried after him.

Jenna was in the rear. At the foot of the stairs she turned to look up at the hosts seeing them off. Cho smiled faintly in farewell. He looked immeasurably sad, and doomed. He'd taken an enormous personal risk to show her Soo-min, and her heart swelled for him. Perhaps he knew he never had a chance.

The main doors opened before they had reached them. From the cold outside came a clatter of steel and thump of running boots. Two columns of armed troops entered the building, running past them on either side and mounting the stairs, holding submachine guns with bayonets fixed. In the final split second before she lost sight of Cho behind the scrimmage of uniform and weaponry she thought she heard him cry out her name.

39

Maram Secret Guest House
Yongsung District
Pyongyang, North Korea

Guards got in on either side of Cho in the back seat of a military SUV and closed the doors. They took one of his hands each, slipped a handcuff over it, and chained him to two metal loops on either side of his seat.

His arrest had an air of unreality about it, a scene from a dream. At the top of the landing outside the banqueting hall his entire group had been surrounded—himself, the First Deputy Minister, and his colleagues. The soldiers parted to let through a captain of the Bowibu, who addressed him without title. "Cho Sang-ho, I have an order for your arrest." He held out the warrant, and Cho heard the intake of breath from his colleagues. The foot of the document bore the signature of Kim Jong-il. He could not look at their faces, could not bear to witness their expressions of shock and betrayal. In that moment, surrounded by glinting bayonets, he felt like a figure in the center of a history painting. The great unmasking of a traitor.

The crimes of his ancestors were finally visited upon him. At last he would learn what they were. And after his escapade this evening, he could not say that his arrest was without cause—unless, that was, he had got away with it, which, in the chaos of the city lockdown, was possible.

A third guard sat in the passenger seat next to the driver. Cho felt no fear, only a strange sense of relief—that an ordeal long dreaded had finally come. He was getting it over with. The strain of maintaining a facade over the last weeks had taken him to the limits of his endurance.

With a curiosity verging on indifference, he tried to think whether they would shoot him tonight, or wait until dawn. In a cellar, in the back of his neck? Or by firing squad tied to a stake? Or perhaps they were planning something altogether more public, which might take a few days. He did not care, if it meant that his wife and son were not harmed ... He clung with all his heart to the hope that he'd done enough to distance them from him. He wished he could explain it all to Books and tell him that he loved him very much. He wished he could comfort Yong-ho and say that none of this was his fault. He was consumed with a need to know where they were, whether they were safe, and a sickening thought came to him: that he would not be told his family's fate, and not knowing would torment him as he entered his final hours.

The guard in the passenger seat was signaling with his hand out of the window at each city checkpoint they passed, and Cho saw police on motorbikes stationed at every one. Was this all for him? In case he gave them the slip again? It gave him a vague satisfaction.

The car entered a district in the east of the city and turned into the courtyard of a complex of gray buildings, two stories high, that was surrounded by pines. It did not look much like a prison, more a type of barracks. The handcuffs were removed and he was ordered out. On the steps of the main entrance, in the wan light of a lamp, stood the man with the silver hair and the plain black tunic.

"Welcome to the Maram Guest House," he said, and to Cho's surprise, shook his hand. "My name is Ryu Kyong. I've been looking forward to meeting you." He had a strong grip and an avuncular, handsome face, cragged around the eyes and with two deep lines on either side of his mouth, like parentheses. His hair was parted on the side. He dismissed the car with a nod. "Come, please."

He had not used an honorific form of address, rather the register used for children, but his voice carried such authority that, far from sounding disrespectful, it made Cho feel like a child in his presence, or a student, and he wondered whether this man, Ryu Kyong, had been a part of his early life in some way.

With two guards on either side of Cho, the man led the way up a flight of stairs and along two corridors to a small room. It was clean and sparsely furnished with a bed, a lamp, and a wooden table and chair, above which hung the Father-Son portraits. A washbasin occupied one corner. The brick walls were painted a pale green, as in a sanatorium, which caused something in Cho's memory to connect. Maram Guest House ... It was where they held purged members of the elite. The floor was of a dark, polished wood that gave off a pleasing warmth. On the desk were sheets of blank white paper in a neat stack, and a selection of blunt pencils. At the foot of the bed was a folded set of blue overalls, which he was asked to put on. They watched him change. The guards took away his belt, shoelaces, and his uniform and medal. He felt no regret.

"You're hungry, perhaps?" Ryu Kyong said.

Cho had just come from a banquet. "No."

"Make yourself comfortable, then. Get some sleep, and when you're ready, write everything down, from the beginning, in as much detail as you can. Take all the time you need."

"Write what down?"

"Your confession." Ryu Kyong smiled with understanding. His eyes looked deeply into Cho's, reading him, and Cho saw empathy and intelligence in them. "Confess the crime that has brought you here."

Before Cho could pick one of the questions beginning to swarm in his head, Ryu Kyong left, and locked the door with a click.

40

Airspace over the Sea of Japan

A grim atmosphere pervaded the cabin. The visit had been a major embarrassment for the governor, whose humiliation at the banquet Chad Stevens was even now writing up, tapping away on his laptop in between swigs of bourbon, his face chuckling in the pale light of the screen. Jenna knew they were all wondering how the hell they were going to spin this in Washington tomorrow, and she should be trying to help, but her mind kept replaying the events of the last hours on a loop in fast-forward.

Her own twin, seeing her, meeting her eyes, piercing her heart with such pain and joy, had left her with a strange afterglow of jubilation and anxiety. She was as restless as if an electric current were passing through her. Eventually she asked Stevens for a shot of his bourbon, an attempt to calm herself.

Stevens, she knew, would be more than happy to shoot the breeze with her over a drink, but she did not trust herself. One prompt, one nudge, and the whole Soo-min story would come tumbling out of her. She was grappling with her urge to unburden herself on one hand and her fear on the other—fear of the consequences for her sister if this got out. In her whole life she had never come so close to a moment of psychic intuition, a conviction that her future and

Soo-min's had been powerfully relinked. Somehow, how she conducted herself from now on would affect Soo-min, too.

She turned to the window to see the bright, three-quarter moon in a cloudless sky, and, far below, the dim, snowbound sheep fields of Hokkaido.

Soo-min had looked healthy and not unhappy, but who knew what mask she wore to survive in that place? The memory of the escape from the villa was a blur.

A thought came to her that turned the bourbon to bile in her mouth.

Had those bastards in Pyongyang made the connection between her and their secret prisoner who never left that compound? If they knew, if they gave the smallest indication that they'd figured it out ... Jenna closed her eyes. She'd be compromised, a walking security breach. She would have to make a full statement to Fisk and resign her position at once. She could not expose herself to blackmail, or give that vile regime leverage in Washington. Her spirits slid into anxiety again.

She wished she could change out of her eveningwear into something more comfortable, but her luggage had been thrown into the hold in the haste for takeoff. Rummaging in her handbag for something to wipe the makeup from her face, she suddenly froze.

Bent in half in her bag was a tight roll of papers, tied with an elastic band.

She remembered Cho handing her handbag to her as he dropped her off back at the hotel before speeding away to the banquet, probably when he already knew his chances of escaping on the plane were less than zero.

She pulled off the elastic band and uncurled the paper. It was crinkled slightly, as if it had been concealed around a forearm or a calf, had become damp with sweat and had dried. The paper was such a poor-quality photocopy that its print was almost lost in the black murk of light exposure. At its head was the crest of the Workers' Party, and a letterhead.

Organization and Guidance Department

Progress Report of Section 915 of the Party's Strategic Command on
LOCALIZATION and the SEED-BEARING PROGRAM
Juche Year 98

TOP SECRET

Jenna began to read, puzzled at first, but then turning the pages with mounting astonishment. When she reached the last pages she found some sort of appendix with passport photographs of dozens of children. Even though the reproduction was so dark that she could barely see their faces, she knew—she KNEW—that these were the mixed-race, half-Korean kids she'd seen at the villa. Beneath each photo was a number, a date of birth, and the name of a country. She saw Germany, Russia, Iran, Pakistan, but the majority of them, two-thirds at least, were destined for the United States.

Jenna took a mouthful of bourbon, dropped her head back on the seat, opened her mouth, and breathed.

Oh my God...

Her mind was ablaze. She had no idea how she would sustain herself through a nine-hour flight to Anchorage, then another nine to DC.

She looked at the wispy white hair of the governor, slumped in dejection against the window. She hoped there would be some way of letting him know that that the mission had not been a failure. Quite the opposite. It had struck gold.

There was one final page in the bundle, almost indecipherable it was so dark. It featured murky passport-type photos of three unsmiling adults in uniform, two men and a woman. Their titles were Director, First Deputy Director, and Second Deputy Director of the Paekhwawon Compound. The Second Deputy Director's name was given as Ree Mae-ok. Jenna's heart skipped a beat.

It was Soo-min.

41

Maram Secret Guest House
Yongsung District
Pyongyang, North Korea

Cho awoke before dawn. The barred window of his room looked onto a courtyard, in the middle of which was a juniper tree that might have been magnificent in spring, but now gave the place a forlorn air. A thin covering of snow had fallen overnight, and patches of it glowed yellow in the security lights, but when he looked up the stars shone icily.

He lay back on his bed, which was soft and warm, listening to the rhythm of his breath, and felt a clarity of mind he had not experienced in years. It was as if he was standing on a mountaintop on a crisp early morning and could view his past in perspective like a long, forested valley. He got up, splashed cold water on his face, and after pacing the room for a while—six steps from door to window, four steps from wall to wall—sat at the desk and began to write. His strokes were cramped and hesitant at first, but soon the words began to flow and gather pace, his sentences becoming a river running through the valley basin. When his stomach started to rumble and a guard entered with a bowl of noodles, a hard-boiled egg, and a cup of hot black tea on a tray, it was a wrench to put the pencil down. He wolfed down the food and continued writing.

Something in Ryu Kyong's kindness had encouraged Cho. He felt drawn to the man, not only because he was puzzled by the contrast between his civilized demeanor and his role here, as a jailor for enemies of the state, but because in that cragged, humane face he imagined he'd seen a profound understanding, a knowledge of him. It was the face of an uncle he could confide in.

As the pages filled, Cho became possessed by an all-consuming thought: that every word he wrote was the truth. He had devoted his life to the Great Leader and the Dear Leader. He had been hard-working and motivated by their teachings. He had shone with that most prized of all virtues: loyalty. He had even acquired that revolutionary virtue that was never mentioned but which was just as important: self-deception. What had he to confess? His career was spotless, his life blameless. He would surely be exonerated, and so would Yong-ho. Somehow, Ryu Kyong would see this. Cho could not be held guilty for the crime of some unknown ancestor, any more than he could help the shape of his ears.

He paused for a minute. What was this crime that had ruined his life, decades after the act? He had no idea, but as it had almost certainly been committed before he was born, he tried to think whether there were any clues in his earliest memories.

He remembered the aura of love surrounding the nurse who had cared for him at the orphanage in Nampo, a large villa that had been a rich ship-owner's home before the Revolution. He remembered singing "We Are Happy" from the heart. The first words he had learned to write were "Thank you, Great Leader Kim Il-sung, for my food." He had bowed to the great man's portrait almost before he could walk. He had grown up in the sunlight of that smile. And as deep as his love was for the Leader, so too was his hatred for his country's mortal enemy: America. The teachers had seen to that.

He recalled, so vividly as he wrote, the day his life changed forever, when the children had crowded to the windows to see a gleaming black Volga bringing a man and woman from Pyong-yang. He was four years old. He and Yong-ho were called out of their class and invited to recite a poem for the visitors in the direct-or's office. The couple had laughed delightedly and treated them with great affection, giving them candies and juice from a hard-currency store, and the director crouched down to the boys' height and told them they were blessed with great good fortune: "This man and lady are your parents. They have come to take you home." Cho remembered his confusion and happiness. From that day on, his life had been charmed. His new home was a large house in the Mansu Hill neighborhood of Pyongyang, where he and Yong-ho had their own bedrooms. Their father, a professor of languages at Kim Il-sung University, and their mother, a political instructor for the air force, had obeyed the Great Leader's call to adopt orphans. But they were also generous and caring, having no children of their own, and treated Cho and Yong-ho as their sons. Gradually his memories of the orphanage became hazy, and he even forgot he'd ever been there, remembering this fact only at odd moments in adolescence as his curiosity about the world sharpened. When once he'd asked his mother about his origins, she became someone he didn't know. "The past is the past," she'd said, in a tone she had not used with him before. "Never ask that question again."

At age eleven his head was shaved and he was enrolled in the elite Mangyongdae Revolutionary School. He excelled at soccer, Manda-rin, and English, encouraged by his father; Yong-ho at basketball, physics, and mathematics. At university Cho studied hard—to study well was an act of devotion to the Leader—and relished his military service, which appealed to his sense of hierarchy and discipline. The proudest day of his life was being accepted into the junior diplo-matic corps, where he quickly made his mark as a negotiator—his mix of tact and tough talk winning valuable trade concessions for his country and easing a succession of swift promotions.

Cho wrote exhaustively, unaware of time passing.

His dinner went cold on the tray. He had not even noticed the guard bringing it. Through his window the sun had begun to set, filling the room with a citrus-red light, and the security lamps in the yard blinked on.

He described meeting his wife-to-be at a mass dance in the May Day Stadium. She had given him the flower from her hair, which had scandalized her friends. Her family had a strong revolutionary background, and her beauty had entranced him. To make a good political match was fortunate; to fall in love too was an exceptional blessing. Not until the arrival of their son, after two years of trying, did their feelings for each other change. It was as if all their love had transferred to the newborn. His wife attended to Books's ideological education, and something in the task had hardened her, made her cold.

Cho's wrist was aching. He paused and stretched for a while. In the yard a lone guard paraded with a rifle, back and forth, never varying his pace, and when Cho's writing resumed he seemed to find the rhythm of the guard's footsteps. He was nearing the end of his testimony, concluding it with his triumph in New York. How could he have succeeded in that mission if not by drawing on his lifelong hatred for the Americans? On the boundless reserves of love he had for his country?

He dared not write more. He could not commit to words the profound disillusionment that had begun in New York, the feelings for Jenna that he would not even admit to himself, the secrets he had betrayed to her, and yet … he did not rule out talking about them to Ryu Kyong.

When a guard came with his breakfast on the second morning, Cho told him that he had finished. Soon afterward Ryu Kyong appeared.

"You have rested, I hope," he said.

"Yes." Cho stood up straight, a novice in the presence of a wise abbot.

"Good. We have many hours of work ahead of us, you and I."

He again looked into Cho's face, and an intimacy passed between them. *You are in good care*, those eyes seemed to say.

Cho handed him the written pages with a deep bow.

A day went by, then another, and Cho began to lose track of time. He slept a lot, dreaming of his wife and Books, picnicking with them in sunlight beneath the trees of Moran Hill Park. He ate three good meals a day and felt himself putting on weight. He was taken for a half hour's daily exercise in the yard, and looked with curiosity at the two other inmates exercising, until a guard barked at him to keep his eyes lowered.

After three, maybe four days, Cho was shaken awake by a guard. He sensed, from the stillness of the place, that it was after midnight. He was led down one flight of stairs, then another, to a long corridor in a concrete basement, with steel doors leading off to each side. At the end of the corridor he was shown into a room so dark he could not gauge its dimensions. Two pools of light revealed a wooden chair, which he was told to sit on, and a table with a lamp. Damp concrete walls and rusted iron gave off a chill that made Cho shiver. Still groggy from sleep, it took him a moment to realize that Ryu Kyong was sitting at the table, reading, and Cho recognized his own handwriting. For what seemed like an age the two of them sat in silence, as Ryu Kyong turned the pages in the small circle of light, occasionally nodding. When he reached the end, he threaded his fingers together on the table and sat upright, so that the shadows fell down his face. His voice resonated in the cavernous dark.

"Cho, to get to the heart of this matter I need your help. I can't do it without you. Are you willing to work with me?"

"Of course," Cho said. A faintly ominous feeling crept over him.

"For the past few weeks I've watched you. I've wanted to get to know you." He folded his arms and leaned back, so that his face was in complete darkness. "This is a very grave case. A twenty-man

Special Mission Group was set up to investigate your real family, handpicked by the Leader himself, of which I was one. That's how seriously we've taken this, Cho, but it was worth it. You were worth it. It took some digging, but we uncovered the truth in the end."

"The truth?" Cho's voice had no substance to it.

"You see, nothing you've scribbled here explains how you and your brother, both of you grandsons of an executed American spy ..."

What?

"... came to worm and lie your way into such trusted positions."

Ryu Kyong got up and sat on the desk facing Cho.

Cho was too astounded to speak. His mind scrambled to recall what Yong-ho had been told about their real family. When he found his voice he managed to say, "I ... never knew my real father or grandfather."

Ryu Kyong smiled with regret and looked down, almost as if he felt embarrassed on Cho's behalf. "Your birth records showed that you were born into a heroic bloodline, grandsons of a decorated veteran. You might have got away with that, too, if we hadn't contacted the veteran's family to arrange a little get-together for you. His grandchildren denied all knowledge of you. That's when we started investigating in earnest, and sure enough, your birth record had been forged."

Cho had a sinking feeling. The hope he'd invested in his confession was collapsing, built on sand.

"We found the civil registry officer who'd forged the record, and we twisted the story out of him quickly enough. He had been bribed handsomely, it seemed, by your biological mother, to make it appear that she gave birth to you and your brother illegitimately and that the father was of a Class A bloodline. Now, why did she do that?

"The Bowibu, in fact, had a file on your mother. Thirty years ago she was caught trying to change your father's record—your real father's record—to say that he had died in a workplace accident. For that, she was sentenced to an indefinite term of penal labor. A courageous woman, your mother. Twice she took a big risk to protect your future, give you a clean start in life. But what was she covering up?

"Her file led us to your father's. Your biological father …" Ryu Kyong leaned over to retrieve a file from a briefcase next to the desk, and put on a pair of reading glasses. "… was Ahn Chun-hyok. Caught attempting to flee the country by motorboat in October 1977. Sentenced at a people's trial. Executed at his workplace, the Chollima Shipyard in Nampo, in front of the workforce, in November 1977—a month before you were born. Your mother omitted to mention that to the orphanage when she abandoned you and your brother."

Cho's mind was in uproar. He put his hands to his head.

Ryu Kyong spoke softly. "Did we agree you could move?"

Surprised, Cho stilled himself.

"Oh, but Cho, it gets better … Your father's file led us to the identity of your grandfather, Ahn Yun-chol." He folded his arms and began to pace around the table. "He was a colorful piece of riffraff, by all accounts. Some sort of itinerant healer and shaman, a petty capitalist hawking his mystical services along the thirty-eighth parallel during the war. The American army recruited him to carry messages to their advance units near Pyongyang, probably in return for money. After our victory over the Yankees his treachery was exposed. He was executed as a spy in 1954.

"Grandfather and father both executed traitors. That's an impressive lineage, Cho. It's one of the worst cases ever passed to me. I can tell you that the Leader was personally very upset. He has ordered your department at the Ministry of Foreign Affairs to undergo a three-week revolutionary struggle to cleanse itself of your infectious influence. Your former colleagues have been demoted." He waved his hand as if that were hardly worth mentioning. "The question that interests us is how you and your brother got away with it for so long."

Ryu Kyong rested his hands on top of the chair. He was watching Cho intently now, watching his inner turmoil play out on his face, giving him time to come clean. But all Cho could say was, "I am innocent. I've never heard of these men until now."

The interrogator shook his head vaguely, as if Cho were a kid caught stealing but pathetically trying to deny it.

"We've established your treasonous bloodline, beyond any doubt. What we must know now … is how your grandfather's espionage mission was passed on to you, and what his instructions were."

Cho stared at Ryu Kyong. "You can't possibly be serious—"

"How did your American spy grandfather pass on his mission to your father and to you? Was it a written instruction?"

Despair and disbelief were overcoming Cho like a virus. "This is nonsense!"

Ryu Kyong gave a small smile and sighed. Then he flicked a glance into the darkness behind Cho, and Cho became aware for the first time of another presence in the room. A chair scraped back. Leather creaked. His arms were grabbed and his hands handcuffed tightly behind the back of the chair. His stomach turned to ice.

The interrogator turned on a switch. A set of dim spotlights illuminated a stained concrete wall on which rusted manacles and hooks hung from an iron rail.

He resumed his seat with his hands knitted in front of him on the table. In the tone of someone of infinite patience, he said, "How did your American spy grandfather pass on his mission to you? What were his instructions?"

Cho felt caught in a dimension that made no sense. Truth, logic, reason had been turned upside down and inside out. Could they honestly believe he'd been acting on the orders of an unknown grandfather and a father who'd both died before he was even born?

"No one gave me instructions. I have nothing to say. I never knew my biological fam—"

The blow struck his right ear. His vision went blank, and a high, tinny noise rang through his head. He doubled over, trying to jam his head between his knees. He had never felt such a searing, explosive white pain. He whined through his teeth, on the verge of blacking out. His brain was paralyzed. When he looked up, breathing heavily, his eyes were streaming.

Ryu Kyong was not at the table. A match flared, briefly illuminating a dark corner of the room as the interrogator lit a cigarette.

"If you're hoping to convince me that you're not an American spy, save your breath." His posture was relaxed. There was nothing aggressive about him, and yet he had become a master with a dog on a leash, exercising absolute and lethal control. The blow to Cho's ear had made his words sound like the buzzing of small insects.

Ryu Kyong picked up the pages of Cho's testimony from the table with the tips of his fingers and set fire to them with a lighter, tossing them into a metal trash can, where the flames momentarily revealed a large chamber with riveted sliding partitions.

"Last month, during your visit to New York, one of our diplomats, First Secretary Ma, was arrested by the Yankees while conducting important Party business. Was it you who betrayed him?"

"No!" Cho's eyes widened. Ryu Kyong affected not to notice his shock.

"Four nights ago, just before the state banquet for the Yankee jackals, you spent forty minutes alone in the company of one of the female Yankee visitors. You're sure there's nothing you showed her, or told her?"

Cho felt his face burning. There was nothing he could say.

"So, then. Let us safely assume you are an American spy, and a traitor. But that still leaves the matter of your confession."

A feeling of helplessness came over him, a profound weariness. He was trapped in a nightmare in which he was starting to lose all sense of reality, but the process had a crazy transcendent logic on its side.

Ryu Kyong stubbed out his cigarette and looked at Cho as he would a son who after years of wayward behavior was receiving the tough love he'd always needed. "Some water?"

Cho nodded.

He signaled for the handcuffs to be removed and a tin cup of water was put into Cho's trembling hand. He drank it straight down and the cup was taken from him.

"We'll speak again," Ryu Kyong said. "Think carefully about your confession." He left the room, and Cho heard others, maybe as many as five pairs of boots, entering the room and gathering behind him, staying out of his line of vision. He was too afraid to look around.

The hood was thrown over his head so suddenly he couldn't even cry out. He was slammed right off the chair and the kicks came from all directions. In his stomach, legs, ribs, head. He was winded and couldn't breathe inside the rough hood. Rolling about on the floor, uselessly trying to protect his body, dodge blows he couldn't see, the kicks rained down with monstrous savagery, in his spine, his testicles, his hipbone, his ankles. He cried out for them to stop, anything if they'd stop. A thudding, dull kick to his temple made him see orange diamonds, and he lost consciousness.

When he came to, he was on the concrete floor of a tiny cell, lit by a humming electric light behind a wire mesh. Only about five feet long and two feet wide, it was impossible either to stand up or lie down. At his feet was a bowl of thin, salty soup, with a few corn kernels floating on the surface, which had long gone cold. He had no idea how long he'd been out, or what time of day or night it was. Almost at once his body began shivering uncontrollably in the sub-zero temperature, but he could barely move an arm to wrap around himself. His body was a blooming flowerbed of agony, from the crown of his head to the soles of his feet.

The spyhole in the door moved and an eye appeared. He heard a guard speak to another; the door opened and two of them reached in to grab him by his ankles and drag him out, and he realized then that his ordeal so far had been nothing but a routine softening up, a prelude.

His real nightmare was now starting.

42

O Street
Georgetown
Washington, DC
Christmas Eve

Jenna put the gifts in the car and called her mother to say she was on her way. Christmas was a difficult time of year for both of them, a bleak reminder that they were half a family, and it only compounded the ill humor Jenna was already in.

Fisk had been waiting for her at Andrews Air Force Base when the mission had arrived back from Pyongyang the week before. It was after midnight and she'd been grateful for the ride. But when they'd got into his car and she'd said, "I saw my sister," he was so surprised that instead of driving her straight home they'd sat in the empty parking lot while she described the drama with Cho, the mixed-race children she'd seen at the villa, and the dossier Cho had given her. "We have a homeland security threat."

Fisk stared into space, taking this in, before turning the key in the ignition.

Eventually he murmured, "I honestly never thought your sister would still be alive."

Jenna rested her head against the cool glass, and closed her eyes. She was exhausted and just wanted to drop into bed. The car sped from one pool of overhead lighting to the next along the deserted expressway toward Georgetown.

He said, "Could any of these spies be active, from this ... Seed-Bearing Program?"

"The oldest are nineteen, according to the dossier."

"Perfect. So they could already be here, on our college campuses."

"It's possible."

He gave a huff of incredulity. "Jesus Christ Almighty ... long-range missile tests, secret weapons labs, indoctrinated children who look foreign ..."

Jet lag, fatigue, and hunger combined in Jenna to produce a flash of anger. What did he expect? Kim Jong-il's North Korea was a haunted house. *Open the door and you'll find a horror in every room, from the cellar to the attic ...*

He turned into O Street. In a gentler voice he said, "What do you want to do about Soo-min?"

Jenna stared bleakly down the empty street. As with everything about North Korea, there were no good options. "I don't know."

She was getting out when he said, "I'm sorry, but everything about that villa and the program stays classified."

Only once she was inside her apartment did she understand why he'd said that—so that she wouldn't breathe a word to her mother, couldn't give her the Christmas present she desperately wanted to give her: the knowledge that she, Jenna, had seen Soo-min with her own eyes. The knowledge that Han's daughter was alive.

The following day she'd been debriefed at Langley, and sat down to translate the dossier.

She was packed and ready to set off on the eleven-mile drive to Annandale when she heard her home phone ringing just as she was locking her front door. She usually ignored the home phone, but this time something made her pause. The sheer strangeness of recent events was making even the most mundane occurrences seem loaded with significance. She unlocked the door, dashed back inside, and caught it just before it went to voice mail.

A soft-spoken female White House staffer was asking her to hold for a long-distance call.

The White House?

Jenna heard a click as the connection was transferred, and a long pause. And suddenly she experienced an extraordinary sense of predestination, a momentous aligning of the stars.

"Ma'am?" Now a male staffer was on the line, and she knew what was coming next: "I have the president of the United States."

It was all she could do not to throw the phone onto the sofa in fright.

The next thing she knew the familiar baritone was talking to her, Jenna Williams, in her own home.

"Dr. Williams, I just read your report ..."

Her mouth opened. Her mind scrambled, rifling for the memory. *Which report?* She was sweating rivers, rooted to the spot in her coat and scarf.

"... I gotta hand it to you. Not many recommendations make me sit up, but yours did."

Her voice was a whisper. "Thank you."

He's talking about ... Her mind configured and connected. *The "fresh ideas" for tackling Kim.* The report the CIA director had asked her to write, a month ago.

"I must ask you—are these ideas your own?"

"Yes, sir."

"I'm intrigued by your reasoning. It's ... counterintuitive."

Not for the first time she couldn't help feeling seriously out of her depth. "They are a little ... off the wall, I guess."

He laughed, and for a moment she caught a riff of that revivalist charisma. "Radical is how I'd call them. Well, listen, maybe nothing will come of it, because I'll never persuade Congress, but I want to explore them further. I'm sharing your report with the State Department. They'll be in touch. Are you with your family this Christmas?"

"With my mother, Han."

"You both have a very happy holiday."

The conversation had lasted only seconds. She stared at the receiver for a moment in a flushing, heart-racing trance, but already she could feel her mood rising in her chest like soda bubbles, and she let out a sudden scream. She had something to tell her mom after all.

Later, when she saw him on the TV news at Han's house in Annandale, she realized that he'd called her from his vacation in Hawaii.

Three days after Christmas, when she returned to training at the Farm, senior Agency people she didn't know started acknowledging her in the cafeteria, making eye contact, stepping aside to let her pass, as if she had an aura of light. As she was soon to discover, her ideas were already rippling through Washington circles and beyond, causing disturbances in the settled pond of opinion.

43

Maram Secret Guest House
Yongsung District
Pyongyang, North Korea

In the darkened interrogation chamber a new face confronted Cho, an officer younger than himself, sitting bolt upright in a starched uniform. A leather strap from shoulder to revolver belt crackled as he moved. His shiny, smooth head appeared as round and pale as a moon. His eyes watched Cho without expression. His cap, with glossy black visor, was next to him on the desk.

"How did your American spy grandfather pass on his mission to you? What were his instructions?"

Cho felt overtaken by weariness and hunger. He shook his head vaguely.

"I never knew my grandfather or my father ..."

"How did your American spy grandfather pass on his mission to you? What were his instructions?"

His head dropped to his chest and he said nothing. Someone behind him took a step toward him, and he saw out of the corner of his eye something swing momentarily into the pool of light, like the prehensile tail of a monkey. An uncoiling wire cable.

Sometimes they beat him with cables, other times with wooden clubs. He writhed on the concrete in pools of his own blood and urine, howling like an animal. If he lost consciousness, water would rouse him. The first time it happened he found his clothes sopping and icy cold, and his mouth full of blood and fragments of chipped teeth. Rough hands hauled him back onto the seat for the questioning to resume. Other times he'd be whipped with a leather strap, but his legs and arms were so tightly belted to the chair he couldn't move a muscle to shield himself.

Occasionally, from the darkness behind him he thought he heard Ryu Kyong halt the beatings, but the young officer's question was relentless and the question never varied. Once or twice he lost patience and slapped Cho's face with his hands, hitting the raw injury of his ear so it rang with a high metallic chime.

Gradually Cho's body numbed, and in those pauses when he was given a moment to absorb and savor the pain, it bewildered him to realize that he was being asked almost nothing about his fugitive forty minutes with Jenna before the banquet: to the interrogators that was simply the proof of his guilt. What was crucial to them, the momentum driving the questioning, was their desire to know how his treasonous bloodline had stayed concealed, allowing him to deceive his way into a position of such trust that he could pass messages to his Yankee paymasters face-to-face, and for his brother to gain access to the personal affairs of the Dear Leader himself.

Slowly, between blows, Cho began to understand. For a betrayal on this scale, to kill him was not enough. His heart-and-soul confession was required, his begging for forgiveness before he was shot, his protestation of penitence and love for the Leader. Everything hinged upon it. After that, his death was an administrative detail.

He was not sure how many times he'd been tortured when they taunted him with the fate of his family. "Your son has been exiled to a village in the northern mountains—because of you, Cho. Your wife chose to go with him." And when he heard that, something inside him died. *His family, outcasts in a harsh mountain village?* For a few minutes the interrogator watched him sob openly. "Confess now," the man said softly, "and they can come home to Pyongyang. Your son can return to school." But Cho understood the system well enough to know that the interrogator was lying. The *opposite* was the truth. Books would be condemned to a far worse fate—a labor camp, a zone of no return—*if he confessed.*

Son to a confessed American spy.

And the more Cho realized this, and the longer and more vicious these sessions became, the stronger became his will not to confess. It became an almost supernatural determination. It was the pearl he would not yield, the treasure he would never give them. He would die soon enough here anyway. They would not pry it from him before he did.

This was his only weapon, his only chance of protecting his wife and son.

The questioning continued day and night. Sometimes it was the young officer with the shaved head. Sometimes others, all of them young. Only occasionally did Ryu Kyong participate, but Cho felt certain he was often present in the back of the room, observing. Twice, four times, six times, he couldn't be sure, the beatings would suddenly stop and the table was carried toward his chair, where he'd be faced by the sheets of white paper and the pencil. Each time, ever more erratically, Cho wrote the same words he'd written before, or a summary of them. The interrogator would read them, searching for a crack, a fissure through which to break him, then the pages would be torn up in front of his face. Each time, Cho felt hatred, like a blowtorch flaming though his body.

Soon he became delirious from lack of sleep. Interrogators' words sounded as if they were spoken underwater. He lost the thread of the questions, mumbling, "Don't understand," and would be slapped and beaten all the harder.

Apart from a vague sense that days were stretching into weeks, he had no idea how long he'd been in the torture chamber of the

Maram Guest House. One day he was left in his tiny cell and ordered to sit cross-legged with his head bowed, all day. If a prisoner moved so much as an eyebrow the guards would throw open the door and beat him with birch rods. They walked back and forth in front of the cells, watching for the smallest infraction. Suicide, which he thought of often, was impossible. After ten hours sitting in that position he could not walk.

Next day he was dragged to the interrogation chamber by his arms. Ryu Kyong awaited him. He sat motionless at the table, regarding Cho with his benign and meditative face, like some venerable scholar.

He took a deep breath before speaking, his disappointment plain. "Why are you doing this to yourself, Cho? Are you hoping to save yourself?"

Cho was alert, his heart racing as he listened for sounds of movement behind him, but they seemed to be alone in the room.

"You are doing this to me."

"It can all be over in a minute, if you'd like, and I can help." The sheets of blank white paper were on the table. Ryu Kyong held up a pencil. "You won't save yourself, but you'll save your son, who is innocent of your crime. Now, why don't we write it together?"

The words *lying bastard* clouded Cho's mind like poisonous gas. After an interminable pause, in which Cho stared resolutely at the floor, Ryu Kyong left.

That day, he was hung by his hands from the iron rod. His toes barely touched the floor, the manacles cut the flesh of his wrists, and his waist felt as if it were being torn from his torso. Guards beat his legs so many times that they swelled up like tree trunks. Even then, he had not endured the worst. They moved him to a cell so small he had to crouch his body, which was half immersed in cold water. He was left there for two days. When he lost consciousness he was dragged out and awoke again to the white paper and the pencil. The water cell was worse even than when they put bamboo splinters under his fingernails and tore them off one by one, urging him to confess, in between his screams, sometimes coaxingly, other times through abuse yelled in his ears.

He did not confess.

One night he was taken outside for the first time in weeks, and breathed cold, clear air. He was ordered to kneel on the compacted snow of the yard and not to move. Snowflakes touched his hair and face. He knelt there for hours like a stone ornament. After an hour or so the violence of his shivering abated and he became numb and strangely serene, as guards came and went in thick rabbit-fur coats. He could not stand when they ordered him up, and had to be dragged back inside.

Gradually, the torture became irregular. Some days they left him in his cell to starve, or gave him salty soup but nothing to drink, so that his thirst became intolerable, and his tongue gluey. After days without food, his biceps were as thin as his wrists, but his legs were so swollen he could hardly sit. When they next took him from his cell he was amazed to find himself in the warmth of the guards' mess, seated in a corner to watch them eat white rice and steaming pork and mushroom stew from a large earthenware pot. The pain in his stomach was acute and the guards laughed at the look on his face. The white paper and pencil was brought to him, and a bowl of rice and stew left just out of his reach. A hunk of fresh bread was placed next to it.

Cho looked away, and tears streaked his cheeks.

Hours later a man in a dirty white coat entered his cell, felt his pulse and his bones, and rubbed a cool ointment on the injuries that had become infected and were weeping pus. He told Cho to remove his overalls, which were filthy, stinking rags by now, and cleansed his ruined body with antiseptic wipes, gave him fresh clothes, then took out a syringe and injected him with something that sent a feeling of euphoria through him before he fell into an exhausted, opioid sleep.

When he awoke he was looking up into Ryu Kyong's face. The man's arm was around him, holding Cho as if he were a loved and dying child. He spoke gently and with intimacy. They were in a bright, sunlit room with white walls that dazzled Cho. How long had he been in this place? The trees outside the window were budding with bright new leaf. White clouds sailed by like airships.

"The Dear Leader is the brain of our great movement," Ryu Kyong said. "His is the mind that keeps us infallibly on history's rails. He is all knowing and unerring. Would you agree with that, Cho?"

Cho felt happiness flooding through him. What wisdom, what tolerance shone in Ryu Kyong's eyes.

"Yes," he said, feeling a smile spread over his face.

"And if the Leader is the brain, then the Party is the movement's beating heart, and the army is its strength and muscle. Isn't that right?"

Cho nodded, a boy being guided through simple arithmetic.

"The masses—the workers, the farmers, the builders—they are the organs and the nerve system. They are the movement's cells and its lifeblood. They are freed of the burden of independent thought, because the brain takes that mighty responsibility upon itself." Pain came into Ryu Kyong's eyes, and his face filled with empathy. "But if any of the cells in the body are found to be diseased, if a tumor is discovered, even if it's lain hidden for three generations, it can not be allowed to remain, or to grow. You do see that, don't you, Cho? Disloyalty must be cut out, removed altogether, so that the body may remain immortal and never perish."

Cho closed his eyes, not wanting to spoil the beauty of Ryu Kyong's logic.

"If we do not root it out, we commit a crime against our own future. I know you'll understand that. Do it now, and spare yourself more needless suffering. Do it out of love for our people. Write your confession, and the Leader will forgive. Die in peace, with his gratitude in your heart, and your son safe …" Ryu Kyong gently lowered Cho onto a comfortable mat on the floor. He weighed nothing. His body was skin and bone. A bowl of steaming bean-paste broth was brought in on a tray and Cho devoured it like a ravenous dog, with Ryu Kyong watching. Somehow, without Cho noticing, the white sheets of paper and pencil had reappeared, set out neatly on the floor next to the mat.

Cho said, "What have you done with Yong-ho?"

"He confessed quickly and fully. He died with a clear conscience."

Ryu Kyong left and locked the door.

Cho watched the white clouds pass and listened to a jay chirping in the eaves. He watched the shadows in the yard lengthen as the sun moved into the west. He saw that the juniper tree in the courtyard was beginning to blossom, and there were puffs of gnats around it. The air smelled of spring.

When Ryu Kyong returned, many hours later, Cho was seated cross-legged, with his back leaning against the wall.

The white paper remained blank and untouched.

He looked at his inquisitor's face, returning that expression of understanding, and was interested to see not anger in those eyes, or frustration … but fear.

For two days Cho was kept in an ordinary cell with a window and a blanket, and given meals of cabbage soup and corn porridge. The guards left him alone. He fell into a deep stupor and became confused between daydreaming and sleep. He thought often of Books. Once he sat bolt upright, seeing his boy crouched before him on the floor, as clear as daylight, in his red Pioneer's neckerchief, reading from his school textbook. "In one battle of the Great Fatherland Liberation War, three brave uncles of the Korean People's Army wiped out thirty American imperialist bastards. What was the ratio of the soldiers who fought?" Books looked up at him, smiling his cute smile. Cho's tears flowed freely, but when his eyes cleared there was no one there. Other times he thought of the Dear Leader working at his desk until the small hours of the morning, signing arrest warrants, giving orders over the telephone through clouds of cigarette smoke, micromanaging his inner circle's personal lives. He recalled the few occasions he'd met Kim Jong-il. The manner that was both whimsical and pedantic. The way he peered at you with an odd look of irony.

On the third day they came for him, and he was ready. He no longer felt anger. He had made peace with himself. Chains were locked onto his wrists and his ankles. But in the yard he saw not a stake and a firing squad, but a covered green Russian truck. He was ordered into the back and the guards climbed in with him. Before he could ask where they were going, he glimpsed the rifle butt coming down. He passed out.

Cho had no idea where he was. The truck had been driving for many hours. He was the sole prisoner. It was very dark; dawn was hours away. He was ordered out and told to kneel on the ground. In the dim yellow lights he saw a squat gray prison complex spread out before him. He heard dogs barking. Bright searchlights swept across the forecourt area from high guard towers. The walls were topped by coiled razor wire. He was in the arrivals area of a large penal labor camp.

This he had not expected at all. The only reason he could be here, the only reason he wasn't buried with a bullet in his heart, was because he had given no confession.

There was no telling how vast this place was beyond the blinding lights, but he had the sensation that he was entering another universe, where the laws of nature were different.

"Eyes on the ground!" one of the guards screamed.

Terrified, Cho bowed his head. He heard someone approach, accompanied by a barking dog. From the honorific register the guards used to address him, Cho guessed this man was a senior prison official, maybe the Deputy Director himself. The man was handed a form to sign and he chuckled as if given a surprise gift.

"An American spy?" The shadow of his head inclined to Cho in mock respect. "Welcome to Camp 22."

Cho almost laughed out loud at the irony. The camp whose existence he'd denied to Jenna over dinner in New York—how distant and unreal that world seemed—was now swallowing his life into its black heart.

His hands and ankles were unchained. Just as he was being led through the gates a distant rumble sounded, a low bass, like heavy artillery fire, from somewhere far away to his right. He assumed it was thunder, until he saw a fiery orange flare rising toward the clouds and trailing a column of smoke, turning night into day, and realized it was a rocket test. The guards stopped to watch.

He was locked in a holding cell for arrivals, where he could hear the guards dining in the next room, speaking in the coarse accents of North Hamgyong Province.

Soon afterward he was given a plate of leftover food and told to change into a uniform of coarse blue nylon that stank of corpses and congealed pus. Then the same senior official entered the room, cast him a crafty look, as if memorizing his face before it was marred forever, and glanced at an open file. He said to the guards, "Family sector, village 40, hut 21."

Cho's heart contracted and he felt his legs buckling.

My family is here? My wife and son?

In this awful hell? What words of hatred would they have for him, for bringing this upon them? For ruining their lives? He felt such agony and despair he almost fainted. *All this time he could have confessed!* It would have made not the slightest difference. He could at least have given them the satisfaction of his own death!

Nothing escaped the state. Its brutal mechanism would reunite him in prison with his own relatives, regardless of the consequences.

He heard the noise before he knew what it was. A demented wail had arisen from within him. He began punching his own face.

"What's the fuck's up with this one?" the guard said, and kicked him hard in the knee so that he fell to the floor.

In the back of another truck he wept bitter tears. He was resolved now to end his life at the first opportunity. He did not care how. That decision calmed him a little as he contemplated the confrontation ahead. The reproach and anger of his wife. The incomprehension, the trauma of his son. What physical state would they be in? His wife was a beautiful woman. She'd be at the mercy of guards who'd use her in any way they wanted.

Oh, how he could not bear to live another hour.

The ride lasted at least thirty minutes over rugged, bumping tracks, enough for him to gauge the sheer scale of the camp. Eventually he was ordered out. In the light of the guards' lanterns he saw a row of rough shacks made of crumbling mud bricks and straw roofs. An odor of excrement pervaded the place. There were no shackles or manacles now; none needed in this new universe. He was shown to a semicollapsed hovel partly built of corn stalks, with the number 21 painted on the wall. The single window had gray vinyl instead of glass. It flapped in the icy wind. One of the guards pushed him to the door of his new family home, and Cho opened it with a heavy heart.

A lone candle in a jar cast its flicker across a floor of packed earth, which was unexpectedly warm. A bundle of rags occupied one corner, which, to Cho's surprise, looked up. The woman was about sixty, with silver hair, and regarded him with flinty, suspicious eyes. In the dim light he saw a prison face of ruts and shadows.

Cho was too confused to speak.

The guard shoved him into the room.

"What's wrong with you? Aren't you pleased to see your own mother?"

44

Camp 22
North Hamgyong Province
North Korea
August 2011

"Move it, you whores. On the double or there'll be trouble!"

The kitchen was deafeningly noisy, even though no one talked. Guards barked, the radio was playing the same speech on a loop, and from amid the clouds of sour, acidic steam came the constant clamor of metal ladles, pans, and mess tins.

The girls worked the infernal pace of the camp. No one shirked, or they'd lose this cushy number faster than they could fall to the floor and beg before a guard. In the universe of the gulag, a kitchen job was the most coveted. You could pilfer grains from the floor and slops from the pigsty, you weren't breaking your back in a field or a mine, you even had corn leaves to wipe your ass. But the girls had paid a price. Some had been awarded the position for snitching. Or worse, they'd won the protection of a guard, who could do with them what he wanted, in the storeroom, behind the pigsties, in the forest. Girls who became pregnant were taken away and not seen again.

Mrs. Moon avoided eye contact with them. She'd got the job because her police record gave her occupation as "cook." She prepared meals for guards, not prisoners, so she was given soap and hot water to wash with, and wasn't covered in filth and fouled rags like the girls. She ate leftovers from the guards' mess, and could smuggle food out for her son, to keep up his strength.

My son.

For thirty years she had called to her boys in dreams. Sometimes, in the moment between sleep and waking—at dawn, when the channel to the spirit world was clear—she'd feel their presence so strongly she could reach out and hold their hands if she kept her eyes closed. She had never dared to hope that she would ever see either of them again in this world.

But, oh, what a cruel and capricious turn fortune had done her, bringing one of them to her here, to this place.

The night he'd arrived, when she saw him standing in the door of the hut, her incomprehension had taken only seconds to crystallize into recognition. In the candlelight she'd seen her own face in his. Then she knew who he was, and received one of the greatest shocks of her life. They'd stared at each other as if across an expanse of decades. Finally she said, "I am Moon Song-ae. I am your mother."

He was mute with surprise, but as this new reality crept over him, his face filled with conflicting emotions. She got up and tried to embrace him, but he turned away from her. The pain that clenched her heart might have killed her there and then.

For days he did not speak, even though they had to share the hut's single blanket. He was repulsed by her, and made little effort to hide it. Her fear of him was surpassed only by her guilt. And she was eaten up by guilt. It was because of her that he was here. It was the only explanation. She had failed to cover up the family past. She had failed him. What a crow of ill omen she was to him, a stranger from a past that had doomed his life. But they were family and had therefore to share a hut. The fact that they were total strangers to each other was of no interest to the state.

So she spared him, her estranged son. She did not cause him shame by speaking to him. She did not even know what name he went by. She turned over and pretended to sleep when he returned to the hut caked in coal dust, shaking from hunger and fatigue, and left food warming for him in the steel pan. They studied each other when the other wasn't looking. She could feel his gaze. She'd known the moment she'd seen him that he wasn't accustomed to hard labor, and straight away she'd begun to fret. How would he survive mining tiny tunnels, pushing those leaden carts, the ferocity of the guards? How soon could he bring himself to eat the rats and snakes and maggots to stay alive? She worried about this even more than she worried about Tae-hyon trying to feed himself at home without her. Men were useless without their wives.

So she began taking risks for her son. Cabbage leaves and potato peel were easy to smuggle from the kitchen in layers of her clothing. Meat was dangerous, if the guard dogs smelt it, but she succeeded in bringing out small, gristly cuts of pork, which she cooked in a stew and left out for him after she'd gone to sleep.

About a week after he'd arrived she was awakened in the small hours by the sound of his moaning. It was early summer and the sky was already light. He was lying on his side with his back toward her. She bent over him and saw that his eyes were puffy and purple, and his body badly bruised and cut. The guards broke in all newcomers this way. Without a word she lit the stove to heat water and put her arm around him. He did not push her away. She began wiping his wounds, and cleaning him with the hem of her apron. When he fell asleep with his head resting on her lap her tears fell onto his hair.

In the morning he looked her in the face for the first time, and she saw in his eyes the glimmer of acceptance, if not yet a bond.

Another beating a few days later and she nursed him again and dressed his wounds as best she could. She gave him her own food, saying she wasn't hungry. That night, as she lay down to sleep he tried to say something to her but choked on the word *Omma*. She heard him begin to weep quietly. She would give him time. She couldn't rush this.

The following night, he addressed her for the first time. Very stiffly, he said, "Be so kind as to tell me about my origin."

And so, over the following nights she told him. He learned that he was born in the western port of Nampo. His father was a ship-builder, his mother a cook. His birth name was Ahn Sang-ho.

"Your father was a kind man," she said. "And handsome. You strongly resemble him. He had a talent with boats and repaired the fishing fleet at Nampo. Just after we were married he was pro-claimed a model worker. The shipyard held a ceremony for him. Soon afterward, your brother was born and our future looked secure and happy. Model workers were urged to join the Party, so your father applied." Mrs. Moon's eyes drifted to the stove. "Then they ran the class background check, which took months. Your father was born during the war, when many birth records were lost or scat-tered. When they eventually found his, the shock was tremendous. He had been separated from his family during the war. He had only the faintest memory of his own father. An American spy? Who knows if it was true or not? It was in the record, so that was that. It couldn't have been worse. Your father was dismissed from the ship-yard. Overnight we sank to the lowest caste. We had no future. He knew he'd be an outcast doing menial work for the rest of his life. He'd be watched day and night. So he made a plan to steal a motor-boat to take us to the South. It was October. We waited for a morning of thick fog, one of those fogs that lasts all day, so that we could slip past the sea patrols. We would make that fifty-mile journey south without even a compass, but your father was a skilled sailor. When the morning came the fog was like broth. It was perfect. The port was dead quiet. He went first; I followed separately with your brother in my arms, to make it look less suspicious ..." She sighed and her face became bleak with memory. "As I arrived at the port I saw five agents run out of the fog and arrest him next to the boat. They'd had him under close surveillance. He didn't stand a chance. If I'd been a few seconds earlier they'd have got me, too. He was hanged a month later at a people's trial in front of the same crowd that had honored him as a model worker. I was eight months pregnant with you but they forced me to watch from the front row. To protect us I had told the Bowibu that my husband had deceived me about his class background and told me nothing of his escape plan ..." She gave a snort of disgust. "They're always ready to believe explanations like that. But from that day on I was living under a cloud, and I faced a terrible choice. If I kept you and your brother you'd face a life in the lowest caste, with no chance of happiness, a good marriage, or rewarding work. And I was struggling to cope. So I had your birth record changed. I bribed a state registry official in Nampo to make it seem that your real father was from a local heroic family, the family of a veteran we knew well before your father's trial. Then I placed you and your brother in the Nampo Orphanage." Tears rolled silently down her cheeks. "It was the hardest thing I ever did ..." Cho put his arm around her, his mother, absorbing her soft tremors. "... but your future depended on it. I had to hide your background. To make doubly sure, I waited four years, then I tried to have the cause of your father's death changed to 'accident,' and the deadly details removed. I figured that by the time you and your brother were young men, if anyone checked, the truth would have been long forgotten. This time, the registry official denounced me and I was exiled to the northern mountains, a penal farm in Baekam County, where I lived for twenty-eight years." They cried together, their faces glistening with tears, holding each other's hands.

For a while, the miracle of her son made life at Camp 22 bearable for Mrs. Moon. When most families returned to their huts after work drained and wrung of all hope, she and Cho lay awake for hours. She learned of her daughter-in-law and her grandson. She marveled that he had traveled to America. Cho learned that he had a stepfather, Tae-hyon, a collier she'd met and married in Baekam County.

She told him that her own parents had died not long after she was exiled. She thought they had been Christians who met other believers in secret—a memory she'd buried for decades. "There are Christians in this place," she murmured. "They are forbidden to look at heaven, and must keep their eyes lowered."

"And you, Omma?" Cho said. "Do you look at heaven?"

Mrs. Moon stared at the walls. She had no answer.

Very quickly, Cho was making her feel human again, and in Camp 22 feeling human could be fatal. It made a prisoner vulnerable. She'd learned early on that to survive this place you had to forget you were ever human. You had to become an animal. Now, in this hell, her feelings were no longer numbed, her conscience was reawakening, and as July turned to August she felt herself sliding into a black depression. She hid it from him at first, putting on a cheerful face, but soon it was impossible to hide, and she became a serious worry to him. She talked of wanting to die in her sleep, of ending her life. She didn't understand why her body went on living when she didn't want to. He said to her, "Keep hoping, and we'll survive. We have each other. What would I do if you died?" That alone nearly broke her heart.

But it wasn't the privations or the filth or the brutality that was depressing Mrs. Moon.

She stirred the cabbage leaves in the pan, imagining she saw something diabolical in the bubbles of boiling water, and calmly drained them as the kitchen girls scurried about her in a frenzy.

Like the girls, Mrs. Moon had also paid a price for her kitchen job. And what she did was worse than any snitching.

Before Cho, her will to live had banished all feeling. Now the horror reached out to touch her from the shadows, it followed her, whispered her name, brushed the back of her neck, and vanished the moment she looked over her shoulder.

She carried the pan of boiled cabbage out of the kitchen, accompanied by an armed guard. It was a different guard every time. She'd heard them draw straws for this task in the mess room.

She walked the short path through the orchard toward the new laboratory complex, nestled in the head of the valley. Apple trees grew in rows to the right, plum trees to the left, but she avoided looking at them, even when they were in blossom and made the air fragrant. The shallow graves of executed prisoners lay beneath these trees, and the soil they fertilized yielded fruit that was famous. Apples enormous and sweet that fetched high prices in Beijing. Plums so tender and aromatic they were exported to Japan.

Behind the main gates a short concrete drive led up to the complex main entrance. The guard tapped a code into the keypad next to the door, which opened automatically, and they stepped into another world. Clean, brushed-steel surfaces, gleaming white floors, bright overhead lights, filtered air. Scientists in breathing masks and blue overalls passed them in the corridor.

They reached the reception area of the vast laboratory that could be seen behind thick glass and a vacuum-sealed door, in front of which stood a special machine visitors walked through to have contaminants blown from their clothing. The guard asked the receptionist for Chief Science Officer Chung. After a few minutes Dr. Chung appeared, a brusque, balding man with a soft face and lips, also with a respirator mask hanging around his neck. "I need your prisoner today," he said. He spoke in a high, clear voice that was almost feminine. "Will you wait?"

The guard hesitated. "Sir."

Mrs. Moon was holding out the pan of boiled cabbage leaves with both arms straight and her head lowered. He took it from her.

"What's your name, grandmother?" He asked her this every time.

Mrs. Moon raised her eyes. "Moon, sir."

The look he gave her was not a look between fellow human beings. "Let's go, prisoner Moon."

45

Chilmark
Martha's Vineyard
Massachusetts

The Secret Service men stationed outside the windows wore dark polo T-shirts and Ray-Bans, like coaches at some upscale athletics club. A trim young man with a radio earphone put his head around the door. "Evergreen just left the clubhouse, ma'am. We expect the cars in a few minutes."

Evergreen. Who thought up these names?

Jenna's hands idled in her lap. She'd been advised that this slot in the day was relaxation time, and had taken the hint, arriving without papers or laptop.

She looked about at the book-lined study, silent except for the ticking of a brass ship's clock. Titles on ancient history, philosophy. A Greek bust. The house, loaned for the season, belonged to a tech tycoon not much older than she was. Beyond the French windows, patches of light shifted and swayed across a lawn shaded by Scotch pines. At the far end she could make out a private jetty, a spit of yellow beach, and the dark-blue waters of Nantucket Sound, glittering like a spinning coin. Gulls swooped and cried.

A burst of radio static issued from outside, heralding the rumble of a small motorcade. She listened as the leaden, bombproof vehicles circled the gravel forecourt, car doors opening, a deep, woman's voice raised in greeting, a dog barking. Jenna stood, facing the door, and brushed the creases from her dress. A small, biscuit-colored dog came pattering in and jumped up to greet her, then sniffed about busily. It had a coat of tight, lustrous curls, like a Restoration comedy wig.

Just outside the door, the same woman's voice filled the cavernous hallway.

"Too hot out there on the links today!"

"Yes, ma'am."

The secretary of state entered the room, directing the oversized smile straight at her, hand outstretched.

"So sorry to keep you waiting, Dr. Williams. My husband's playing golf with the president. Us *wives* went to watch them tee off," she said, for some reason adopting a southern accent.

Jenna gave a polite smile.

"Well, now." The woman closed the door and paused, taking a moment to retrieve a mental note from a well-stocked mind. She was wearing a loose-fitting lime-green linen smock, as if she'd just been at the easel, or the potter's wheel. "It was good of our friend in Pyongyang to celebrate July Fourth. Even if it was with a medium-range missile test . . ." She slipped off her shoes, and settled into the armchair opposite Jenna. "Which has brought your report back to my desk." She gave a sour little chuckle, enough for Jenna to understand that there had been disagreement in the highest circles over her ideas. "Seems you've become quite influential." The large blue eyes were turned on her like loaded shotguns. "I get it. Sanctions don't work. If Kim has to tighten his belt, the rockets and nukes are the last things he'll cut, right?" She clicked her fingers to get the attention of the dog, which jumped up onto her lap.

A housekeeper entered and put down a tray with a pitcher of iced tea and two glasses. Jenna waited until she'd gone.

328

"It's not simply that they don't work, ma'am," she said. "Sanctions play right into Kim's hands. The isolation they cause makes him more powerful, not less, and rallies his people to him in a kind of defensive nationalism. The deeper we isolate him, the more dangerous he becomes."

The secretary of state gave a little facial mime of frustration. "Sure, all right, but what you recommend is a full reversal of decades of policy. Have you thought about how I'm going to pitch that?" She held up the dog's front paws, turning it into a puppet that moved as she spoke. "A complete lifting of all trade, travel, and banking restrictions on North Korea? Establishing diplomatic relations? Treating a vicious, totalitarian tyranny as if it's a normal country—like *Canada*?"

Jenna said, "With respect, nothing else has worked. I believe the only way to change that regime is to draw it out of its isolation. Start talking. Do everything we can to help build its economy. Empower those small-time market traders and turn them into wealth makers."

"That could take decades."

And Jenna knew then, as surely as she knew anything, that this woman had her sights set on a higher office.

"In the end, ma'am, prosperity will sweep away that dictator. Isolation won't."

The secretary of state put the dog down and took a sip of her iced tea, watching Jenna over the rim of the glass. "That last time we met," she said sweetly, "you suggested killing him."

Jenna didn't blink. "If you won't do that, this is your next best option."

The woman turned to the window. A succession of thoughts seemed to play across her face like the shadows of fast-moving clouds in fall, and Jenna knew it was the exigencies of power she was thinking of—the flak she'd take from Congress, the media reaction, the reputational cost, the horse trading she'd need to start at the UN, the sheer psychological effort of it all—and for one spine-tingling instant, breathing in the smell of books, conscious of the ticking clock marking time, Jenna felt she was at the boundary of some powerful ley line that could change the future.

The secretary of state made a small huff, as if she'd reached some long-put-off decision. She gave Jenna a formal smile. "I'm told you're graduating soon. Feeling ready for active ops?"

Jenna was in the final stages of her training at the Farm. She was not looking forward to the night parachute drops.

"Actually, I've requested an assignment to the CIA's liaison in Homeland Security. Not leaving Washington."

The secretary of state cast her a quizzical look, but nothing in Jenna's gaze betrayed the image materializing unbidden in the front of her mind, like a darkroom picture developing on photographic paper. Of Soo-min surrounded by a classroom of half-Korean children.

46

Camp 22
North Hamgyong Province
North Korea
First Week of December 2011

The day had begun badly at Cutting Face Number 6. A snowfall overnight meant that some of the men had to be spared for clearing the coal-cart tracks, and the work unit was short as it was. Cho led the men in single file between the mountains of scree, thinking that next week was the anniversary of his arrest. He remembered the shock of his first day at the mine, thinking himself in a nightmare beyond his imagination. Soot-blackened skeletons and cripples whose skin dripped pus. A deep, sunless valley with mine shafts ventilating steam. Circling crows cawing above. "Don't think," they'd told him. "Just do. It'll get easier."

As they entered the tunnel the men began whispering their prayers. Who they whispered to—the spirits of their ancestors, the Great Leader, God himself—Cho had never asked. They knew they might not end the day alive.

Cutting Face Number 6 was high up on the valley's slope. It cut into the side of the mountain rather than beneath it, following the meager coal seam through a long, unsupported gallery that ended in a vertical shaft; this connected to the next long gallery, and so on into the mountain, in a series of shallow, downward steps. Only in a place where life cost nothing, Cho realized, would such a mine be built. The natural shifting and settling of rock made the long galleries highly unstable. He had lost count of the times he had dug out corpses with his bare hands after a sudden collapse, or the times the men had clawed their way out after becoming trapped.

He waited at the foot of the first shaft while the men climbed down the ladder. He'd organized them into teams of diggers, pulley operators, and cart pushers, which they would rotate after lunch. The stale, fetid air rose to greet them. Cho barely noticed it any more. This was the easiest part of his working day. It occurred to him that the nonstop hard labor and daily battle to obey orders, avoid beatings, and starvation had saved him. If he'd had the leisure to dwell upon his condition he'd have been dead months ago.

But who was he fooling?

His own mother had saved him. His real mother. Without her, he'd have died in the first week. Of all the surprises he'd experienced in his life, she was the greatest. He had never believed in miracles before.

She had arrived in Camp 22 only three months before he had, but her years of working on a penal farm had prepared her well. She had acclimatized far quicker than most arrivals. From her he'd learned the camp's internal workings, how teams were rotated, what trouble the guards themselves got into if quotas were not met. He learned to exploit the control system in which some prisoners acted as assistant guards. He acquired a sixth sense for snitches. He'd learned which levers to pull to stay alive. And the more he learned the less impotent he felt. He had accepted what had happened to him, and it had given him a peace of sorts. Many prisoners did not survive the first few weeks, the crucial transitional period, because the shock was too great. He'd survived because of her. Because of her he no longer wanted to die.

Cho had always believed that his adoptive mother had loved him. Now he was less sure. She was a remote and formal woman, devoted to the Party. Would she have cared for him, unhesitatingly, when he was as foul and cast down as he was now? He didn't know. But his real mother, this woman Moon Song-ae: whatever she was feeling for him he sensed it was pure and it was unconditional. Though she barely knew him, it was love.

A spasm of worry spread through him. Lately it seemed as if her will to live had completed its transfer to him, leaving her empty and wanting to die. Nothing he said could pull her out of it. He'd even offered to pray with her. She was troubled by something, like a sickness, that she would not speak of. After everything they'd shared, he sensed there was still something she was keeping from him, and it was gnawing away at her soul.

Omma, don't fade away now, not after all this.

At the bottom of the third shaft they reached the new gallery they had been cutting all week. It was tiny and narrow and extended about thirty meters. They had no wood to prop up the ceiling so dared not make it too wide. As Cho entered, something made him stop. He held up the lantern and sniffed. The others seemed to sense it too. Overnight the air had changed. It had turned much colder ... and it was damp. He ran his hand over the wall. It was glistening and wet to the touch, giving off the faint petroleum smell of anthracite.

"This isn't good," said a man called Hyun, whom Cho trusted.

"Probably spring water seeping through," Cho said.

The men looked at each other. It gave Cho an uneasy feeling, too, but it was too late to redeploy everyone now.

"Damp coal is heavier," said another. "We'll make the quota faster."

Cho worked like an animal all morning, hacking at the glittering anthracite, shoveling it backward with bare hands. In the chill air the men were sweating freely. From behind him came the nonstop clinking of picks striking and the coughing of clogged lungs. Tar-black men glistening like worms. It was vital to keep moving. A loaded container had to be ready to go up the shaft the moment an empty one arrived, or the system broke down. If the system broke down, the quota was short. If the quota was short, food rations were cut.

They rested a quarter hour at lunch to devour a handful of boiled wheat. Hyun had found a coiling white snake in one of the galleries, and they cut it up and divided it between them, tearing at the viscous, stringy flesh with their teeth, eating like men possessed.

They resumed work, hacking onward into the seam, but the farther they mined, the wetter it became. Water was now trickling down the walls and pooling on the floor. Cho sensed the men's fear, and decided to abandon the gallery. He was about to tell them to pack up, when something caught his eye. At his feet, wriggling and silver white in the light of the lantern, was a tiny, slender fish.

Suddenly they heard a scream. Cho scrambled past the others toward the foot of the shaft. The unit's youngest member, a nineteen-year-old boy, hadn't loaded fast enough. Two empty containers had come down from the gallery above and one had smashed his hand.

Cho pulled him out of the way. He tried to lift the container to hook it onto the pulley, but the wet coal was heavy and he was beginning to weaken and tire. His legs were wobbling. "Someone help me."

The next thing he knew a sound of falling, splashing water was coming from the gallery and the men were shouting.

The change in air pressure was instant. He turned toward them to yell.

Before he could make a sound the gallery dissolved in a thunderous, groaning roar. The men's cries were snuffed out. A massive deluge of water blasted into the shaft like a jet thrust, knocking

Cho off his feet, and smacking his shoulder against the wall. The lantern went out. One of the containers struck him hard on his forearm. Somehow he caught hold of the pulley rope, but couldn't haul himself up with one arm. The torrent rose up over his head, engulfed him, and the world went black and silent. He was flailing his legs in complete darkness, clinging to the rope. Bubbles rumbled from his mouth.

After what seemed like a minute he had the sensation of rising quickly, his body scraping against the side of the shaft. Suddenly he could breathe; a voice shouted his name, and he was being hauled from the water by the pulley operator in the gallery above. The water had risen forty meters up the shaft, and even as he was being dragged out he heard it subsiding behind him. He was laid on the floor, gulping in great mouthfuls of air, then blacked out.

When he came to, he was icy cold and his teeth were chattering. He wanted to cough but could barely move. His body was so numbed and weakened he couldn't tell for sure where the damage lay, but his shoulder didn't feel too secure and his forearm had an unnatural-looking kink in it. He closed his eyes and groaned. A whimper he recognized sounded next to him in the dark. The teenage boy was saved.

"Where're the others?" Cho croaked.

"Just me," said Hyun. "The five inside the gallery didn't make it." He sat on his haunches and covered his face with his hands. "We were mining under a fucking lake."

Cho closed his eyes and focused on his breathing. *The irony.* The men had often joked that if they kept tunneling they'd reach the other side.

Outside the mine Cho was laid down on the snow by his remaining teammates. He'd dislocated a shoulder. That could be fixed, but not the fractured forearm, unless a prisoner with medical training could bind it in the camp infirmary, which, as everyone knew, was death's waiting room. If he'd been healthy and strong he'd have been in agony, but he felt only numbness and discomfort. Not even the cold was bothering him. Most likely he would be shot right here. He was no more use as a miner. Cho looked forlornly at the teenage boy, whose face was streaked with tears, and winked at him, to say *Put it out of your mind.*

Two guards were trudging toward them and Cho's heart sank. The larger one, a pig of a man who kept a whip in his belt, was in the lead, but the other was one of the older guards. The older ones, Cho had learned, were softer and less strict about the rules. Hyun removed his cap, fell to his knees, and lowered his eyes to explain what had happened, but to the men's surprise the guard said, "This one healthy?" He was pointing to the teenage boy.

Cho said, "Yes, sir."

The boy was pulled away by the arm toward an open-top jeep parked next to the coal-cart tracks below, which ran between the slopes of black moraine. Cho had only just noticed it. In the back sat four prisoners. Standing next to it were two men in blue overalls, with respirator masks and clear goggles hanging from their necks.

The older guard leaned over Cho's face. "Well, this *is* your lucky day, isn't it?"

Cho's shoulder was fixed and his arm bandaged and put into a makeshift splint in the infirmary. Within hours he was assigned to lighter work, on a construction project two valleys farther along from the mine. He almost smiled when he understood he was to push a flat cart of loaded goods, which, with luck, he could manage with one arm.

After the mine, this was a vacation. It was late afternoon. He felt sunlight on his face for the first time in months. At the entrance to the construction site a passing farm cart hit a pothole and spilled radishes all over the road, which had the line of prisoners dashing to and fro, grabbing the vegetables and devouring them on the spot, despite screams and kicks from the guards. Cho had never much liked radishes. Now they were the most heavenly things he'd ever tasted.

The construction project, which lay at the head of the valley, and at the end of the railroad that ran through the entire camp, was an annex to a new laboratory complex, he learned. His coworkers were cleaner and in better physical shape than the miners. He guessed they hadn't been here as long. He was assigned to a unit of fifty prisoners, divided into teams of ten. Their task was to unload materials from the trains that arrived twice daily from the port at Chongjin, and goods from the trucks that came by road from the north, from China. He saw the unloading of massive stainless steel centrifuges from one; from another, desk computers, packaged in white boxes with an apple logo. Whatever this laboratory was, it had an extraordinary budget.

Toward the end of his first day on the project, work came to a halt at the sound of a whistle.

"Line up, heads up, you scum!" a guard screamed. A muzzled dog barked.

The prisoners shuffled into a long line in front of the trucks with their heads lowered and their hands behind their backs.

"I said a line!" The guard kicked an elderly prisoner who was too slow. The man's skeletal body struck the side of a truck like a sheaf of straw.

"No need for that, Sergeant," said a light, clear voice.

A man was inspecting the line, followed by a guard. He was dressed entirely in a white bodysuit with the tight hood circling his face. Clear goggles and a respirator mask hung around his neck. His rubber boots were also white.

"I am Chief Science Officer Chung," he said, smiling genially. "I'm looking for three healthy men to work for me inside the lab complex. You'll be warm and well fed, and in return we may ask you for some blood samples ..."

Cho sensed a wave of desperation run along the line.

The doctor was looking each prisoner up and down, as if he were a livestock auctioneer. "You, professor," he said to a tall young man. "How old are you?"

"Twenty-six, sir."

The doctor lifted the man's eyelid with the tip of a gloved finger and examined the inside his mouth. A nod to the guard, and the man was yanked from the line.

"Gently. Please," said Dr. Chung with a reproving laugh.

Cho puffed out his chest, and pulled himself up to his full height, wishing he could scrub his face with snow and rub color into his cheeks and lips.

The doctor stopped in front of the man immediately to Cho's right. "How old are you, father?"

"Forty-three, sir."

The doctor moved on a step, and he was in front of Cho.

His eyes scanned Cho's face, and in that moment Cho pictured his own appearance through the doctor's eyes. He hadn't seen his own reflection in a year, but he could clearly imagine the yellow, hollow-cheeked ghost man. The human ruin with the deep stink of the long-term prisoner. The musty, sweetish odor of the camp.

The doctor moved on.

Moments later another selection was made. A young lad who couldn't have been in the camp more than a few weeks was pulled from the line.

The whistle sounded again, and the unselected went back to work.

Later, Cho described his day to his mother in the hut as she stirred the rice for dinner. He thought she'd be pleased to know he had easier work, but she kept her back toward him and said nothing, and he attributed her silence to her depression.

They ate without speaking. The meal was barely three mouth-fuls. Then she snuffed out the candle and got under the blanket.

He was almost asleep when she spoke. In the dark, her voice sounded unnervingly calm.

"If that doctor comes again, you must hide. If you can't hide, have a coughing fit. The guards will think you got black lung in the mine and you won't be selected."

"What d'you mean?"

Cho turned over and stared in her direction but she had returned to silence.

47

Camp 22
North Hamgyong Province
North Korea

After a week laboring in the sunlight and open air, Cho's skin stopped weeping pus. He felt stronger. His day divided into day and night, rather than endless dark. He was no longer in the perpetual delirium of exhaustion he endured in the mine. His forearm was healing in the makeshift splint, though it was sorely sensitive to the touch, and the bone was not setting straight. He had to lift and carry with his right arm.

A stoic man in his thirties had shown Cho the ropes at the construction site, orientated him, warned him which guards were killers and which would turn a blind eye. Cho marveled that natural human kindnesses endured, even in this place. The man's name was Jun. His back was bent in half, so that he had to crane his head up to look at Cho. His skin was leathery and stretched tightly over his bones like all the prisoners, but to Cho's astonishment his eyes were blue. He was the grandson of an American POW from the Korean War, he said. He had been born inside the camp and had never left it.

After the mine, the temperature on the surface almost stopped Cho's heart. Sweat on his brow turned icy in the lacerating wind that swept down through the narrow valley. The air seemed to crystallize in his nose. The bare skin of his fingers stuck to the steel cart he pushed. His day became a minute-by-minute battle to stay warm, but again Jun helped, showing him how to steal empty burlap sacks when the guards weren't looking and wrap them around the body beneath the thin nylon prison clothes.

Once again Cho could not believe his good fortune. The building had to be completed at such breakneck speed that the prisoners were fed two cups of food each day, one of mixed grains and one of boiled corn, double what Cho had received in the mine, though here on the frozen surface he'd found no grubs or rats for protein.

The guards had never risked venturing down into the mine shafts, but here they stayed close to the prisoners, with rifles on their backs and rabbit-fur hats pulled low around their ears. He was becoming a veteran prisoner, he realized. He never looked the guards in the face but had an instinct for when their eyes were upon him. He kept his ears open and an eye out for the smallest detail that could give him an edge, and keep him alive.

And as he worked, Cho noticed a most curious detail.

They were pulling cement sacks from the train wagon when he whispered to Jun.

"The guards ... Why don't they enter the lab complex?"

Jun barely moved his lips. "They're afraid."

He fell silent as one of the snitches passed into earshot.

Jun lowered a sack onto Cho's handcart, close enough to his face to speak almost inaudibly. "... The place was heavily guarded until a year ago. Then a guard's wife gave birth. The baby had no arms or legs. Another was born blind."

Jun flicked him a look of warning. Gossip was a dangerous commodity in the camp.

It was Sunday and snowing hard, but trains still arrived with building materials and departed laden with coal; trucks had to be unloaded. The prisoners worked under a barrage of oaths and blows. The guards kicked and whipped the prisoners as if they were lower than animals. "Move it, you traitors, you sons of bitches!"

They'd been at work since 6:00 a.m., and Cho had eaten no more than a mouthful of rice for breakfast, and some cabbage leaves his mother had smuggled out in her apron. He watched Jun pick up a heavy cement sack from the train wagon and heave it onto his crooked back as lightly as if it were a pillow. Cho, his arm still in a splint, pushed the cart with one arm, his wooden clogs slipping on the frozen black mud.

Suddenly his feet slid from under him and he landed hard on his wounded arm on the ice. Before he knew it a rifle butt had smashed into his shoulder. Pain shot down his spinal cord like a lighting strike.

"What's this? Sabotage? GET UP!"

Cho scrambled painfully to his feet, and had just got himself upright when the kick of the boot struck the base of his spine. For a moment the agony made his vision go white, and his eyes watered. He'd been shivering all day but now felt a sudden fire burning through him. Even his fingers on the cryonic cold of the iron hand-cart were suddenly hot and sweating.

The snowstorm was blowing up into a full blizzard. Fine grains stung his face and eyes. He could barely see two meters ahead. The prisoners carried their loads in a single file. He could just make out the bent-over shape of Jun lugging the cement sack. They were approaching the entrance of the annex.

Suddenly they were in a full whiteout. Zero visibility, an empty dimension. He heard a sharp yelp, and through a clearing in the swirls of snow saw Jun lose his balance. The sack tumbled from his back, hit the ground, and split wide open. Pale-gray, ashy cement lay across the road like a cremation. Jun dropped to his knees, took off his cap, and went dead still, head lowered, awaiting his fate.

Three guards ran to him and surrounded him, staring at the spill. The prisoners stopped moving.

"You, son of imperialist scum, how long have you been here?"

Jun was trembling violently. "Thirty-two years, sir. All my life. Please."

The guard turned to the others. "Thirty-two years in Camp 22 is long enough, wouldn't you say?"

He drew his revolver and shot Jun at point-blank range in the head.

The noise echoed off the steep valley sides, and the small body flopped to the ground like a child's toy. The line of prisoners turned to stone, and something inside Cho broke.

It seemed to happen in slow motion. He heard a voice roaring. It was his own. He was lunging at the guard, with his good arm extended like a spear. He caught the look of surprise on the guard's face. The other two reached to their holsters. Cho grabbed the man's wrist, which still held the revolver, but a starving, emaciated prisoner was no match for three fed, trained killers.

He felt himself being yanked violently backward and his legs kicked away. Next his view was of the gray-white sky, and the faces of three guards. A boot covered in ice and mud pressed down on his windpipe, as the revolver was aimed in his face.

Cho closed his eyes. For a delirious moment he saw his wife and son bathed in light, somewhere far away and happy. He saw his mother, as a young woman. He saw Jenna across a candle-lit dinner table, giving him her radiant smile.

The revolver cocked with a fluid click. The finger squeezed.

"Oh-ho, hold on there," said a high, clear voice. A patter of rubber-booted feet was approaching at a run. "Not so fast, comrades. This one's fighting fit, isn't he?"

In the periphery of his vision Cho saw blue lab overalls and a white, gloved hand extended toward him.

"Come, sir. Let me help you up."

48

Department of Homeland Security
Nebraska Avenue Complex
Washington, DC

Jenna's breakthrough came by pure chance.

Her time was up at the CIA's liaison in Homeland Security. In three months she had not turned up a single clue—nothing that might link a young migrant entering the United States with the children of the Seed-Bearing Program, with that villa in Pyongyang. Fisk told her the Agency had other priorities. "Wrap up there tomorrow. We need to discuss your next op." One by one she took down the passport photos and visa copies pinned to her board. All were of half-Asian young adults who had been briefly held by US immigration because of some anomaly in their backgrounds or documents. All had been allowed to enter the country. She'd put a strike mark through every one of them.

It dismayed her to think she'd wasted her time, and even now it was a wrench to give up. All she'd needed was a clue, a crib to unlock the puzzle, but it had never come.

"Bailing out, huh?" The overweight young guy in the cubicle next to hers was making a daisy chain out of paper clips. At first she'd attributed his stale odor to lax hygiene, but she soon started to think of it as the smell of low morale. It seemed to pervade this whole place.

She shuffled the passport pages into a neat pile and stared at it thoughtfully for a minute. She knew that if any of the children from that villa had been infiltrated into the United States they would have carried passports that disguised their country of origin and traveled via a transit country. And that transit country would have to be on the exceedingly short list of North Korea's friends in the world, countries whose security services did favors for each other. Cuba she'd rule out—almost no one from Cuba arrived through normal immigration channels. China, too, she thought very unlikely. Beijing wouldn't want to get involved in Kim's covert ops. That left Syria, Iran, Pakistan, Malaysia, Russia, and Vietnam. Arrivals from the first four of those countries were monitored closely by the CIA's Counterterrorism Center for any links to Al-Qaeda or Hezbollah, and several times she had tagged along with CIA officers to Dulles, Logan, and JFK airports to observe some wide-eyed, sweating student being interrogated by Homeland Security behind a one-way mirror.

At first she'd assumed North Korea would use false passports: after all, they'd been forging everything from hundred-dollar bills to erectile dysfunction medication. She'd made exhaustive inter-agency cross-checks for any young adult caught at immigration bearing a false passport from a country on that list. But after three months without a lead she began to suspect that these kids may be entering the country with fraudulently issued *valid* passports. And that made her task impossible. With a valid passport from Syria, Russia, or Vietnam, there was nothing stopping a young adult applying for legitimate visas for work, tourism, study. They would not be detected. Background checks, biometric data, profiling would have nothing on them. Trying to solve this by herself now seemed absurd. The task required an international team effort with the CIA station chiefs in all those countries, and she knew that senior figures at Langley harbored doubts about the Seed-Bearing Program. *Indoctrinated young adults who look foreign? Trained as spies and assassins?* Some days she had simply given up on the task and had returned to Langley to monitor the spysat traffic. Simms showed her the latest worrying images of the secret lab in Camp 22, which appeared to be expanding. A second building was in the process of construction.

Her phone rang, and her spirits sank when she saw it was Hank from Counterterrorism, a morose divorcé whose offers of dinner she'd twice declined. She'd accompanied him to the airports half a dozen times.

"Got another one at Dulles, if you're interested? Arrival from Malaysia."

She cast a forlorn glance at the pile of passport photos on her desk, ready for the shredder, and heard herself say, "Sure thing, Hank. Why not?"

At Washington Dulles International Airport they were greeted by a tough-looking young female immigration officer Jenna had not met before. She explained that she herself was of Malaysian-American descent.

"Never had one like this before," she said, "it's like the kid's … some kind of ghost."

Perhaps it was the spooked look on her face but the skin on Jenna's back was suddenly chilled to gooseflesh.

In an interrogation room behind a one-way mirror sat a young woman whom Jenna knew without a doubt was mixed race, and half East Asian. Her eyes were almond shaped and bright, her skin tan colored; her glossy black hair was tied into a long braid. The detainees she'd seen in that room invariably sweated or fidgeted, exhibiting the full range of nervous symptoms. But this one sat bolt upright, cool and comported, utterly expressionless. There was a curious neutrality to her clothing: new Cargo hooded top, new Gap baseball cap, new white sneakers—the kind of look an older generation thinks a teenager wears.

"Name is Mabel Louise Yeo," the immigration officer said, "Aged eighteen; speaks perfect American English; valid Malaysian passport; genuine student visa. Enrolled at George Washington to study applied physics in September. Said she just returned home for a few days for a family occasion. Provides a home address in Kuala Lumpur. Everything checks out. But … there's something off about her."

"Her body language," Jenna said.

"Actually, it's her language. She doesn't speak a word of Malay. I said hi to her and told her I knew her home neighborhood." The officer ran a palm down her face. "Total blank. So then I questioned her in English. But it's like she sticks to a script. The moment we go off script she clams up. Wherever this kid's from … it's not Malaysia."

"May I speak to her?" Jenna said.

"Ghost kid," Hank said. "I like that."

Jenna opened the door. The instant the girl saw Jenna's face she gave a yelp of surprise and leapt from her seat. Before any of them could react, she had thrown her arms around Jenna in an embrace.

In her astonishment Jenna found herself pressing the girl's cheek to hers, stroking her hair, as if she were a little girl who'd got separated from her parents.

In North Korean dialect she whispered, "You must be tired after your long journey."

49

Camp 22
North Hamgyong Province
North Korea

Mrs. Moon made her way through the fruit orchard toward the laboratory complex, carrying the pan of boiled cabbage leaves. The guard behind her kept flicking at a cigarette lighter. To the left she saw a work unit hacking at the ground, their bodies black against the pristine snow. Another pit amid the trees. *They'll run out of room,* she thought, and imagined, not for the first time, the faces of the faraway consumers of these fruits, their reactions if they knew what made the apples and plums so extravagantly lush. And each time, the same thought followed: the secret was safe. No one left Camp 22, even as a corpse.

Inside the complex she waited while the cabbage leaves were taken away and treated. She would soon be working here, Chief Science Officer Chung had assured her. The new annex, almost completed, was a staff refectory with kitchens. And she would be the kitchen block leader, responsible for its prison workers and given a coupon for soap and a new set of clothing. This news, which guaranteed she would survive the winter and have enough to eat, simply completed her depression.

Dr. Chung was in high spirits. Mrs. Moon sensed the growing importance of his work, and of this facility. Pyongyang was sending inspectors every week. A political agitation team had visited, and festooned the laboratory and the corridors with slogans on long red banners. LET US MAKE OUR COUNTRY A FORTRESS! SCIENCE IS THE ENGINE OF SOCIALIST CONSTRUCTION!

Half an hour later the pan of cabbage leaves was returned to her by a scientist wearing a full white bodysuit with goggles and respirator mask. She angled her head away from the fumes and stood behind Dr. Chung in the entrance to the chamber while he delivered his address to the prisoners. The guards would not enter the laboratory itself, so the process was kept orderly with a deception.

"On behalf of this facility's administration I bid you welcome. Just as we scientists work to defend our country against its enemies, so you are being given a chance to redeem yourselves, and help secure the welfare of a stronger Korea. We will feed you and look after your health, and in return you will help us test new vaccines. Before we take the first blood samples, please eat these cabbage leaves and digest them, as they have been soaked in vitamins, iron, and glucose. If any of you are diabetic and not allowed sugar, make yourselves known ..."

Mrs. Moon entered, holding the surgical pan of cold boiled cabbage leaves.

Smile at them, woman, Dr. Chung mouthed to her, miming a smile with his fingers.

She could not look at them. They were sitting naked around a drain in the floor in a bright tiled chamber watched by security cameras. Not all of them were fooled, she knew.

Hungry, suspicious eyes turned toward her. She moved from one to the other, robotically forking a large cabbage leaf into their cupped hands. Even the smell of it was warning enough. This test held eleven prisoners, all male, seated on the tiled bench, holding their hands in their laps to protect their modesty.

The sight of a forearm in a splint made her raise her head, and she found herself looking into the eyes of her son.

Mrs. Moon was paralyzed. The security camera was trained on her from the ceiling corner. Suddenly the pan slipped from her fingers to the floor with a clatter. She muttered an apology and picked it up, taking a moment to bend up straight, then forked a leaf into Cho's hands. She forced herself to turn to the next prisoner. She focused all her effort into not looking at Cho.

When the last prisoner had been served she hurried out before it began. The door sealed shut behind her.

Cho watched the emaciated men devour their leaves in seconds. Their bodies were all bone cage, grime, and patches of hair, and these were the healthy specimens. If they had any suspicions they were too hungry to care. The moment his mother left the room, the chamber door sealed with a pressurized hiss and a ventilation system began to hum. He stared at the leaf in his hand and crunched it into his mouth. It was fresh and crisp and sour. Untainted, slipped from his mother's apron in the moment she'd dropped the pan. He munched it and watched, his chest filling with foreboding, thinking how vulnerable nakedness made a man.

It began like an earth tremor. The first prisoner who'd eaten the cabbage, a small man in his thirties with missing teeth, began shaking. Suddenly his seizure was so violent he fell to the floor and twisted and writhed, screaming like an animal as his mouth and nostrils frothed with blood. Then it began in the prisoner next to him. In the next moment four of them were on the floor with blood bubbling over their faces and froth pouring out of their mouths. They howled like beasts being slaughtered.

Cho was too shocked to move. He could but watch. Limbs flayed out and kicked, in a stinking bath of blood and excrement. Death worked quickly from one to the next, twitching each into stillness. It had taken no more than ten, twelve seconds for them to die.

Cho stared at this vision for a moment, alone on the bench, then retched.

Moments later the door hissed and opened. Two scientists in white hazmat suits and respirator masks stepped in. One was holding some sort of digital timer.

He said, "You—eat the cabbage."

Cho was panting. His voice was hoarse. "I ate it."

The scientists stepped across the bodies as if they were cushions, their white rubber boots becoming smeared with blood. "Open your mouth."

Cho opened his mouth, showing globs of green cabbage on his tongue.

They pulled him by his arms from the chamber and closed the door on the horror. Cho was standing in a blinding white antechamber. One of them walked away shouting, "Fetch Chief Science Officer Chung."

He was naked, and realized he was standing next to his mother. Perhaps it was the nakedness, and an irresistible sense of shame, but out of nowhere he began to weep.

His mother's voice next to him was a whisper. "You are strong, Sang-ho. You are good. Find a way to escape this place. Find a way. Do it for me."

Cho wept like he hadn't wept since he was an infant.

He said, "I don't want to be without you."

She moved her head to one side as a camera trained on her. "My life is over. I've killed too many here. Not even I will allow myself to live. But you—tell the world what you have seen. Tell the world what happens here."

Without looking at him her fingers touched his gently. She took his hand and squeezed it behind her back, out of view of the cameras. It was her farewell, he realized. It took all his effort not to turn to her. Then she clasped his hand shut, and he felt a hard, ball-shaped object in his palm, the size of a chestnut.

"Use this for bribes." Her voice was pure air. He barely heard it over the humming ventilation. "It's worth at least five thousand yuan."

Dr. Chung was stomping toward them, and stopped to listen as the duty scientist explained. The doctor was so worked up he hadn't put on his respirator mask. Cho heard the words *possibility of natural immunity.*

Dr. Chung shoved the scientist out of the way. "Natural immunity to scytodotoxin X?" he shouted. "One *microgram* of that is enough. That old bitch must have helped him!"

Cho's head dropped to his chest.

"Well now," Dr. Chung said, baring his teeth, "What are we to do with this *cheat?*"

If guards had witnessed this, he'd have been beaten to death on the spot. But there were no guards present.

Cho sank to his knees and entreated, clasping his hands in front of his chest. "Not the mine, sir. Please. I'll do anything in the camp. I'll empty the shit tanks. I'll do corpse duty. Not the mine."

An expression of happy recklessness overcame Dr. Chung's face. He waved his arm in a wide arc. "Send for a guard!" he said in a singsong. "Throw this filth back down the mine."

The next morning Cho rejoined the work unit at Cutting Face Number 6. Hyun stared at the splint on his arm. Cho knew what he was thinking. He wouldn't survive a week in the mine with a still-healing fracture. Hyun patted his shoulder, and handed him a lantern.

The march to the new seam took about thirty minutes. It was on the third gallery down and veered sharply right, away from the shaft that connected to the flooded fourth gallery, the watery tomb of his five teammates. Cho dragged his feet and hung back until he was the last in the line. He hoped that what he was about to do would look like a suicide. It was as good as suicide. Even if his hunch was right, his chances of survival were terrible. If it was wrong, he was dead. There could be no coming back.

He waited until the team had turned a corner of the tunnel, then he slipped away, quickly doubling back to the mouth of the flooded shaft. Leaning over the edge he held out the lantern. The ladder was still in place. It disappeared down into the water, which glinted like black marble. Where was it from, this water? If only he could be sure. A spasm of dread swept through him. Even if he could make it through, he might easily find himself in some narrow cavern with no way out.

Cho heard his breathing become shallow and his heart thumping in his temples. He was filled with a premonition of death.

Footsteps were approaching fast. Someone had been sent running back to find him. He put the lantern down, and felt the adrenalin singing in his chest.

He filled his lungs with air, and closed his eyes.

Don't hesitate. Do it now.

He jumped.

Time seemed to slow down. Frigid air rushed past his ears. He hit the water like a dart. A shock wave of cold passed through him. Water thundered past his face as he shot down, down into the shaft. When his fall began to slow he grabbed the ladder's rungs and pushed himself down to the bottom. Already his lungs were bursting. He had nothing to hold on to now, and nothing but touch to guide him. He was floating in a black void. His hands pawed at the walls at the foot of the shaft, trying to find the gallery opening. *It should be right here.* His arms flayed as he fought a rising panic. He extended his hand out as far as he could, reaching with his fingers ... and touched the smooth cold face of a corpse.

His eyes bulged. He cried out, losing great bubbles of precious air, and felt a fresh surge of terror. He pushed the body out of the way.

A jab of sharp pain as his forehead hit rock.

Was this the gallery? He was clawing along its sides, feeling for the roof, and his lungs began to spasm and heave. The roof was intact. The collapse must have happened farther up. How far? Twenty meters? More? He scraped at the rock with his nails, pushing himself along in the tiny narrow space, braising and shredding the skin of his hands. Water entered his inner ear, bringing a sepulchral change of acoustic in which he could hear every bubble, every swirl. Then his face brushed the splayed hair of another human head, and horror burst through him once again.

The corpse seemed to block the whole space. It was bloated to the touch. Frantically he punched at it, trying to push it downward and in doing so felt his body begin to fail. His lungs were imploding. They were seconds from surrendering to water.

This is it, Cho Sang-ho, said a voice in his head. *This is where it ends.*

In a final desperate lunge he shoved the body downward by the shoulders. Some fusion of will and terror was giving him a force beyond the physical. Next thing he knew he was touching not rough coal, but smooth slippery stone, a mound of boulders that had fallen from above. And in his inner ear he heard the sound of water moving, flowing. His feet had traction now, on the boulders. He kicked like a sprinter, and then he was rising upward through water. He could hold his breath no longer.

One second, two ...

Suddenly he surfaced, and air and sound burst over him again. The air he gulped in great heaves gave him such a head rush he felt on the verge of fainting.

He was still in pitch darkness. From the echoing drips he guessed that he was in a narrow cavern, just as he'd feared. But the water was moving quickly.

Gently it carried him along while he panted and caught his breath, but soon he was swimming with it, paddling like a dog. The cavern became narrower and the flow stronger. Ahead of him he

354

could hear the gurgling of an outlet. He braced himself, and let the water pull him feet first into a noisy pothole. His teeth gnashing in terror, he became stuck, with water roaring over him. Frantically he wriggled himself free, slithering through a space only a skeleton could slip through.

He emerged into another cavity, coughing, gasping, and at once felt the draft of fresh air on his face. Not daring to believe his senses, he saw the faint pallor of daylight. He stood up, and waded toward it. He was exhausted and faint, cut and bruised everywhere, and bleeding from every limb. But he was alive.

Oh, he was alive.

He fought his way through an opening overhung with dead bracken. He blinked. The daylight was as shocking as the cold. A large pine had fallen across the mouth of the cavern and he had to clamber over it. The torrent fell in a short waterfall toward a white-water stream that roared between boulders.

Panting, he stepped carefully over the rocks next to the waterfall and collapsed onto a patch of dead grass, coughing and crying. Almost immediately he began trembling with such violence he could barely lift himself back up into a kneeling position.

He was in another deep shaded valley, one of the many that fed into the broad valley basin where the camp was located. He glanced about at the steep slopes covered in thick pine forest. The sky was an arctic white. Crows circled far above, but of the camp there was no sign.

He had come right through the mountain and out the other side. He could see no watchtower, no electrified fence.

He was out.

50

North Hamgyong Province
North Korea

Cho clenched his teeth against the chattering and let the faint warmth of the sun touch his face. The white stream foamed through a narrow gully, but over the noise he heard birdsong, for the first time in more than a year. His exhilaration lasted only seconds. Some internal clock had started ticking. He was icy and wet. He had no shelter or food. He'd been so focused on making it through the mine that he'd given no thought to what came next, but he knew he did not have much time.

He entered the forest and began fighting his way through dead undergrowth, up the steep, rock-strewn slope. His body was so weak from hunger he had to stop every few steps. The crest of the narrow valley seemed impossibly high and was serrated with sharp rocks, but he had to find his bearings and figure out which way to go. He knew this wild region only from folktale and legend.

He stopped again when he thought he heard a scratching. He listened, and over the wheezing of his breath realized that the sound was coming from a mossy crag to his left. Peering into the cracks between the rocks, he saw a glassy black eye look back at him. A brown rabbit, fallen and trapped. In a reflex movement Cho grabbed its ears and pulled it out. He wrung its neck and tore away the fur, devouring the raw meat in voracious, unchewed gulps. It tasted as sweet as syrup. Within minutes there was nothing left but fur and bone. Wiping the gore from his mouth, he rested a moment. He felt the difference immediately. The nourishment turning to energy in his body.

He renewed his climb and tried to think.

Hyun would not report him missing until the end of the working day, toward 11:00 p.m., when the work unit returned to the surface for the evening roll call. Death by accident was a daily occurrence in the mines, and often the bodies were never found. Suicides were common. Would the guards presume that he'd jumped or fallen into the flooded shaft, and leave it at that? No, they wouldn't ... He'd ranked too highly for them to chance it. He had caused too great an upset at the top. Pyongyang would want confirmation of death.

They'll order an immediate search for the body.

With heavy remorse he realized that it was Hyun and his men who would be sent down into the water to find him. It was their lives he'd gambled with.

He had twenty-four hours at most, he calculated. Twenty-four hours before the camp issued an all-points bulletin and alerted the checkpoints and the border authorities. He had nowhere to lie low and regain his strength. He had to make it to the border as fast as he could.

But even if he got there, what then?

One step at a time.

By midmorning he was nearing the summit of the valley. A low cloud had descended. Despite the cold and his damp clothes, sweat stung his eyes, and his body was aflame from the effort. With one immense final lunge he reached the rocks at the top.

For a moment he saw nothing but swirling gray vapor, and then the clouds parted and he had a steep-angle view of Camp 22, spread out below and far into the distance. A slave kingdom, so vast he could not discern its boundaries. Plumes of steam rose from the cutting faces of the mine shafts. He could see hundreds of work units toiling on the endless brown fields. From the garment factories came the hammering of distant machinery. He turned his gaze southward, toward the prisoner villages, which stretched as far as the eye could see, and felt his chest clutch as he thought of his mother. He could make out the execution site, and the black smoke pouring from the crematoria. A flash lit the horizon, followed by a distant rumble, and a rocket climbed its way toward the sky over the East Sea.

Cho looked at his hands and saw that he'd clenched his fists. He was shaking.

Good and loyal people suffered and died in this pit. How deceived they'd been before they'd entered its gates. How utterly he had deceived himself, all his life. His eyes filled with tears. This is what lay hidden behind the scenery. This was the black heart of the cause he'd served.

Overhead a crow circled and cawed, a harbinger of ill omen. But Cho did not feel cursed. For a moment the sun pierced the churning cloud, sending a gilded shaft across the black landscape below. He felt salvation upon his shoulder. He saw the purpose of his life laid bare.

I will be a witness. I will survive and bear witness to the world.

He tried to keep beneath the cover of the trees as he scrambled down the other side of the peak, heading northwest, but twice he had to cross open pastures where his trail was obvious in deep snow. Farther down he saw some scattered farmhouses and barns. Snow had begun to fall in large spinning flakes. If only it were enough to cover his tracks.

The first barn stood in a field that adjoined a thicket of pine trees to the right, beyond which was a densely wooded slope that led down to a railroad. He stopped and listened—dead silence—and started searching the barn's exterior. He was in luck. A set of farm laborers' overalls was hanging from a hook on the outside door, left out to freeze the lice. The fabric was ragged and covered in patches. Cho lifted it down and tried the door. Inside smelled powerfully of dung and moldering straw. An aged brown ox lying on the hay turned its vast head indifferently toward him and snorted. He slipped inside and changed clothes, finding also a too-large pair of rubber boots. Before burying his blue prison garb beneath a mound of silage, he pulled away the string where he had crudely stitched his pocket closed, and removed the hard cellophane ball his mother had pushed into his hand. He held it up and studied it. The reflected light of snow filtered through slats in the barn's wall, bouncing off the tiny white crystals beneath the cellophane.

Bingdu. About forty grams, he reckoned.

Looking about for a surface he could use, he found a fragment of broken windowpane on the floor, which he wiped and laid on his lap; then he sat on a hay bale and slowly began to unwrap the cellophane, in the process tearing off small pieces.

How long had his mother kept this hidden on her? Why had she brought it to the lab complex yesterday ... ?

Cho stopped and stared into space.

So she could kill herself. At a moment of her choosing. All she had to do was overdose. Swallow the lot. Her heart would stop. His eyes misted. It was several minutes before he could force himself on.

Taking extreme care, he used his fingernail to separate portions of the powder into smaller cellophane balls until he had ten of them, gleaming like pearls in the white light, plus the remainder in a larger ball.

Some process of decay beneath the mound of hay was causing it to give off a faint warmth. He slipped the pearls of *bingdu* into a pocket of the overalls and before he knew it he had covered himself in hay and had fallen asleep.

*

He opened his eyes to the sound of men's voices.

He had no idea how long he'd been sleeping. The light through the slats had turned a faint neon blue, and his hunger had returned with a vengeance. His face was numb and frozen.

The voices were outside, talking about the missing overalls. The door creaked open and Cho shrank into the hay, seeing the glow of a kerosene lamp light up the barn. A man and a teenage boy entered. Their clothes and hats were powdered white. Cho prayed to his ancestors that it had snowed enough to cover all his tracks and not reveal that he'd entered the barn and hadn't left.

"Appa, no one's hiding in dung," the boy said in a strong Hamgyong accent. "The thief's gone."

The father lingered for a moment, seeming to notice the broken windowpane Cho had used to divide the *bingdu*. Slowly they left and closed the door.

Cho lay dead still, his nerves on full alert. He waited several minutes, then got up as softly as he could. He opened the door with caution, and peered about. It was snowing heavily. The tracks of the farmer and his son led away to the left. It was about thirty meters across the field to the cover of the pines. He stepped out into deep, fresh snow. His leg sank as far as his knee. He could only walk by taking giant, exaggerated steps. A farm dog barked, setting off a dozen other barks farther down the valley.

Then he ran, wading across crisp snow, into the woods.

It was darker beneath the pines where the snow had not penetrated. He kept moving, swiping branches aside, weaving between trees, downhill toward the railroad.

This was the track that carried coal from Camp 22 to a destination he guessed was Hoeryong, about ten kilometers to the north. He'd seen it from the summit, the small city on the banks of the Tumen River, the border with China. He'd be lucky to make it there by evening. How long had he been asleep? From the sky it looked like midafternoon, and darkening. What a fool he'd been!

That farmer or his dog would find his tracks and alert the Bow-ibu before he'd covered two kilometers. His escape window had radically narrowed.

Cho heard distant dogs barking behind him and felt an electrify-ing surge of adrenalin. He began to run, tripping and falling on the sleepers and loose chippings.

Hoeryong was in darkness except for a few sparse lights around the statues and monuments. He felt sure a city this size would have an informal market where he could buy what he needed. Sure enough, along the platform of the railway station he saw several dozen ajummas packing up their wares by the blue beams of pencil flash-lights. A coal brazier gave off more smoke than light. He approached a woman whose head was muffled in rags. She was putting away small bottles of home-brew corn liquor and cartons of Chinese cig-arettes, the Double Happiness brand.

He said as little as possible as he made the transaction. A Pyong-yang accent would advertise him like a flashing sign in these parts. She cast him only the briefest glance, but in it he saw avarice and suspicion. His stomach clenched as she examined the white pearl of *bingdu* in the pale glow of her flashlight, opened it, and snorted a tiny mound of it from the tip of a latch key. Moments later he was walking away with a bottle of corn liquor and ten cartons of cig-arettes in a plastic bag.

A group of railroad workers were eating hot broth at a makeshift canteen in the street outside Hoeryong Station, their faces lit by a tiny bright spark in a jar—a lamp that burned rapeseed oil. The vendor accepted three cigarettes from Cho in payment for a bowl, and he joined the men at the table. His only thought was to wolf the food down and leave. He had no documents if anyone challenged him. His best chance of escape across the river was *tonight*. But as he savored the broth, which had fresh noodles and stringy, mari-nated pork, he felt overwhelmed. This was the first real food he'd tasted in a year, and its effect was instant and humanizing. Already the animal-slave life he'd been leading seemed unreal to him, a nightmare. He looked at the faces of the railroad workers. They were blackened from oil and coal soot, but to Cho's prison-camp eyes they seemed a picture of health, and he was reminded that he hadn't seen his own reflection in a long time. He craned his head around and peered into the glass of a dark window in the station building behind him. Even in the dim light the sight was enough to make him gasp, and a feeling of profound pity for his destroyed body overcame him. His head was a gray skeletal bulb where his hair had fallen out in patches. A bare scalp was crisscrossed with scars from beatings. Sores and boils from starvation and lack of sunlight covered his face, his skin an old rag drawn tight over bone, which made his eyes huge and dark. It was his own face, no doubt about it, and it had changed almost as much as he had inside.

"Where're you from, citizen?"

The railroad worker's face was an unsmiling black mask. The others had stopped eating and were watching him. Suddenly he was aware of how much the farm overalls stank.

"From Chongjin," Cho mumbled, conscious of his accent. "I ... have been very sick. I've come north to buy medicine."

Something softened in the man's eyes, and Cho sensed that his answer had passed a test: people here were accustomed to visitors hoping to slip into China to buy goods impossible to obtain at home.

"Any tobacco on you?" the man said.

Cho took out a pack of cigarettes, and offered them around.

"Double Happiness," the railroad worker said appreciatively. He put the cigarette behind his ear and went back to his broth. Cho thought that was the end of the exchange, but then the man said, "The river's too wide to cross here unnoticed, and the ice is thin. Head westward along the Musan Road until it gets narrow and frozen solid. There's a quiet spot about six watchtowers away."

"If a guard stops you, offer him crackers and cigarettes," one of his friends said.

"And promise a gift on your way back," said the other, lighting up. "A bottle of Maotai is very nice, or Chinese cash. Tell them you'll only be a day or two and ask the times of their shifts."

Cho could not believe his luck. He bowed and thanked them, and gave them each a full packet, which they accepted. Ivory smiles in coal-soot faces. He stood and bowed again, but was distracted by movement behind him. He turned to look and his heart almost stopped.

A figure was walking away carrying a pot and a brush. In the very window in which Cho had seen his reflection, his own face now stared back from a black-and-white flyer.

WANTED FOR MURDER

CHO SANG-HO

And beneath the image of his face:

DANGEROUS!

REPORT ANY SIGHTING TO THE MINISTRY OF STATE SECURITY

Murder? He felt his legs turn to paper.

For a second he was too panicked to turn back to the men.

Already? The Bowibu were hunting him already? Hyun must have reported him missing immediately. Cho couldn't blame him, if it earned him an extra cup of cornmeal. He was fixated by the image, from which he felt an odd dissociation. It was the face of his previous life. Clean shaven, hair glossed back, complacent, arrogant, entitled. A photo taken from his Party file. His epaulettes were just visible at the sides.

"Thank you, citizens." He wished the men a good night.

They raised their cigarettes in farewell.

As soon as he was out of sight he began to run. *Wanted for murder? Oh, my ancestors!* He remembered this trick: high-ranking cadres were accused of heinous crimes if they defected, and the Chinese police were notified, too. One thing was clear: they were determined to catch him, and this realization ignited an equal and opposite determination in him. He would not be taken.

But as he dashed down a deserted westbound road, fortified by food and rest, he forced himself to slow down. He himself had seen his own transformation. It was impossible to imagine anyone matching that photo with this face.

At a bus station on the western edge of the city his face stared from every lamppost. He found another informal market and exchanged more of his *bingdu* pearls for Chinese yuan, rice crackers, a woolen hat, and more cigarettes. From a vendor selling electronics spread out on a mat he bought an illegal unregistered Nokia cell phone with a charger, and a China Mobile fifty-yuan phone card. The vendor explained how to use the phone card, adding, "If you can find anywhere to charge the phone, that is."

He could find no one selling a kitchen knife or anything he could use as a weapon. He'd feel safer if he had something to defend himself with. The remaining cash he used to buy a pencil flashlight, a razor blade, and packet of cigarette rolling papers. With a tremendous effort he remained calm and spoke as little as possible. No one seemed to cast him a second glance. He was a vagrant, a nobody, and he stank like a rank goat.

On the road out of the city he passed through an industrial area of rusted smokestacks and silent factories. After pausing a moment to check he was not being followed, he slipped into the shadows of a freight yard and found a disused garage. Crouching down on the oily concrete floor he turned on his pencil flashlight and carefully took out the largest remaining ball of *bingdu*. It had occurred to him that he could at least turn the *bingdu* into a weapon of sorts. Keeping his hands steady, he slit a Double Happiness cigarette lengthways with the razor blade and tipped the crystalline powder liberally onto the tobacco, so that the tobacco was laced with the drug. He resealed the cigarette with the rolling paper and examined his handiwork. It was almost impossible to tell that it had been doctored. Anyone who accepted this cigarette from him and smoked it would receive an overdose big enough to stop the heart. Death would come in a puff of euphoria. He returned it neatly to the packet, turning it upside down so that he knew which one contained the drug.

Soon he was out of the city and following a winding, unpaved track that ran along the Tumen River, the border itself. It was far colder here. The river to his right was a road of ice, pale and translucent, as if it were absorbing the starlight. Too dark to see the Chinese bank. Every few meters stood a sign. BORDER AREA! STOP! But what alarmed him more was the absence of any tree cover and, at each of the narrower points, a blocky concrete watchtower, where he could see the tops of guards' helmets moving about behind slit windows.

Cho felt a wave of panic.

Cross now, a voice in his head said, *before you're challenged.* It was dark enough for him to slip across unseen. Why not here, in front of a watchtower, where they'd least expect it, and before he ran into a patrol?

An unbearable agitation overcame him, and he found his legs carrying him toward the ice, his faculties overridden by panic. The far bank was no more than forty meters away. He'd be across in under a minute. He stepped down the bank. His right foot stepped onto the ice and the blood sang in his ears.

"Halt!"

The voice rang out of nowhere. Cho stood frozen.

"Hands up! Turn around."

Slowly he raised his hands and turned to see a single soldier, still a teenager from the sound of his voice, pointing an AK-74 at him.

Barely out of Socialist Youth League. The soldier turned on a thin flashlight that was attached to the barrel.

"What are you doing here? It's a restricted area."

"Comrade, I ..."

"Do you have anything to eat?"

Surprised, Cho signaled to the plastic bag he was carrying, and lowered it. Slowly he handed a packet of rice crackers to the soldier, who snatched it and shoved it into the tunic pocket of his coat. Encouraged, Cho handed him an unopened packet of cigarettes and the small bottle of corn liquor, which all disappeared into pockets. The boy wore a camouflage helmet and a pair of enormous canvas boots.

"Show me your ID."

Cho held up his palms. "Comrade, I'm just an ordinary fellow, hoping to visit relatives over there who'll give me the medicines I need. I'll be back tomorrow night at the same time, with a gift of rice for you, and a bottle of Maotai."

There was a pause as the boy took this in.

"You're from Pyongyang ... ?"

"Yes." The word was out before Cho could stop himself.

The boy reached into his tunic breast pocket and pulled out a flyer. The flashlight was directed into Cho's ravaged face, and then back to the flyer. Then again. Cho squinted in the bright beam.

"What is your name?" Louder now, excited.

Cho had never thought of an alias. He hesitated, and the boy's whistle was blowing before he could speak.

To his astonishment lights came on everywhere, along the bank, on the roof of the watchtower, finding him and converging on him, as if he were an actor on stage.

Cho turned and ran, ran for his life, skidding and falling on the ice. Getting up and running. He heard his breath snorting in his nose like a bull.

Voices shouted behind him, and a siren rose from the watch-tower. He knew the border garrison was not allowed to fire at the Chinese bank.

"Stop or we shoot!"

The farther across he got the safer he'd be ... Second after second, meter after meter, he got closer, and saw China taking shape in the dark. Tree and hill and field.

Something shrilled past Cho's ear. Shards of ice struck his eyes like glass where the first bullet hit the frozen surface, followed by the whip-crack sound of gunfire.

Another bullet thunked into the trunk of a tree ahead of him.

He was just a short distance from reaching the bank when he felt a sensation like a massive shove to his left leg, followed by the crack of another shot. He fell, skidding across the ice on his face.

For a second or two he felt no pain, though he knew he'd been hit. Then pain seared through him like a lightning bolt, blinding him. He cried out. It was hard to breathe. When the next bullet passed so close to his ear he could feel the lash of the wind, something almost supernatural in him propelled him on. He got up, supporting himself on one leg, feeling an adrenalin rush. Next thing he knew he was grasping root and branch and hauling himself up the bank, up from the ice.

The searchlights from the North Korean bank seemed to lose him, their beams sweeping from side to side penetrating the black woods, making long shadows of the trees. Cho crawled forward without stopping. He plowed through deep snow, trailing blood, shielding his face from bare branches. His body was getting heavier, sinking in the soft powder. He fell onto his chest and caught his breath. Half his face felt shredded and burned where he'd skidded across the ice. His calf was on fire. He could feel the scorch of the bullet's heat. The overalls on his leg were black with blood. The searchlights went out and for a moment he was in pitch darkness, but he knew the soldiers in that watchtower would already be on the radio to the Chinese border force. *Emergency! A murderer has escaped …* They'd request clearance to send the Bowibu agents across to put him down, like an escaped zoo animal. He'd lost the bag with the rice crackers and provisions. But he still had the packet with the doctored cigarette in one pocket, and the cell phone and charger in the other.

He blinked the sweat from his eyes and turned over in the soft snow. Ripping a shred of fabric away from his leg he fashioned a tourniquet and tied it at the top of his calf, clenching his teeth as he tightened it, his breath hissing in his nostrils, and rubbed snow on his wound. How bad was it? *Bad.* Torn viscera, shattered nerves from ripped flesh. A gaping hole in his leg from heavy military ammo. His foot had no feeling and was hanging limp, but the bullet must have missed the bone by a millimeter. A bloody trail in the snow! Could he have made this any easier for them? He felt a sudden surge of euphoria, which he guessed was a hormonal effect of the shock. Reaching for a fallen branch to use as a crutch he heaved himself up and stumbled on.

Ahead the trees thinned out and he saw a road piled high on either side with cleared snow. Beyond the road, only half a kilometer or so away, were the lights of a farmhouse, and beyond that he could make out the pale-blue outline of a range of bare hills. He forced himself up the ridge of plowed snow and was about to lower himself onto the road, with the pain from his calf shooting orange stars through his eyes, when he heard a car. He would flag it down, he decided, and plead for help. Trust himself to fortune, or die out here. He did not think he could make it as far as the farmhouse.

It was the lights that made him suddenly hold his breath. The flashing sapphire and ruby of a police car. He rolled onto his back and remained as still as stone. There was no time to flee. The car moved at a slow crawl. A police radio crackled behind a closed window. It proceeded past him and he breathed.

By the time he reached the farmyard his breathing was ragged and he was struggling not to faint from blood loss. He knocked on the door. A powerful smell of pigs hit him. A dog growled inside. Footsteps sounded, and the door opened, casting a wedge of yellow light across the ground. He saw the silhouette of a man's head.

"Who are you? What d'you want?"

Cho struggled to focus his eyes. The man's outline became blurred and fuzzy. He couldn't see the face. He felt nauseous suddenly.

"If you've come from across the river, I can't help you."

His head began to spin. The door closed in his face. Next thing he knew the ground rose up to his cheek and he blacked out.

Cho regained consciousness to a sound of sniffing and the sensation of a wet nose touching his ear. His calf was throbbing and numb. A coarse, sun-beaten face was peering down at him. The man was about fifty, and eyeing him with the glinting suspicion of a peasant. A chemical reek of disinfectant reached Cho's nostrils. His eyes tried to take in his surroundings. He was lying on his back on a tiled kitchen floor in front of a stove fire, which cast a reddish glow. The room was plain and poor, with a set of bashed metal pans hanging above a sink. A dog was busily nosing about him, taking in the stink of blood and filth.

"What happened to your leg?" the farmer said, in the singsong accent of a Korean Chinese.

From near his feet Cho heard a sharp intake of breath, and realized that his left leg was resting over a steaming bowl, where a large woman with bright red forearms was attempting to clean his wound with disinfectant. Each dab made him flinch.

"An accident ... as I crossed the river," Cho said feebly. No point denying where he'd come from. "Thank you for helping me."

"What trouble are you in?"

Cho screwed his eyes shut. "Do you have painkillers?"

The farmer plodded off and returned with a bottle of amber liquid.

"Made it myself." He touched the bottle to Cho's lips and Cho felt the spirit burn its way down his gullet like lava. He coughed, and when he spoke his voice was pure breath. Farmer and wife were both standing over him now.

"Please. Could I charge my phone ... ?" Cho feebly pulled it from the side pocket of his overalls.

The couple exchanged looks. Reluctantly the farmer took it from him. "The socket's in the next room."

"I'll get out of your way as soon as I can and won't trouble you."

"Rest here for now," the farmer said without taking his eyes off him. "We'll talk later."

The woman dried his calf and put a towel under it, and the farmer administered another generous slug of moonshine.

All his strength had drained from him. Again he drifted off, in and out of consciousness, with no sense of passing time. He dreamed of hushed voices arguing in the next room. When he awoke the fire in the stove was lower and his brow was beaded with sweat and feverish, his back stiff and painful on the hard floor. He raised his head and saw the dog watching him from a mat in the corner. The farmer was speaking Mandarin in the next room, then the kitchen door opened a crack and he saw the man peering at him.

"Please," Cho said. "My phone ..."

"Rest, rest," the man said in a hush.

Cho raised his voice to a shout. "Give me my phone!"

The farmer entered the room, glowering at him. He handed Cho the cell phone, which was warm from charging. Cho turned it on.

His hands trembling, he entered the code from the phone card to add the fifty-yuan credit, having no idea whether it was enough, then punched in the number he had memorized almost a year ago. He could not think what time it was in Washington.

Jenna sounded impossibly distant, a voice speaking from another world.

He hadn't a second to waste. He gave no greeting; he simply told her where he was, and in between labored breaths, in English so that the farmer wouldn't understand, began to outline what he knew of the human experimentation program inside Camp 22.

"I was a prisoner there. I saw it."

She said, "This is an open line ..."

She was warning him. The Chinese security forces had ears on all cell phone calls to numbers outside the country, and this one would raise an instant red flag. The caller was in a remote border area speaking to someone in Langley, Virginia. But that didn't matter now.

"Just listen. In a few minutes I'll be dead anyway. Your friend Fisk was right. Kim Jong-il's nuclear threat is a bluff, a smokescreen for something much, much worse ... The objective of the long-range rocket testing is to bring the United States within range of a nerve agent called scytodotoxin X, a WMD that will poison the food and water supply and kill millions. That's the payload the warhead is designed to carry. I've seen what one microgram of this stuff does to a human body in just ten seconds. You can't imagine it."

The suspicion on the farmer's face was turning to naked hostility at hearing English spoken. He said, "Are you a spy?"

Cho said, "It's been good to hear your voice."

"Wait." For the first time Jenna sounded panicked. "What is your precise location?"

A vehicle was pulling into the yard outside the window and the kitchen ceiling became a kaleidoscope of flashing of red and blue lights.

"It's no use. Good-bye, Jenna."

"Hey!" The farmer tried to wrest the phone from Cho's hand, but Cho just wanted to hear her say good-bye.

Static filled the line, and telephones rang in faraway Langley. Jenna's voice was cool and controlled.

"Please pass the phone to that person in the room with you. Tell him I need a word."

51

CIA Headquarters
1000 Colonial Farm Road
Langley, Virginia

"Isn't the intel worth more than the asset … ?" Fisk grimaced in that sheepish way he had when he was detaching himself from his principles. "Seriously? An operation on the ground in China?"

"He's the most valuable source we've ever had inside the North," Jenna said, trying not to raise her voice. "He's given us high-grade intel on not one—"

"Okay, okay—"

"… but *two* covert North Korean operations. I'm damned if we're going to throw him under the bus in China."

"But the *risk*…"

After a long argument in his office, Fisk had relented.

"I'll need a safe house in Yanji, local liaison, and a weapon," Jenna said.

He dropped his head back in his seat with a defeated sigh.

Approvals were sought all the way up to the national security advisor and within hours an operation had swung into place for Cho's exfiltration to the United States on a false US passport. Upon arrival he would receive the asylum offered all North Korean defectors.

"We don't have time to get you an official diplomatic cover," Fisk said, rubbing his face. "The Chinese will smell a rat. You'll be operating as an NOC." He nodded as she visibly baulked. "You're sure he's worth that much to you?"

Nonofficial cover was the most dangerous overseas status for a CIA operations officer. If caught, she would be at the mercy of China's security forces. She would have no diplomatic immunity or protection. She would have to deny any connection to her own government.

"If this goes wrong, Jenna," he said, suddenly angry with her, "it's on you."

52

Yanji
Jilin Province
China
Saturday, December 17, 2011

The cold of Manchuria took Amy Miller's breath away the moment she exited the glass doors of Yanji Airport. Luckily she didn't have to wait. A driver was holding up a sign with her name and took her straight to her hotel, which was in a business district of neon signs and glitzy towers of emerald-green glass. Even the city's downtown area looked rundown and tawdry, she thought.

She beamed at the desk manager as he took the number of her passport; she gave her occupation as travel agent on the guest registration form, and a home address in the Arlington Heights district of Milwaukee, and asked in English if there were any other delegates to the North China Travel Fair staying at the hotel. Not until she'd tipped the porter, locked the door of her room, and got into a steaming hot shower did Amy Miller begin to feel like Jenna Williams again.

Yanji, in the Jilin Province of northeastern China, was a small city less than fifty kilometers from the North Korean border. Its large population of ethnic Koreans spoke Mandarin as a second language. Jenna had visited several times when she was an academic—she'd learned her North Korean dialect in Yanji—and each time felt she was in a frontier town where anything could happen. The place had a buzz to it, and not in a good way. Undercover Bowibu agents were free to hunt down escaped North Koreans, underage girls were trafficked into seedy massage parlors and never seen again, and the riches from crystal meth put the city authorities in the pockets of violent gangs.

The CIA's station chief in Shenyang had arranged a safe house for her that was a five-minute walk from the hotel, but she knew that "safe" here was a relative term. Her presence in the city was sure to have been noted by the Chinese state security police, and the chances of their already having her under some level of surveillance were pretty high. She would have to exercise extreme caution.

The safe house was an apartment on the eighth floor of a dingy block with landings that smelled of congealed pork fat. When she got there, after a long detour in which she'd doubled back and walked around several other blocks in opposite directions to make sure she had no tails, she found Cho under a blanket on a sleeping mat, drifting in and out of reality in the worried presence of Lim, a young bespectacled CIA asset from Shenyang who worked as a software programmer for the People's Armed Police, and an off-the-books surgeon whom Lim had procured to treat the gunshot wound to Cho's left calf, which had begun to redden and swell. Lim was keeping Cho stupefied on oxycodone, because the surgeon, whom Jenna suspected worked for the city's gangs, had declined to operate until he'd been paid his considerable cash fee, which Jenna had given to him before she'd taken off her coat. Lim had handed her a thick padded envelope containing a compact Beretta 8000, her preferred sidearm, with a loaded double-stack magazine.

The pig farmer had done exactly as she'd instructed: Cho's cell phone was still in the farmer's hand when he'd opened the door to the Chinese border police. She'd heard every word of his Chinese-accented Korean as he spoke to them. "He came here asking for help, about two hours ago. I told him to turn himself in. What took you so long? He could be anywhere by now."

She had made good on her offer, and the next day the farmer had found a small fortune in his bank account. In the early hours she had succeeded in sending a car to pick Cho up and transfer him to Yanji.

She knew that his disappearance in China would no longer be a matter for the Chinese border police, but would by now have been escalated to a state security level, probably under political pressure from Pyongyang. There wasn't much time. It was vital she got him out of the country in the next twelve hours. She had his US passport on her. The CIA station chief was arranging his flight out from Shenyang—an eight-hour drive away—on medical insurance documents.

The surgeon was a small, tough-looking Han Chinese who worked on his knees in silence. She watched him clean the wound, pick out tiny fragments of bullet casing with tweezers, stitch and close the entry and exit holes, and wrap a clean bandage around the calf. He cut away the rotted swaddling around Cho's forearm, gently felt the healing bone, and rebandaged it. On the table he placed two glass vials of a strong sedative and a packet of disposable syringes. "His blood pressure must be kept down. Give him one injection before the drive to Shenyang. Another for the flight."

Lim showed the surgeon out and then left to buy clothing and food. Cho had nothing to wear and would need plenty of nourishment before the long journey to Shenyang. Jenna was only now beginning to worry about that part of the plan: police checkpoints along the way routinely examined motorists' IDs.

She boiled a saucepan of water on the tiny hot plate in the kitchen, made herself a cup of green tea, and sat on the floor with her back to the wall as it began to snow again in swirling flakes and the world outside the window became a diffuse white, an empty space. It was 2:00 p.m. As soon as Lim returned with the provisions she would wake Cho and assess his fitness to travel.

She watched his breath rise and fall, and this had the effect of making her slip into a meditative state. The wall clock ticked. The heated floor gave off a scent of chemical forest. On the table, the room's only other item of furniture, were Cho's entire worldly possessions: a packet of Double Happiness containing two cigarettes, a few crumpled notes in yuan, and a couple of small cellophane-wrapped balls of some mysterious white powder. Nothing else to his name. He must have ditched the cell phone.

He could be anybody, she thought, picking up the cigarette packet and turning it over in her hand. A nobody. An everyman. His body was just bone and sinew, but the tight skin made his face strangely serene, like a young boy's. She adjusted his blanket, pulling it up to his chin, and felt a strange inclination to brush his cheek, smooth his brow. All that arrogance she'd seen in New York had fallen away. She was not religious, but it seemed to her that his soul had been unburdened, and was now so humbled and light it could float through the snow clouds. It reminded her of something Solzhenitsyn had written. You only have power over a man so long as you don't take everything from him. But when a man has been robbed of everything, he's no longer in your power. He's free.

When she saw him in Pyongyang he was already in serious trouble. *Condemned to Camp 22, a zone of no return ... and escaped?* She shook her head in silent amazement. He must have gravely offended the regime. She tried to think what law he might have broken, but then she remembered there were no laws that mattered in North Korea, except one, for which the severest punishment was imposed if it was broken: absolute loyalty to the Kim dynasty.

"Don't touch those."

She was startled out of her reverie. Cho's eyes were narrow slits.

377

"I ... don't smoke. I won't touch them."

"Throw them away. I filled one of them with crystal meth ... in case I needed to ... kill someone with an overdose."

She nodded dumbly, and put the packet into her jacket pocket. She would dispose of them properly in a garbage can in the street.

His voice was barely above a whisper. "You ... saved me. Why?"

He was turned on his side, watching her, his face half hidden by the pillow. She sensed that his pride did not like her seeing him like this.

"You showed me my sister. I got you out. Wasn't that our deal?"

It was so quiet in the apartment they could hear themselves breathing.

She said, "Why Camp 22?"

He looked at her for a long time before answering. Then he gave a faint smile and lay back, staring at the ceiling. "You could say it was my destiny ... written in the stars before I was even born."

"You survived," she whispered.

He nodded very slightly. "Through the love of my mother."

Before she could ask him what he meant their heads turned to the door at the sound of the elevator opening in the corridor outside. Jenna knew it was only Lim returning with the provisions, but she was instantly on her guard. She left Cho's room and closed the door behind her, then she followed procedure, taking out her Beretta and turning the safety catch off. She had checked the magazine that morning and cleaned the bore and the bolt. She had fifteen rounds. She waited for the agreed signal: two double knocks on the door. The signal was given. She unchained the latch and opened the door ajar. Suddenly it burst open inwards, almost hitting her in the face. She raised the Beretta, aiming it with both hands.

Lim was outside. His lip trembled. He mouthed the word *sorry*.

The man pointing the Glock 17 to Lim's ear had a shaven head and wore a cheap black leather jacket. Four Chinese state security police in navy uniforms stood behind him. The man in the leather jacket spoke calmly in Korean. "Drop your weapon."

Slowly Jenna lowered the Beretta to the floor.

"Now step forward."

Faster than she could react a rough hood was over her head. To warn Cho, she screamed, as loud as she could, until a hand covered her mouth. Her hands were grabbed and cold steel cuffs were slipped over them.

Leather Jacket said, "Not another sound, and we'll do this the nice way."

They escorted her along the corridor, past the prying eyes of neighbors, into the elevator, and took the hood off her. Her legs were wobbling. They had seen through her cover like a bad disguise. She was just surprised they had found her so soon.

The door closed and the elevator began its descent with a shudder. She thought of her mother, and of how she would explain this to her. She thought of Soo-min, and of Fisk and his disappointment. Miserable way to end a career.

Leather Jacket had his back toward her. Two of the Chinese police were behind her. The other two, she supposed, had gone into the apartment to arrest Cho.

"Where are we going?"

Leather Jacket said nothing.

Outside the building's entrance she was shown into an unmarked black Volkswagen Bora sedan. The two policemen sat either side of her in the back. Leather Jacket got into the passenger seat next to the waiting driver.

The car signaled and turned into the traffic flow, the windshield wipers creating a blur of sleet and neon. Jenna shivered without her coat. She was wearing jeans, her running sneakers, a light sweater, and just a padded black sleeveless vest.

She tried to think, and guessed they were taking her to Shenyang, the nearest big city. At best she'd be charged with illegally entering the country on false documentation, and used as a bargaining chip after Beijing had lodged a diplomatic protest in Washington. At worst she'd disappear into a secret prison, find herself locked in leg irons, and opened up like a can of beans. Cho wouldn't be so lucky. Whatever they had in store for him it was nothing good, and she discovered in that moment that it was his fate she was worried about, not her own.

A strange calm came over her in this moment of crisis. When others panicked, the operations officer calculated. Surely she could negotiate for Cho's release with the intel he'd already given her ... The Chinese were just as alarmed as Washington by the Kim regime's lethal capability. She had to judge this correctly.

The early evening rush hour had slowed traffic to a crawl in downtown Yanji, but after about half an hour the roads became quieter. The car had passed every turning for the expressway and it was now clear that their destination was not Shenyang. By her estimation they were heading south. The tower blocks became sparser, the suburbs petered out, and soon they were leaving the city environs altogether, barreling southward through industrial parks and bare farmland barely visible in the wintry gloom that was fast descending.

Jenna's equanimity began to evaporate, and her mood gave way to fear.

South of Yanji there was nothing but the North Korean border.

Her breath became shallow; she felt dampness beneath her arms.

"Sir," she said to Leather Jacket, "could we talk?" Leather Jacket remained immobile in the passenger seat. "I have it in my power to create a highly beneficial outcome for all of you," she said, glancing at the two policemen, "if you'd just pull over so we can talk for a minute."

The car picked up speed.

A red sun was setting behind turbulent snow clouds, and onward the road stretched, southward into eddying snowfalls.

Oh my God, no.

The two Chinese policemen peered down at Cho, lying on his sleeping mat beneath a blanket, with his arms out of sight. A lapel radio crackled.

"Get up. Get dressed," one of them said in Mandarin. He turned on the ceiling light and cast his eyes about for Cho's clothes, but saw none.

Cho regarded them with interest. Their appearance in the room had not surprised him completely. Jenna's cry had alerted him. They were both young, barely into their twenties. Plain faced. Dull eyed. Had they even finished their training? The guards he'd been accustomed to were seasoned killers, unmatched in ferocity by any other class of people he'd ever encountered. But the Chinese state security forces had sent two kids to arrest him. He, Cho, who had escaped Camp 22. He gave a weak smile. His previous self would have felt quite insulted. He'd bet his last yuan they'd never fired their service revolvers.

"Come on, get up," the same one said again. He had a bumpkin's accent.

"I can't move," Cho said evenly in Mandarin. "I've suffered a massive trauma to my back. If you want to take me out of here it will have to be on a stretcher."

"What're you talking about? Show me."

The policeman took off his gloves and pulled back Cho's blanket. Cho's hands were beneath him, as if he were supporting his back, holding his spine away from the pressure of the floor. The policeman attempted to turn Cho over, but stopped when he let out a sharp cry of pain.

The policemen looked at each other.

The lapel radio gave a burst of static. *"Come in, Wang. What is your progress? Over."*

381

The one on his knees said to the other, "Fetch the stretcher from the van."

The landscape was becoming more barren, turning into an endless stony plain, undulating, rock strewn, reaching as far as the eye could see. Here and there it was patched white with snowdrifts. Jenna could see no signs of habitation.

After a while the road began running parallel with a railroad track. The sun had almost set. Some meteorological trick of the light created a display of peach and tangerine clouds. The car slowed and pulled over. They were in the middle of nowhere. There was nothing out here but the road and the railroad. She was alone, handcuffed, in hostile territory. Her fears began to morph into black terror.

A secret murder. They'd chosen the right place.

Unable to keep the tremble from her voice she said, "Sir, whatever it is you want, I will obtain it for you with one phone call …"

Leather Jacket chuckled. "Shut up."

She tried to think, think of a strategy, but her hands were out of action, she had no space to kick, and these four were armed. She suddenly felt an immense sadness for herself. For her unfulfilled self. For the future she would never see. She was staring ahead as Leather Jacket lit a cigarette and lowered the window to smoke. The driver turned on the radio … Peng Liyuan singing a patriotic ballad, backed by a male-voice chorus. He was drumming his fingers on the wheel. Leather Jacket was watching out of the window.

Yet it was very strange, this murder, with none of the shiftiness and dark energy of a foul act about to be committed. But who was she to reason why? It would happen. Why else drive here? Perhaps they were waiting for her executioner.

The policeman to her right muttered something in Mandarin to the others and held up his cell phone: no signal out here.

Leather Jacket started slightly, and flicked his cigarette out of the window.

About a mile away on the horizon to the north, moving slowly toward them like a dark-green hedgerow, was a train.

Leather Jacket took something from the glove compartment, exited the passanger door, and clambered up the shale escarpment of the railroad bank. Standing on the tracks, he held up an orange flag in one hand and a flashlight in the other. He was signaling to a train heading toward North Korea from ... where? Beijing?

Jenna watched the scene intently. The train's headlights flashed once, acknowledging the signal. It had already cut its speed.

Minutes later it was in front of them, rolling to a stop in a long hiss, couplings banging together, a screech of brakes. A reek of carbonized steel reached Jenna through the car's open door.

It was immense, much higher than a normal train. The front of the engine car was adorned with a large white star between two red flags. The carriages were painted dark green. Some were window-less; others had black tinted glass. Two were mounted with antiaircraft guns: one near the front, the other at the rear of the train. Gleaming brass Korean letters on the side of the engine car bore the name STAR OF THE NORTH.

Doors opened and dozens of helmeted troops jumped out onto the chippings.

Leather Jacket opened the car's rear door. Jenna was herded out and held by her arms between the Chinese policemen so that she stood on the gravel facing the train.

She began to shiver.

The soldiers had taken up positions at intervals along the length of the entire train, holding their Kalashnikovs at forty-five degrees. For a few moments nothing happened. Sparse snowflakes continued to fall. An icy breeze flapped their long coats. Finally, an officer appeared in a train door and beckoned to Leather Jacket with a flick of his finger.

The man removed the handcuffs from Jenna's hands and, almost courteously, led her forward by the arm, up the shale embankment toward the train. The officer reached down and helped her up the three ladder steps into the carriage. The heavy door closed with a thunk behind her.

Cho watched the policeman's face, pale in the reflected glow of his cell phone as he checked his messages with one hand, and picked his nose with the other. Outside dusk was falling. They heard the elevator. His colleague had returned.

"No stretcher in the van," he said.

The other looked at Cho. "Right. We'll lift you ourselves."

Again Cho spoke calmly and evenly. "If I'm returned to North Korea paralyzed from the neck down, how will that look for you two? How will your captain explain it?" He smiled at them. "You'd better find a stretcher."

One of them swore, and said to the other, "Radio the boys in Onsong Station. See if they have a stretcher."

In the soundproofed interior, Jenna heard her breath sound shallow.

Piped Korean folk music played softly. The officer pointed the way forward, pushing her gently in the small of her back through a series of compartments—a conference room with a long polished table, a lounge furnished with ornate, comfortable sofas and a mirrored bar, a communications room with banks of flat screens and seated army officers speaking on radiophones. One of them stopped her and scanned her from head to foot with a handheld metal detector. He took her keys and phone from her.

In the next vestibule the officer told her to wait. She stood to one side as about a dozen women in long silk *hanbok* dresses flowed out of the compartment ahead of her. White-powdered faces turned briefly toward her as they rustled past in a cloud of sweet fragrance.

They were holding musical instruments—zithers and flutes. The officer reappeared. Again Jenna was propelled forward by a hand on her back, and she found herself in what appeared to be a long dining compartment, empty except for two soldiers standing guard at the far door, and a small aged man in beige seated at a dining table, eating alone. The door behind her closed. The women's fragrance still hung in the air.

"Dr. Williams?" the old man said, raising a napkin to his mouth. "Thank you for coming." He stood with some difficulty and smiled at her. "Please join me."

As if in a dream, Jenna could only stare. The man was Kim Jong-il.

53

Forty Kilometers South of Yanji
Jilin Province, China

Somehow she motioned her body forward. Her limbs were on a kind of autopilot, while her mind had closed down in shock. She could not take her eyes off him. He sat back down. His attention had already drifted back to the food.

A dozen saucer-sized gold dishes were spread out before him. From one of them he picked a tiny morsel with silver chopsticks and chewed slowly.

A place had been laid for her with a crystal goblet.

"Please," he said, gesturing with his chopsticks for her to sit.

The window blind next to him was drawn against the glowing landscape outside and the lamps in the compartment were shaded by orange glass, but the low lighting couldn't hide his frailty.

Jenna sat.

Facing her, stooped in his seat, was the Lodestar of the Twenty-First Century, the Dear Leader, a man whose image had been carved in marble, cast in bronze, painted in oils, mass-produced in screen-prints, patterned in vast mosaics of glass, displayed by a hundred thousand schoolchildren holding up colored cards, and projected onto clouds in the sky. His name was graven in letters six meters high on the rock face of Mount Paektu, it was intoned in voices quavering from loudspeakers, it was sung by army choruses, invoked by toddlers in thanks for food on the table, praised by orators before massed rallies. It was a name that had authored hundreds of volumes on everything from nitrate fertilizers to the art of the cinema, a name given to countless schools, universities, factories, tanks, and rocket launchers. It was a name shouted by cadres in a desperate act of loyalty as they faced the firing squad, a name that haunted the dreams of defectors, no matter how far they fled from his realm.

Yet absolute power hadn't halted the decay of his body. The famous bouffant hair was dry and sparse; she could see patches of his scalp. Deep lines bracketed his mouth and caused his cheeks to sag as he ate; his skin was creamy gray and liver spotted. With the outsized glasses resting on a small, feminine nose, he resembled not so much a man as a homunculus, kept alive by raw power.

"I use to have such an appetite on these journeys," he said vaguely. "Now food has lost its taste." He pointed to a dish with his chopsticks. "Chilled flowering fern cleanses the palette. Quail's egg jelly goes well with the grilled pheasant, shot on my own range. This one's fried octopus with ginkgo nut, prepared by my sushi chef. But can you guess which is the best food on this table?" He looked at her with amusement. "The bread! Flown to me this morning from Khabarovsk."

His voice was thin and parched, and impeded by a slight stammer. The left arm had a tremor to it, and one side of his body seemed subsided, as if from a stroke.

This man has fewer than five years left to live, she thought.

"I'm … not hungry."

An immaculate young man in a white jacket appeared at Jenna's side, bowed to her with his hand pressed to his heart, and poured a spirit into her glass from a golden bottle, which he left on the table.

"Baedansul," Kim Jong-il said, turning the label toward her. "Distilled for me by the Foundational Sciences Institute. At eighty proof, my doctors won't let me touch it now. Doctors ..." He gave a wry snort. "When they attend to me their hands tremble. But if they didn't tremble ... that's when I should worry."

He was drinking what looked like watered-down red wine. He raised his glass to her in a toast, but she did not move.

"Why have I been brought here?"

He stopped eating and his expression changed minutely, becoming less benign.

He signaled to the young attendant to remove the dishes, then raised his hand and with a flick of his wrist ordered the soldiers behind him to leave.

They hesitated. "Great General, we—"

"Leave us." He closed his eyes. Raising his voice had enervated him. The soldiers left through the rear door.

His mouth settled into neutral expression but the tiny eyes were as bright as pins.

"America's symbol is the eagle, is it not? A bird that soars. And Korea's pride is the mountain landscape that scrapes the sky. There is no obstacle we cannot overcome if we decide together."

Jenna could think of no response to this gnomic remark.

"If people treat me diplomatically," he went on, "I become a diplomat, and I wish to be treated diplomatically, Dr. Williams." He swirled his glass and took a sip. "For years my father was a guerrilla fighting the Japanese occupiers in Korea. He'd spend whole winters holed up in caves in the mountains of Ryanggang Province with my mother and a devoted band of rebels. By day they'd be outfoxing the imperialists, by night singing songs around fires in the snow. It was a simple, heroic life. Then came the Revolution in '48, and my father was no longer the leader of a small band of rebels, but of a country of eighteen million people. So our new nation became an extension of the life he had known. We are a guerrilla nation at war with the world. That's the state I inherited. It is who we are. There is nothing I can do to change it, without it falling apart."

388

He gave the sigh of a man who had drunk deep from the cup of life's experiences, and was tired. He put his glass down.

"We're not dissimilar, you and I," he said, giving her a thin smile. "Your life, like mine, was shaped long ago by unhappiness and events beyond your control. Neither of us had a choice in the person we became."

She felt her ears burning as she sensed, in some vague and unformulated way, that she was about to be blackmailed.

"You don't know me," she said. A faint feeling of nausea was beginning to ferment in her stomach.

Kim Jong-il raised the window blind a few inches and peered out. The black Volkswagen sedan that had brought her here was still waiting down on the rough road parallel with the track. Leather Jacket was standing next to it, braving the cold to smoke. The helmeted soldier below the window stood as immobile as a statue. Snowflakes were sticking to the barrel of his Kalashnikov. The last light of the day had retreated to the horizon in a palette of ominous reds and purples. A few stars pierced the sky between the clouds.

He said, "A year ago you wrote a secret report for CIA director Panetta urging a radical change in America's attitude toward me. Your idea was to sweep away all sanctions and embargos on my country, all restrictions on travel, banking, and trade. You argued for nothing less than a sea change in American policy. It was a bold, audacious proposal. The secretary of state was opposed to it, but under pressure from the White House, it seems, she discreetly shared your ideas with the Chinese and the South Koreans, and later with the Russians. She was most surprised, judging from her e-mails, that their response was not negative. Last week, in an e-mail to your president, she wrote that she had become convinced of your recommendations. She is ready to go public with them and lobby the UN ..."

Jenna stared coldly at him. *So here it is.*

"... and once she does so, the president will give her his full backing."

Kim Jong-il turned back to her. The dying light was reflecting in his glasses so that she could not read his expression, but his voice turned cold.

"You will tell the secretary of state that you have reconsidered your report. After much soul-searching, you have developed grave doubts about it. It is your expert opinion that all sanctions and embargos against my country must remain in force in perpetuity."

A long pause passed before Jenna said coolly, "Your country is poor and isolated because of sanctions."

"You think I don't know what you're doing?" A current of anger had entered his voice, but then he seemed to force his expression into something more conciliatory, and she sensed the momentousness of what he was saying. "My people are innocent children. Exposing them to the storms of the global economy, and with it all the pernicious influences of the modern world would … put them under stresses they could not endure."

Jenna muttered, almost to herself. "But while they're hungry and poor and kept in the dark they can't rise up against you." She felt a spike of pure loathing for this man. "What makes you think I'd do any such thing?"

"I should have thought that's perfectly obvious." He pressed a button in the side of the table.

The doors behind him at the far end of the compartment opened, and a woman in a pale-blue silk *hanbok* dress appeared.

Jenna jumped to her feet.

Her sister's black hair was tied back, and a white powder had been applied over her caramel skin. Her face was expressionless, a grotesque doll, her eyes blank and glassy.

Without looking at her, Kim Jong-il raised a finger and beckoned her forward.

Jenna watched appalled as Soo-min glided toward her like a vampire. She felt herself begin to tremble and realized she was crying.

*

A stretcher had been found. Both policemen were by now in a thoroughly bad mood. The one who'd had to fetch it was shining with sweat and swearing but Cho was oblivious, staring at the ceiling from his mat, not moving a muscle. They lay the stretcher on the floor next to him.

"Careful," he said. "I suggest you each go either side of me and lift me very slowly, with one of you supporting the weight of my head."

They crouched either side of his mat, putting their hands beneath him to lift.

"That's it," Cho said, grimacing. "Slowly, slowly."

"Soo-min … it's me." Jenna's face was streaking with tears. She held out her arms. "It's Jee-min."

Soo-min stopped at the dictator's side. She kept her eyes lowered, avoiding Jenna's gaze, but Jenna sensed her sister's emotions roiling behind the facade, like flames behind glass. Kim Jong-il reached feebly for Soo-min's hand, taking it and pressing it to his shoulder, an intimacy that made Jenna feel sick to her stomach.

"I'm delighted to be the agent of your reunion," he said.

Jenna lurched forward and threw her arms around Soo-min, but her sister remained stiff and unresponsive, as if Jenna were a stranger.

"Please, embrace," Kim Jong-il said with a wave of his hand. "We are all family here."

Slowly Soo-min reached her arms up like a manikin and placed them around Jenna's shoulders and Jenna felt her sister's heart beating violently. Their cheeks pressed together. Soo-min's skin was flushed hot.

"My dear sister," Soo-min said in a strange voice that sounded disconnected from her body, like a tape recording. Her face froze into a smile. "I bid you socialist greetings, and wish you well in your endeavors for my people."

Kim Jong-il's face had lost its weariness and had become animated with cunning.

Soo-min released Jenna. She bowed deeply to him, whispering, "Great General," then inched backward toward the door, her body bent over.

Jenna began to follow, until Soo-min glanced up and flashed a bright, clear warning with her eyes. As quickly as she'd appeared, Soo-min was gone.

Jenna's mouth had gone dry. She reached for the clear liquid in the crystal glass and took a gulp before remembering that it was an eighty-proof spirit. She coughed and felt her face catch fire. Her leg was trembling. She sat down again before she collapsed.

Kim Jong-il chuckled softly. "I wish I could join you in a glass of that ... Ah, but ..." he patted his heart. His small fingers were as white as grubs. "I hope you and I now have an understanding? I personally will guarantee your sister's safety." His eyes hardened. "I regret that the same can't be said for the traitor Cho Sang-ho, however. He will be returned to our care tonight."

Jenna felt the alcohol go to her head. An unbearable agitation filled her body. Not sure what to do with her hands, she put them into the pockets of her padded sleeveless vest and touched the corner of a cigarette packet.

Cho's cigarettes.

It was a curious sensation that overcame her at that moment, as if she had suddenly seen a simple solution to an impossible equation.

"I fear we've shocked you, Dr. Williams. You're shaking. Sip your drink."

"Forgive me ... a cigarette would help, if you'd permit."

"Of course."

She took the packet from her pocket.

"Double Happiness," he said with a note of regret. "China's best brand. Another pleasure forbidden to me."

He pressed the button in the side of the table.

She opened the packet and put a cigarette shakingly to her lips. She had no idea which of the two Cho had doctored. She was playing Russian roulette. The male attendant appeared with a thick glass ashtray and a chrome table lighter, which Kim Jong-il took from him.

"A beautiful woman shouldn't have to light her own."

He flicked the lighter and held it to the end of her cigarette.

She took the tiniest of puffs, watching the tip glow a rose color. It had the unmistakable taste of tobacco, and she felt her shaking begin to calm.

Then she committed herself to the act, fully and without a second thought.

She offered him the second cigarette.

The conflict played out on his face as he resisted temptation.

"Alas. Doctor's orders."

"A pity," Jenna said, dropping her head back on the seat and exhaling the smoke. "It would have been a tale to tell my future children, that I shared a smoke with the most powerful man in Asia."

The delight on his face was almost childish, as if her remark had conferred all the license he needed. "In that case, it would be unsporting to refuse."

He slid the cigarette from the packet and put it to his mouth.

Feeling a rush of destiny, she picked up the heavy chrome lighter and lit it for him, noticing that the lighter had been engraved.

IN FRIENDSHIP, FROM V. V. PUTIN, 2001

He took a deep drag, and closed his eyes in pleasure. "Tell me," he said, with the smoke coming out with the words, "whose idea was it to rescue Cho from that wretched riverbank? Yours?"

"Yes."

"You're a genius." He chuckled again. "Your CIA operation was so swift it caught the Chinese napping ..."

Without taking her eyes off him she took another puff, a deeper drag this time. It had been years since she'd smoked a cigarette. She'd forgotten the light-headedness. The effect that was both calming and stimulating. She was watching his face intently for any sign of the crystal meth taking effect. An overdose, Cho had said. Big enough to kill.

"I adore rescue stories," he went on, taking another drag. "Especially in movies. Stories that grip the audience and define their emotional response."

"Except that this rescue ends in the death of Cho and the continued incarceration of my sister."

He seemed not to hear and turned back to the window, suddenly thoughtful. "This really could be a movie." He was holding the cigarette up an angle next to his face, like a film siren. "The theme should be devotion to duty, and the innate goodness of the Korean soul ..."

She took another nervous puff. The smoke wasn't burning her throat in the way she remembered. In fact, when she exhaled it looked more like a kind of mist ...

She felt her wrist.

Her pulse was racing. And a light sweat had broken out on her brow. The faint nausea she'd felt since entering the compartment was intensifying, and mixed in with it was a thin but unmistakable ripple of euphoria.

Oh, SHIT

She stubbed the cigarette out frantically.

Kim Jong-il was still talking away, gazing out of the window. Her face was becoming hot and flushed. How much had she smoked? Three, four drags ...

"Out of love for your sister, you crossed the world in search of her, and in doing so found your true calling—to serve the people. *That* will be the plotline. You did not have your sister's advantages, of course, not having experienced the riches of socialism, the liberation of our ideology, the intoxicating thrill of a mass movement ..."

The drug's latent power was kicking in. Her lungs were filling deeply as she breathed. She knew her pupils were dilating.

"... But it is the Korean in you that triumphs over the baser race mixed in your blood ..."

Somewhere near the top of her diaphragm a tingling, kindling feeling of elation was threatening to flood her whole body.

"I will give my screenwriters on-the-spot guidance for this script." He turned back to her. "I will edit it mys—"

He froze, caught by her transformation. He was seeing her eyes lit large and bright, her shoulders heaving like some powerful beast. She felt as if she were growing in stature in front of him. The feeling of nausea was evaporating, leaving her with an exhilarating clarity of mind, and a kind of hyperacuity—her senses felt alive to the tiniest detail. She could almost see the labored beat of his weak heart. She could hear the soldiers talking in the guardroom behind the far door.

In a low voice she said, "You asked me if we have an understanding." She began to rise slowly from her seat. "We do not." Her eyes remained fixed on his. "There is no bridge I won't burn ... no earth I won't scorch ... to get my sister back."

Kim Jong-il watched her unfold to her full height, a distinct wariness in his eyes now, a look of alarm. His fingers still held the half-smoked cigarette. Suddenly his left hand moved to press something concealed beneath the table. A panic button.

The door at the far end flew open and the two soldiers of the Guard Command came running to the Leader's aid, holding AK-74s. For three seconds she was invisible to them. His need was all they answered. Both were tall and heavily built, like hundred-meter sprinters, but that did not concern her.

In Newtonian physics, the power of a strike increases quadratically with the speed of the strike, but only linearly with the mass of the striking object.

Kim Jong-il was pointing at her. Both turned toward her.

In other words ...

The nearest one moved to grab her. She spun her body ninety degrees and shot out her leg in a devastating side kick to his cheek. The ball of her heel connected with a soft crack of bone.

... speed generates more power than size.

395

He went down like a tree, crashing to the seat next to Kim Jong-il. The second soldier moved to draw a handgun. In a lightning-fast movement she swiped the heavy chrome lighter from the table and pitched it with the full force of her arm. It struck him in the eye—with such impact that it broke in two and the lighter fluid splashed over the table and curtain behind him.

For a moment the only sounds were her breathing and the groaning of the soldier whose eye she'd smashed. The other was unconscious.

She felt a mantle of power settling about her shoulders. She was invincible.

Their rifles were in fact AKSUs, she saw, as she pulled one off the unconscious soldier, the shortened version of the AK-74 designed for close-quarter firing. She liked its grip, its heft. She flipped off the safety catch.

Kim Jong-il coughed. For an unreal moment she had almost forgotten about him. He was hammering his knuckle on the window, trying to draw the attention of the soldier standing guard outside, the top of whose helmet could be seen below. But the glass, vacuum sealed and blast proof, closed in all sound.

He coughed again, a violent hacking cough, and unzipped his jacket at the collar. Blindly he felt for his glass. She picked up the crystal goblet of Baedansul that had been poured for her, eighty proof, and put it into his hand, watching with fascination as he gulped it down. His cough became a kind of hoarse retch, his face now turning a deep plum color.

Jenna shook her head. She was being distracted. *She had to find Soo-min.*

She was about to run in the direction Soo-min had taken when the door opened behind her. Two more soldiers were staring into the compartment in disbelief. They fumbled for their sidearms.

She leveled the AKSU at them. The carbine blazed in her hands on full automatic, pumping out rounds. It had a kick of a recoil.

Wounds opened like poppies in their chests, knocking them back-ward. Another soldier appeared behind them. A burst of firing, and she cut him down, too.

A wave of euphoria surged up from the toes of her feet to the crown of her head. She was Diana the huntress, a goddess shooting silver arrows. She swept the smoking muzzle of the AKSU back to the other end of the carriage.

A radio earpiece had fallen to the floor, issuing a crackle of fran-tic radio traffic.

Every soldier on the train was about to converge on this compart-ment unless she created a diversion. The dictator's lit cigarette had fallen to the floor. She picked it up and flicked it at the lighter fluid dripping from the table behind.

A *whumpf* of bright, pure flame raced across it. A second later, one of the window curtains caught fire, billowing an acrid white smoke.

At once the klaxon blared along the length of the train, drowning out all other sound. Outside, the soldiers were running from their posts.

She wasn't sure why she took one last look at Kim Jong-il. Per-haps it was an awareness of a shared moment of fate, or simply curiosity. The desperation of his coughing was silenced by the klaxon. His breathing was constricted; he was suffocating, a man in a vacuum, and his eyes had begun to bulge like eggs. What little it was taking to squeeze the life from his diseased heart. A tiny, toxic mix of alcohol, smoke, and terror. His glasses had fallen to the table. For one instant his eyes met hers, as though imploring her. *Die*, she thought, as his body jerked from the convulsion in his chest. The large head shot back, then with a slow exhalation of breath slumped onto his chest.

The two policemen were crouched either side of Cho. They had removed their gloves, caps, and jackets and were fully focused on inching him toward the stretcher.

"That's it," Cho whispered through clenched teeth. "Keep going."

They were sweating profusely. He could see the pulse beating in their necks.

Suddenly the blanket surged violently. As fast as a lizard Cho's thin arms were out, his fists drawn back.

One of the policemen turned to him, eyes bulbous with incredulity. The other fell forward onto all fours. A bubbling noise came from his throat.

A syringe was plunged in each of their necks.

One of them struggled with Cho's fist and pulled the needle out. The syringe was empty. He'd received the full dose.

Jenna ran, holding the AKSU at an angle to her body. She had boundless energy and a single desire: to find Soo-min.

She sprinted toward the far doors and into a small deserted guardroom. To her left, the train door to the outside was opening, letting in a freezing wind. A helmeted soldier was clambering in. In two sharp movements she drove the butt of the AKSU into his face, and delivered a pushing kick to his upper chest, sending him flying backward. The door was massive, made of thick, blast-proof steel. She pulled it closed with both arms and pressed down the lock.

A small corridor led past a restroom. The klaxon was amplified by the confined space. She opened the next door carefully and locked it behind her.

The scene she saw might have stunned her, but in her altered state of mind she simply felt a radiant smile spread across her face.

Soo-min was seated with a gathering of children. About seven or eight of them, boys and girls, hid their faces in the flowing folds of her blue silk *hanbok* dress or beneath her arms. A few of them had covered their ears against the noise. The blinds in the carriage were drawn. The only light came from a wall-mounted flat screen playing a children's animation. The space was arranged like a comfortable living room, with sofas and armchairs.

She knew that these were some of the half-Korean children she'd seen at the villa. One of the boys turned to look at her. He was East Asian, but with chestnut-brown hair—and she suddenly saw herself through his eyes. A drug-crazed armed Westerner in jeans who looked exactly like the woman protecting him.

Still holding the AKSU at an angle, Jenna held out her left hand, shaking her fingers, urging her sister over the noise of the klaxon. "Soo-min, come!"

A massive blow struck the door behind her—a boot kicking it in. The children began to cry and howl.

Soo-min's eyes sparked with terror. She got the children to their feet, and herded them to the far door of the carriage, away from Jenna. They clung closely to her as they ran.

A shouting of soldiers' voices and a thumping of boots sounded behind the locked door.

Jenna went after her sister, but as Soo-min shepherded the last of the children out of the far door she closed it, and turned her back against it protectively.

Jenna switched to English. "Susie, let's go."

The exit Soo-min had closed was their only way out.

Another massive blow struck the door Jenna had come through.

Her sister was frozen to the spot, her expression hard to read. It showed fear and confusion and something else, something that disturbed Jenna, but at that moment she was distracted by the sudden lurch of the floor. The train was starting to move.

Cho sat slowly up on his elbows, watching his captors writhe and gasp on the floor. Their motions were slowing. That sedative must be strong. Either that or they were going into some kind of shock, which, given their youth, was possible. For the first time he noticed that he was completely naked beneath the blanket. He stood upright on the mat and tested his weight on his heavily bandaged calf. He wasn't feeling bad at all, and guessed it must be an effect of the oxycodone Lim had given him for the pain. What had happened to Lim?

A gurgling noise on the floor distracted him. One of the men was reaching for his gun holster. Cho lunged toward him before he could pull it, tugged the man's riot baton from his holster belt, and without emotion struck down on the man's skull. Knockout blow. The other had already rolled onto his side. Cho waited a moment, baton raised, then heard a quiet snore coming from his throat.

Without wasting a second Cho began to undress the unconscious policeman, who was about his own height, though Cho's prison-camp body had nothing like the build of the man's arms and shoulders.

A short while later, a thin man in the navy uniform and boots of the Chinese state security police rode down to the lobby, disabled the elevator buttons with a hard blow from a riot baton, and emerged onto the slush-covered sidewalk. The icy street glowed like wet blood under the crimson neon signs. He checked the jacket pockets, finding a cell phone, which he flicked into a trash can, and vehicle keys. He pressed "unlock," and watched as the indicator lights of a new, unmarked BMW minivan parked ten meters away flashed and pinged amid the dark line of parked cars.

"Oh, yes," Cho murmured.

The compartment door was kicked wide open and three, four soldiers burst in holding semi-automatic rifles. Jenna did not hesitate for a millisecond. She opened up with the AKSU, cutting them down with a burst of bullets until she'd emptied the clip. Thick gray smoke poured in from the fire in the dining compartment.

One soldier lay screaming on the floor from a stomach wound. She took his magazine from him and reloaded. Between the blasts of the klaxon she heard men choking and realized that the fire in the dining carriage must now be a blaze, stopping more reinforcements from getting through.

She leveled the AKSU again and squeezed the trigger, firing into the smoke in the corridor. She could just make out the shapes of two bodies and the flickering orange glow of flames coming from the dining compartment.

Jenna ran back and grabbed Soo-min by her arm, hauling her through the kicked-in door of the compartment, toward the heavy train door in the guardroom, holding the weapon in her other hand.

The train door would not unlock while the train was in motion. Jenna motioned for Soo-min to stand back. She fired three rounds at the glass, which shattered in a thousand flashing, deafening fragments. A roaring, freezing air from outside took her breath away as the door opened. The train was picking up speed.

She clasped Soo-min's hand tightly and shouted, "Jump with me."

"To where?"

"Home."

Their eyes met, and in that briefest of seconds, as star and flame reflected in Soo-min's eyes, Jenna knew that her sister was not lost to her.

A large, powdery snowdrift approached. They jumped, and the burning train roared southward into the night.

Cho fastened the safety belt and turned the ignition. The powerful engine engaged softly and the dashboard lit up. Full tank. Again the lapel radio crackled.

"Wang, do you copy? Come in. Over."

Cho hesitated. The bumpkin Mandarin wasn't so difficult. He pressed the button. "Eh, Wang here. It's going to take us a while. The prisoner's injured on a stretcher and the elevator's bust. Over."

"Copy that. We're sending support. Over."

"Uh, no, no, we'll manage. We, uh, need the exercise. If I don't get back to you it's because we're carrying the bugger."

He tore the radio clip from the fleece collar, opened the door, and dropped it into the flowing gutter. He was leaning over to the glove compartment to look for a roadmap when he noticed the glowing console set into the dashboard. Mandarin characters flashed ENTER DESTINATION. Puzzled, he touched the screen, then tapped, tentatively: S − H − E − N − Y − A − N − G.

The display configured, showing him a route via the G1212 Jilin-Shenyang Expressway, and a large red arrow.

DISTANCE: 717 KM.

TIME: 7 H 44 MIN.

He shook his head. *Incredible.* It was like witnessing magic. Then a soft, female Chinese voice nearly made him jump out of his seat.

"In four hun-dred me-ters," the voice commanded, *"exit left on-to the G-1212 Express-way."*

Jenna got the men out of the Volkswagen Bora by yelling for help. They were walking toward her holding flashlights—Leather Jacket, the two Chinese policemen, and the driver. She was holding up a stumbling, shivering Soo-min, dressed in nothing but a flowing silk *hanbok*. Behind Soo-min's back, in the folds of her dress, Jenna held the AKSU. When they were close enough for her to see their faces she raised the weapon and fired a single shot over their heads. The men froze. The Volkswagen's headlights were pointed away from the scene and the men's faces were in shadow. Her objective was to reach the car. Her teeth were chattering now. From the sound of them, so were Soo-min's. The temperature was falling fast.

"Drop your weapons to the ground," she yelled into the wind.

No one moved, and she wondered how many of them understood Korean.

She fired another shot into the ground in front of them, sending up a blast of gravel. They raised their hands to their eyes.

"Drop your weapons or the next shot takes out a kneecap and the one after that puts a hole in a lung!"

Slowly they took out their handguns and dropped them.

"Lie down on the ground. Facedown."

They got down onto their knees.

"My darling sister," Jenna whispered, without lowering her aim, "please collect their weapons."

The men must have thought they were in a strange dream. A North Korean woman from the Dear Leader's personal train was floating among the rocks and ice like a lady from a folktale, picking up their weapons, unmanning them, while the train had passed in flames toward the horizon.

One minute later Jenna and Soo-min were strapped into the seats of the Volkswagen, driving off fast over the wilderness toward Yanji.

Jenna was coming down off the high she'd experienced on the train. The meth was wearing off. She was returning to steel-plated field-agent mode, calculating probabilities, her mind probing ahead for danger.

She felt the vast volume of questions she had for Soo-min building up like pressure behind a dam, but questions could wait until they reached Shenyang. All she could do now was glance occasionally at her sister's profile as she drove. She could not believe the miracle of her sister's presence next to her. Soo-min, Susie. So much to say to her and all the time in the world to say it. Soo-min just stared at the road, eyes limpid and glassy, saying nothing, breathing in short, shallow huffs. Jenna recognized the symptoms of shock.

Somewhere near the city limits of Yanji she threw the AKSU and the handguns into a field and accelerated up the entrance road toward the expressway. The police would be tracking the car by transponder once the alarm was raised, so they abandoned the vehicle in the bus station of Changchun at 11:15 p.m. There Jenna hired, for a generous fare, a taxi off the street to drive them the rest of the journey to Shenyang.

54

The G1212 Shenyang-Jilin Expressway
Ninety Kilometers East of Meihekou
Jilin Province, China

Cho had been driving for about two hours. He felt rested and alert, if a little hungry. He'd found no snacks in the minivan and dared not visit a service station. His biggest worry was having to stop at an expressway tollgate—the obvious place for the police to trap him. The alarm had surely been raised back in Yanji by now. But there were no tollgates on this expressway, just yellow signs for ELECTRONIC TOLL COLLECTION. He had turned off the satnav but couldn't shake the feeling that he was still being tracked. Lieutenant Wang's wallet held a small amount of cash. Cho had already resolved to ditch the vehicle in the next city, Meihekou, which he'd reach in an hour or so, and buy a bus ticket for the rest of the way to Shenyang. He'd have to find a change of clothes. They'd be on the lookout for the police uniform.

Worry about that later.

He was traveling westward through the foothills of the Changbai Mountains. The expressway curved and undulated through the landscape, now and then crossing a suspension bridge that spanned a deep valley gorge. What a bleak province Jilin was in winter. A murky orange glow behind the mountains to the left was all that remained of the daylight. It looked like a chemical reaction. Thick snow blanketed the hills, now pale gray in the gloom. To his right he saw the lights and flares of a vast shale oil refinery and caught its toxic stench.

The road unrolled endlessly from the dark. It had been gritted and salted but was still icy at the edges. He gripped the wheel tighter. Traffic was sparse, and speeding. A giant truck overtook him, rocking him in its slipstream, spraying him with brown slush. He dared not go faster, dared not give the highway patrols any reason to stop him.

He turned on the radio. Some music would calm him. A Chinese girl band, playing something state approved on zithers and xiaos. His bandaged calf was beginning to throb painfully again. He took another oxycodone capsule from his shirt pocket, forced it down without water, and once again distracted himself with thoughts of his son.

There was not one hour of one day during his months in Camp 22 when he had not thought of his boy. Books, his only child, his little man. What was the joke behind the nickname? Cho wished he could remember. He pictured the upturned little face with the cute grin. The puzzle book that always seemed to be in his hands. An innocent kid who loved animals. In the dim reflection of the mirror, Cho caught himself smiling and saw his eyes swimming with tears. He would give anything to know what had happened to Books. The smile faded from his face. He would never, ever know. The chance that he might be dead was too terrible to consider, though it had haunted him in dreams. Cho did not really believe his son was dead. But it was unimaginable that he'd been allowed to return to Pyongyang. Had he been told to despise and condemn his father as a traitor? Almost certainly. Would he believe it? Cho hoped not. He hoped his boy would keep the truth in some corner of his heart that the Party would never find, and this comforted him. He believed his son had a child's insight into his old father that no other adult had. Of the boy's mother, however, Cho was more certain. Intuition told him that they'd got to her quickly. In fact, he had started losing her long before his fall, and it surprised him to realize that he only saw that now. How she must loathe him. How she must curse the day she had ever met him.

It was curious, but whenever he tried to picture the three of them as the family they might have been, happy together, posing for a photograph on the seaside at Wonsan in summer, perhaps, or in another life, somewhere else entirely, in New York City, with the Statue of Liberty behind them, it was not his wife's face he always saw next to him, but Jenna's.

Jenna, who had crossed the world to rescue him, a wretched nobody who had lost everything. A husk of a man. She did not know that he knew her real name.

He shook his head gently. To have the freedom to love a woman like that ... he dared not imagine it.

He tried to think where she could be now, and felt worry gather in his chest like heartburn. He hoped she was unharmed. The Chinese had secret prisons, black sites invisible to the West, where there were no rules for interrogating spies. But he reminded himself that she was an American citizen. That in itself conferred magical protection. She came from a universe governed by laws and human rights. They could not mistreat her, as they could him. Somehow, she would be all right.

Cho glanced in the mirror again. The headlights of a lone car were some distance behind him, driving at the same speed. Was it following him? It had been there a long time.

Between patches of fast-moving snow cloud he saw the pinpricks of tiny cold stars. A bright half-moon was rising, its light turning the snow a dull blue. The whole firmament was above him, revolving, indifferent, and this thought made him feel very small, and his problems irrelevant. His brother was dead. His dear mother, who had never stopped loving him or believing in him, was almost certainly dead, too. What was he but a temporary assemblage of atoms, impermanent, like everything else. He would go the way of all things. The world would spin without him. No one would remember him.

He had not noticed the moment at which the oncoming traffic on the other side of the barrier had stopped. All lanes heading in the opposite direction were empty. An accident up ahead?

Then something flashed in his mirror, and he saw the lights, about two kilometers behind him.

He couldn't tell what it was at first. A broad mass of multicolored lights, like some sinister fairground attraction, was keeping its distance but creeping closer, until he saw that the lone car following him had been joined by three others, moving abreast, one in each lane, with more following behind, all with headlights on full beam and hazard lights blinking, and red and blue emergency lights rotating, a silent bank of approaching light.

He felt no surprise or fear.

Cho turned off the music on the radio. Now there was just the hum of the engine, the rumbling of the wind, and the distant rotors of a helicopter, drawing nearer until he could make out the rhythm of its blades. He glanced up through the sunroof but couldn't see it.

The few cars on the road ahead of him were pulling over onto the hard shoulder.

The next moment he was blinded. A stark white beam from above was upon him, moving with him, illuminating him in the minivan's interior like the ray of a magnifying glass on a hapless ant. He had the sensation of being suspended in the gliding pool of light. He tried to keep his eyes on the road.

Cho smiled faintly to himself.

So, they were taking no chances. He had incapacitated two policemen, after all, and had stolen Wang's belt and holster with its Type 92 service handgun. He was an armed criminal fugitive.

He felt remarkably calm. His breathing was steady.

The expressway was cresting a low hill. He put his foot down and accelerated. The police cars behind him increased their speed.

On the other side of the hill he saw the trap. At the end of a long bridge was a roadblock with dozens of police cars, lights strobing. The bridge spanned another valley gorge. In the blinding glare he couldn't see how deep it was. Finally, he took his foot off the gas pedal.

Toward the middle of the bridge he stopped. He turned off the engine, and sat still for a while. The helicopter's flapping was very loud now, directly above him. The bridge around him was bathed in a blue-white glare, like a stage set. The phalanx of police cars behind him had also stopped, at a safe distance near entry to the bridge.

A metallic voice overhead blared, *"This is the People's Armed Police. Step out of the vehicle, with your hands in the air."*

The amplified voice did not bounce or echo. It was swallowed by the dark, and Cho sensed that the drop beneath the bridge was very deep.

He exhaled slowly. Never had he felt so alive, so present in the moment. So ... at peace.

Of all the endings offered to him since his troubles began, this, he knew, was the right one. The one he was destined to take. Perhaps nothing he had done in his life could have changed this ending. There were no accidents.

Slowly he got out of the car. He stepped onto the road and feebly raised his hands. Lights were trained on him from above, behind, and from in front. Ahead, he saw the silhouettes of helmeted police coming toward him.

"Stay where you are," thundered the voice from the sky.

He turned and saw them approaching from behind.

His breath made a long plume of white vapor in the freezing air.

He looked up, wanting to see the stars one last time, but the helicopter's light dazzled him, its downdraft tore at his clothes and hair.

I'm ready, he thought. *I've been ready for a long time.* He dropped his arms.

"Keep your hands raised!"

In four long strides he reached the crash barrier.

"Stay where you are!"

In two stiff movements he had clambered over the barrier railing.

"Halt! Do not move!"

He was holding on to the railing and leaning out over a dark chasm. The breath of night howled through the valley, lacerating his face, numbing his ears, freezing the tears in his eyes. Below he saw empty void. Oh, it was deep enough all right.

It was time to let go.

As he fell, with the wind rushing through his hair, he released all need to understand, all need to know. And in that moment he understood everything.

55

US Consulate
Shenyang
Liaoning Province, China

The guest rooms of the US consulate—a sprawling, concrete Brutalist block—reminded Jenna of an East German budget hotel, but she had never minded hard beds. Soo-min had barely stopped sleeping since they'd arrived here, on edge and exhausted, at three in the morning twelve hours ago.

It had pained Jenna to report to the CIA station chief that she had failed in her mission, that she had lost Cho Sang-ho, the most significant North Korean asset ever to attempt defection. If not for him, the truth about the rocket program might never have been discovered. But when she had recounted the events on Kim Jong-il's train in a Flash Critical report sent to Charles Fisk via JWICS, the Joint Worldwide Intelligence Communications System, the CIA's own internet for encrypted top-secret communications, Langley's reaction had surprised her.

She had expected a dressing down for the carnage she had caused, a formal reprimand, a suspension from duty pending an inquiry, but Fisk was impressed. "You refused to be blackmailed and you recovered your sister, an abducted US citizen." The CIA director was briefed immediately and had been pleased to inform the president of Kim's death before the news broke. In fact, twenty-four hours after the event, North Korea had still not announced it. "I'm truly sorry about Cho," Fisk said, "but our immediate priority now, as soon as you're back, is to debrief Soo-min."

What?!

Perhaps Jenna had a blind spot for her sister, but she had not seen that coming.

"You said she may have been a member of Kim's entourage, maybe for years," Fisk said. "She could be a gold mine of information, and she has inside knowledge of the Seed-Bearing Program. She knows every one of those kids. With her help, we'll find them."

And do what to them?

Jenna felt immediately and fiercely protective of Soo-min. It worried her that her twin had said so little during the journey to Shenyang. She had not even asked after her own parents, and Jenna decided to wait until the moment was right to tell her of Douglas's death. Only once had Jenna seen her exhibit any kind of reaction, when she'd shrunk in terror and hid her face at the sight of the police guards outside the consulate's gates. Jenna had squeezed her hand and kissed it. "You've nothing to be scared of. You're not a fugitive. You're an American citizen." Soo-min had not yet uttered a word in English.

"I'm concerned my sister may be suffering the effects of severe trauma," Jenna said. "She may not react well to questioning."

"We have personnel at Langley trained in debriefing assets with PTSD," Fisk said, and logged off. End of conversation.

Later, lying awake in the guest room, she watched Soo-min breathing gently. Asleep, when her face was soft and in repose, she looked the way Jenna remembered her. But Jenna knew the moment her twin would awake the mask would come back on, and again she would be guarded, watchful, distant. An enigma. She seemed to carry some darkness inside her like a tumor. Jenna had put on the necklace with the tiny silver tiger for Soo-min to see, and waited for her to open her eyes, hoping to catch her unawares.

"Who is Ha-jun?" she said quietly, in Korean. Soo-min did not move, and for a while Jenna thought her sister had willfully not heard her. "You whispered the name in your sleep.

Soo-min sat up then. Her hair fell across her face, but she kept her eyes steadily on Jenna. In a voice barely above a whisper, she said, "My son."

You have a son? Jenna felt something in her heart give way. "Was he one of the children at the villa?"

Soo-min nodded almost imperceptibly, her face expressionless.

"He's still there?"

After a pause so long that Jenna thought her sister had permanently returned to silence, Soo-min said, "He was taken from me … when he was eight years old."

"Why?"

"Many reasons."

Jenna had a daunting sense then of the vast unexplored subjects ahead of them, like new continents emerging from the mist.

Slowly, haltingly, as if learning a new language, Soo-min began to answer Jenna's questions. It was as if she were feeling in the dark for mental tools she had long ago discarded, and Jenna saw that this was only a tiny beginning. The process of Soo-min's return to the world would take time, maybe months, even years.

Disconcertingly, she spoke Korean in the strong accent of the North. For more than a year, she said, she and Jae-hoon, the boy from the beach, had been held in a guarded residential complex shared with four Japanese couples who had been kidnapped many years previously. "Our handlers urged us to marry. Jae-hoon is the father of my son." A regular and menacing presence at the complex, Jenna gathered, was Sin Gwang-su, their abductor. But after Soo-min's son was born, mother and son were transferred to the villa of the Paekhwawon Compound, and for reasons that were not clear to

Jenna, they did not see Jae-hoon again. Soo-min claimed not to know his fate. It was as if her memories that led up to the arrival at the villa still bore the glimmer of a path she could describe, and each time her eyes met Jenna's, Jenna strongly sensed the magnetism that had always linked her to her twin reaching out, trying to sync, but not quite connecting. Once the story reached the villa, however, all became mystery once again. Whatever her role had been there, she would not say, the secret was locked behind too many doors, but Jenna had seen for herself that Soo-min had had a strong bond with the children there. It couldn't have been easy to leave them.

Then Jenna said, "Why were you on Kim's train?" and the light went out of Soo-min's eyes; she lowered her head, and said no more.

It's forbidden to speak of the General.

She gave no sign that she recognized the silver necklace.

At dinner the consul said, "You have friends in high places. I just got an e-mail from the secretary of state herself. Your sister will be reissued with a temporary US passport. You're both out of here tomorrow."

After that Jenna called her mother and asked her to wait in the arrivals building of Washington Dulles International Airport tomorrow. She gave Han the flight details.

"Since when did I have to meet you off planes?" Han said.

This was the moment Jenna had fantasized about, the news she'd longed to give Han, but now she felt nervous, as if she were presenting a gift so fragile that it might break in her mother's hands.

"Soo-min is with me."

The line went silent. Jenna could feel the shock like a blast under water.

Han tried to say something but her voice thickened when she spoke her daughter's name, and then she and Jenna were crying in silence together, hot tears rolling down their cheeks, thousands of miles apart.

"Let me speak to her," Han said.

"She's not herself yet, Omma. Better to wait until you see her."

That evening, Jenna thought a lot, too, about Cho. If she was honest with herself, losing him in Yanji had been more than a professional failing. Each time she pictured him, in the room of that safe house, shyly watching her from behind the covers, the light of snow clouds reflected in his eyes, too dignified and ashamed for her to see his body, her heart stirred with feelings of . . . loss, affection, regret. No one she had ever met had been tested in the way he had. She'd read enough history to know that extreme conditions—as in battle, famine, concentration camps—brought out the worst in humanity; only in rare and special people did they bring out the good. The man she'd seen in that room had not become an animal, or a monster. He had shone with humanity. He had found himself.

56

Beijing Capital International Airport
Beijing, China
Monday, December 19, 2011

The twins sat side by side, sipping coffee in the transfer lounge. They wore identical suede boots, skinny jeans, Benetton t-shirts, and puffer jackets. Years ago, as girls, they had never dressed identically. Why Jenna had bought the same clothes for them now she wasn't entirely sure, but she had a vague awareness of wanting to reforge a shared identity with Soo-min, and the fact that this hadn't felt spontaneous troubled her. Soo-min wasn't used to the jeans and kept scratching her legs. In one of her few utterances at the airport, she admitted that she had only worn *hanbok* dresses for years.

Jenna told herself that with help, Soo-min would slowly get back to her old self. If she had problems coping with the stresses of the free world, and with the loss of her son, then she, Jenna, would be her rock and her guide. She would do whatever it took to make her sister's life normal and happy.

They were about to leave for their gate when the TV screen on the wall caught their attention. A live broadcast on China Central Television News, subtitled in Mandarin, was from North Korea. Two days after the event, the news was finally being announced. The anchorwoman was dressed in a black *hanbok*. Her eyes were red from crying and her face deathly pale.

Jenna watched impassively. "Here goes ..."

"Our great comrade ... our Dear Leader ... General Secretary of the Workers' Party, Chairman of the Defense Commission, Supreme Commander of the Korean People's Army ..."

The woman's voice was choking with emotion. Jenna said, "Our flight's called. We should go."

"... KIM JONG-IL ..."

Soo-min was watching screen with an odd look on her face, a kind of rapture.

"... Genius of Geniuses, Guiding Star of the Twenty-First Century, Father of the Nation, Leader of All Socialist Peoples, Bright Sun of the Juche Idea, Friend of Children ..."

She seemed unable to tear her eyes from the screen. Gently Jenna got her to her feet and led her in the direction of the gate.

On the long moving walkway, she tried to divert Soo-min's attention, telling her of Han's disastrous "introductions" to some comically unsuitable men, but Soo-min seemed not to hear. The news was being relayed from every screen they passed.

"... suffered a myocardial infarction on board his train, caused by the excessive mental and physical strain of his lifelong dedication to the people's cause ..."

In the lounge next to the gate Soo-min remained transfixed by the screens. A strand of her hair had come loose and Jenna tucked it back behind her ear, but she did not notice. She was in a trance.

"... all over the country, spontaneous demonstrations of inconsolable sorrow are erupting as workers run from factories and offices in disbelief. Their only thought is to unite with the mass public grieving ..."

The footage cut to crowds crying and wailing on the snowbound streets of Pyongyang. People falling to the ground and hitting their faces with their fists, people sobbing and appealing to the sky with their hands.

The scene seemed to electrify Soo-min. Suddenly she covered her mouth with her hand to suppress a sharp cry. Passengers in the lounge turned to stare. Before Jenna could say a word Soo-min had shot out of the seat.

Jenna went after her. For one surreal moment she thought her twin was escaping her, but then she saw her enter the restroom.

The flight for Washington began to board. Jenna started toward the restroom, then stopped, realizing that Soo-min wanted a few minutes to herself. Boarding had almost finished when she finally emerged. Her eyes were puffy and sore, but whatever turmoil she had experienced had been contained and extinguished. The mask was back on. She had recomposed her face. She was cool, remote, placid. She even managed a smile at Jenna as she approached.

Jenna took her hand. "Are you all right?"

She nodded.

The airplane rose through gray drizzle, up into the sunlit plains above. Soo-min's face remained pressed to the window, gazing out at the bales of white cotton cloud. Jenna was beginning to realize that her sister's mind was in a far stranger place than she could imagine, and there may be no easy way of reaching her there. The plane angled its way eastward toward the Pacific, flooding the cabin with morning light. She looked at Soo-min's profile, and reminded herself that she, Jenna, had also been through hell by losing her twin. Time had healed her and made her stronger. Time would do the same for Soo-min.

"Home in thirteen hours," she said, and clasped Soo-min's hand.

This made Soo-min jump, and she looked at Jenna. For the briefest of moments—the merest fraction of a second—the mask slipped, and Jenna again saw anxiety, bewilderment ... and something else, something steely and purposeful.

With sudden insight Jenna asked: "Why did you jump with me from that train?"

Finally, Soo-min turned in her seat toward Jenna and took both her hands in hers. For the first time, she spoke in English.

"Because my son is in America."

57

Camp 22
North Hamgyong Province, North Korea
Thursday, February 16, 2012

The cell was a concrete square, barely large enough to lie down in. Two thin blankets and a bucket for bodily needs were its only contents. Mrs. Moon had been held in the camp's internal prison for about two months, she reckoned, but it was hard to be sure. She had no window. Each day was identical to the next, and the normal measures of time seemed to have changed their values. Minutes could drag like hours, but the weeks flew. She was let out for the morning and evening roll calls, which were held in the huge assembly ground next to the camp's main administration building, so she knew when it was day and when it was night, and had a vague sense of the month passing. She'd even spotted signs—a fresher smell of earth in the air, a formation of gray-winged loons flying north—that told her spring was not far off. These tiny details stood between her and insanity.

The morning roll call had passed without incident. But she had been back in her cell only for a minute when the door unlocked again and a guard ordered her out. There was a time when this would have filled her with foreboding—to be singled out under guard always meant something bad—but now she was merely curious. She had long lost interest in living. She inhabited a state-less zone, which wasn't actually life, and, strictly speaking, wasn't quite death. To her surprise the guard led her into the main administration building, to a reception area she had not been in before. It was gleaming and smelled of floor polish. On the wall behind the main desk was a portrait photograph of a plump young man she did not recognize.

A group of about twenty prisoners was assembled there, men and women, ragged and dirty. They were surrounded on three sides by about a dozen guards, standing along the walls of the reception as if this were some sort of ceremony. About six or seven of the prisoners looked even older than her. White-haired skeletons and bent-over cripples.

So, they weren't going to be beaten to death. They wouldn't have been brought here for that.

An officer in high polished boots emerged from the office door. The guards snapped to attention. The prisoners bent over in a full ninety-degree bow.

"Prisoners ..." The man in boots paused, waiting for them to stand upright. His voice was quiet and clear. He was reading from a text. "Today, on this sixteenth day of February, the Day of the Bright Star, when our nation remembers the selfless and miraculous life of our Dear Leader Kim Jong-il, whose death will forever be raw in our hearts, and whose spirit endures eternally, I am authorized by the Central Committee of our great Party to tell you the following."

The air in the room tensed. The prisoners were holding their breath.

"To honor the memory of his late father, our new leader, the Great Successor Kim Jong-un"—the officer drew out the vowels with sonority—"has, in his boundless mercy, granted clemency to ten prisoners whose petitions have moved him, and to all prisoners in the camp older than the age of sixty years."

Mrs. Moon's eyes popped wide open. A few of those on either side of her cried out and started weeping. Mrs. Moon stared about her. The guards looked as amazed as the prisoners. Before she could begin to take in what this meant, one by one the prisoners began falling to their knees.

With a struggle she got painfully down on her knees. One of the older prisoners lost his balance and toppled over. No one helped him.

The man in the polished boots shouted, "Long live the Great Successor!"

They shouted, "Long live the Great Successor!"

Goatshit and chickenshit! I'm surviving this place?

"Long live the Great Successor!"

I have no right to live.

A random set of oversized factory overalls was given to her in a folded bundle. Since no one was released from Camp 22, the administration office did not store prisoners' original belongings. She was handed a form.

"Read it carefully and sign it," the guard said. It stated that she could not reveal anything about Camp 22 to anyone in any form of writing or speech. "Open your mouth and you'll be marched back here faster than you shit corn."

They were a motley group that walked toward the camp's main gate. Like shipwreck survivors, she thought. A few of them, she could see, were too old and broken to enjoy their liberty for long. Their bodies would not recover, and the horrors would revisit them in dreams. She hobbled behind them in the flapping overalls, under the gaze of dozens of the guards who'd come to watch the spectacle, their faces a mix of puzzlement and suspicion. What they were seeing went against all their instincts, all their impulses and training.

It was midmorning. The sky was a chill cornflower blue, and sparrows flocked and chirped in the yellow grass. Mrs. Moon felt no lightness in her heart. What was she being released to? Nothing but a larger, country-size prison. Why hadn't she died here, at a moment of her choosing, and been forgotten, a corpse fertilizing a fruit tree?

On the other side of the gates a small crowd waited. Some of them waved and wept as they spotted faces in the group. A child ran into the arms of a father. A son embraced his mother and wept. The camp must have informed the families beforehand to make sure they were all picked up and did not become vagrants.

Mrs. Moon saw one thin, stooped man standing apart from the others, and something inside her melted. His face lit up like a boy's when he saw her. Tae-hyon's clothes were threadbare and patched. His coat hung from his skinny shoulders like drapes, and he'd lost so much hair he was as bald as a rivet. He looked pathetic! How had he managed? That any husband could cope without his wife was a miracle in her book.

"You survived, then," she said.

He was holding out a green apple for her. And he had something else for her, too, which he slipped from his jacket and pressed into her palm once they were out of sight of the gates.

She opened her hand, and her face wrinkled into a smile. It was the first time she'd smiled in a long time.

Bless my ancestors. A Choco Pie.

"From a balloon," he whispered. "In the forest yesterday morning."

They set off hand in hand along the dirt road. It had not rained all week and the sparrows were fluttering and bathing in the dust along the road edge. The farther they walked from the camp gates, the sweeter and cleaner the air became. Mrs. Moon tilted her face toward the faint warmth of the sun and breathed in. Spring was not far off.

Epilogue

The morning air, fresh with mist, dampened the boy's hair as he climbed the trail. Pine needles formed a carpet beneath his bare feet. The dawn's light was piercing the forest in slanting rays, slowly dissolving the small white clouds that clung to the valley's upper slopes. In the distance to the west the mountains' limestone crags were brightening from amber to gold.

The boy stood still for a moment and listened. He could distinguish between the songs of a jay and a sparrow. In fact he could identify the five types of local pine, knew the name of the tributary flowing through the valley toward the Yalu River, and could tell the geological periods in the layers of the rocks strewn along the path. He knew there were more species of beetle than of any other animal on earth. At night he could pick out the brightest stars of the constellations, remember their distance in light years, and calculate his own weight in each of the planets' gravities. All this he kept to himself. The villagers had taunted him for his accent, stolen his shoes, called him names he didn't understand, and beaten him with sticks. But in no time at all, it seemed, he'd become as dirty and ragged as they were, his speech as coarse, and he was so hungry he'd swallow live caterpillars and bite the heads off dragonflies.

He put down his sack of firewood and kneeled to inspect his deadfall trap—a simple flat rock propped up with a stick. If he was lucky he caught a rabbit or a squirrel, but all his traps had been empty this morning.

Suddenly a large brown hare, freshly killed, landed softly on the ground next to him. He leapt to his feet, reaching for his foraging knife. Sitting on the rock carved with the ancient Chinese script was an old woman, watching him.

"Seems I get up earlier than you," she said.

Her silver hair was tied back in the old Korean style, with a needle through the bun, and she wore a faded, Chinese-style padded jacket. Her eyes were twinkling and narrow and her face had the boniness of one who'd endured a lifetime of hardship.

"Are you the young man known as Woo-jin?"

The boy stared at her and said nothing.

"They said I'd find you on this trail." She took a large bundle off her back and untied it. From inside she produced a small bamboo basket and gave it to him. He took it from her without bowing, and threw off the lid to find four vegetable dumplings, which he stuffed ravenously into his mouth.

"I've been wandering this province for months," she said, watching him eat. "Looking for you."

The boy ate without taking his eyes off her, his face expressionless.

"That dumb look doesn't fool me, young man. I know you can read the script on this rock. And I see your father's face in yours."

The boy stopped chewing. His eyes opened wide in surprise.

"You knew my father?"

"Hoh, he speaks!" The old woman's face creased into wrinkles as she smiled. "How long is it since anyone called you Books?"

The forest was still except for the song of the sparrows, and the distant splashing of a mountain stream.

"Who are you?" he said.

"My name is Moon. I am your grandmother."

Author's Note

The idea for this story came to me during a visit to North Korea in 2012, when my small tour group was suborned into some of the daily rituals of the cult of Kim. On each day of the tour we were asked to pay our respects by lining up and bowing before one of the innumerable statues of Kim Il-sung, the country's founder and self-styled Great Leader. To refuse would have risked getting our two guides, a friendly man and a woman with whom we had formed a real bond, into trouble.

To outsiders like me, the sheer strangeness of life in North Korea could imbue even everyday occurrences with an epic quality. I left the country determined to learn more. My research revealed that the experience of my visit had barely scratched the surface, and that the truth about North Korea was even stranger than I could have imagined. What follows is factual information relevant to events in the novel.

The Abductions Program

In the 1970s and early 1980s the North Korean state actively abducted civilians from beaches in Japan and South Korea. These were not important military or political targets, but random people—teenage couples watching a sunset, a divorced man walking a dog, a local hairdresser, and so on. The motive behind this bizarre criminal enterprise has never been fully explained. Some of the victims were put to work teaching local slang and customs to spies and assassins being trained to infiltrate Japan and South Korea; others had their identities stolen; a tiny number were brainwashed and sent back home as spies, but the majority of them had no obvious use to North Korea. They were housed in isolated compounds for decades and permitted only limited contact with the North Korean population, or they died in mysterious circumstances. For years these abductions were the stuff of urban myth and conspiracy theories in Japan, until 2002, when, during a visit to Pyongyang, Japanese prime minister Junichiro Koizumi was stunned to receive an apology from Kim Jong-il for the abduction of thirteen Japanese citizens (the true number almost certainly runs to several hundred). It was the only public apology Kim had ever made. He hoped it would trigger the release of billions of yen in war reparations from Japan, but it backfired on him spectacularly when the Japanese public reacted with outrage and demanded the abductees' release.

In addition to the Japanese and South Korean victims, there are believed to be victims from at least twelve countries, including eight from Europe. The most detailed investigation of the abductions is Robert S. Boynton's excellent account, *The Invitation-Only Zone* (Farrar, Straus and Giroux, 2016).

The Seed-Bearing Program

Perhaps because he could never be sure that his kidnap victims were successfully indoctrinated and loyal, Kim Jong-il apparently scrapped the abductions program in favor of the Seed-Bearing Program, which came to light only in 2014 with the publication of Jang Jin-sung's extraordinary memoir *Dear Leader* (Rider, 2014). In an account reminiscent of an episode of *The Twilight Zone*, Jang, a regime insider who worked as a Party propagandist, describes how North Korea sent attractive female agents abroad to become pregnant by men of other races—men with white, brown, or black skin. At the same time women of other races were kidnapped and brought to Pyongyang to have sex with male North Korean agents. Their half-Korean children were born in Pyongyang and looked foreign. The aim was to create loyal spies who were North Korean born and bred and thoroughly indoctrinated. These children live in strict segregation from the rest of the population. Their needs are attended to by Section 915 of the Organization and Guidance Department, the shadowy body through which the ruling Kim exercises power.

Gangster Diplomats and Bureau 39

In the 1970s the North Korean government found it increasingly difficult to fund its embassies abroad and ordered them to become self-financing. Using diplomatic pouches, which are exempt from customs searches, North Korean diplomats began smuggling gold, illegal ivory, counterfeit dollars and pharmaceuticals, and hard drugs manufactured to a high purity in North Korea for sale to local crime organizations. Border guards and sniffer dogs have discovered these diplomats' contraband many times. Some embassies have also been involved in the abductions of local citizens, others for channeling wealth into Bureau 39, the secretive slush fund for maintaining the Kims' luxurious lifestyle and for buying their cronies' loyalty. For the best account of North Korea's illicit economy, see *North Korea Confidential* by Daniel Tudor and James Pearson (Tuttle Publishing, 2015). This book also offers the most convincing explanation for why Kim Jong-un had his uncle Jang Song-thaek, the brains behind Bureau 39, executed in 2013.

Christians

North Korea has no freedom of religion, except, of course, for Kim worship. A few defectors have testified to the existence of secret Christian "house churches" in the cities. These have tiny congregations that change their meeting places frequently for fear of discovery, rather like the early Christian church. They read from verses of the Bible copied by hand onto scraps of paper. Anyone caught in possession of an actual Bible faces execution or a life in the gulag. Two large churches in Pyongyang, replete with hymn-singing congregations, are sometimes shown to foreign visitors. Jang Jin-sung's memoir *Dear Leader* confirmed what many had suspected about these churches: that they are a cynical sham designed to deceive foreigners and to obtain international aid. They are run by the United Front Department of the Workers' Party and the congregation members are UFD operatives.

The Gulag

Generally, there are two types of labor camp in North Korea. In the first category are camps for those sentenced to "revolutionary reeducation through labor," from which, if they survive their punishment, prisoners may be released back into society and then monitored closely for the rest of their lives. The second category, operated by the Ministry of State Security, the Bowibu, are the extremely harsh "total control zone" camps for political prisoners. Inmates there have little hope of release and are worked to death as slaves in farms, factories, and mines. About 80,000 to 120,000 political prisoners are estimated to be held in total control zone camps, according to Daniel Tudor and James Pearson (*North Korea Confidential*).

In both types of camp, conditions are life-threatening and unsanitary. Torture, beatings, rape, infanticide, and public and secret executions are common, as is extremely dangerous work without safety equipment or protection. Most prisoners, however, die of illness and malnutrition, as food portions are tiny and many resort to eating rodents, snakes, and insects to survive. Daily life in the camps is attested to in a number of astonishing defector memoirs, most memorably *The Aquariums of Pyongyang* by Kang Chol-hwan (Basic Books, 2001) and *The Eyes of the Tailless Animals* by Soon Ok Lee (Living Sacrifice Book Company, 1999), both of whom escaped North Korea after their eventual release. Soon Ok Lee's account is one of the few to bear witness to the brutal treatment of Christians inside the camps. The descriptions of Cho's torture in chapter 43 are based on Soon Ok Lee's account of the torture she endured in prison.

On rare occasions, a prisoner might be pardoned or granted early release on a special date, such as the Leader's birthday, but, as with Mrs. Moon's release at the end of the novel, this is purely arbitrary. Prisoners are also allowed to petition the Leader to plead for clemency. These letters go through the Organization and Guidance Department, and, once in a while, some fortunate individual is miraculously freed. On one occasion, Kim Jong-il apparently sent a gold watch to a prisoner whose plea for mercy had moved him, but did not allow his release.

Some analysts have wondered about the purpose of the labor camps. Starving, emaciated prisoners are only fractionally as productive as well-fed healthy workers. The camps make no economic sense in terms of their contribution to the wealth of the country. Sadly their main purpose is to serve as instruments of control. Just as a functioning democracy must have free elections, so a totalitarian dictatorship must have concentration camps if it is to maintain control through terror.

Guilt by Association

Often, three generations of a convicted prisoner's family, including children and the elderly, are made to endure the punishment alongside the prisoner. A family will share the same hut inside the camp.

Children born in the camps—most famously Shin Dong-hyuk, whose amazing story is told in *Escape from Camp 14* by Blaine Harden (Viking, 2012)—bear the guilt of their parents and can expect to grow up, work, and die inside the camps.

North Koreans also carry the perceived guilt of their ancestors under the *songbun* system. In her memoir, *The Girl With Seven Names* (HarperCollins, 2015), Hyeonseo Lee describes how this caste system, unique to North Korea, divides the population into three classes: loyal, wavering, and hostile, depending on what the father's ancestors were doing just before, during, and after the founding of the state in 1948. If your ancestors included workers and peasants, and fought on the right side during the Korean War, your family is classed as loyal. If, however, your ancestors included landowners, merchants, Christians, prostitutes, anyone who collaborated with the Japanese during the period of colonial rule, or anyone who fled to the South during the Korean War, then your family will be classed as hostile. The hostile class—about forty percent of the population— are assigned to farms, mines, and menial labor. Only the loyal class gets to live in Pyongyang, has the opportunity to join the Workers' Party, and the freedom to choose a career.

In the novel, the events that befall Colonel Cho are based loosely on the experiences of Kim Yong, who, as a child, had been adopted from an orphanage by a loyal family in Pyongyang. When his birth records were checked prior to an important promotion, however, he learned that he was the son of an executed traitor who'd spied for the Americans during the Korean War—the worst imaginable class background. The nightmare that then begins for Cho really did happen to Kim Yong. He was deported to a total control zone, Camp 14, where he was put to work in the mines, and later to the less harsh Camp 18, where he joined his family, after his former colleagues appealed on his behalf. His riveting escape, described in *Long Road Home* (Columbia University Press, 2009) is still one of the best of the defector memoirs.

Camp 22 and Human Experimentation

Also known as Hoeryong Concentration Camp, Camp 22 is a vast, isolated total control zone in the northeast of the country where the brutality of the conditions defies imagination. There is no prisoner testimony, as far as I know, from Camp 22. The description of the camp given in chapter 14 comes from satellite monitoring and the evidence of former guards.

Kwon Hyuk, a former head of security at Camp 22 who defected to South Korea, and Ahn Myong Chol, a former guard, have described laboratories containing sealed chambers for chemical weapon experiments on human prisoners, with gas pumped through a tube into the chamber and scientists observing through glass windows. Three to four prisoners would be murdered at a time, often a family unit. At Kaechon Concentration Camp, Soon Ok Lee described an experiment in which fifty healthy women were given poisoned cabbage leaves. All fifty died within twenty minutes of vomiting and internal bleeding. She gave testimony to the United Nations Commission on Human Rights in New York in 2013.

The Dear Leader's Train

Kim Jong-il was afraid of flying—possibly because he'd ordered the bombing of Korean Air Flight 858 in 1987, killing 115 people, in a bid to deter visitors to the 1988 Seoul Olympics. After that, there was always the possibility of a reprisal against him. Most of his journeys were undertaken in his private armored train, which had seventeen compartments, including luxury living quarters and a satellite communications center. He preferred to travel at night, when scrolling American spy satellites couldn't track him. In 2001, he even made the 4,500-mile journey from Pyongyang to St.

Petersburg (which he insisted on calling Leningrad) by train. It took twenty-one days. Traveling with a large entourage, Kim the gourmet sampled the local cuisines and had fresh fish and game flown out to him en route, and even wines and cheeses from France. He was in such high spirits that he regaled his courtiers and Russian guests by singing patriotic Soviet songs. It was perhaps fitting, then, that he died on this train on December 17, 2011, according the official North Korean state media, suffering a myocardial infarction (heart attack) while traveling on one of his endless field guidance tours.

Rockets and Missiles

Eagle-eyed readers will spot that I've taken liberties with the dates for North Korea's satellite rocket launches. To date, it has launched five, in 1998, 2009, two in 2012, and one in 2016. Only two of these apparently succeeded in putting a satellite into orbit. The rocket program's real purpose, however, is almost certainly to test the technology needed for long-range intercontinental ballistic missiles (ICBMs) capable of striking the United States. Such missiles have to leave the atmosphere and reenter without their payload burning up. After several test missile launches in summer 2017, and the launch of Hwasong-15, a powerful ICBM, in November 2017, it is now clear that North Korea has mastered, or is very close to mastering, this technology.

Further Reading

I would not have been able to write this story without reading the histories, journalism, and memoirs of a number of authors. I've enjoyed the research as much as the writing, and many of the works in which I've found the details for the story have been of an astounding standard. Some I've mentioned above. What follows is a further small selection. I should say that any liberties taken with truth, or any historical inaccuracies in the novel are mine alone.

Barbara Demick's *Nothing to Envy* (Spiegel & Grau, 2009) is a brilliantly readable account of how ordinary people found ways to survive the famine of the 1990s, some of them unlearning decades of ideology in order to become market traders.

The Real North Korea (Oxford University Press, 2013) and *North of the DMZ* (McFarland, 2007) by Andrei Lankov, whose wry humor was much appreciated, are both superb general introductions to North Korea, as is *The Impossible State* by Victor Cha (Bodley Head, 2012), a veteran foreign policy adviser to President George W. Bush. I'm indebted to Dr. Cha for the scenes in which the North Korean diplomats are treated to a night out at the 21 Club in Manhattan, and the American mission arrives in Pyongyang.

The Hidden People of North Korea by Ralph Hassig and Kongdan Oh (Rowman & Littlefield, 2009) has some fascinating descriptions of the imperial lifestyle of Kim Jong-il. At the opposite end of the social scale, *Under the Same Sky* (Houghton Mifflin Harcourt, 2015) has first-hand information about lives of the *kotchebi*, the vagrant street kids of North Korea, written by a defector who used to be one of them, Joseph Kim.

Finally, *Blowing My Cover* by Lindsay Moran (Putnam, 2004) and *The Art of Intelligence* by Henry A. Crumpton (Penguin Press, 2012) both provide extraordinary insights into the day-to-day activities of a CIA operations officer.

I cannot recommend these books highly enough.

Glossary of Korean Words
Used in the Book

ajumma

Sometimes translated as "auntie," *ajumma* is a term for an older married woman. In some contexts it is a term of respect, in others, it can be pejorative. It is often used to denote matronly, pushy, hard-working, no-nonsense women.

appa

Father (informal).

banchan

Small side dishes of food such as fried fish, toasted seaweed, or kimchi, served alongside a main Korean meal.

bingdu

Literally, "ice." A North Korean slang word for crystal methamphetamine.

Bowibu

The Ministry of State Security (*Gukga Anjeon Bowibu*) is North Korea's much-feared secret police, which also controls the concentration camps.

bulgogi
Literally, "fire-meat," bulgogi is a favorite Korean dish. Thin, marinated strips of beef are sizzled on a griddle, often in the middle of a restaurant table, and eaten rolled up in a leaf of crisp lettuce.

capsida!
"Let's go!"

chima jeogori
A traditional Korean dress consisting of a *chima* (short jacket), worn over a *jeogori* (long dress wrapped high on the body). It is commonly worn in North Korea, but usually only on special occasions in South Korea.

Chollima
A mythological winged horse common to the East Asian Cultures. In North Korea it is the name given to the regime's equivalent of Mao's Great Leap Forward, or the Soviet Union's Stakhanovite Movement, intended to energize the workforce into overfulfilling quotas.

dobok
A loose-fitting outfit worn to practice Korean martial arts such as taekwondo. *Do* means way. *Bok* means clothing.

hanbok
The word for the combined *chima jeogori* dress.

kisaeng
An artist, musician, or courtesan employed by the imperial Korean court to provide entertainment, a tradition that died out at the end of the nineteenth century.

kotchebi
Literally, "flowering swallows," it is the term given to North Korea's vagrant children, who, like swallows, are constantly in search of food and shelter. The *kotchebi* became numerous during the

famine of the 1990s, when they migrated to the cities after their parents had perished of hunger.

kwangmyongsong
"Bright star," "brilliant star," or "guiding star," a name sometimes given to Kim Jong-il, and the name of North Korea's space satellite program.

mandu
A meat-filled dumpling, served hot. *Mandu-guk* is a soup of *mandu* served in a beef or anchovy broth.

man-sae
"Live long!" Shouted by crowds in North Korea, it is an expression of victory, or to wish long life to the ruling Kim. The phrase originated in China to wish the emperor ten thousand years of life.

noraebang
A Korean version of karaoke in which private, soundproof rooms are available to rent to groups of friends.

-nim
Or *seonsaeng-nim*, commonly translated as "teacher." A respectful, honorific form of address used for a senior person of knowledge and skill.

omma
Mother (informal).

sassayo
"Come and buy." *Tteok sassayo*: "Come and buy rice cakes."

soju
A traditional Korean clear spirit, made from rice, wheat, barley, or potatoes, usually drunk neat.

soondae
Blood sausage (cow or pig's intestines) stuffed with kimchi, rice, or spicy soybean paste.

ri
A Korean unit of distance, equivalent to about 400 meters (a quarter mile).

-yang
An honorific form of address used to a female on formal occasions.

yangnyeomjang
Soy sauce with garlic, peppers, chili flakes, onion, and sesame seeds.

yontan
A circular charcoal cake burned for heating everywhere in North Korea.

Acknowledgments

I have been very fortunate in having the support and encouragement of a world-class agent, Antony Topping of Greene & Heaton, whose belief in the novel saw it through from a rough and sketchy draft to a finished story. Kate Rizzo at the same agency and Daniel Lazar of Writers House in New York have also been indefatigable on the book's behalf. I'm filled with admiration for both of them.

My editors, Jade Chandler of Harvill Secker in London and Nate Roberson at Crown Publishing in New York, have been amazing. Their forensic reading of the book made me realize I was dealing with some of the brightest people in the industry.

A major thanks goes to one remarkable family I've known for many years: Claudia, who reads, sometimes multiple times, my rewritten chapters; Giles, who demonstrated to me the basics of taekwondo; Barret whose knowledge of deadly neurotoxins I'd never have found anywhere else, and Nadia, who invited me to her home in Menorca, providing a perfect environment for me to think and write.

My parents, too, have on many occasions provided a peaceful home away from London for me to write without distraction, sometimes for weeks on end. They have always fully supported me in everything I've done, and in that I am extremely fortunate.

A great deal of travel was undertaken for this book. I'm indebted to my hosts in Washington, John Coates and Ed Perlman, who graciously sheltered me for a prolonged stay during Hurricane Sandy in 2012, and to Dr. Josiah Osgood of Georgetown University for my tour of the Georgetown campus.

I'll be grateful all my life to my hosts in Seoul: Mrs. Choi, Yoon-seo, and Yang Jong-hoon, professor of photography at Sangmyung University, who taught this uncouth Westerner much about Korean etiquette and culture, and imbued in me a deep love for Korea.

Huge thanks goes to Kim Eun-tek, who connected me with the defector community in Seoul and whose tact succeeded in arranging numerous interviews with people whose stories weren't easy to tell. I must also express my deep appreciation for the endlessly patient Keunhyun, who answered my online queries at any time of the day or night.

Most importantly I would like to thank Seth Yeung, one of the most marvelous people I know, for putting up with a lot when I was writing this book. His life has changed mine, immeasurably for the happier.

Finally I would like to thank the human rights activist Hyeonseo Lee, the only North Korean I've had the honor and privilege to call a friend, for sharing her story with me. Her courage, intelligence, and sheer power of will inspired many aspects of this novel.